A SONG OF SILVER AND GOLD

MELISSA KARIBIAN

A SONG OF SILVER AND GOLD.
Copyright 2022 © Melissa Karibian.

Cover design by Elizabeth Jeannel

ISBN 978-1-956037-10-4 (hardcover)

ISBN 978-1-956037-09-8 (paperback)

ISBN 978-1-956037-08-1 (eBook)

First Edition

First Edition: June 2022

This eBook edition first published in 2022

Published by Hansen House

www.hansenhousebooks.com

HH
Hansen House

To those questioning or unsure. And to those that have always known, deep down. You are valid and you are loved.

*"Sing me no songs of daylight,
For the sun is the enemy of lovers
Sing instead of shadows and darkness,
And memories of midnight"*
-Sappho

Prologue

O sailor in the lonely night
Whose ship has crossed the ocean
Fierce as you are with all your might
May join me with your devotion

Come one come all
Don't worry, don't be afraid
Come let the water stand tall
And join a pretty young maid

Let go of your worries
Let go of your fears
Join hastily with hurry
Let me wipe away your tears

The piercing, golden eyes of the siren stunned the pirate into silence. Her voice had the means of captivating any poor soul who could hear her song. Completely out of control, the pirate stood motionless, mesmerized by the pretty face that stared back.

As the icy water splashed the pirate's face, it engulfed them in frozen darkness. The devilish creature had overturned the paddleboat. The pirate frantically searched the ocean around them for any sign of *her*, but the moon had disappeared behind a patch of clouds, leaving them in the dark.

Before the pirate could even attempt to swim up and catch a breath, a ripple in the water revealed the siren's glistening skin. Her scales lit up and illuminated her entire body. Her laughter contorted her once beautiful, flawless face into something ugly and sinister as her sharp teeth sank into her victim's neck.

Chapter One
Kae

The sword's tip dug into the skin at the center of my collarbone, momentarily distracting me from the pounding headache of my hangover. The sharp metal bit into my skin, giving enough pressure to make me stand still, but not enough to draw blood. The man at the other end flashed a wicked grin at his victory. I raised my sword and dropped it, feigning defeat.

I had never been one to take losing with my head held high.

The sword relented and gave me enough space to duck and swipe my right leg out, knocking the tall man off his feet.

Dalton was just over six feet, towering above me with very tippable long legs. His dirty blonde hair clung to his temples in damp strands, a clear indication that he was trying to work off the rum from last night.

He fell down hard with his breath whooshing out in surprise. The wooden deck soaked through his pants, still damp from last night's light rain. I grabbed the dagger from my belt and pointed it right at his nose, the black metal shimmering despite the cloudy skies. Dalton rolled his eyes and pushed it to the side.

"You're such a sore loser, Kae," Dalton grumbled, a wrinkle forming at his brow.

I smiled cheerily and helped my best friend rise to his feet.

"*Captain* Kae," I corrected him in a tone an octave lower than my natural one.

He may have been my closest friend, but that did not mean he could undermine my authority.

"Captain Kae," Dalton repeated, mocking my voice quietly so that no one else heard.

He was a jerk at times, but I knew Dalton would take my secrets to the grave. I shoved him hard in the shoulder and we both nearly collided into the mainmast.

He rolled his eyes again in response.

A slight breeze due east picked up. My heated skin welcomed it as the gust billowed into the white sails. The ship rocked gently along the small turquoise waves, lethargic as an overfed cat. Just one glance at the sea made me want to jump into the warm waters and swim the rest of the way.

"We're just about due for docking! We've arrived!" The shouts from my first mate, Ruff, echoed across the main deck of my ship.

He was one of the few that took exact scheduling seriously. I gave him a thumbs up and went to collect my sword.

"How do you two have this much energy after all that drinking last night?" Ruff questioned as he made his way over to us.

He had barely drunk the night before, which was a rare occurrence for him. Instead, my first mate had decided to call in early.

Dalton and I shrugged simultaneously.

Though I had tried finishing an entire barrel of rum by myself, most of it had come back up later in the night, leaving my head mostly clear.

Truthfully, I had slept no more than three hours. The nightmares that riddled my dreams had followed soon after. Nightmares about sirens—always sirens—had ruined all hope of a good night's sleep, the night before, and most nights for that matter. The dark circles under my eyes had taken up permanent residence over the last few months.

Dalton had greeted me at dawn, asking if I was awake and wanted to spar. I had gladly accepted, wanting to sweat out the horrid night with the clash of swords. Fighting had always helped me focus my jumbled thoughts. I never turned down more practice, as the streets of whatever kingdom we visited were my teachers. Bar fights, my mentors. Two years with a blade in my hand and it had quickly become an extension of myself.

"Years and years of experience." Dalton winked at Ruff, who scoffed in return.

Dalton made his way up to the helm of the ship to assist in steering.

I entered my quarters below the helm, shutting the door softly behind me before I placed my sword inside a locked cabinet. The rest of my clothes and some jewels greeted me. I grabbed my travel bag, feeling the light weight of its contents in my grip. Without dwelling too long, I turned the brass key, feeling as though I was leaving a finger behind.

Hopefully sometime soon I could come back to visit my sword before dust collected on its blade. With another turn of the key on the door to my quarters, I backed out onto the main deck one final time.

My men hurried about the ship to prepare for docking the *Mar Daemon*. They had all declined joining Dalton and I for drinks last night. I wasn't offended. They were eager to return home, wanting to spend the last night at sea sober to better remember it. Chatters of what awaited them back in our home kingdom, Avalon, filled the sea-salted air. It had been a little over a year since we'd all left the Golden City. The names of girlfriends passed their lips. No name came to my mind.

"And you, Captain? Who've you got waiting back home? A man like you must be drowning in lasses!" a scrawny boy named Kipp addressed me.

Kipp was one of our best fighters, despite his bony stature. He could not have been older than fifteen. It was obvious he had lied about his age to get around my prohibition of children joining the crew. Still, Kipp made up for his youth. He was our best sharpshooter on board—his skills with a crossbow were unmatched.

His sand-colored hair was tied back with a bandana and sweat gleamed his brown skin. He had been training below deck, though I hoped it was for fight stances and not letting arrows fly loose where the rest of the men slept. I eyed the crossbow slung across his narrow back, held by a strap of leather. I would bet five gold coins that Kipp slept with the weapon, always itching for a fight despite being queasy at the mere sight of blood.

At his comment, I absentmindedly tugged my tricorn hat further down on my head, making sure not a single strand of my curls was seen. Kipp looked at me expectantly, and I smirked at him.

"A man like me never ties myself down. I suspect I'll be collecting new hearts to break real soon," I said with confidence.

Kipp lapped up every single word with bright eyes.

As the anchor lowered and the *Mar Daemon* made its way to the port of Avalon's harbor, the conversations jittered to a stop. The ship jolted with its successful docking. My eager crewmates looked to me for a final sendoff. I had never much enjoyed giving speeches. I hated speaking in front of crowds, but as captain, speeches had become part of the job, if for nothing else but motivation.

"This year has been a test of our endurance and our survival. We lost Haz and Crook and we honor them every day. We honor all of those lost souls who were taken too soon from us by those monstrous sirens. Our vengeance has led to the deaths of seven sirens just this past year. And while we are now home to celebrate, we must also carry our friends' deaths with us. So, drink deeply tonight, lads, for you have earned it. Enjoy tonight and every night, and when the sea calls, may we sail again!" I finished my harangue with a clenched fist in the air.

The crew shouted with glee and raised their swords back at me.

One by one, the pirates walked the plank onto the port, wishing me luck back home and saying goodbye. They carried all sorts of bags, boxes, and trunks as they left, their belongings accumulated after an entire year at sea. Some left with more than they brought, making wagons a necessity.

Dalton nodded at me as he left with only a small burlap sack slung across his back. I knew I would run into him at some point at the local pubs, so this was not a final goodbye.

Ruff lingered behind, being the last to leave. He had been hounding me all of yesterday to join the crew for drinks once we were back in Avalon. I assumed he wanted to get in one last word about my decline to partake in the festivities.

"I just think it's right for a captain to be with his crew at the end of our big journey. We went through so much together. You should be there with them," Ruff said, continuing our argument from yesterday.

He knew I tended to distance myself from the crew, yet he kept bothering with this for some unknown reason. I hated lying to him. He was a close friend, as close as friends could be, yet I couldn't help the piling of secrets that I kept from Ruff.

It ate away at me.

"Look, you know I understand all of this. I want to drink myself to death with my crew. They laid down their lives for this cause. But I have further duties that cannot be avoided. I hope to see you soon, my friend." I clapped Ruff on the back, trying to appear lighthearted.

Ruff sighed and outstretched his hand for a shake. We slapped our palms together and then slapped the backs of our hands before shaking hands in a tight grip.

I smiled at Ruff, and he returned his own before he walked down the dock, heading toward the pubs that lined the harbor. He gazed back over his shoulder, mouth open as if to say something.

With a shake of his head, Ruff waved and kept on walking. I walked in the opposite direction, heading toward a more refined living arrangement.

I entered a deserted alleyway that was free of any onlookers. Though I cast backward glances to ensure I wasn't followed.

Ruff meant well, but that did not mean he wasn't suspicious. He had reason to be, but I hoped for both our sakes that he actually went to the pubs.

Opening the bag that I brought with me, I reluctantly pulled out the pristine navy coat and threw it on. I dreaded wearing it in the warmth as sweat instantly began to trickle down my back. Summers in Avalon were always brutal. But there was no other way to hide the sailor's garb without stripping. I kept the coat on.

I took off my hat, letting my curls fall free, and placed it inside the bag next to the other headpiece that I avoided looking at. Losing the hat atop my head was as detrimental as a fish parting from the sea, but it gave me away.

I ensured nothing was out of place and buttoned up my coat before I walked down the overcrowded streets of Avalon, stealthily making my way toward the center of the city.

I was in the outer sector of the kingdom, meaning I had nearly an hour of walking to reach my destination. Avalon was arranged in ring-like sectors that represented the three social classes: lower, middle, and upper, with the wealthiest of the city housed in its interior. At the very center was a castle that housed the royal family.

Knowing I had plenty of time to reach the castle, I stopped by local vendors, trading bronze coins for delicious fruit-flavored sweets. Berry tartness flooded my taste buds. A small child watched me eat while he played by himself in the street. I offered him a piece, and he took it, running away without another backward glance.

The smell of cheap alcohol and freshly caught fish filled the air out here, where the outer sector touched the harbor. I tried not to let my delicate, hungover stomach get too used to the stench and pressed on.

The kingdom's academy came looming above me next. Long, black metallic spires topped the gothic towers. The stained-glass windows looked as if they had just been recently washed, kept as pristine as the teachers demanded. I stopped at my old school to watch students file out with gleeful expressions and loud voices. Distant memories called out to me like the whispers of ghosts. I shuddered and trudged on.

The main street of the middle sector cut directly through the kingdom's marketplace. I kept walking through, not trusting myself enough to avoid being tempted by all the goods offered at the multiple stalls. If I so much as glanced at what was being sold, my pockets would immediately empty. I breathed through my mouth when syrupy sweets wafted through.

Past the marketplace, most of the sector dwelled. The buildings pressed against one another like a school of minnows swimming upstream in a river. A variety of stone and painted wood apartments meshed together, distinguished by housing or storefronts alike.

From most windows hung flower beds filled with tulips, roses, and dangling ivy that nearly reached a floor down.

On the balconies of some apartments, occupants enjoyed the summer air while leaning against the railing, waving a lazy hand to fan their dripping faces.

The middle sector was by far my favorite, not for the sights of liveliness, but for the smell, too. Fresh cinnamon wafted from the bakeries, promising delicious fried sweets to any that entered. The smell of spilled ink hit me when I walked by the mailer's quarters. My nose scrunched up of its own accord.

Still, there was also the sweet nectar of flavored rum that sloshed out of drunken mugs and ran through the grooves of the cobblestone road, leaving the ground near the local taverns slick and sticky.

Shouts of those men living their happiest lives filled the air, melting with the bangs of a blacksmith's hammer against flattened metal. I smiled at the brand-new swords up on display. The one hidden back on my ship could do for an upgrade, but that would be for another time—another place.

The end of my journey drew nearer and nearer as I entered the inner sector. This part of the city was home to Avalon's wealthiest and most influential families. Horse-drawn carriages filled the streets instead of pedestrians here. The rich didn't believe in walking everywhere and displayed their wealth through the design of the most intricate carriages.

I had heard that the Manko family—the wealthiest family in Avalon, second only to the royals—had theirs built entirely out of porcelain, if that was even possible. The luxurious houses were more spread out than in the outer sectors and were far bigger than the small families that inhabited them needed, I was sure. They towered above me.

I kept my head down as I continued to walk, not wanting to look directly at the obscene wealth. Not when I knew so many who suffered more than they ever deserved.

The wall surrounding the castle loomed above me in a mixture of gold and marble. I walked alongside the wall until I approached the nearest guard station. I knew that once I alerted royal guards, there would be no turning back. It wasn't like I had any other choice. I was sure the King and Queen would send out a search party if I did not arrive by nightfall.

My breath caught in my chest, fluttering within my lungs like a trapped bird. That's what I would be once inside those walls. Trapped again in an old life. It was as if the walls were enclosed around me, shrinking until I could no longer breathe.

As fast as it came, I shoved the feeling aside. There would be no fear today. I took a step forward. Then another.

I approached a man dressed in the colors of the commander of the royal guard. I smiled innocently and gave a little wave. We stared at each other for some time and then, without missing another beat, I reached into my bag and placed the headpiece atop my head.

A golden crown with alternating rubies and sapphires sparkled in the sunlight. The commander's eyes widened, and he scrambled to get a carriage ready for me. As if just remembering, he bowed to me before barking orders to anyone within earshot. I had to be barely recognizable, what with my short hair and dirty face.

Another much younger guard was sitting in the box seat of the horse-drawn carriage that approached. He jumped down and opened the door for me. I thanked him and stepped inside. It would take some getting used to being doted on again.

The carriage moved forward as we entered the gates to the castle's grounds. Many fountains and rose bushes lined the road with posh décor. I smiled at the memory of getting caught swimming naked in one of those very fountains.

Endless, pristine yards of grass, the richest shade of green, stretched out on either side of the road. Beyond that was the royal cemetery, adjacent to the lavender field. When the breeze picked up ever so slightly, the wafting scent of lavender reached the open carriage window. I delighted in the smell.

The carriage came to a stop, and the guard opened my door again. The trip ended all too soon. I begrudgingly accepted his outstretched hand and descended the two steps to the ground. I could get down on my own, but knew I had to play my part.

The man led me through the open doors of the castle. Marble accents lined the pillars and door frames, and the gold accents that lined the marble exterior glittered under the sun. It was a color I had grown to loathe. I never dared to voice my distaste for showing off the ridiculous amount of wealth in ugly decor aloud, especially in front of the King.

The guard marched on, not slowing his pace to sneer at the castle like I did. We were headed in the direction of the throne room.

It had been a year since I had been within these walls. Returning brought both familiarity and repressed memories bubbling up to my mind's surface. Though the somber air seemed to have dissipated in the months following the death of Avalon's beloved prince, there was still something awfully sobering about this place.

I hated it.

I hated how quiet it had become in my absence. Not just quiet. Lifeless, hollow. Void of any sort of warmth, a mirror of my own cavernous heart.

I hated that *he* was gone. Every little thing reminded me of him. I tried to shake my head clear of his face, hoping the pain would disappear. I wished it were that simple. I marched onwards.

The guard and I reached the majestic double doors that led to the throne room. My breathing was rapid and shallow. The two guards that stood on either side of the doors gave one look at me and bowed their heads. They both pulled on the handle of the doors, opening them outward. I took a deep breath and held it for a few seconds before exhaling.

Here we go.

Chapter Two
Kae

"Now announcing to Your Royal Majesties, the fair and grandiose Princess Kaelyn has returned!" The young guard was smiling widely with pride as he broke the news to the King and Queen.

Every single member of the royal court ran toward me and began asking a million queries. I sensed a feeling close to claustrophobia rise. Questions about my trip, how I was feeling, if I had eaten today, what I was wearing, what happened to my hair, did I find a husband, and more all spilled from their lips like liquid. Or perhaps being shot at me like arrows was a proper analogy.

I grimaced, trying to show how uncomfortable I was without making a scene.

"Enough! Leave us with our daughter. Tonight, we celebrate her safe return with a grand ball. I hope that you all have already started the preparations," the Queen decreed with her chin raised.

The court members scrambled out of the throne room to continue their planning of the celebration. Their princess and only heir to the throne had finally returned.

I watched them leave and avoided eye contact with my parents.

"Perhaps we can all catch up after the ball. I've grown tired of sitting up here all day listening to people complain about their petty squabbles and mundane lives," the King said.

He stood up from his golden throne and descended the pristine marble steps. The Queen hastily followed after him. He didn't so much as greet me as fully ignore me. I expected nothing less from my father.

"Kaelyn, why don't you go up and wash yourself? And please change out of that horrid coat." The Queen gave me a once-over as she noticed my squalid state. "It's from last year, isn't it? I sent your dress to the maids for tonight. We'll meet you in the ballroom."

She wrinkled her nose in disgust and dismissed me with a single hand. She was also less warm to me when my father was in the room.

"Of course." My pithy response didn't go unnoticed by my parents as I left them and made my way toward my chambers.

I was glad that my conversation with the King and Queen was put off until after the ball. I didn't have the energy to lie to them right now. I was hoping the warmth of alcohol would make things easier when we finally did have our little catch up. Nerves ate away at me at the thought of them discovering how I *really* spent my traveling year.

Though I wished I didn't have to lie at all. I missed my mother and how close we'd been when I was younger. I didn't wish I could say the same for my father. I wished things were easier between us, that I was the perfect daughter he wanted me to be. Facing him was going to make the night seem as long as day.

The long halls leading to my bedroom were decorated with statues and paintings by famous artists from across the seas. The open doors of the many rooms on either side beckoned me with promising distractions.

I stopped in front of the grand library. Not that I cared much for books apart from the few I'd found on ships and sailing, but the training room for the royal guards was just beyond the bookshelves. I was already itching to get a sword in my hand again. Perhaps now that I was eighteen, my parents would allow me to finally enter that room as a fighter, rather than a keen observer.

Time ticked by as temptation called me to the sparring ring. The thought of how cross my parents would be if I arrived late to the ball motivated my legs to keep on walking.

As I entered my bedroom, three maids were waiting for me, not to my surprise. The maids immediately got to work in stripping their princess down and getting me into an already-running bath.

I wasn't looking forward to it. The months of built-up dirt and grime gave me a shield of protection against the world. It disguised my true identity. And replacing my freeing men's clothes for a dress was less than ideal.

I could easily move around, fight, breathe in the clothes I so often wore. The thought of wearing a corset made my ribs ache. Then there was the way I was perceived, in a different, masculine light that made me feel as though I floated on a cloud. No feeling could compare. If it were more acceptable for women to don trousers over ballgowns, I would have a field day.

Despite myself, I sighed as I lowered my body into the warm water. My aching muscles relaxed, and some tension released while I sat in the tub. I was most grateful that none of the women commented on the male clothing that was hidden under my coat. One mumbled about getting them washed and left right away. Though I didn't recognize any of these maids, I knew that most who worked for the royal family were loyal and not ones to gossip.

There were dire consequences, if otherwise.

"If you don't mind, I'd like some time alone," I asked.

They shot each other wary glances.

"Please. I assure you all that I know how to dress myself."

"Of course, Your Highness. We will return soon for your hair and makeup," one of the maids said quietly.

I tried my best to give a reassured smile that did not look fearful at the promise that sounded like a threat. The maids quickly filed out, leaving me alone at last.

I paled at the thought of what their return would entail and lowered myself further until my head was fully submerged underwater. The warmth covered me like a childhood blanket. The salt and dirt that had become engrained in my skin for a year washed away like the shedding of a second skin.

Captain Kae dissolved in the soapy water, leaving Princess Kaelyn behind. After a minute, I came back up for air and sighed. I already missed my days out at sea, and I hadn't even been home for half a day.

With another sigh—I was doing a lot of that since returning—I got out of the tub. I dried myself off with the fluffy white towel that was draped on the counter. I made my way out of the bathroom and shut the door behind me.

My furniture was made of dark mahogany wood, lined against cream-painted walls. The windows with flowing curtains led to the open door of my balcony. I took in the familiar sights and felt myself ease just a bit. This comforting familiarity felt strange. My bedroom was nothing like the captain's quarters back on the *Mar Daemon*. Three of my bedrooms could fit into this royal suite. Still. I grew up here. Fairytales were told beneath warm covers, reluctant baths scrubbed away mud and scoldings.

I plopped down on the enormous bed, pinching the soft sheets in my hands. They were nothing like the rough wool blanket that donned my hard mattress on the *Mar Daemon*. I couldn't help but compare the two.

My skin felt scrubbed raw. My deviant, short hair was certainly going to produce whispers behind my back tonight. I loathed the gawking and attention that pretentious rich elitists gave me. I pretended not to care, though deep down their rejection stung. But I wouldn't let that stop me from doing what I wanted, regardless of the stares. As if they knew anything about me.

A shudder went down my spine. I had always wondered in my months at sea what would disappoint my parents more: that I was a pirate captain that hunted sirens or that I was attracted to women instead of men. When the rumors had spread that I was spotted in brothels kissing women, my father had grown red in the face with embarrassment. As if the horrid things were being said about *him* instead of *me.*

My mother was quick to come up with lies and explanations to cover things up. My brother showed neither contempt nor support. I much preferred his neutrality over the reactions of the other two. I never brought it up to them again. It was obvious my father would welcome a pirate scoundrel over an "abnormal" daughter.

"Ready to be dressed, Your Highness?" One of the maids poked her head in the doorway.

I hadn't realized how long I had been laying there, thinking about the first time I had kissed a woman. How freeing it had felt. The feeling of her soft lips against mine and her auburn hair entwined in my fingers.

"Yes, sorry. I didn't get a chance to pull my dress out of the closet."

"No need to apologize. It's my job, after all." The maid crossed the room and began pulling the components of my outfit out of the drawers.

Still wrapped in only a towel, I stood up and allowed the maid to dress me. I had nearly forgotten in my time spent out at sea how *long* it took to be properly dressed, instead of hastily throwing on trousers and the like. All the lacings to be tied, the layers of undergarments. The itchy material. I allowed myself to be tightened into this contraption of a gown without so much as a whimper.

A second maid came in with her arms full and placed the makeup she was carrying on my vanity. I took a deep breath, like bracing for battle.

The many lies I had thought up over the last year ran through my mind as I rehearsed what I would eventually say to my parents once we spoke later tonight...

My parents believed that I left Avalon a year ago to study different cultures. My father and I had agreed I would embark on a yearlong journey studying the ways of life in the other kingdoms. So, when my coronation day came, I would be adept at handling all foreign affairs with ease.

They had not been there to see me off, unknowing that the crew I had promised them that would take care of me did not exist. Instead, *my* crew was not compiled of trained guards or the like, but the pirates I had grown to treasure above all else.

I technically didn't lie about visiting kingdoms and learning new things. While at sea, my crew and I stopped at the coastal cities to restock on food and supplies. And I could never deny my crew the opportunity to drink and party on land, with a little stealing from the rich thrown in there.

My voyage had been driven by vengeance. My older brother, Edmonde, had been killed by sirens a year ago. The attack sank his ship, killing most of his crew. He had been traveling to meet his betrothed in Vrolon, a neighboring kingdom.

Since then, I made it my mission to wipe out the demons responsible for his death. I would give my last dying breath if it meant taking down a siren alongside me.

"Is the corset too tight, Your Highness?" the maid dressing me asked.

I barely had any room to breathe, but shook my head anyway. The corset could have been pulled tighter, but I wasn't willing to risk passing out in front of everyone tonight. They led me to the chair in front of my vanity, where the two went to work on my makeup.

"Shall I do her hair while you paint her face?" The third maid entered, addressing the other two.

"Yes, make sure to style it with jewels to match her dress and crown," the eldest said while she slipped heels on my feet.

I sighed. This was nowhere near the comfort Captain Kae's clothing brought me.

No one knew my little secret, except for Dalton. He was the only person who knew Captain Kae was a woman. My navigator and close friend had walked in on me changing by accident toward the beginning of our journey last year. He had immediately covered his eyes while my face turned red.

I had explained why I did it—apart from the way the clothes felt more freeing physically. They also made me more confident, stronger. I felt as if they'd prevent me from being perceived as weak or less than.

Dalton had claimed he would keep my secret and offered his own in return to make things even: he liked both men and women. I was so relieved not only to have a confidant but also a friend who was so like me.

I missed those times, being able to truly be myself while we both spilled our guts to each other in the middle of the night after everyone else went to sleep. The ghosts of our laughter rang in my ears.

"We're finished, Your Highness." The voice of one of the maids snapped me out of my thoughts.

The bloodthirsty pirate I had transformed myself into was no more. A glance in the mirror was like staring at a stranger. The haircut I had blindly given myself months ago was now shaped into something anew; a style that I had originally tried going for.

My curls were even and pronounced, reminding me of dark chocolate swirls in my favorite childhood sweets. One of the maids had placed small rubies in my hair that glittered like blood droplets whenever the light caught each jewel. The dark red color dripped into my dress, outlined by golden lacings that looped at the bodice.

Gone were the layers of salt and dirt that once served as my makeup. Instead, my eyelids were painted a shimmering gold; my lips were a bold crimson shade. Blush highlighted my cheekbones. Reds and golds were everywhere, reminding me of both a massacre and treasure. I lifted a hand and watched my reflection do the same. That was really me.

"Thank you. This is perfect," I replied.

Though I was against the dress, the rubies, even the makeup, I had to admit I looked stunning. *Princess Kaelyn* looked stunning. I looked not at all myself.

I could play dress up for just one night.

"Will you be needing anything else, Your Highness?" The third maid caught my eye in the mirror.

I shook my head and reached my hand up to touch my cheek. The maids bowed their heads and left my room.

Not wanting to stare at myself any longer, I got up and almost stumbled. I wasn't used to wearing pointed heels anymore. My boots had always been flat and simple. At certain times, drunken times, I even walked around the main deck barefoot, allowing the sea-salted wooden floor to soak into my skin. I walked a few steps, trying to balance myself before it returned like muscle memory.

"Greetings, Your Highness." Two unknown court members stood at my door.

I couldn't seem to get any alone time.

"Hello. And you are?" I walked over to them.

"I am Harrye, advisor to the King." Harrye introduced himself.

He wore an affable grin that showed off his straight teeth. His suit jacket had tassels on the shoulders, indicating his high status to the King.

"And I am Nikias of Vrolon. I am a foreign ambassador," Nikias said.

He had a more nervous demeanor. His eyes refused to meet my own, and he bounced his foot against the ground.

Vrolon was one of our neighboring kingdoms—Evrelon, the other. For centuries, we'd had strong alliances with the two. It had been natural for my brother to be betrothed to the princess from Vrolon. A means in my father's eyes of further strengthening our ties to them.

The name of the kingdom felt like a punch to the gut, as it reminded me of Edmonde.

"Pleased to meet you both," I said after a few seconds of awkward silence.

Several of my father's court members had retired just before I left a year ago due to their age. Harrye and Nikias must be some of the few that replaced them.

"We'll be leading you to the ballroom, Your Highness," Harrye said.

He was much taller than Nikias. Younger, too. He had to be only a few years my senior. It might have explained why he was smiling at me so much, but I hoped it was merely a pleasantry.

I nodded and allowed them to lead the way down the dimly lit halls. I tried my hardest not to envision a younger version of myself running alongside Edmonde as we raced through the castle in fits of giggles.

Before the thought could even dissipate, we stopped at the entrance to the large ballroom. I took a deep breath and wondered if it was too late to bail and hide somewhere—anywhere—so long as it wasn't here.

"The woman of honor, Princess Kaelyn Amarant!" A servant dressed in a dark navy suit addressed the crowd as we entered the room.

Cheers and applause followed the announcement. I did my best to remain poised as I smiled and waved at the crowd that had gathered. There had to be over a hundred people here, the sea of faces unrecognizable as they all laid their attention on me.

It had been a while since I had been in this ballroom. We hosted the winter festival here shortly before Edmonde had departed on his fateful trip. Still, nothing had changed about the room in the many, many months since then.

The twenty windows that lined either side of the rectangular ballroom could light up the room with brilliant sunrays during the day. Now, night leaked in, but could not get very far. Ten chandeliers hung from the ceiling, each lit with dozens of flickering candles. Crystals dangled from each branching arm.

The marble pillars that surrounded the perimeter were wrapped with golden garlands. Tables lined near the walls, surrounded by many guests. It allowed for ample space in the center to be used as a dance floor. The warm colors of the candlelight set the mood, but I was not sure if they were enough to shake my jitters.

I gracefully walked over to join my parents at the long table at the head of the ballroom. I was starving and the smell of roasted meat filled the air. Plates upon plates of Avalonian delicacies were laid out like a feast before us. Chicken, bread, cheese, wine goblets filled to the brim, heaping plates of rice, and various small *tapas* plates emitted a combined aroma that had my mouth watering.

"My beautiful daughter, what a transformation the maids have performed on you. You look absolutely radiant." My mother beamed at me in a way that truly made me miss home.

Her eyes were soft, and she placed her hand atop my own.

"But your hair! Why would you cut it so short?" my father critiqued.

Ah yes, the reason I hadn't missed home. I braced myself. Being home came with the constant belittling comments and snide remarks about my appearance, my actions, my words.

"It was a terrible accident. I got a sticky tar-like substance in it when I was visiting Eayucia. You know how they are with their inventions." I smiled sheepishly as I fibbed through my teeth to my father.

We both took long sips from our goblets while my mother shook her head.

"The both of you better stay sober. Tonight, is a night of celebration and remembrance. I won't have you make fools of yourselves," my mother said in a commanding voice.

My father and I glanced at each other before I downed the rest of my drink. He cast me a glance and finished his drink while my mother rolled her eyes and excused herself from the table.

I watched as my mother made her way over to one of our many guests. Their table was near our own, signifying their high status. The Manko family. The wealthiest and therefore the most pretentious. I plastered a fake grin on my face when my mother gestured over at me with a hand.

Eugene Manko, their only son, waved at me. I waved back, knowing full well that the two of us had been sworn enemies since age six. Tonight, was reserved for peace, so I didn't dare make a scene with the most entitled prick in the room.

I called a waiter to refill my goblet to the brim. My father noticed and had his refilled, too. I scoffed to myself. The only time the two of us seemed to get along was when there was wine involved. He was a competitive one and took these unspoken drinking games as connecting with me.

I, however, didn't care for them. They were just my only excuse to get drunk while in his presence. That, and the only time that my father was tolerable, was when there was wine in his veins. He seemed happier, more caring. It was a lie.

Then again, I, too, slipped into a more truthful persona when drunk. Captain Kae would come out. I felt more myself with a drink in my hand. It shed away my nerves and allowed comfort in being me.

I took a deep sip of the dark purple drink, dreading when I would have to get up and converse with each of the guests. I misplaced my manners as I slurped it down, again ordering another refill while I dug into the feast laid before me. I was already feeling its effects, and as I ate my meal, I lost track of just how many times my drink was filled.

The last memory of the night I had was eventually standing up and stumbling in my heels as the entire room spun.

"Rise and shine, mi amor!" My mother's voice woke me up with a start.

Instinct made me grab for the non-existent dagger under my pillow, and I groaned at the empty space, remembering where I was—*who* I was.

"Buenos dias," I replied groggily in the dead language of Avalon.

My mother was persistent in keeping some of the dialect alive before the new common language took over. I wasn't nearly as fluent as she was, but I tried to speak it now and then to remember how. It always pleased her whenever I did, though my accent was not nearly as thick as hers.

I grumbled at the sudden burst of light and sat up.

"Good morning, how did you sleep?" my mother asked from where she stood by the curtains.

She scanned my face, and I knew she saw the dark circles under my eyes. I yawned and rubbed at my eyes to answer her question.

Razor-sharp teeth and sinister golden eyes had raided my nightmares yet again. I had not slept well despite the lull of the wine I had consumed the night before. I could still see them in flashes, even when looking at my poised mother.

"Perhaps if you hadn't drunk yourself silly, you would not be feeling so improper." My mother said. "Your father and I await to speak to you over breakfast. We are meeting some foreign diplomats later today, so hurry up and get dressed."

It was far too early to be scolded by the Queen, so to avoid any further argument, I sprang out of bed. I got dressed in the bathroom and noticed that someone must have changed me out of that horrid dress and into a loose nightgown.

Ruffling my fingers through my hair, I grabbed my crown off the dresser and walked beside my impatient mother. There was no way she would wait for the maids to come and help me get ready. Besides, I craved the simplicity of dressing myself.

As we entered the dining hall, I took note of my father seated at the head of the table, a hand to his head. He scowled in contempt, his eyes closed, as though he hadn't noticed that we were in his presence.

"Your pain is your own doing, my love. Maybe next time, think twice before playing a drinking game with our daughter at *her* ball." My mother huffed and sat down beside her husband.

My father's eyes remained closed in, what I assumed, was an attempt to relieve the pain that came from a strong hangover in a brightly lit room. I sat across from them and chowed down on the warm breakfast placed in front of me like I'd never left my ship and I were seated with my crew instead. My mother's lip turned down at my manners, and she opened her mouth as if to say something, but merely sipped on her coffee instead.

I felt fine. There was only the faintest of throbbing right between my eyes, but nothing more. I had suffered worse nights. One night in particular was so bad that I had nearly let slip my secret concerning my true identity to both my crew and total strangers. At least this morning I knew where I was when I woke, even if it had taken me a second to remember.

"Tis not my fault that I underestimated how well Kaelyn could handle her wine. It's not becoming of a lady to be that accustomed to the effects of alcohol," my father said in a tone that did not seem like a compliment.

I knew he was annoyed with the fact that I had beaten him in his own imaginary drinking game.

I smiled slyly at him and tore off a piece of toast.

"While I do agree, Kaelyn merely rose to the occasion that you presented," my mother said before she heaved a sigh, shaking her head as she looked between us.

My father remained silent at that.

The rigid atmosphere lingered for the rest of the morning as I regurgitated the lies that I had been creating over the past few months. I recounted stories of my study abroad that included helping the elderly in one kingdom, giving back to orphans in another, and even speaking with the king of Evrelon about potential suitors. If my parents took to reading fairytales, they might see a suspicious resemblance between my stories and the ones written in children's books.

And yet, at least some of my lies came from truths. Of helping those less fortunate by giving them some of our stolen goods, knowing the rich wouldn't miss any of it. I *had* spoken to someone in Evrelon, but it wasn't the king and it definitely was not about suitors. If my drunken memory served true, the kind gentleman and I talked about our past relationships with women, though mine were a lot more fleeting.

My father perked up when I mentioned suitors. Marrying a prince from Evrelon would give us an even more advantageous alliance. My mother appeared to have zoned out at one point and only looked up when Nikias entered the room.

"Forgive me for the intrusion, Your Royal Majesties. The foreign ambassadors have just arrived." Nikias stood there with the corner of his lip turned down, as if he could sense the tension in the room.

He cast an uneasy glance at the three of us.

My father dismissed him with a wave as he rose out of his chair.

"Will you be joining us, Kaelyn?" my mother asked, though I suspected that she already knew the answer.

I had never hidden my distaste for politics. I would only attend at their insistence.

"I think I'll take a walk. Perhaps I will join you all later for dinner," and with that, the three of us exited at opposite ends of the room.

My parents headed toward the castle's main entrance while I returned to my bedroom.

I was pleased to see the clothes that I had arrived in were washed and folded in a neat stack on my bed. A bolt of fear struck me at the thought of my mother discovering the clothes before I had.

I stripped down and slipped into my brown pants and white shirt. I slipped into a large dark brown jacket that I had taken from Edmonde's closet and pulled my mud-covered boots up. Then I replaced my crown with my tricorn hat.

A glance into the mirror revealed Kae staring back at me. Kaelyn would be left behind in this bedroom, like a forgotten mask. My shoulders dropped in relief at the familiarity of my appearance.

The sight of Edmonde's old jacket tightened my chest. Without thinking, I wandered back into the hallway. Three rooms down, and I was in front of his door. With a careful turn of the knob, I found my brother's bedroom in the same condition as I had last seen it.

My mother had insisted on keeping it untouched for a short while, but it seemed that no one could bring themselves to clear it out. I crept toward his closet and pulled out a dark blouse. One that had sleeves flowing like the river just outside the kingdom. He had worn this to one of the bars we went to for his birthday. I rubbed the soft fabric between my fingers as I headed back to my own room.

My bedroom resided only on the second floor of the castle, dangerous, but after a year at sea facing sirens, I wasn't afraid of heights. With Edmonde's shirt tucked into my belt, I glanced at the ground far below. I climbed out of my window and found my footing in the loose stones that I had knocked out years before. They acted as small ledges to balance my weight on.

Slowly but with years' practice of sneaking down that very wall, I descended the castle and landed on the grassy ground in silence. I half-crouched down and snuck my way alongside the main path that led to the gates of the city. A carriage obscured me from view, allowing me to pass the castle's wall without the guards' notice.

I let out a sigh of relief once beyond the castle walls and into the city. I was back to feeling like myself again almost instantaneously. With plans to hopefully run into some of my crew at the local taverns, I made my way toward the kingdom's harbor with a sudden spring in my step.

Chapter Three
Aqeara

I stared at my reflection in the sunken mirror, observing the non-existent flaws in my pores. My fiery red hair flowed in rhythm to the ocean's lethargic movements. Humming a new tune that I had recently come up with, I smiled at my new shells now covering my breasts with a perfect fit. I had just returned from swimming all around the cove this morning and was ecstatic at finding these light green clamshells.

"They do not really match your tail though, do they? You should have gone for the emerald green ones. Those were lovely!" Hyrissa exclaimed.

Small bubbles rose to the cave's ceiling as she spoke.

Hyrissa looked at me with a similar shade of envy. As the youngest princess of the royal family, Hyrissa was not yet allowed to wear colorful shells as they were a sign of coming of age. Instead, less-appealing seaweed fashioned into a covering lay atop her midriff.

I was older, though, and got to exchange my dull and cracked white shells for these new ones. It was very common to match one's shells in the exact shade as one's tail. Most sirens did it as a trendy fashion statement. It annoyed me to see the same color twice. How positively boring!

"Yes, but I do not care to match my tail exactly. I wish to don as many colors as I can. Honestly, I should have gone for the lavender ones. You know men are always after pied treasures. I want to be as colorful as their jewels to lure them in." I did not remove my gaze away from my reflection as I spoke to my cousin.

I ran a delicate finger through my hair and let it part itself naturally. It was true, from what I was aware of at least, that humans loved colorful things. Their sunken ships were filled with sparkling jewels and other treasures that littered the ocean floor.

So, as a warrior, I wanted to make myself as variegated as possible: my red hair against my green shells and tail, along with my bright golden eyes, which stood out against my porcelain skin.

"Oh, you and your obsession with hunting men. I have given up on tasting the flesh of humans. They never venture this far out into the sea, and I am forbidden to leave the city's borders," Hyrissa said, and I knew she was starting to go through one of her fits.

"That rule has not stopped you before," I reminded her as memories of us sneaking out to visit shipwrecks came to mind.

My cousin shot me a look.

"I give up! I shall eat common bannerfish for the rest of my days," Hyrissa said, crossing her arms over her chest.

She drifted, rather dramatically, to the bottom of the room and onto the pale sand. Her golden hair flowed out wildly around her. I was used to the antics of my younger cousin. I rolled my eyes and swam down next to her.

Before I could open my mouth to offer comforting words, a siren swam to the rock opening of Hyrissa's room and bowed at the sight of the two of us.

"Good morning, Your Majesty," Noerina greeted a grumbling Hyrissa and then turned to me.

"There has been a sighting of the hunters' ship. After months of searching, we found them docked at the port of the golden city. We should move at once." Noerina spoke in a formal, authoritative voice.

Noerina was the head of my warrior troop. One of the oldest sirens alive, she was therefore automatically given a higher ranking than I, much to my distaste. Her bright orange hair stood out in stark contrast to all other sirens. It almost seemed to glow when under the sunlight, a feature that no other siren had. It added another intimidation factor to Noerina's authority, which I had no choice but to respect. On top of her high-ranking, and therefore ability to use compulsion on us, Noerina was not one to be trifled with.

As for her mention of the hunters' ship, I rose off the ocean floor.

"I will meet you with the rest of the troop at the edge of Meyrial's border. Thank you, Noerina," I said.

Noerina nodded at my apparent but nonchalant dismissal. She bowed toward Hyrissa and left.

This group of hunters had killed seven sirens in the past ten months; a number that caused unease throughout the kingdom. For as long as sirens have existed, men have tried to hunt us down. Usually to no avail, though there was the off-chance that the occasional siren met her terrible fate. Seven dead in just one year was frightening.

That was an entire troop of warriors. There were only two left: mine and one other. The rest of the troops disbanded to procreate. It was against our laws to be a warrior and mother, so many gave up their ways to raise offspring and help repopulate our species. Besides the hunting, sirens also met their unjust fate in nets or at the ends of fishing spears. I, for one, did not care to produce youthlings of my own. I loved my position in protecting my kin.

"I have a proposition for you," I said after I was certain Noerina was out of earshot.

Hyrissa was still lamenting on the ground. Her arm draped over her head. At the mischievous tone in my voice, she straightened up and swam toward me. Her golden eyes were gleaming. It was not the first time I had suggested something dangerous that usually resulted in us either getting yelled at or nearly eaten. If anyone asked about the latter, the great white shark had come out of nowhere.

"You sneak out with our troops and join us in taking down these men. You can finally get your taste for human flesh and put those singing skills I have been training you for to the test," I said, seeing my idea come to fruition in my mind.

"Oh, how wonderful! I will be delighted to come. What about your commander?" Hyrissa clapped her hands in glee and fretted about her seaweed top.

"Noerina would not mind once we get far enough away from the city." I said with a shrug. "It will be too much of a hassle to make you turn back around and travel home by yourself. Besides, this is the chance you need to prove yourself to the Queen that you are capable of venturing beyond the city's walls!"

Hyrissa was the youngest of the queen's seven daughters. I knew the queen would not notice if Hyrissa was gone for a day. We had snuck out multiple times under her nose and nothing bad had happened before.

I wordlessly handed Hyrissa my old set of shells, hoping to better disguise my cousin, who was covered in the seaweed of youths.

"Yes! You are right, Aqeara. Let me fix up my hair and we must leave at once. I cannot wait to finally kill a man!" Hyrissa was beaming as she spoke.

She hummed to herself as she changed into my old white shells and fixed her hair in the mirror. It was the tune we'd been practicing. I watched as she rehearsed her facial expressions, and couldn't help but smile.

I knew once Hyrissa got her taste for men that she would not be content with just living off of fish like the rest of Meyrial's citizens. Sirens could easily survive off just fish, as it was our primary diet, but nothing compared to the energy human flesh gave us. But only warriors, those who have lured men to their deaths got to reap the rewards.

"I am ready! You are my favorite cousin, you know." Hyrissa swam out of the cave without waiting for a response.

"I am your only cousin," I muttered under my breath.

I scanned the waters as we exited the castle, to be sure we weren't spotted.

The castle was at the edge of Meyrial, the siren city, and the border walls where we were to meet my troop were on the opposite side. The castle inhabited only the Queen, her seven daughters, and me. And it was made of a mixture of coral and stone, formed out of multiple caves stacked on top of one another, which closely resembled the structure of a human castle. The varying bright colors stood tall against the vibrant blue sea.

Hyrissa and I swam past the many siren homes in a blur. Meyrial's marketplace was overcrowded with fish traders and fashion merchants and citizens shopping in the midday sun.

I had to tug Hyrissa along when she protested to stop for a bite. We would soon feast on a much better meal.

We slowed as the border wall loomed within view. The warriors were already gathered, talking amongst themselves as they waited for Noerina's orders. Hyrissa broke off to avoid anyone's attention, remaining several paces behind while I checked in with Noerina.

"We are all here. Let us get a move on. The current should be in our favor today. Our sea god is looking out for us," Noerina called.

She looked to the heavens above the ocean, silently asking for Idros to bless our mission. I caught sight of Hyrissa hiding behind a tall strand of seaweed.

She nodded at me.

Without another word, the eight of us departed toward the golden city, though not entirely uniform, I had to fight to keep a safe distance behind the rest of the troop. I was itching to sink my teeth into these siren killers. I'd only had the chance to hunt down five humans, not nearly as many as my fellow sisters. I was eager to prove myself.

Hyrissa swam closely behind me, angling herself so that my body would block Noerina's view of her if she happened to glance back. Though my cousin wore cracked shells, I was glad I thought to switch the seagrass for them. Idros knows how horribly she would stand out without them.

There was a current that flowed straight to the golden city near the borders of Meyrial. It was faster for travel than swimming the whole way and always gave me a jolt of energy. When we reached an opening, we all threw ourselves forward one by one and yelped in anticipation. Our swift movements were barely detectable to the traveling fish as we cut through the ocean in flashes of color.

As expected, the current filled me with jitters. I knew this would be one of the most memorable and honorable fights of my life. My blood sang for what was to come.

"Do we swim through this the entire way there?" Hyrissa asked in a low voice.

She kept up with us with a sense of swiftness and alacrity. She had always been the fastest swimmer out of her sisters.

When I looked back, I saw her expression had changed. The worried lines were enough to reveal Hyrissa's stance about crossing the open ocean. The creases were gone as quickly as they came.

Hyrissa always liked to appear impassive, but I knew her better than that.

"Do not worry, these currents are safe for sirens. Nothing but small fish travel through them." I tried making my tone light, but serious. "You are the furthest outside the city you have ever been. You finally get to use your voice on the humans. This will be the most momentous day."

I remained at the back of the troop, hoping no one would bother turning around. None had yet.

"You do not suppose mother will be angry with me when she finds out? Oh, she must be proud if I can manage to kill a hunter. She must be," Hyrissa reassured herself.

She was good at that, calming herself down when her stress threatened to overcome her. I remained silent, not wanting to disturb her encouragement. What good would it do to mention that if she failed today, the Queen would be deadly furious?

Nearly halfway to the golden city, we broke off from the current to hunt a school of yellow fish that had gathered to our right. It would give us the boost of energy we needed to keep swimming and to take out the hunters once we found them.

"You may hunt two fish each and then we are to return to the current." Noerina ordered as she swam like a lightning bolt after her prey. "We will waste no more time than absolutely necessary before we reach the hunters."

I captured my meal and ate in silence. I knew this would not fill my belly, but the imagined taste of human flesh already created an insatiable appetite for the predator in me. This would have to do for now.

I was lost in thought as I floated beside Hyrissa.

"Hyrissa? What are you doing here?" A familiar voice sent a chill down my spine.

I looked up to meet the golden eyes of my eldest cousin, Clagoria.

As the siren queen's oldest daughter, Clagoria was next in line to the throne. She had joined the siren warriors when she became of age, just before me, though she was not part of this troop. She was the head of the other remaining one.

I could not believe I had not noticed her before we left. She must have taken the place of the feeble Merenah, who had injured her tail the week before.

Clagoria's brilliant blue hair, resembling the ocean far up north near the icicles, had a sharp distinction against her red face filled with apparent anger. Hyrissa whimpered and glanced at me for help. She looked like a young seal pup seeking its mother's protection against a killer whale.

"She wanted to come along and prove herself to the Queen. I was the one who suggested the idea. I take full responsibility for her." I tried not to speak too fiercely to my cousin, and I did not dare say anything like a challenge to the future queen.

This was not the first time the two of us had gotten into a heated argument. There were still fissures in the boulders bordering the kingdom that had suffered our last fight. I could not even remember what it had been about.

"This is not a simple mission, and you know that, Aqeara. These hunters are dangerous."

"I have heard her songs. I know she is capable." I kept direct eye contact with my cousin, refusing to back down.

"Her first hunt should not be with these men."

"I have trained with her for many years. You have witnessed how strong she is."

Clagoria let out a rather final huff.

"Fine. If you are so certain about this, I will hold you accountable for my little sister. You are responsible for her safety." Clagoria did not spare her sister a glance as she swam back toward Noerina.

The two spoke with bowed heads, their voices not carrying through the waters. Her threat remained unspoken, but I knew the consequences of what would happen if I made a single mistake today. Clagoria always hounded me for perfection.

"Everyone! Time to get back on course." Noerina led us back to the current as we continued our journey.

Hyrissa swam alongside me now that she did not have to hide. We twisted through the snaking ocean current as a more unified group. A familiar bend up ahead told me we had reached the halfway point to our destination. The sunbeams provided crystalline light through the clear water.

The ocean was warmer as we traveled, caressing my skin in a welcoming gesture.

"She hates me." Hyrissa said quietly, bringing my attention to her. "I know she does. She finds me annoying; do you agree? Like I am the spine of a sea urchin lodged in her side."

Her shoulders were more relaxed than when we'd left, and her breathing came out steadier. She knew she would not be getting scolded today, especially if she managed to kill a hunter. Which was why she had come in the first place.

"Clagoria does not hate you, she cares deeply for you. You must be prepared to use the techniques we have been practicing. If you do not lure a hunter into the water, this excursion will have been a waste for you, and I am certain Clagoria will see to it that I receive some sort of denouncement." I fussed with my shells while I spoke.

"I am ready. I have been working on my song and practicing my tone. You do not have to worry about me." Hyrissa grew more determined.

I was glad.

We both flapped our tails harder and swam closer to the rest of the warriors.

Chapter Four
Aqeara

Hours passed. The thought of our future prey looming ahead kindled the jitters within us. We were starved, unable to draw forth any energy until we tasted human flesh.

The warm and shallow waters were the first sign that we were nearing the kingdom. A ship loomed overhead, ready to dock at the nearby port. I noted that it was not the ship belonging to the hunters. The bottom was small, perhaps meant for local fishing trips.

As we reached the harbor's port, we fanned out in search of the familiar wooden carving of a woman that adorned the hunters' ship. Other ships—not the one we wanted—floated in the harbor, anchors digging into the sandy floor. The metal chains swayed in tune to the ocean's rhythm like long seaweed kelps. The water turned to a shade of turquoise in these shallow parts. I did my best to avoid the lobster traps floating by.

Hyrissa stayed close to me in our search, her eyes wide with wonder and overstimulation. Several times her mouth opened as if to speak, but she remained silent and took everything in.

"Here!" Clagoria called out after several minutes of searching. She sent out a sound that bounced off nearby objects, letting us know her location.

We all raced to meet her. I paused several feet from the ship and craned my neck up to look at it. This vessel carried the men responsible for the death of seven of our sisters. My blood boiled. They deserved to meet the same bloody fate they bestowed on their victims.

No one may kill a siren and live to tell the tale. The faces of those stolen from us flitted through my mind. I did not linger on the dark thoughts. It would only drag me into that endless void of grief. Sirens looked out for one another. We protected our own.

And the hunters destroyed that. They had caused so much fear amongst our kind.

Noerina sneered and pressed a hand to the bottom of the hull. She was trying to feel for any vibrations that indicated there were humans on board. She shook her head in annoyance.

"There is not a living soul on the ship. They must have gone ashore already," Noerina stated, disappointment echoing in her tone.

I grunted in frustration.

If the hunters departed, who knew how long it would be before they returned? I breathed through clenched teeth at the thought of delaying our mission. Revenge and hunger alike fueled me to keep some of my dwindling patience in check.

"Perhaps we can break surface and see if any of them are on the docks?" Domora asked.

Noerina nodded and the eight of us swam to the surface. I poked my head out and looked around the winding docks.

Nothing.

"We need to spread out again. Get everyone on all sides of the dock and look for men in pirate's clothing," Clagoria suggested.

Pirates were almost always covered in mud or blood, unkempt and disgusting compared to noble sailor-men. I had told Hyrissa as much in our lessons. Those were the humans who hunted sirens. Those were the humans we wanted to kill.

"Meet back at the bottom of the hull in fifteen minutes. Make a call if you spot anything," Noerina said.

She dismissed us with a single nod, and we all went separate ways. Hyrissa followed after me.

"If you are going to prove yourself, try tracking on your own," I said to her.

Hyrissa's eyes widened in excitement, and she nodded eagerly. Her tail flapped as she disappeared around a corner, leaving nothing but bubbles in her wake.

I swam to the other side of the boat and popped my head out again above the surface. Below, the docks were nothing more than long supportive wooden beams that spanned from the bottom of the ocean floor to above the ocean's surface. But up above, the flat boards nailed together held humans, creaking under their weight. The sun tried its hardest to lift the soaked wood free of seawater.

From here, I could see part of the kingdom, with strange structures in the distance. I focused again on the harbor. A few men sat at one end of the dock, but they were not hunters. They carried no weapons save for a fishing rod.

Fishermen, I thought to myself. I swam back down and continued my search. My hands twitched at my sides at the lack of hunters in the harbor.

I swam closer to the docks and resurfaced. As far as my eye could see, the docks were mostly empty. Two women were laughing and walking toward the fisherman. None of them were threats.

I shook my head and plunged deeper to remain out of sight. I started toward the direction of our meeting point, hoping to find Hyrissa. We had a better chance of searching together.

Nothing could have prepared me for the sight before me. The young siren was half out of the water, feasting on the corpse of a small boy. He could not have been older than ten or twelve in human years. His dark skin was torn open at his bent neck. Blood streamed out at a steady rate into Hyrissa's mouth and the surrounding water.

"Hyrissa! What in the name of Idros are you doing?" My shaky voice reflected the fear and rage that threatened to overcome me.

Sirens only named our sea god aloud when we were stressed or asking for a blessing. It was considered bad luck otherwise.

It was one thing to kill an adult man—a hunter. But a child? Children were so young. Damned if they could grow up to become hunters, but I could not stomach the sight of harming something so innocent. But most importantly, children were always surrounded by multiple other humans who were always alert and protective of their young. I knew a novice like Hyrissa did not stand a chance against more than one angry human.

I quickly rose to the surface and yanked the body away from Hyrissa, who hissed at the removal of her prey. Her eyes were pitch black and yellow scales had appeared on her cheekbones, a common occurrence when sirens were hunting.

Hyrissa's razor-sharp teeth were covered in blood and flesh. When we fed, our primal instincts kicked in. To remove one's prey was an act of war. She moved forward as if to attack, but froze at the sound of danger.

At the sight of what was before them, the two women who I had spotted previously watched the scene before them in terror. One of them let out a scream while the other gagged. Their cries for help caught the attention of a few nearby men who rushed further to investigate.

Before we could react, we had been seen. I pulled Hyrissa down beneath the surface, risking her predatory wrath but not caring. She needed to get out of harm's way before the humans came to attack us.

In the moment, I feared Clagoria's anger at Hyrissa being hurt more than a couple of angry, murderous humans.

I made a high-pitched noise in the back of my throat, a warning cry for my sisters. Hyrissa looked up from her meal instinctively at the sound, and her eyes slowly faded back to the golden hue they normally were.

She let go of the boy's body and gave it one last glance as it sank to the bottom of the ocean.

"*Hyrissa!*" Clagoria's voice was laced in venom, her eyes alit with pure fury.

Before she could censure her sister, several more humans fell into the water. Melodious tunes caressed my ears.

The other sirens, because of their hunger or adrenaline, sang to the men that approached the docks. Splashes of human bodies hitting the water mixed with the sirens' songs. It was a mass feeding frenzy.

I was soon engulfed in clouds of blood and harmonious tunes. Through the chaos, all I could do was focus on Hyrissa. Hyrissa, satisfied with her meal, distanced herself from the mayhem.

She looked at me as if to say, *See? I did this. I fed our troop.*

That smug grin was replaced with a look of shock an instant later. She looked down at the arrow that struck her chest directly above her heart. It had come out of nowhere, lodged securely in her ribcage. Without thinking, she pulled the arrow out before I could rush to her and stop her from doing that very thing.

I did not have to further investigate to know that the arrowhead was made of *zephlum*, a metal found deep in the caves on Zephlus island. Little could kill a siren faster than decapitation or *zephlum* to the heart.

My heart dropped as if I had sunk to the very bottom of the deepest trenches in a matter of seconds. This was not happening. It was a blur, too fast for me to comprehend what this meant. By the time I got to Hyrissa, wrapping my arms protectively around her, I knew it was too late.

I screamed as the life left Hyrissa's eyes. Her mouth was still open in a perfect *O* from shock. Red flooded my vision, but it was no longer from the human blood. In my embrace, her body turned into a cloud of sand. It was what happened when a siren died; her body was given back to the ocean.

The sand slipped out of my fingers and I floated there. Alone.

My heartbeat thundered in my ears. A ringing noise competed with it, though I had no idea of its source. My breathing came out rapid and shallow.

Hyrissa's cloud of sand slowly dissipated into the ocean, never to be seen again. She was gone. I nearly choked on a sob at the thought.

I snapped out of my grief when an arrow whizzed past my head, missing me by two inches. I refocused my energy and rose to the surface to see who was responsible for the death of my best friend.

"Hunters!" Noerina spat out in answer to my unspoken question.

She was hidden beneath the dock, floating above the surface of the water.

One look at my broken face and the absence of Hyrissa by my side told Noerina everything she needed to know. The princess was dead. Murdered.

Her face crumpled and matched my rage. It took over her features in a deadly manner. I tore my gaze away from her to see a scrawny young man standing above her on the dock. He was aiming a crossbow directly at my face. I opened my mouth to sing but was beaten by Noerina.

I have swum hundreds of miles
I have come to the land above
I have traveled just to find you
My darling sailor, my love

The young man slowly lowered his crossbow, entranced by the soothing lullaby. His cheeks were flushed, eyes wildly looking for the source of the voice. He was on the young side, lanky and skittish. The perfect prey.

I broke my attention from him and looked to where Clagoria and Domora were fighting off three other men. The humans were no match for their coy smiles and sharp teeth. Even in the middle of a sea of blood, they were hauntingly beautiful. They would lure the hunters soon enough.

The other three warriors, Arriris, Genilyn, and Tolia, had fled the scene. Or at least, I hoped they had managed to get somewhere safe. I could not bear the thought of losing a single other siren today.

I snapped my focus back to the man as Noerina revealed herself from under the dock. She was still singing intently. Scales lined her cheekbones. She was in predator mode, focused, yet at ease in her predatory state.

The man locked eyes with Noerina and jumped.

"Kipp! No! GET AWAY FROM HIM!" One of the men fighting Clagoria and Domora roared at Noerina.

I sunk my head a little lower toward the surface to hide from the view of the shouting one.

He ran over to where the young man had jumped off the dock, his sword raised and gleaming with the same sparkling black of *zephlum* as the arrowheads. I knew he was no match for Noerina, but I still swam closer as the man paused. Recognition flitted across his face, stopping him in his tracks.

Noerina barely looked up in acknowledgement as she snapped the neck of the young man. She sank her teeth into his shoulder, pulling away a large chunk of flesh. Blood billowed out from the open wound, staining the turquoise water a bright crimson. The predator in me, restless from lack of human prey, moved forward.

"Stay back," Noerina commanded in a possessive tone with the full force of her ranking.

The sound of her compulsion forced me to snap out of my hunting state. I swam backward to give her space and watched as she tore out another chunk from the human's neck.

I licked my lips and looked away for just a moment to see if my cousin and Domora were faring well. There was so much blood, I could see little of anything, but a large splash in their direction told me they had at least one hunter in the water with them.

They were winning.

"*You.* You killed him! And Kipp!" The man quickly recovered from whatever had previously paused him and jumped right onto Noerina and her victim's body, sword raised to swing.

He straddled Noerina with a murderous look in his eyes. The man aimed his sword at my commander's head, and she screamed as she was separated from her meal.

She reared on him with pitch black eyes as the discarded body sank to the ocean floor. I had half a mind to go after it and finish the meal, but I was rooted to the spot.

At the last second, before the sword could graze her neck, Noerina's hand shot out to catch the blade. She let out a small yelp of pain as the *zephlum* cut into her palm. Her blood sizzled out of the wound before it could quickly heal shut. Just having the metal touch our skin was like touching acid.

To my surprise, the man was unphased as Noerina's grip tightened on the sword, drawing even more blood. She did not intend to let go.

I felt helpless, floating—watching. I would have offered aid had it not been for her direct order. I could not move closer. The magic compulsion in her voice kept me floating there, watching the two fight for their lives.

It was only when I saw the gleam of a dagger that the man produced from his belt that I screamed and tried to swim forward, feeling the order block me yet again. The man drove the dagger into Noerina's heart. Bones cracked as the blade cut through ribs.

He squinted in the water and looked at my face with a startled expression, but quickly pushed away from my commander's body to swim back toward the dock. Noerina turned to me, mouth open as if to say something. I was immobilized, frozen from shock, as Noerina became nothing more than a cloud of sand. Her final words left unsaid.

Relief washed over me as Clagoria and Domora swam to me unscathed. I could see the hunters they'd not killed swimming toward the docks. The blood began to dissipate, a mixture of siren and human alike.

As the three of us joined together, an arrow shot through the water in front of us. Domora cried out in surprise and we all fled from the docks toward the safety of the open ocean, cloaked temporarily by the already fading crimson hue.

The floor dropped down abruptly, no longer shallow and near land. We soon caught up with Arriris, Genilyn, and Tolia, who were swimming in small circles.

They relaxed when they saw us. The three were the youngest in our troop, save for Hyrissa, and were newly trained warriors. We had expected a swift sneak attack, not an ambush, and the three novices would not have survived. It was good they had fled.

"Where is she? Where is Hyrissa?" Clagoria spun around and focused on me once we were a safe distance from the harbor.

Hyrissa. Noerina. Both dead. Both billows of sand returning to the sea.

I said nothing as my body continued to run hot. We were safe, but that did not stop my heart from thundering like a tropical storm. My stomach felt as if I had just swallowed a rotten fish whole.

It had been my idea to bring Hyrissa along, after all. I did not think… We were supposed to have the element of surprise.

I could have sworn I taught Hyrissa not to attack children. That seeing young boys, even alone, meant their older, protective humans would be nearby, eager to strike anything that threatened their young. Hyrissa had been so careful in our sessions, working on her song and how to spot the perfect prey.

Hunger must have gotten the better of her. She was supposed to be scouting, not hunting. I should have never left her alone. I was supposed to protect her. She was dead because of me.

Noerina was dead because of me.

"Answer me!" Clagoria swam in my face, and I made no move to swim back as she yelled.

She was my commander now, by default. Her commanding compulsion moved my mouth before my brain processed the words. It was meant only to keep us safe, ensure we followed orders and didn't make mistakes... like attacking children. It stung to hear Clagoria use it on me. In all my years of living, I had never seen her this angry before.

"One of the hunters killed her. Noerina killed that hunter before another got to her. Clagoria I—" Clagoria cut me off as her hand sliced through the water, barely detectable to the eye, and slapped me across the face.

The other sirens swam back, mourning their loss at a safer distance. Or perhaps avoiding her rage being turned on them as well. I stood still and allowed the sharp pain to shoot across my cheeks. My tears flowed into the ocean, though I was certain they weren't from the pain.

"This is your fault!" Clagoria spat at me and I did my best not to flinch. "My commander is dead. My little sister is dead. Royal blood has been spilled."

I tried to not even twitch under the gaze of her wrath. Any sign of weakness would only anger my older cousin even more. I remained silent as the guilt ate at me, settling in my gut and threatening to heave out.

"You are banished from Meyrial. If you dare enter the city, you shall—you shall be beheaded at once. I never want to see you again. Ever." The power in Clagoria's voice was thick as she enunciated every word, even when her voice broke on the last word.

The four onlooking sirens expressed their shock in a chorus of gasps, but none dared to speak.

"But Clagoria—" I silenced myself as I saw the hurt and anger in her eyes.

"You will stay in this exact spot until the moon rises. Only then may you continue your lifelong banishment wherever you seek," Clagoria said.

Without another word, she turned her back on me and swam away. The others followed her, casting sorrowful glances over their shoulders as they left. I watched as the five sirens gradually became smaller and smaller, and continued staring even after they disappeared in the distance.

The moonrise would not come for several hours. I thought of the hunters. I was still near the harbor. Were they following after me on their ship?

I would welcome death with open arms should they encounter me in my paralyzed state. Perhaps I would get the chance to avenge Noerina and kill her hunter with the ridiculous hat. That would be an honorable death, one I feared I did not deserve.

Though I did not much like my commander most days, she had taught me everything I knew from perfecting my song to protecting myself from the hunters. She had taken care of us. When a sea urchin's needles were stuck in my tail, she had yanked them out for me and shed tears on my wounds.

The teardrops of sirens had healing properties. And though I was full-on sobbing now, no amount of healing from my tears could mend my broken heart.

My sobbing intensified when I thought of Hyrissa. My poor little cousin just wanted an adventure and to follow in my footsteps. What kind of warrior was I if I could not save the life that meant the most to me?

Hyrissa was to become of age next winter. She would have earned her own shells in a massive ceremony. Now she was gone forever.

Tear after tear streamed down my cheeks as Hyrissa's face burned into my vision. I succumbed to the pain in a way closest to what I imagined drowning was like. A perfect irony. A deserved death.

Chapter Five
Kae

The ocean seemingly returned to its normal hue of crystal blue, the ever-lapping waves having washed away the blood and remains.

The sirens had escaped after I missed all three of them with the last arrow in the crossbow. Sharpshooting was certainly not my expertise.

I sat on the dock fuming, heart racing, dripping saltwater everywhere. A small puddle had formed around me, soaking into the old wood. I couldn't bring myself to stand. My legs had given out on me long before the water had slowly faded back to its normal color.

Instead of trying to get up, I stared ahead, waiting for our sharpshooter to come out of the water. Kipp needed to come get his crossbow. He would surface, water pressing his hair to his temples, and tell us we needed to go after those demons. Why wasn't he surfacing?

Ruff and Dalton limped their way over to me, nursing minor injuries. Nothing major, some scrapes and bruises here or there, but otherwise intact. The tension in my shoulders dissipated slightly at the sight of them. They were okay. They would be okay. The three of us sat in silence, engulfing ourselves in the weight of the past thirty minutes.

It was only a mere hour ago that we had met up at the tavern that overlooked the ocean, sharing mead and discussing our next expedition. Then the screaming had started. The four of us tried fighting off the multiple sirens with wax coverings in our ears.

I'd never known they could fight back with this much aptness when their song couldn't reach us. They were bloodthirsty and faster than I had ever seen before. Dalton, Ruff, and I were desperately trying to fight off two sirens while they tried to drag us into the blue-green water. Their mouths had been covered in blood; their eyes black as night.

One had somehow managed to pull Dalton in the water and Ruff had jumped in after him without a second thought. The screams of the onlookers still rang in my ears. Or were they my own?

The two had managed to get out alive. That was when I noticed Kipp had not been by my side. No nightmare could match the jolting feeling as I watched Kipp raise his crossbow to fire. There had been no wax coverings in his ears and I knew it was too late.

Kipp would not be coming out of the water. He was gone. My memories blurred, blood mixing with screams. Adrenaline still coursed through me. My breathing was rapid as I tried to calm down.

We were silent, but Ruff's shoulders moved as sobs raked through his body, bringing me back to the present. Kipp was like a younger brother to Ruff; the two were always joking around—inseparable. He was like the entire crew's little brother. Losing a member of my crew brought back the feeling of losing Edmonde all over again. What was worse, the two had died at the hands of the same siren.

"I'm so sorry for your loss, your Highness," the survivor off Edmonde's ship had murmured, a bandage wrapped around his hand.

He leaned onto a cane with tears in his eyes. I stared at him from a long dark tunnel, my vision caving in. My mother's cry echoed in my ears as I spiraled into grief.

Weeks later, when I went to meet up with the same man, he told me my brother's killer had bright orange hair. All sirens seemed to have distinctive colors, so it was easy to spot the very same siren that had taken my brother snapping the neck of my friend.

I'd killed her. Edmonde was avenged. Kipp was avenged. It had to count for something. It had to.

"We should gather the rest of the men. Let them know what happened," Dalton said, pulling me out of my memories.

I discreetly wiped the corner of my eye on my already soaking shirt sleeve before I looked up at Dalton.

His dirty blonde hair was dripping still, leaving his skin looking far more pale than I was used to. Dalton's usual easy-going demeanor was gone from his face. He looked like a ghost compared to the charming, energetic version of him I knew. It pained me to see my best friend so sullen.

"I think I need a drink," Ruff said.

I turned to look at him, but Ruff had already stood up and was making his way to the pub down the street.

Dalton and I shared a look before we both rose to our feet and quickly followed. As we walked, I made sure my hat was secured on my head. I wondered to myself if Ruff had noticed how much smoother my face had gotten since I had been back in Avalon. It had been a concern earlier today as well, when I first met up with them at the pub that afternoon. No one had made a comment, but was it noticeable now?

Perhaps in the erratic events of the day, he hadn't noticed. I didn't let my concerns overwhelm me as we walked through the doors of the bar. I didn't have enough energy in me to care any more about my identity at the moment.

Before entering the pub, I glanced back at the horizon. No signs of sirens or lost ones. The harbor was hauntingly calm, as if nothing life-changing had happened on those docks. The ocean lethargically swayed without a care in the world.

The gentle chatter of customers during the daytime hours was comforting background noise. The pub wasn't too crowded, as it was still early, so we made our way to the back and sat down in a private booth.

A barmaid came over and took our orders—three pints of beer—and left us to ourselves.

No one spoke. My eyes darted between my two friends, who were looking in different directions, their eyes glazed over. I hated being alone with my thoughts. I'd much rather distract myself with something—anything but thinking about Kipp.

The barmaid returned with three glasses filled to the brim with the golden liquid.

"Here you go." She flashed a dazzling smile at Dalton, who grabbed his drink without once looking at her and slid the other over to Ruff.

I grabbed my own and thanked her, but she left with a huff, clearly not used to being ignored.

We sipped our drinks in silence. Ruff quaffed down his entire drink in mere seconds and called back the barmaid to order another. I much preferred rum or wine over this wheat juice. I stared at the liquid in contempt and took a small sip, though I wasn't even sure I could stomach it at all after today. I was surprised Ruff could.

"I agree with what you said earlier, Dalton." Ruff said. "We have to inform the crew. As soon as we can raise the sails, we must go after those disgusting monsters until all of them are wiped out from existence."

Ruff gulped down half of his second drink before the barmaid even left our table. He gave an apologetic look after he slammed his cup down. She raised her eyebrows but said nothing, leaving to fetch him another.

After she left, Ruff did little to hide the way his hands shook.

Even I was shocked at how angry Ruff seemed. He usually never spoke his feelings aloud. Dalton nodded to my first mate and the two of them turned to look at me. They needed their captain's approval.

I would rather have been in that awful dress with a face full of makeup than deal with everything right at that moment. I needed time alone to collect my thoughts and my bearings. To plan. To breathe. To process.

"Dalton, send word out immediately that we are to depart tomorrow morning." I said with neither malice nor elation in my voice—I did my best to keep it as neutral as possible. "We'll head straight to Zephlus to restock on weapons and then set about to hunt down that group of sirens."

Dalton placed some bronze coins on the table for his drink. He left the pub without another word. The barmaid stared at Dalton's retreating figure and placed more drinks on our table.

"What's a handsome man like him leaving after one drink?" she said.

Neither Ruff nor I had the energy to respond. She seemed annoyed, but said nothing else, retreating to the other side of the pub. Any other time, I would have pondered if Ruff knew about Dalton's preferences, but I was far too exhausted to even think clearly.

Ruff went to reach for the drink in front of him, but I quickly dragged it toward myself. He shrugged and leaned back in his seat with his arms crossed in front of him. The tattoos that covered both his biceps were on full display, as were his muscles.

I knew this was what he did to intimidate others. It helped prevent many drunken bar fights, but it didn't work on me. I stared at Ruff's green eyes, now cold with grief and anger. I could have argued he always looked like this.

"The adrenaline of nearly dying and everything else that happened today might be making me bold here, but I think it's time we cut any secrets. Especially between us." Ruff reached for another drink that the barmaid had dropped off where Dalton was sitting.

He didn't break eye contact with me as he took a tentative sip.

My eyes widened before I caught myself and took a deep breath. He looked at me expectantly.

Did he know I was a woman? The princess of Avalon? He was my first mate, he should know, but what would he think?

My heart was racing, and I could feel myself starting to sweat, but I was getting way ahead of myself. I channeled my anxiety through restlessly tapping my foot below the table, out of Ruff's line of sight.

"What secrets are you referring to?" I took a large gulp of my beer and regretted it.

The lukewarm taste of dry grass made a permanent residence on my tongue.

We locked eyes. This was a showdown between the two of us. I was his captain. I had to remain strong. Ruff sighed and finished his beer, glancing around the room as he did.

Ruff leaned forward as he spoke, his voice slightly hushed. "I know you're a woman, Kae. Maybe you dislike being one. Or you think you can't lead us if you are. I really don't care what your reasoning is. What I do care about is that I am your first mate, and you can't even confide in me. Don't you trust me?"

My jaw dropped slightly, and blood crept into my cheeks. Though I felt faint, I also felt a large weight had been lifted off my chest. He knew. I wasn't sure how, but he knew.

"I'm not sure how to answer that. Yes, and no." I stared down at my lap as I spoke, then looked up to see his reaction. "Yes, I'm a woman, and I was afraid you and the crew wouldn't listen to a word I said if you knew. And no, it's not that I don't trust you. Of course, I trust you. I had my reasons."

Ruff shook his head. "No, you don't get to do that. Not now. Not after—" he cut himself off before saying Kipp's name. "Tell me your reasons, Kae."

Ruff would not break eye contact. The bags under his eyes seemed to have deepened in the past hour. He was tired. We both were. I picked at the skin on my nail bed before answering him.

"I'm the princess of Avalon. Heir to the throne." I said in a hushed tone, not wanting anyone else to overhear. "It was more about keeping my true identity a secret from everyone more than anything else. And I don't particularly care for my royal status, so I thought as Kae, I could leave that all behind in Avalon once we sailed in the open seas."

Ruff's eyebrows shot up.

It was easy for those from the outer and even middle sectors to not know what their princess looked like. All my life, Edmonde and I were kept locked in the castle, only leaving when we went away to the academy. We only got to interact with children of the elite and wealthy families in the inner sector. That is, until I grew bored with being kept within walls and began sneaking out at night.

"Well. That certainly is news," Ruff said, toneless, vague.

He stood up and tossed enough coins to cover both of our tabs. I tried protesting, but he shook his head. I stood up as well and followed him outside the pub. It was nearly sunset.

"This doesn't change anything, you know." He said with a sigh. "Though I need some time to process this. You're still my captain and my friend. I follow your command, no matter what."

Ruff paused and turned to me.

"I have to admit, Kae, you could have told me. I didn't much like piecing together the puzzle slowly and alone. And then when you came out of the water in the harbor…" Ruff looked directly into my eyes, "… it was like everything clicked into place. Why you were always so secretive about your quarters? Why you absolutely *had* to return home and not drink with the crew."

"I'm sorry," was all I said after a brief pause.

It was all I could say, but Ruff seemed satisfied with my response. Maybe it was the way my voice broke on those two words.

"I should have told you a lot sooner. You deserved to know." My fingers fumbled with the hem of my shirt. "You're one of my best friends, you know that, right?"

Ruff smiled and nodded.

"No more secrets." I extended my hand, and Ruff shook it.

He nodded to himself again, lost in whatever he wanted to say next.

I couldn't seem to stop myself from filling the quiet gaps.

"Dalton also knows." I added, and Ruff did not seem at all surprised. "He accidentally walked in on me changing once, so I had to explain myself. Just so you know."

"You guys are close, of course he knows. But now I also know, which will make him feel less special." Ruff's smile was warm, and I laughed.

Dalton was always in need of an occasional ego check.

"Does this mean I'll see you tomorrow for departure?" I asked, painfully aware of how small I sounded.

I hoped I wasn't being too precipitous about leaving Avalon so soon. We had to begin our journey at once. Every last siren had to die, especially those who fled.

A brief flicker of fear crossed my planning thoughts as I tried to figure how best to break the news to my parents. I would have to deal with that later.

"Aye, Captain." Ruff sighed. "While I would take your secret with me to the grave, I don't think the crew will mind. I suggest telling the men before we depart. It isn't right keeping secrets when we're all supposed to trust each other with our lives. Sleep on it. I'll see you at dawn."

Ruff saluted and gave my shoulder a small nudge before he left.

I let out a deep sigh of relief.

That had not gone how I'd expected, but I needed one less thing to worry about. I knew deep down that Ruff was right. If they were all willing to die for my cause and put their trust in me to lead them, it shouldn't matter if I was a woman. I had led them to victory. I had saved them from their boring lives for one filled with adventure and purpose. I would tell them tomorrow.

Without another thought down that winding path, I forced my legs to return home. It left me feeling strange.

Did I consider the *Mar Daemon* my home? Or the castle in Avalon?

Despite being a princess, I was alien to the royal scene. Acting a certain way and being watched by everyone was never something I enjoyed, but I knew that I would have to take the throne one day. I was now the only heir.

Yet here I was, preparing to sail again in the morning. I planned what lie I would come up with to my parents as I walked back to the heart of Avalon. Perhaps I would simply just disappear into the night without another word.

Chapter Six
Aqeara

*T*he sounds of harmonious melodies filled the hull of the sunken ship. We had spent the entire day swimming between the three large shipwrecks that surrounded Meyrial in the shape of a triangle, in and out of the damaged holes wrecked by cannonballs and aging wood.

The wreckage we were currently exploring was just outside the city walls, but not far enough to get us into serious trouble if we were caught. Exploring the human ships was a favorite pastime of ours. Hyrissa loved to scavenge for human trinkets as much as I did, collecting our shiniest findings and hiding them in our caves back home.

We also loved playing this game of guessing what each object was used for by the humans. It was humorous, as most sirens knew little about them. My primary source of knowledge about humans was what Noerina taught me, or what I heard in passing conversations as sailors shouted to one another on their ships.

My cousin took handfuls of the colorful stones that littered the floor, throwing them up into the water with glee. The jewels slowly *descended back to the ground, glittering in the sunlight and filling the ship with its reflected colors. A dozen rainbows danced along the walls of the ship's corpse.*

"Look at me!" I said, drawing the attention of Hyrissa.

She turned to me as I picked up a rusted fork. I smiled and imitated my cousin's jocosity, hoping to elicit a laugh, as I brushed my hair with the trinket. We both knew humans used this for eating, but I found it funny. Hyrissa's peal of laughter was contagious.

"Oh, look! This one is much larger." Hyrissa called as she grabbed something buried under a pile of wooden boards.

It looked similar to the fork I held in my hand, but several times larger. It looked more like a weapon—perhaps a spear—rather than an eating utensil. Hyrissa and I laughed in unison as she struggled to comb through her hair with the pronged ends.

There was no laughter now. There were no sun rays lighting up colorful stones nor were there fun trinkets used to comb hair. My memories were clouded with the blood from the attack. Hyrissa's contorted face in her final moments was all that came to mind when I thought of her now. My heart was being shredded into thin strips.

I knew that Clagoria's compulsion had run its course. The moon had risen. I could move, but I had nowhere to go. I could never return home to Meyrial—I would have to survive all on my own. The beams of moonlight illuminating my face broke me out of my guilt-ridden trance.

"I'm sorry, Hyrissa!" I shouted, heartbroken, to no one in particular. It did not seem that there was another living soul for miles. Then I whispered, "I miss you."

A bright light, small and shiny, illuminated the water before me. It was mesmerizing to look at, only it reminded me of an anglerfish. I blinked past the startling light and inhaled a sharp breath at what the light was attached to. A creature that almost resembled a siren stared back at me. Though their torso looked much like mine, their body was that of a slithering eel. Their skin was covered in blue scales. Glowing yellow eyes met my own. Instead of hair, the creature had tiny serpents swimming around their head.

"Missing someone? But someone is found! What are you doing all alone, little siren?"

The sibilant whispers echoed out of the creature, though their mouth remained shut. They resembled the anglera species that the Queen would describe in the stories she told me as a youthling. Anglera were evil sea demons known to lead sirens astray. They were to be avoided at all costs, known to steal the souls of innocent sirens. I always thought it was a way for the Queen to get us to behave as youthlings, but I knew a demon when I saw one.

"Don't be frightened, siren. Your grief is only temporary. Little do you know, your sweet Hyrissa can be returned to you."

My insides turned cold as ice, and I stiffened when the anglera circled me. Their long, dark body was threatening, as if poised for attack. Or to wrap around me and squeeze out my soul.

"How do you know who I am? Can you really bring back my cousin?" I demanded in a tone that made me sound stronger than I felt.

I was grateful for it. I did not want to be perceived as gullible or weak, despite feeling frightened to my core.

"Salophine can help you." The anglera said. *"She knows all. More than you think, more than you will ever know."*

They tilted their head and regarded me. My hesitation seemed to unnerve them.

"Come. Let me take you to her. Not too far from here."

Every word that escaped their mouth was a hiss of nails against coral. Their beady yellow eyes bore into my soul before a bulb of light was brought down within view again. I stared at it, and my mind went blank. Something swirled within that small bulb, like a lighthouse calling a boat to safety in a terrible storm. I found myself unable to look away from it. My thoughts of doubt subsided, and I relaxed.

They were nice. They could be trusted. It was almost like another voice spoke the reassurances in my head. *I can trust them.*

I did not dare move a muscle for fear this being would disappear. I could not risk losing the opportunity to bring my cousin back, even if it would lead me to my doom. But this anglera was nice. I straightened my back and lifted my chin. I spoke to the bulb with intensity.

"Take me to her, then. Take me to Salophine." As soon as the words left my mouth, I felt dizzy.

Once my eyes left that of the anglera, I immediately grew fearful again, as if I had blinked out of a trance. The same feeling that came when I had traveled too far down some of the deep, dark trenches south of Meyrial erupted. The pressure hurt my head and built up until I felt it might explode.

The anglera came to view once again as they lifted their bulb away from me. They swam behind me. I turned around and gasped at the sight before me. There was an oval of swirling water in the middle of the ocean that had not been there before. It appeared to be an opening to a current, only there was nothing behind it. Water rushed around it, sounding like a waterfall crashing down into the sea off a cliff. I stared when the anglera swam into it and disappeared. They did not come out on the other side of this strange phenomenon.

I swallowed hard at the sight of it, knowing they wanted me to follow them through this portal. I could not guarantee my own safety if I crossed the threshold, and the tips of my fingers felt numb with cold at the thought. Taking a single deep breath, I swam forward and resisted the urge to shut my eyes as I entered the oval.

I was startled to have found myself inside a cave. I should not have been able to see a single thing, but hundreds of glowing jellyfish floated alongside the walls and ceiling. They lit up the cave almost as well as sunlight. It was absolutely radiant. For just a moment, I forgot why I was here.

"I see you have met my chimera." A voice spoke up from the darkness where the light of the jellyfish did not reach.

I swam toward the voice with a sense of trepidation.

"You mean the anglera was just an illusion? They seemed so real," I wondered aloud and gasped when the owner of the voice emerged out of the darkness and into the bioluminescence.

The Queen had once told me dark and scary stories of sea witches when I was young. She believed in the powerful creatures that haunted nightmares and stole young and naïve sirens away. I always thought it was her way of scaring me and my cousins from leaving Meyrial, swimming too far, exploring too much, getting lost in the depths of the sea.

The sea witch that floated before me matched the Queen's descriptions far too closely, as if the Queen hadn't been telling a story, but retelling a memory. Her thin onyx hair floated around her head in wisps. Her bright crimson eyes terrified me. The sea witch's skin was a dull gray, reminding me of a corpse. Attached to her siren-like torso was a long, winding tail that matched her crimson eyes. Elegant scales lined the sides, and her webbed end flickered in tune to the ocean's movements. I had never seen a being with black hair before, as all sirens were born with colorful hues that drew in our prey.

"The anglera is an illusion I created, but they are very much real when I want them to be." Salophine said, her voice deep. "They can speak to you—touch you. My anglera was called to your distress, little one."

Rows of sharp teeth reflected the light off of the surrounding jellyfish.

She swam past me to a side of the cave that was aligned with numerous human jars and bottles. I tried not to dwell on her addressing me as little. I puffed out my chest in an attempt to appear like the fierce warrior I was. I would not be underestimated.

The anglera that lingered in the corner of my eye evaporated into a puff of smoke, disappearing as quickly as they had appeared.

"They mentioned my cousin, Hyrissa." I said as I eyed her closely. "There was a chance of her being brought back to life. How is that possible? Her body turned to sand already."

Everything inside me screamed for self-preservation. My tail twitched, wanting to swim away from this cave and strange creature. She had powers I could only ever dream up, if the Queen's stories proved to be veritable. Though, the Queen never lied to me before.

The sea witch procured several odd containers, not looking at me while she laid them down on a flat stone surface.

"Yes, that is why you came through the portal. You want your friend back. I can make it happen. I am known to help those in need of it."

Salophine opened a bottle and took a sniff. She made a face of disgust and set it down.

"What I require is nothing short of difficult to obtain." Salophine added. "You must be the one to get the key ingredient for this spell to return Hyrissa to the sea of the living."

Salophine continued to grab bottles and pour them into a larger container.

"What is this ingredient? Can I really bring Hyrissa back with just a simple spell?" I asked.

Doubt flooded my mind, but I pushed it aside at the slight taste of hope.

"The dark magic involved can bring her back, though do not mistake this spell as simple. What I need is for you to steal the heart of the one who loathes you the most. A hate-filled heart is the key ingredient I need."

"Who hates me the most? It must be Clagoria. She absolutely despises me." A prickle of anxiety struck as a cloud of black smoke rose out of the container that Salophine was mixing all her ingredients in.

Salophine disappeared into the back of the cave and came out with a large white sphere. It looked like a pearl, only it was not opaque. It shimmered in translucence.

"Here, look into this. It will show you the heart you must carve out for me," Salophine said as she dropped the orb into my outstretched hands.

I faltered a bit, nearly dropping the thing. It was heavier than expected. I felt foolish staring into it, but focused on the orb, anyway. A familiar face bubbled to the surface, and I almost dropped the orb again.

The face belonged to Noerina's killer, the hunter with the ugly hat. His silver eyes were staring out at something unseen by the current perspective of the orb. The focus on the man's face zoomed out, revealing his surroundings. He was on his ship again with the crew of hunters, barking orders to anyone who listened.

"*Yes, Captain Kae.*" The voices of the crewmen echoed back to him.

Kae. His name was sharp and acidic, just like him.

So, he was their captain. The image kept zooming out until I could see the entire ship. A name amongst the string of commands stood out to me: Zephlus. They were sailing to Zephlus, restocking on their *zephlum* supply. It meant they were after me, as well as Clagoria and the others.

"I will more than enjoy stealing this heart." My voice was cold and unyielding.

Seducing this lowlife and taking his heart would be easy. Meyrial and all of its inhabitants would have to welcome me back. My honor would be restored. Everything would go back to the way it was.

Noerina's face flickered through my mind, but I shook my head. Meddling with dark magic was bad enough already—who knew what the consequences would be if I brought back two souls. Besides, with her gone, I could be head of the warrior troop.

The cold thought made me wince.

"For the spell to be successful, you must steal this human's heart by the next full moon. That is the longest amount of time I can give you before your cousin's soul is lost to the sea of dead forever." Salophine lifted the container, shoving the other empty containers off the rock's surface.

"That sounds reasonable," I replied.

"It is also the longest amount of time that this other spell will be in effect."

"What spell is this?"

"The one that makes you human."

"*What?*" My voice was shrill with surprise.

Surely Salophine could not be serious. What good would I be as a human? Had she gone mad?

"For this to work, you cannot tarnish the human's heart with your siren magic. Once your hands touch the heart, it will be inadmissible and the spell will cease to work. You will have legs only temporarily." Salophine swirled the container in a fast motion.

My stomach lurched.

"But—"

"Let me finish. You will only be a human until the next full moon. That is the longest I can give you. Once you steal the heart, no matter how early the moon's phase is, you will return to me and be transformed back to your siren state. If you fail to steal the heart by the full moon's peak, you will remain a human forever." Salophine stared at me as she spoke in a grave tone.

I shivered. Being trapped in a human body meant I could never return home again.

"And what of payment? I do not expect you are charitable when it comes to a spell this costly." I twirled a strand of hair between my fingers. It was an awful nervous habit of mine.

Salophine smiled as she eyed my movements.

"I do not ask for much. I am a rather benevolent being. All I ask is that you give me your voice."

"Excuse me?"

"Just your singing voice! You will still be able to speak. But you will never sing again. Not as a human, nor as a siren. That is my price, which is fairly reasonable for the life of your cousin," Salophine said as she eyed the contents of the container. It had turned from black sludge to a light brown. She transferred it to a glass bottle.

My mind spiraled. It took everything in me to not breakdown right in front of her. If I went through with this, I would never lure a man to his watery grave ever again. My warrior status would be stripped away. I would have to marry and reproduce. Years spent on creating tunes and lyrics would be lost.

But I would get Hyrissa back. I would get my honor back. My city would once again be my home. Clagoria would respect me, even worship me for my sacrifice. The Queen would be most pleased. There was no question. I would give up my voice to fix the damage that I had inadvertently caused. I knew I had to do whatever it took to see Hyrissa's laughing face again.

Salophine was unwavering, staring at me with an almost hungry look while I contemplated my fate. It made me uneasy.

"Okay. I will do it," I said after several moments of thought.

Salophine let a bone-chilling grin stretch across her face. She swam hastily toward me, her red tail swishing around the cave.

"Excellent. Now that we have an understanding, prick your finger and let some blood drip into the bottle." Salophine handed me the spine of a fish while she held onto the glass bottle.

I grabbed it and, without a second thought, stabbed the sharp end of the bone into my thumb. I squeezed hard enough until blood flowed out from my skin. Salophine brought the bottle forward, and I stuck my thumb into the opening. The blood floated down and touched the contents inside. Once a muddy brown, the contact of my blood turned the sludge inside the bottle into a bright, glowing orange. It resembled the jellyfish above me.

Before I could question what happens next, Salophine ripped the bottle from my hand and forced it to my lips. The sludge was most foul as it hit the back of my tongue and made its way down my throat. I swallowed and nearly threw it back up. Not even the rottenest of fish tasted like this.

"What is that taste—" My body jerked back and slammed into the wall behind me, cutting off my speech.

Choking noises came from deep within me. My hands flew to my throat as my eyes widened. Salophine simply stared at me, offering no help, not even so much as an explanation.

I screamed as the gills on my sides began to burn. It was like boiling water from a geyser pressed into my skin, cooking me alive. My fingers tried to feel the fire that consumed them. Instead, they grazed across smooth skin. My gills were gone. I could no longer breathe underwater. Black spots appeared at the sides of my vision. My heart raced, thumping frantically in my chest.

I inhaled water. My body was convulsing out of my control, shaking and contorting. Something cracked in my chest, and I screamed as bones crunched beneath my skin.

The feeling of my lower half being sawed off threatened to overcome me. I did not even want to look down. In my century and a quarter of living, I had never known pain like this.

As my consciousness faded, Salophine swam forward. She was just a blur to me, barely visible within my waning vision. I thought I saw her red eyes flicker to gold, but I must have imagined it. The sea witch opened another one of her portals. With a flick of her wrist, a large current swept me through it.

Chapter Seven
Kae

My parents would have discovered my rashly written letter by now. I'd written of some dire emergency, and that I would return as soon as possible.

It was short and to the point, which my father would surely appreciate. No long-winded prose, no explanations. Just that I needed to leave for an unexplained purpose, with the mention that I might return with a betrothed. I made sure not to disclose the gender of said potential spouse.

I stood at the helm, facing my crew. We would depart in mere minutes, heading for the next adventure. But Ruff's word of advice came to mind.

"We will rid the ocean of the nefarious sea demons and find victory once more! I thank you all for coming along on this seemingly spontaneous journey with me, despite only being home for a day. Your loyalty and willingness to join me in seeking justice for our lost crew members are not unnoticed. Kipp was a fine young man taken from us too soon. Today we sail for Kipp!" I raised my sword high into the air.

There was a prolonged silence out of respect for our fallen friend.

"Kipp!" A chorus of shouts rang back after a minute. My men raised their swords above their heads.

"To Zephlus!" I shouted.

We all bellowed with excitement at the journey ahead of us. The largest weight had lifted itself off of my chest, knowing that I had found purpose again. I never felt more alive.

"And one more thing before we officially depart." I added once the shouts had died down. "It is with a begrudged heart that I must tell you all that I have been keeping secrets for the past year. And you know me, I like establishing trust. I want to come clean."

They regarded me with mostly confusion as they lowered their swords and sheathed them back at their sides. An expectant hush settled across the ship.

I took a deep breath. I wanted to do this, to tell them all. This journey would surely differ greatly from the last. I could feel it in my bones. So, I knew I had to start it off right. I had to tell the truth and be free of the weighted secrets to truly be myself. They would have to live with it or leave my ship.

Ruff nodded to me in encouragement.

"I am a woman."

Several gasps outmatched the winds as I removed my hat and shook my curls loose.

"And also, the princess of Avalon."

I tried to maintain a neutral expression. I wanted to appear strong and confident to remind them I was still the captain they'd always known. The truth slipping out felt like swallowing a mouthful of sand. It scratched my throat and left it raw.

Dalton spat out the water he was sipping on. I had forgotten he didn't know about the princess thing. His eyes went wide, but eventually allowed a smirk to crawl on his face.

Ruff gave me a thumbs up, but no smile crossed his face. Always the serious one.

"I lied to protect my identity," I continued. "But that is not the only reason. I wasn't sure if you lot would back a female captain. Either way, if it's a problem, you are free to walk away now before we depart."

I looked at the crew expectantly, waiting for them to shout, be angry, but they didn't.

"Yer daft if ya think we'll be leaving ya." Birch, a man of few words, spoke up.

The rest hurrahed their agreements.

"It means nothing to us. You're still our captain," Barnes said at the helm.

I turned to smile at him beside me. The rest of the crew grinned up at me. A few gave supportive shouts while some hollered. I couldn't help but smile back, to feel that surge of emotion that threatened to break the surface. I schooled my features back into place.

"Now get back to work," I said flatly.

"Yes, Captain Kae," and the crew broke off to their posts, chattering amongst themselves as they went.

I helped Barnes turn the ship safely away from the harbor, giving him words of encouragement when a bead of sweat trickled down his temple. As we headed out of the harbor, I snuck a glance back at my crew.

They would follow me in seeking revenge for Kipp and countless others against the sirens. I would never have expected this amount of loyalty from every single one of them. It put me at ease.

When I eyed the horizon again, I had the oddest feeling I was being watched, which was ridiculous because, of course, I was being watched. My crew glanced up as I barked out commands, getting the *Mar Daemon* swiftly on its course.

When I was certain Barnes was well off, I descended the stairs onto the main deck to help. The coarse feeling of rope in my hands anchored me to the ship. It was a welcomed and familiar feeling, even if it burned my skin whenever the rope slipped through. My palms were calloused enough that the pain barely registered.

In just twenty minutes, Avalon was a speck on the horizon. At the rate the wind was aiding us, the *Mar Daemon* would reach the shores of Zephlus by nightfall. I wasn't entirely sure where to go from there. The harbor fight proved that our weapons needed replacing—the metal had grown dull in the last year and would deteriorate soon.

After we restocked and purchased more *zephlum* weapons, I would have to ask around for siren sightings. This island was always the most reliable when it came to that. Secrets and gossip were always eagerly exchanged for some coin. And more often than not, they proved to be veritable.

Last year, I threw small pouches of gold at whoever had a trustworthy siren encounter and we'd promptly sail in the given direction. It had taken a while to grow accustomed to the ways of

Zephlus, but my crew didn't complain, soaking in the revelry while we found our headings.

I had a feeling I would do the same thing all over again.

As several of the men worked with the ropes and sails, Ruff was practicing his sword combat with Birch, our best swordsman. It appeared to be smooth sailing, and little need for me.

I made my way to the set of stairs in the center of the ship. They led down below deck, where the sunlight was not as strong. Several lanterns were lit to compensate. A stack of rum barrels took up the left side of the ship. To my delight, there was still a full barrel left.

I grabbed a mug and filled it to the brim with the light brown liquid.

There was a small corner hidden behind the rum barrels where a mattress was lined against the wall. I had stolen it from a kingdom I could not remember and used it as my little hideaway. The mattress was hidden from view, tucked away in a shadow. It allowed me to get lost in my thoughts for a little bit. My own private oasis. I was as alone as I could be on a ship filled with eleven other people.

"Figured I'd find you here." Dalton's voice appeared out of the darkness, though I had not been startled.

I was used to this arrogant man appearing out of nowhere. I would never tell him I enjoyed the company, though I had a suspicion he knew it, anyway. My best friend had a calming presence about him. What I found annoying was that he found me not after two minutes of silence.

"Well then, you would know that this is where I require peace and solitude," I retorted as Dalton sat down beside me.

He leaned back so his head was against the wall.

"I admit I should have guessed that you are royalty. I mean, you get so proper at talking whenever you're really drunk." Dalton laughed at some distant memory.

I rolled my eyes at him and playfully punched his shoulder.

"I should have blackmailed you or convinced you to sleep with me when I figured out your secret. Could've gotten some coin out of it," Dalton said.

He wagged his eyebrows at me, which earned him a sharp laugh from me.

"A little blackmail could get you some coin. Perhaps you can borrow some of my dresses back home and get lucky with one of my suitors. Besides, I don't have a need for any of them." I tried keeping a serious face as I spoke, but ended up breaking into a fit of laughter.

Dalton shook his head, a wide grin plastered his face. He grabbed my cup and took a deep swig of the rum.

We often joked like this with each other. It was as if all tension in my muscles disappeared whenever Dalton and I spoke as our true selves.

Though I had come clean to the crew about myself, I knew Dalton still hid his secret in fear of the other men in the crew hating him. But I also knew he disliked lying; he always wore his heart on his sleeve, secretly feeling far more than he let on.

A sailor at a bar made shrewd comments once; it had been just me and Dalton there. He gave Dalton a black eye just because my best friend was acting "too feminine" and "giving eyes to the other sailors".

It was entirely untrue, and I broke that man's hand. Yet Dalton's demeanor shifted that early night last year. He was terrified of our crewmates acting that way toward him. It pained me seeing him hide who he was.

"Perhaps I could. I'd enjoy spending another night with Zechariah again. And I'm sure a dress would make for acceptable wooing," Dalton teased and handed me back my glass.

I smirked as my best friend brought up the prince of Zephlus and an illicit affair last summer between the two of them. I finished the rest of the rum in a single gulp and placed the cup on the ground beside me.

"You don't need a dress to woo the prince again." I noted. "You've got charm radiating off you in anything you wear."

Dalton sighed instead of reveling in the compliment like he usually did. He sat up as if to leave, but turned to look at me.

"If only we were like the others. Life would be easier that way, wouldn't it?"

"We could always get married and have our own string of lovers on the side," I proposed, and Dalton snickered.

"And have me on the throne? Oh, I *do* like the sound of that," Dalton said as he menacingly rubbed his hands together.

I had a brief glimpse of what that would be like—Avalon in revelry and ruin.

"It could be a viable option, though," I said in a serious tone.

Dalton flashed me a somber look as he stared back at me.

"Would *you* want that option?" he asked.

He knew me better than most.

"If it's one of our only choices to live as our true selves, perhaps. Though I don't think I dislike you enough to succumb you to political meetings," I said, leaving the rest unspoken.

I barely wanted to be on the throne as it was. I wouldn't lock my best friend away in that cage as well.

Dalton laughed heartily, but his eyes did not match his mood.

"I'll accept your proposal, regardless. Worse comes to worst, I suppose I'll look good with a crown on my head." He gave me a little salute before returning to the main deck, presumably to help Barnes at the helm.

It was a nice backup plan; a way for us to secretly be ourselves. But if I had it my way, we both could love whoever we wanted out in the open, no fears or regrets. I very much liked my difficult life, despite everything. I wouldn't change it for the world.

I went to refill my glass but thought the better of it. Instead, I left my little corner and went back onto the main deck, leaning over the side railing. The endless ocean stretched out before me, beckoning me.

I looked up at Dalton at the helm, admiring how at ease he was—how natural it looked for him to stand behind that wheel. Out at sea, I was a different person, more at ease, more in my own nature. I truly belonged out here, with no rules but my own. No one told me who to marry or what to wear or say or think. It was freeing beyond compare. I had no beliefs in our sun god, Atdia, nor did I believe in superstitions, but being in the middle of the ocean felt as close to destiny as I could get.

And if I married Dalton, if I chose the royal life instead of what I truly desired? It would be a noose around both our necks.

The sun was just setting. We were almost to the island. The closer the ship got to the shore of Zephlus, the more determined I became. It was rash, throwing myself into this journey, knowing it would distract me from processing Kipp's death just as the first journey had Edmonde's.

I had allowed myself to cry all night last night. Then come morning, I buried the sentiment deep down. I would not be weak. I had to move on. Despite the time I took below deck to regain my composure, from here on out, I could not afford to let fear and grief consume me. I had to be better. For Kipp. For Edmonde. For every lost soul.

The sky exploded into a kaleidoscope of reds and oranges and pinks. The red hues reminded me of a specific face: the siren. The one with the fire for hair and a green tail. It had watched me murder its own, trying to save Kipp.

I knew this siren had to be the first to go, preferably by my hand. Otherwise, I had no doubt it would come after me for revenge. Sirens had no other emotions, save anger and bloodlust, if that counted as one. They wouldn't allow those who killed their own kind to get away unscathed. Devious little devils, the lot of them were.

It was my fault Kipp was gone. I should have paid more attention to him, should have noticed his ears clear of wax coverings.

But now was not the time for rumination. I would avenge his death by killing them all.

"Thinking about sirens?" Atty's voice came from beside me.

I looked away from the skyline to one of my greatest hunters on board.

"How'd you know?"

"You get that look in your eyes. I know it, I've had the same. Especially after Kipp…" Atty trailed off, looking out at the sea.

He and Birch had trained Kipp. They taught him everything he knew about combat.

"I was just trying to strategize about the next move once we've restocked," I said.

I glanced back at the setting sun, barely visible above the horizon.

"Of course. Maybe we'll pick up a new crewmate while in Zephlus. We're in need of another hunter," Atty said as he broke away from the railing.

I nodded and walked to my quarters. If we were to hire another hunter, I would need more loot on my person before heading to the island. Good hunters came at a price—usually a steep one.

I grabbed my old satchel that hung on my bedpost. It was filled with jewels and coins I had smuggled from the royal treasury in Avalon before I left. They were a few lesser-valued items, nothing that would be missed. These could buy essential information about sirens on top of the *zephlum* weapons we'd be purchasing.

There was a wooden floorboard under my bed that, when pried at just the right angle, came loose, revealing a hidden nook to hide treasured belongings. I emptied some jewels and coins inside, not wanting to carry too much on my person while in Zephlus.

"Captain! We're about to dock." Arden, our gunner who enjoyed explosives a bit too much for my liking, poked his head into the door frame of my room.

He stood there, waiting for a response. At this angle, I knew he couldn't see my hiding spot, but I tensed nonetheless.

"Thanks, Arden." I said. "I'll be out in a sec."

Arden nodded and closed my door behind him. Then I made sure to properly replace the board before I left my room.

The *Mar Daemon* had slowed in speed. Zephlus' harbor was only yards ahead. I scanned across the ship for any sign of Ruff or Dalton. Dalton lounged at the other side of the ship, having just finished his part in helping the ship dock. I walked over to him, feeling the wind and swiftness of the currents as the ship bobbed along. With a wave of my hand, Marsden and Dyer threw heaving lines over to the dock.

"I thought you were sailing the ship into the harbor," I observed.

I looked at Barnes at the helm. He was our novice sailing master under Dalton's wing, and that gave me slight concerns.

"My apologies, Captain." Dalton joked. "I was just giving Barnes some practice. I was below deck, making sure I had my wits about me. Can't leave that behind, now, can I?"

I narrowed my eyes at his response, but shrugged. Dalton was always odd. I didn't mention how askew his clothes were since I last saw him—he enjoyed appearing unkempt and rugged. It added a certain charm to his demeanor.

I left Dalton and made my way up the stairs to the helm, standing beside Barnes at the wheel. I inclined my head and Barnes stepped aside. I turned the wheel, angling the ship to be parallel to our docking spot. The *Mar Daemon* groaned under my hand, but it listened all the same.

When I looked up, my entire crew was out on the main deck. They all looked at me. Barnes made his way back downstairs, giving me the floor.

"Feel free to drink merry tonight. Ask around for any siren sightings." My voice resounded throughout the ship, and I tried to hide its edge. "It's late, the *zephlum* shops are closed for the day. We'll gather intel tonight and hopefully by morning tomorrow, we will have new weapons and a new course."

It was nice not having to fake the tone, letting my voice be its normal pitch instead of lowering it, pretending to be a man.

Many bellowed their glee in return. As I descended the steps, the crew began exiting the ship. No doubt eager to hit the taverns and parties.

Zephlus was known for its debauchery. The king and his two sons threw extravagant parties every week. Last year, we stayed for an entire month reveling in the kingdom's festivities. I'd forgotten half of it in a drunken stupor, but I do remember having my broken arm in a sling for weeks after. I didn't even remember breaking it. Nor did Ruff remember streaking naked across the local courtyard.

Dalton met up with me and threw an arm around my shoulder. He was almost a foot taller than me and constantly teased me for it. I looked up at the small scar just below his ear where my dagger *accidentally* nicked him when the teasing became a bit too relentless. I smiled fondly at the memory.

"It seems the men are splitting up in their gaiety to cover more ground in siren sightings." Ruff said, emerging from below deck. "I'm assuming I'll be joining the two of you. Make sure you don't get yourselves killed by the end of the night. Or imprisoned."

I was surprised he didn't come up earlier when I was addressing the crew. Ruff had a startled look on his face as he glanced at Dalton's appearance. I tried to decipher the meaning behind it, but came up short.

"Just because you broke us out of prison in Eayucia that one time, doesn't mean you get to hold it over our heads for the rest of your life," Dalton muttered.

Ruff smirked. "It does, too."

Ruff addressed me, ignoring Dalton's sputtering at the dismissal. "Captain, will you be requiring my company for the night?"

The two of them got into pointless arguments at least twice a day.

"Of course. I always have the most adventurous times with you two scoundrels," I said and laughed at my friends' faces.

We got off my ship and disembarked on our night, following the few scraggling crew members on our way to the taverns, likely to cause a bit of mischief of our own.

Chapter Eight
Aqeara

Small waves lapped at my feet when I came to. I inhaled and coughed up water. The salt burned as it scraped against my throat. What was once smooth as a dolphin, essential for living, now felt like acid.

I tried taking in my surroundings and let out a small scream when I saw what was in place of my tail. A pair of pale legs that perfectly matched the skin color of my torso were attached to me. I stared and wondered if they would disappear if I took my eyes off of them. But no, this was not one of Salophine's illusions.

The little toes wiggled, and I gasped. I bent my legs and stretched them out again. Looking down, I noticed my shells were gone. I was completely naked, which would not bother me were I still a siren. But humans were always covered. This was wrong.

I shivered. Not from the cold—there was a nice tropical climate here—but from just how vulnerable I was. My heart hammered in my chest. At least that part of me remained the same.

The beach spanned thirty feet between a line of trees to where the waves crashed against the sand. Nothing but endless amounts of sand. No sign of life anywhere. I shivered and wrapped my arms around my chest.

Standing up was impossible. I wobbled over and shot my hands out to catch my fall. Pain shot up my palm from a jagged shell.

How ironic, I thought, *that the one thing used to protect my heart now cuts me like a blade.*

I sat back down and stared at the thin stream of blood that trickled from my palm. My skin was not healing even half as fast as it normally did. It did not seem to be healing at all.

Huffing in impatience at the stinging sensation in my hand, I tried once again to stand up with more caution. My brain willed orders to my legs. It appeared I was on a shoreline. There were trees up ahead and hopefully some sort of civilization passed them.

My heart ached at the mere thought of turning my back against the sea. Against what was once my home. I had to fight the shudder that rippled through me as I removed my gaze from the water. But looking ahead gave me a twinge of excitement.

Hyrissa and I had loved spending our days in shipwrecks, pretending to be humans with their little treasures. Perhaps this was my chance to experience it. And once I brought my little cousin back, she would be delighted to hear all of my stories.

As I trudged on—as best I could, given the new legs—the sand gave way to a darker, softer type of sand I was unfamiliar with. The trees had large coconuts attached, ripe for the picking.

Only after decades of listening in on pirates and sailors talking about human things and describing what they missed in great detail did I learn to recognize objects. Siren warriors passed down information from generation to generation. Knowing as much as we could about humans helped us in luring them away from their land and into the sea.

There was no beaten path in the ground that I could follow. Small critters crawled on fallen leaves, some flew lazily in the air around me. I tried my best to avoid stepping on sharp branches or rocks that were hidden in the dirt, waiting to penetrate the soles of my new bare feet.

After a few minutes of no new change in scenery, I began to panic. If this was how the humans lived, it was no wonder they fell into their watery graves so easily. I was hopelessly lost, both directionally and mentally. Maybe I was trapped on a small island and would starve. I kept trudging on.

Several more minutes passed before a clearing formed ahead. Beyond the trees was a large pathway made of stone, with human houses lined up on either side of it. I had seen similar homes whenever we hunted near smaller islands.

Men out at sea talked often of how they missed home. That is, before we lured them out to their doom. Sometimes I would find myself listening to their stories before opening my mouth.

Many people were walking to and fro as I stepped out onto the pathway. I took another step and froze when a human looked at me with widened eyes. I opened my mouth to sing, ready to be on the offensive, before I remembered I could not do exactly that.

"Oh dear! What happened to you, you poor thing? Come, come! Let's get you inside and covered!" The woman stepped toward me, and I took a step back.

I beheld my naked body and was aware that I was not the threatening predator I once was. Now I was a meager human. And this woman was not trying to kill me. What reason did she have?

I sighed with a mix of relief and contempt and followed as the human led me to the nearest home.

The least Salophine could do was conjure me some clothes, I thought.

"Don't mind the state of the place. I told my husband to clean up before we moved back to our winter housing. You think men listen?" The woman said over her shoulder.

I tried not to laugh at her statement.

"Men listen to me just fine," I muttered under my breath, stepping through the front entrance after her.

"Oh my, excuse my manners. What's your name? And what happened to your clothes? What luck that you ran into a seamstress, huh?" The woman made a tsk-ing noise as she disappeared behind walls that led to other rooms.

She was much older than me—in human years, at least. Her brunette hair had turned gray in many spots. The woman's rich brown skin bore a few wrinkles around her eyes. She gave off a motherly aura, and I felt safe here. I also knew that women did not hunt sirens, they were immune to our song. Noerina had told me so.

I looked around the place and wished more than anything that Hyrissa was here beside me. There were so many little human trinkets that I had no name for. Wood lined the doorways in thin beams. The walls were painted a light blue, the color of the sky during the day. A table took up the center of the area to my right, with a large chair-like structure positioned near it. It looked comfortable and inviting.

"My name is Aqeara." I said in the human's language. "I was inside a shipwreck."

My accent startled me. My throat felt scrubbed raw, as if I were still choking up seaweed. The thought left an uncomfortable pit in the bottom of my stomach. There was no underlying melody when I spoke. I would never be able to use the human's language to sing again.

"Oh dear, lost at sea, you poor thing! I have many questions, but first, let's get you dressed," the woman fretted about and handed me a thin dress that felt like clouds.

I bowed my head in thanks.

"Let me see if I have bandages for your hand," she crossed the room in quick yet determined strides before adding, "Oh, I'm Helene, by the way!"

Helene soon returned with a larger dress. She patiently waited for me to maneuver my way into the thin slip of cloth. I did my best to act like I knew which limb went into which hole. The gown covered me from my torso down to the top of my knees. Helene wordlessly handed me a larger green dress with a smile on her face. The color almost matched my old shells perfectly. The familiar shade warmed me.

"Here, try this on. I think you're the same size as my daughter." She left me with the dress as she disappeared into another room again.

The clothing intimidated me. There were so many strings crisscrossing throughout the dress. I had no idea how to even begin putting it on. This was far more complicated than a single string of seaweed I used to tie my shells. I was already covered in one dress. Why must I put on another?

"I am not aware of how to put this on!" I called out, wincing at how gravely my voice sounded.

I tried to clear my throat and swallowed a few times. The older woman came back with several pieces of cloth. She set it down next to her and picked up the dress.

"Lift your arms up." Helene instructed, and I brought my arms above my head. "I know this one's a bit complicated. It's on the more expensive side, you see. It still requires the under slip, but I'm working on having one sewn into the dress itself."

Half of her words went through one ear and out the other, but her voice was soft, and I found myself smiling at her. Once the dress was over my head, it clung to my body like a second skin.

Helene went behind me to tie the strings at my back. I sucked in a breath as she tied them too tight for comfort. How could anyone possibly breathe and talk in such a contraption?

"A perfect fit! Now have a seat and let me get a look at that hand." Helene pointed to a chair, and I sat down. "Where did you say you were from, again?"

She immediately went to work cleaning my wound. I winced at the stinging pain, but Helene's grip was firm and would not let me retract my hand. She neatly wrapped it so that as I flexed my fingers, the bandage did not unravel.

"I am from... Soledel. I was sailing to Zephlus to meet a friend before the ship sank. I woke up on shore here," I lied, though not fully.

I *was* meeting someone in Zephlus, or so I hoped. I was not accustomed to having to lie like this and had given little thought to a plan. Yet when I said the first kingdom that had come to mind, my shoulders sagged in relief.

Soledel was a kingdom known for worshipping sirens. They were isolated, blocking off the rest of the world that saw us as demons. It is the only human kingdom that I would ever consider safe for sirens, and the safest lie for me to tell.

"Soledel? But I thought… oh never mind. You're lucky to have ended up here. This is Zephlus, my dear!" Helene smiled at me before I had a chance to analyze her.

I couldn't believe my luck.

"This is Zephlus?" My heart raced as multiple more questions bubbled to mind. "Do you know where the *zephlum* sellers are?"

Perhaps Salophine purposely dumped me here. She knew the hunters would arrive on this island soon if they were not already here. I had to find the captain before it was too late.

"Yes, they're on the west end of town. I'm afraid the shops are all closed for today, it's getting late. Why don't you wait here while I get you something to eat? We can both head down the road to the shops tomorrow. I really don't mind the company. My husband's gone out for a business meeting." Helene walked away and threw the bloodied rag she used to clean out my cut into a bin.

As soon as she was out of sight, I stood up. It was a little too quickly. I swayed on the shoes she had given me with their nubs at the end. What strange contraptions humans dressed themselves in. What use did these shoes possibly have?

Time was my enemy. It was imperative that I began my search for the hunters as soon as possible. Hopefully, they had not made it to the shops before they closed. I would wait all night for them to come in the morning.

A mirror hung right by the exit of Helene's home. The mirror was not similar in design to the one in Hyrissa's room, but its purpose was the same. I paused when I saw my reflection. Salophine must have altered my face so that I would not be easily recognizable by the hunters. The face staring back at me was almost foreign, but there were hints of me hidden if I stared hard enough.

I still had my same porcelain skin, but now freckles lined my cheeks. My once brilliant red hair had been muted to a darker, more humanlike red. My eyes were no longer bright and golden; they were now duller and close to amber. She had slightly altered the shape of my face, but I was still beautiful.

For a human, at least.

The luring beauty of a siren was gone. I held a hand up to my cheek and pinched the skin. It was real. I opened my mouth and observed that my teeth were flat instead of razor-sharp. It was a strange feeling.

The dress was something new. It covered my legs and made me forget I had them for just a moment. I kicked a leg out to observe my foot was still there. There was a beauty to this piece of clothing. The top hugged my breasts how my shells had. It resembled a thinly veiled sort of protection over my heart.

The sound of something being dropped snapped me out of my self-admiration. I needed to leave before Helene convinced me to stay. Lying to a woman who had shown me nothing but kindness and hospitality ate at me. I ran out of the home, nearly stumbling on my way out. These shoes were a mistake waiting to happen.

Warm colors flooded the sky as the sun was just about to set. Brilliant shades of pinks and purples exploded before me. My heart tugged at the sight.

Hyrissa had loved sunsets. She would beg Clagoria to take us to the surface, where we could watch them. Clagoria had only allowed us to go on the solstices, but it had been cherished regardless.

The solstices were the only time Clagoria was not as insufferable, as they were widely celebrated in Meyrial. Sirens were at their most powerful during these times of the year. They were a time of happiness spent with loved ones.

I blinked back tears. *Soon*, I thought to myself. Soon I would reunite the three of us together again. We could watch the sunset every night if Hyrissa wanted to.

I marched on into the city of Zephlus. I tried to keep my features neutral, my movements unnoticeable. I mimicked how the people moved around me with confidence. Being surrounded by this many people left me anxious, but I knew I had nothing to be worried about. I was human like them.

Their heads were either held high with purpose or slouched as if not wanting to be bothered. Either with warm smiles and small nods to passerby or downcast eyes and shuffling feet. It was fascinating how different, yet similar, they all were.

The buildings were a similar color to the dirt from the forest and the leaves of the trees above it. Muted tones that made it seem like the buildings had been carved from nature herself. Clothes hung on thin ropes that were attached between balconies, swaying in the breeze to an unheard rhythm, not so unlike the currents that tugged brightly colored fish about the sea floor. Floral scents wafted through the air as plants lined the front entrances of many buildings.

The scream of a woman jolted me out of my observations, rooting me to the ground. I whipped my head around and zeroed in my focus on her. She was laughing; her face red from her glee. She slapped the shoulder of another woman beside her as the two giggled. Not a scream of terror, but one of laughter. I took a few seconds to calm my nerves before I continued on.

A thought came to me then as I walked down the street. Humans were not only a threat to sirens, but to themselves as well. Once on an excursion, my troop had encountered a ship. There were women on board, which was unusual. We rarely came across women at sea. It was not until we broke surface that we heard their screams and knew they were there by force. They were in pain, forced to do things they did not want to do. It did not take long to cause the men to jump overboard into our open arms. I had enjoyed ripping the head off one of the men that night. He had been my first kill.

I shook the memory away and turned down another street.

Zephlus was formed like a grid, its homes lined up in streets that turned in perfect right angles. This kingdom, though beautiful in its monochromatic aesthetic, lacked bright colorful architectures that I had come to admire about humans. My green dress did not seem to draw too much attention. Some women wore gowns though, none were brightly colored.

A large flag waved in the wind to my right. Its colors were two stripes of black on either side of a brown stripe in the middle. Two *zephlum* swords were crossed in the center. This must be the flag of Zephlus. Several pirate ships that I have encountered at sea had their own versions of these flags.

The part of the kingdom I had now entered smelled acrid. There was no name I could give it. The sounds of a man upheaving his stomach contents twisted at the pit of my own stomach. I scrunched my nose against the smell and pressed on past him. Melodies and shouts filled the air, both enticing and intimidating.

I hadn't the slightest clue where I was going. I was heading west, that I knew for sure based on a glance at the setting sun. The symbols on signs in front of shops were foreign to me. While I could speak the human's language, I could not read it.

Frustration grew as I realized I had walked in a square, making four right turns until I was back in a spot I had been in about several moments before. I huffed out a sigh and decided to just walk into the first building on my left. Music floated out of it like turtles in a current. Perhaps I could ask one of the musicians inside where the shops were.

The lantern light from inside engulfed me as I left the ever-darkening streets of Zephlus behind.

Chapter Nine
Aqeara

Music filled my ears from the moment I stepped inside. It was unfamiliar, yet reminded me of home all the same. I had never heard music being played without a voice before. A small trio stood in the corner of this establishment, only playing with instruments. Sometimes when I broke surface near a ship, I would listen to the sailors sing their shanties while playing instruments. But without their offkey singing? It sounded lovely.

I stood awkwardly while I took in the room. People were shouting at one another over the songs, but not in anger. There were bright smiles all around as they laughed in merriment. Seats lined up in front of a long table.

A man behind the table walked over to me as I sat down.

"What can I get for the lady?" the man asked as he cleaned out a bottle.

I was not sure what to answer—if *zephlum* would be appropriate to ask for.

"Whatever he is having," I decided and pointed to the man that sat a few seats down from me.

The seated man winked at me. The man behind the table shrugged and started pouring liquid into a cup. They sold drinks here, not *zephlum*. I had no form of payment. I knew humans traded shiny coins for things, and cursed myself for not thinking of that before.

The seated man got up and settled in the empty chair beside me. He threw down three silver coins and smiled again.

"Drink's on me, but it might be strong for a lass such as yerself." The man flashed a toothy smile, and I noticed he was missing several teeth. "What's yer name, sweetheart?"

Any warmth that radiated from Helene was lost on this man. He made my heart rate rise and not in a good way.

"Aqeara," I replied curtly grateful the melodic tones were gone from my voice.

I took a sip from the cup in front of me and tried not to make a face at the odd liquid. I did not appreciate being challenged. The man stared at me while I drank, and his smile became more menacing.

"Ah-keer-ah. What an interesting name for a pretty girl. Ye here all by yerself? Ye don't look like yer from here." The man slurred his words and inched closer to me.

I leaned away while remaining seated.

Memories of drunk men harming innocent women flooded my mind again. The man's hand grabbed my thigh and tightened. My dress was thick but I felt the warmth from his sweaty and disgusting hand.

I was going to be sick.

I opened my mouth and tried to sing—nothing but air came out. My siren's voice was gone. I had no means of protecting myself. I could not even seem to speak. I braced myself for the horror that was to come. My knuckles were white from clutching the sides of my chair. If I could hold on tight enough, the wretched man could not steal me away. My heart was thundering in my ears, blocking out the music.

"Please get off me," I said in a quiet voice, barely a whisper.

I could muster nothing louder than that. The man's hand traveled upwards. The sick and twisted smile remained on his face. I closed my eyes and took a deep breath. I killed men twice the size of this one with more fight in them. Siren or not, I refused to let a man be my end. I was a warrior.

"Get your hands off of her!" a voice shouted from behind me.

It distracted the man from me—he turned to see who had yelled at him. It was all I needed to gain my strength back. I grabbed his thumb and twisted it backward until I could hear a satisfying snap.

The man cried out and stumbled away from me.

I stood up and lifted my leg to kick him where I knew men were the most delicate. Years of attacking them led us to learn a thing or two about where they were weakest. Another cry came out between his lips.

Grabbing my drink, I walked away to a table on the other side of the room. It was much smaller with only two chairs on either side. Hopefully, my display would serve as a warning against any others that tried their hand at me.

The musicians kept on playing their instruments, either oblivious or accustomed to fights such as these breaking out.

"Hey, are you alright? That was seriously amazing what you did back there." Another man plopped down in the empty chair across from me.

I recognized his voice as the one that distracted my assailant. There was something else familiar about him I could not quite place. I took another sip of my drink as I looked at him. I liked how this liquid burned on the way down to my stomach. It provided warmth.

"I am okay." I said. "Thank you."

I was not sure how to act with this new man. I wanted to be closed off from anything like before happening again, but he had come to my rescue. This one was younger than the other. He had wavy dark blonde hair atop his head. He was tall, lean, and muscular. If I were to fight off this one, it might prove a bit more difficult.

His smile, however, did not give off a fighting aura. His stature was relaxed and nothing about him raised any alarms. If I were in my siren state, I bet he would be easy to lure in.

"The name's Dalton, by the way. I saw what that pig was doing to you and thought I could step in, but it seems you got yourself taken care of." He winked and took a sip of his drink.

I could not tell if the wink was flirtatious; it seemed to be only friendly. But what did I know about the inner workings of a human's mind? I only knew they were suckers for pretty faces.

"I am Aqeara." I smiled and finished my drink. "I appreciate your rescue attempt, anyway."

I felt fuzzy, similar to how I felt at pufferfish parties back home when sirens would purposely get stung by the small creatures to make us hallucinate. It felt like we were floating in a bubble. That same feeling buzzed through my veins, making my head feel as if I was floating. Perhaps that was why the musicians were used to fights.

Dalton smiled at me in return, but it soon vanished. He stared at something behind me. I turned around in my chair to see what Dalton was looking at and gasped. The man whose thumb I had broken was back and flanked by several equally menacing men.

"That's him! The guy who slept with your wife last year! He's stealing my girl," the man shouted to one of his friends, who broke a bottle in response.

He held the jagged edges out toward Dalton with malice in his eyes.

The man's statement took me aback. I had just broken his thumb and hopefully rendered him unable to reproduce—in what world did I belong to him?

"Aqeara, get behind the bar. Now!" Dalton ordered between clenched teeth.

He motioned toward the long table where I had been sitting before. Dalton then unsheathed a sword from his side that I had not noticed when he'd sat down.

The rest of the people inside scurried out, including the musicians and the server behind the long table. I picked up the ends of my dress and ran behind the bar, ducking down behind it and poked my head out slightly to see.

The six men approached Dalton with a predatory slow walk. They knew they outnumbered him. I did not have a weapon on me to aid him; I had only ever needed my voice and teeth until now. Being wobbly on my feet with slightly fuzzy vision did not help the situation.

"Honestly, your wife?" Dalton said, tauntingly. "You're just angry that *you* were caught flirting with *me*."

The man with the broken bottle hurled it toward Dalton with a growl. Dalton barely had any time to duck before it soared over his head and came straight at me.

I yelped and ducked down again as the glass shattered against the wall. Broken pieces sprinkled all around me, and I shielded my eyes. There were several shouts followed by the sound of sword on sword.

He was really fighting them all. I frantically searched around me for something—anything. The shelves that lined up the bar proved useless in holding any potential weapons.

"C'mere pretty, pretty." A voice came from my right.

Another man curled his finger in a beckoning motion and licked his lips. My stomach dropped as he moved to grab my leg. I kicked him square in the chest and tried crawling backward. He was fast and circled his fingers around my ankle before I could get out of reach.

"You bitch!" He pulled me toward him and shoved me onto the ground.

My head hit the floor hard, knocking my vision out of focus. A bottle was within reach of my flailing arms, and I grabbed it firmly by the top. I swung as hard as I could against the man's temple. He fell over instantly.

The bottle cracked open in the momentum and shattered, spraying brown liquid all over the man's unconscious body. I crawled away and searched for another bottle before anyone could investigate the noise.

It took a bit for my eyes to adjust from the fall, and I blinked rapidly in the dim lighting. The back of my head still throbbed from where it had hit the ground as I tucked my legs underneath me in an attempt to make myself small.

"Dammit, Dalton, we leave you alone for *five* minutes and you're already picking fights!" A woman's voice rose above the other shouting voices engaged in combat.

More grumbling and yelling filled the air.

"I didn't ask for this!" Dalton shouted back.

I was still behind the bar, unable to see the fight unfolding. Another large bottle was tucked under the bottom shelf. Just as I was about to lift my head above the bar counter, a body slid across the tabletop and landed right beside me.

I screamed and jumped back, feeling my dress rip as it caught on some broken glass. The man straightened up and faced me.

We stared at each other for mere seconds, but it could have been forever. This man was not a man. A *woman* stared back at me. And not just any woman, the siren hunter. Kae. The captain whose heart I had to carve out.

The blood drained from my face and my head spun. The captain tilted her head and squinted at me. I prayed she would not recognize me now that I was human.

"What are you doing back here? You're going to get hurt. Get out." The hunter's voice was icy as she pulled herself up onto her feet and slid back over the tabletop to join the fight.

I helplessly stared at the space where she had just been, growing furious at myself for freezing yet again.

The captain was a woman. Without her ugly hat, her face clean of any dirt and grime, it was obvious. She was entirely different in demeanor than when I had first met her back at Avalon's harbor, where she had been far away on the docks and not inches from me as she was now.

She looked younger than I expected, closer to my age than I had originally thought. In human years, at least. Sirens aged differently than humans did and though I have been alive for a century and a quarter, I was still on the younger side of my lifespan.

Her being a woman meant it would be even harder to seduce the captain and get close enough to cut out her heart. Sirens had only ever hunted human men. I did not know if humans experienced same-sex attraction—like sirens did.

Noerina had never mentioned it before in my training. This set my plan back by a lot. Though, if she dressed like a man, perhaps it meant she felt like the men she sailed with. And those men were easily lured into the siren-filled waters.

She also had covered her ears when we had attacked at the harbor, so she must have been susceptible to our songs. My head grew heavy with all the confusion. I could not think straight.

I realized then it had gotten eerily quiet.

I got up and looked over the counter. The bar was now empty save for three unconscious bodies, including the one I had knocked out. Neither Dalton nor the captain were anywhere in sight.

Dalton. *Dalton.*

That is why he looked so familiar. He was a siren hunter. He was there that day in Avalon, fighting off Clagoria and Domora with one other man. A wave of disgust washed over me as I remembered sharing a friendly smile with him earlier. Infuriating hunter vermin.

Dalton ran back into the building. He was panting hard and sweating. A red welt had formed on his cheek, and his shirt was torn. The captain and another man—the other hunter I saw back in Avalon—walked in after.

"Are you hurt?" Dalton called over to me, but I was not paying much attention to him.

The captain stared at me with narrowed eyes. Goosebumps rose on my arms under the gaze, and I felt a familiar well of something… good rising in me. I ignored any rising attraction and internally kicked myself for even thinking of her in such a way. Sure, she had a pretty face, but it was a pretty face I would tear the heart out of nonetheless.

"I am alright," I slid my gaze from the captain over to Dalton, then smiled sweetly. "Thank you for protecting me."

I batted my eyelashes at him and smiled. The third hunter grew red in the face and the captain rolled her eyes. Good. I was hoping to somehow make her envious. Annoyance was a sign of jealousy. It might have meant she preferred women after all.

"Of course. Well, I must leave you with my two friends here. They'll escort you home. This is Kae and Ruff. I'm to be meeting a friend soon, so goodnight, guys." Dalton held up two fingers and strolled out of the bar.

The remaining three of us stood there awkwardly, unsure what to do now.

"Where's he off to?" the man introduced as Ruff asked.

"Where else? Someone's bed probably," Kae said quickly.

I focused on her tone. It was intimidating, sure, but also soft. She was speaking of a close friend. I made a mental note of it and tried to keep my thoughts from spiraling. I knew I had for form a plan—secure a place on her ship.

"Your hand, it's bleeding," Kae said and motioned to where my hand hung at my side.

To my amazement, my bandaged hand was dripping blood. The wound must have reopened during the fight—my guess on the broken glass that scattered on the floor. I had felt no pain. The bright liquid was fascinating to stare at. Little scrapes like this one would have been healed by now had I been in my siren form.

"We have a kit on my ship. I'll clean up your wound and maybe you can tell us a bit about yourself." Kae suggested, much to Ruff's surprise. "Dalton claims you snapped one of those brute's fingers and knocked out another. We could certainly use someone with your fighting prowess."

Ruff lowered his raised eyebrows and shrugged.

"Better to get a move on before those idiots come back looking for a second beating," Ruff muttered.

I nodded and joined them as they left the bar. Perhaps this would all be over quicker than I thought.

The two hunters led me in a zigzag through the rest of the city. I struggled to keep up. Admiring the architecture of buildings, the music coming from multiple parties, the way people laughed and spoke, how they dressed—I hated to admit I was drinking in everything around me.

We finally made it to the docks, and I stopped walking. The ocean after the sun had set looked dark and foreign to me. It was minatory as larger waves crashed below against the docks. I shivered, fully aware of what happened the last time I was at a harbor. It was strange being on the other side.

"Are you coming? This one's ours!" Kae shouted from beside the lowered plank of her ship.

She waved at me in a way that did not at all seem welcoming so much that it was commanding.

I rolled my eyes and walked toward the hunters' ship. I looked up at the wooden carving of a siren at the front of it. Most men had human women adorning their ships—it was what we assumed was at the front of theirs. It shouldn't have surprised me that the siren hunters had a carving of the very thing they sought to kill. They could not even capture the proper beauty of my kind in this simple, crudely done carving.

Kae, Ruff, and I boarded the ship. The parchment-white sails were down, tied to large wooden poles that loomed high above me. Intricate patterns of swirls were carved out along the railings of the ship. I cataloged the different familiar structures I had encountered during my trips to the shipwrecks. It was more lifelike up close, floating above the water and perfectly intact—like it was its own living being.

"It is beautiful." I gasped, much to my surprise.

Kae shot Ruff a baffled look within my periphery to which I ignored. She then mumbled something about getting medical supplies and disappeared down a flight of stairs that led beneath us.

"So, where are you from?" Ruff asked.

Though he was taller than me—only slightly—and insanely muscular, he seemed harmless. Judging by how he fought the men at the bar, however, I knew to steer clear of his bad side.

"Soledel," I answered with the same lie I told Helene earlier.

Ruff made a face of disgust, typical for a siren hunter to think ill the kingdom that worshiped sirens.

"The siren worshipers?" Kae said as she returned with a dark brown bottle and cloth wrappings. "I wasn't aware people left that kingdom."

I scrunched my nose.

"They educate themselves on what they do not understand instead of fearing with blind hatred," I shot out in a tone that could cut ice, or at least I hoped that was what I sounded like.

I glared at the two hunters, overtly aware of how many lives they took in the past year—in the past few days. My body involuntarily shuddered at the thought, but Kae didn't seem to notice.

"You're not seriously defending sirens, are you? I was wrong in suggesting we have an open position. Just let me clean your cut, and you can leave," Kae said flatly, looking at me as if I said something unintelligent.

Ruff looked uncomfortable and headed toward the other side of the boat, fiddling with some ropes.

"You said you needed another fighter. I can fight and easily learn the ways of the sword. You hunt sirens. I have a wide range of knowledge about their species. You need me." I wanted to stare down Kae as I spoke to assert myself, but my gaze went down to my hand as she unraveled the old bandages.

The cut had opened up and deepened during the fight. Kae shot her head up.

"How did you know we hunt sirens?" Kae asked and her eyes narrowed.

Sweat dripped down my backside.

"There are many tales of the siren hunters. You have a carving of one on the front of your ship. It is how I knew." I brushed over the lie a little too quickly, feeling her eye me suspiciously. "It was why I sought you out. I want to see the sirens up close. I can teach you more about them. Perhaps with more knowledge, you can have some shred of sympathy toward them," I added for good measure.

Kae tilted her head slightly, but said nothing.

"And what happens when we encounter a siren and decide to kill it, anyway? What then?" Kae's features were cold and impassive.

"Because if you try to stop us by putting my crew in danger, I'll have you join your beloved sirens in the depths of the sea."

If I hadn't been so annoyed with her, I might have been terrified. She was only acting like this because she was still grieving over that Kipp fellow. Human lives were so vulnerable and fleeting. Could she not just get over it?

"Fine. I betray you; you throw me over. Understood. Now, will you take that giant stick that is so far up your OW!" I screeched as a burning sensation engulfed where my cut was.

I retracted my hand and shot her a glare. Kae only smiled sweetly in response, though it did not seem sweet at all.

"Relax, dulzura. I just poured alcohol to clean your wound. Can't have it getting infected, now, can we?" Kae spoke in a nonchalant voice.

My hand still stung when I let it rest in Kae's calloused hand. She had spoken in one of the human's older languages that was not the common tongue. I assumed it was an insult.

"And as for your offer, I'll give you a trial period. We're heading south tomorrow after we buy more *zephlum* weapons here. You behave and give us valuable info on the sirens, and you can stay with us. Deal?" Kae did not look up as she spoke, still wrapping my hand with new bandages.

She had practice doing this—bandaging wounds. I could tell by the sure way her fingers moved to tie up the bandage. The pain had lessened in intensity. My eyes lingered on her hands, roughened with callouses and thin scars.

"Deal." I did not let any triumph show on my face.

I had until the next full moon to woo this uptight wretch and get close enough to cut her heart out. It was plenty of time. Perhaps I would allow myself to experience being human for a little while longer before finishing the deed.

After all, I would never get this opportunity again. The more information on the vulnerabilities of the hunters I could get, the more valuable I would be when I eventually returned home with Hyrissa.

I smiled to myself. This journey was just the beginning.

Chapter Ten
Kae

The next morning, everyone met up at the *zephlum* shops, bright and early—much to the hungover protests of my crew. The sun shone down on us with few clouds in the sky. I could already feel the prickle of sweat start to bead beneath my coat. I pulled down my hat farther onto my head to block out the rays.

Our potential new member, Aqeara, had slept in a room below deck that was separated from the others. We used it to store miscellaneous things that had no place anywhere else. I had tried cleaning it out the best I could, making a mental note to throw some of the useless junk out. A moderate cot lined one wall. The room itself felt suffocating, but Aqeara didn't seem to mind, and I had left her to sleep.

I had nearly sprinted out after showing her the room. Close proximity to someone I found annoyingly attractive was a potential recipe for disaster. I didn't know why I offered her a position on the crew. It was true I was getting desperate to find someone on this island who seemed capable of holding their own in a fight and wasn't a drunk, but I would be an idiot to deny that I didn't also choose Aqeara based on looks over skill.

We all had our vices.

"Have you gotten any news about our next heading, Captain?" Atty asked as he rubbed his eyes.

I nodded curtly in return.

Before I found Dalton in the middle of a six-on-one bar fight, I had just met up with a well-trusted informant.

"We are to sail immediately to Naivia. I have confirmation that there's a man located there who might have a heading to the siren kingdom," I said in a hushed tone and glanced around to see if Aqeara was nearby.

I didn't want the siren sympathizer to overhear this news. Atty let out a low whistle.

"Do you know what this means? If we find their home, we could really have a chance of wiping them all out." Atty's grin turned sinister, and I matched his expression.

"We can finally be rid of those horrid creatures," I agreed, and signaled my men to head inside the shops.

A few crewmen were missing. They probably had far more interesting nights than I had. I hoped they would return to the *Mar Daemon* in time for departure or there would be some serious scolding.

Aqeara seemed lost in thought, several feet away. There was a glaze in her eyes as she stared at the library sign. Her eyebrows furrowed, and she huffed a sigh, muttering something to herself that I could not hear. Before I departed to do my own shopping, I walked over and gave Aqeara a handful of gold coins.

"Buy yourself some new clothes that aren't ripped and better fitted," I said as I dropped the coins into her outstretched hand.

Aqeara's dress was tattered in multiple places from the fight last night. Even brand new, her corset did not fit her properly—it was *very* tight at the bodice. I tried my hardest to maintain eye contact. Aqeara's eyes widened at the coins, and she gave me a sly grin. Without another word, she turned and walked in the opposite direction of where the clothing shops were. I wondered whether she would return or just take my money and run.

A shooing motion was all I gave my men before they walked into the weapons shop of their specialty. The owners of each small shop sold a different type of weapon made of the siren-killing metal, and the men separated accordingly.

Ruff disappeared into the crossbow shop and a sharp pang struck my chest. Kipp had been the expert with crossbows. He had been teaching Ruff how to use the weapon in the final days of our last journey, before we'd returned to Avalon.

I had dropped Kipp's crossbow in frustration after missing those sirens on the dock and had broken it in my anger. Ruff was looking to purchase a new one. He told me he had spent hours the night before trying to fix it with no luck. Though, I suspected it was more for sentimental reasons than practical use.

A fresh wave of sorrow threatened to wash over me. I channeled that grief into something more useful. Rage. I clenched my fists at my sides before taking a deep breath.

I walked in the opposite direction of the *zephlum* shops. Just a few blocks down, there was a local jeweler with a craftsmanship I had liked the last time I was here. There had to be a name for spending coins on unnecessary things to get rid of dreadful feelings. I just hadn't come up with it yet.

The small stand blended in with the many other street vendors that lined up the sidewalks of Zephlus. There was nothing flashy about it that would draw the attention of customers, yet it was still here when I strode up to it, meaning it had to have been doing well in business.

Behind the little stand was a stranger—not the owner I had encountered last year. She was petite and stout, eyes narrowed in a way that made me assume she was always expecting the worst of people. I stood in front of her and the woman's dazzling smile threw me off guard. It wasn't what I was expecting from her demeanor.

"What can I get for ya?" The woman's teeth were a pearly shade of white, except for the golden one that twinkled against the sunlight.

"Got any new rings this season?" I asked as I skimmed my eyes along the cloth table.

There were many pearl necklaces, gold bracelets, and a plethora of other jewelry made of various gems. The woman ducked down behind the table. Metal clanged as she rummaged through her products.

"I have these new rings fresh on the market. Price is a bit steeper 'cus this is genuine silver. Five gold pieces a ring." The woman never faltered with her smile.

I grinned back at her and rummaged through the handful she placed on the table.

My hands were currently bare of all jewelry. I had been blindfolded, walking in an alleyway a few months ago, and had my rings stolen clean off my fingers, as well as the coins I had on my person.

They had also stabbed me in the side, but that was less remarkable. Men were such cowards.

I felt naked without my rings. My fingers needed something to fumble with. The rings helped, and not having any had been something I never quite got used to. Especially the more masculine rings that were unlike the ones that filled the jewelry box in my bedroom back home.

"How about these three?" I picked out my favorites after careful consideration.

One was twisted and bent to look like a snake with two small ruby stones for eyes. Another looked like it could have been a family heirloom. It had a thick silver crest in the middle that resembled an octopus, with tentacles spreading out across the band. The third ring had a polished teal stone in the middle of a thin silver band. I placed the rings on my fingers and was aware my movements captured the gaze of the woman. My fingers wiggled as I slid the rings on and I smirked. A laugh nearly escaped my lips as she audibly swallowed.

Still got it, I thought.

"I- Uh, will that be all?" The woman regained her composure and smiled again. "Twelve gold pieces."

The discount did not go unnoticed. I winked at her and handed the pieces over, suppressing a proud grin as the faintest blush rose to her cheeks. A glimmer of sunlight reflecting off a familiar surface caught my eye as I turned to walk away.

"Are these pearls made of *zephlum*?" I asked.

The necklace lying on the corner of the table was a simple string of small black pearls pressed against each other. My suspicion was confirmed when my fingers grazed over the familiar metal.

"Aye. The owner is trying out new jewelry welding the metal. This one here is eight gold pieces. A first and only of its kind... for now." The woman didn't even finish her sentence before I shoved the eight coins into her barely outstretched hand.

I clasped the necklace around my neck.

"Thanks," I said over my shoulder as I headed in the direction of the weapons' district.

The streets weren't nearly as crowded as they usually were during peak hours. It was still early out, the sun still fairly low in the sky. There was a nice crisp to the air that was rare around this time of year. I welcomed the slight breeze as I made my way back to the shops, specifically the one that specialized in swords.

The sword shop in question was more refined and established than the street vendors. For one, it was in an actual building rather than a well-stocked cart. It was also the most popular *zephlum* shop on the island, which gave the owner a lot of liberty in keeping up with both the interior and exterior of the building.

The shop was small, yet cozy. The owner kept the place neat— not a speck of dust or a tumbleweed in sight, despite quite a few bouncing along the streets outside. Wooden beams lined the doorways, stone stacked up on top of each other to create the walls.

Graying stone, weathered on the outside yet scrubbed down on the inside.

Cutlass swords with various handles and designs lined the walls. They all glittered in the same black metal that promised sure death to sirens. Though *zephlum* was the only material known to kill them, it did not have a long lifespan—the metal deteriorated and grew dull after extended use. Which was the reason we'd come to restock on new weapons.

A tall and disheveled man was the only other customer in the shop. I made note of the stranger who, upon further inspection, turned out to be Dalton.

"Enjoyed your night, Dalt?" I greeted my friend just as Doc and Birch walked in. Dalton opened his mouth with a response and promptly closed it as the doctor and swordsman settled within his peripheral vision.

"Trying out a new sword, Doc?" Dalton called out to Doc as the doctor beheld the different swords.

Birch lifted his head in silent greeting toward Dalton and I. He went straight to one of the swords on the wall opposite of where we stood, knowing immediately which one he wanted. Birch was a man of few words. It took us all a solid month after first meeting the hunter to translate what his body language meant.

"It appears Birch here has made a fair point that I learn to defend myself. I just bought a small dagger to use in case of a siren encounter. I am now simply following Birch to obtain his own new weapon," Doc said and pulled out a dagger that was resting in his new holster.

The hilt was engraved in a spiral pattern that wrapped around the entire handle. I was impressed by the detail. It had to have been expensive, but Doc was from the wealthier side of the middle sector in Avalon. It explained his posh dialect compared to the others.

It also didn't help that he was the oldest of all of us at nearly twenty-six years old, adding maturity to his disposition.

"I'll take two o' these." Birch—whose arms were covered in tattoos, had a nose ring and a buzzed head, on top of a large scar running down his face—handed his pick of swords over to the trembling shop owner.

The man nodded meekly and gave his price for the swords. It was at face value. Birch handed the money over with a satisfied look on his face. He turned and walked out with Doc at his heel.

"My night was, err… uneventful." Dalton began albeit quietly. "I ran into Zech at the tavern we met at last time. He was dashingly handsome as always, nearly as charming as me. He even offered to buy me a few drinks. I dunno. I felt different this time. Maybe I don't fancy him as much as I thought I did. Or maybe I do. Ugh." Dalton stared blankly at the wall of swords in front of him and tugged at the strands of his hair in frustration.

"Either way, I acted like a total prick and ruined any chances with Zech. I blacked out on rum and woke up outside by the dumpster to the sun rising." Dalton's once-cheery voice now oozed with resentment.

He picked up twin swords at random and paid for them. The knobby handles, made of pure gold, contrasted against the curved, glittering black metal. There were small skulls engraved in the middle of each handle. The design suited Dalton's style.

"You were really looking forward to spending time with the prince. What happened? Maybe it's because you're yearning for another." I smirked and raised a brow as I chose my own cutlass sword after careful consideration of my options.

The sword I chose had a silver handle that spiraled in a vertical pattern. The grated grip almost resembled lace. The blade was longer than Dalton's but had a smaller curve. I practiced a few moves, ignoring Dalton's reaction.

Dalton stiffened at my comment, pulling me away from my minute observations. He dropped his weapons and fumbled for a bit before muttering in objection. Red blush crept up his neck to flush his cheeks. I pressed on the teasing.

"It's the lass, isn't it? Well, you'll be pleased to know she's joining us. The little siren lover wants to *educate* us on the sea devils. She could give us vital information, maybe even the location of their kingdom. Plus, we do need another fighter after…" I trailed off, not wanting to finish my sentence.

We both knew why we needed a replacement. The shop owner named his price to me, and I placed the coins on the counter.

"It is *not* Aqeara." Dalton was a little too curt in his response. "It isn't anyone. Just drop it, Kae."

His tone was off, exasperated at an unseen source. He looked annoyed, his eyes glancing skyward before falling to the floor.

I fastened the sword to my belt and held up both hands in reconciliation. He stormed out of the shop with me right behind him.

"Sorry. That came out harsher than I intended," Dalton muttered, and I knew from his tone that he was angrier at himself for an unknown reason than at me.

He rolled his shoulders as if brushing off the built-up tension.

"S'fine," I said and shrugged it off.

I knew he meant well.

"It'll be nice to have a new member on board. Keeps things interesting. But really, I'm fine. I appreciate the sentiment." Dalton looked far from fine, but he still flashed a grin, anyway.

I smiled and punched him in the shoulder. I didn't want to argue any further. He was my best friend after all. Dalton, renouncing any feelings for Aqeara, somehow put me at ease. Like the tension I was carrying in my shoulders had relaxed.

It's because you don't trust her, I thought to myself. *You don't want your best friend getting hurt.*

Yeah, that had to be it.

And there she was, the woman of the hour. Aqeara nearly ran into Dalton and me as she exited a shop that sold mostly small weapons like daggers in haste. She looked startled as she was in the middle of sheathing her twin daggers into her new belt and hadn't noticed us in her path. I, on the other hand, noticed everything. Aqeara had gotten a little spend-happy with the money I had given her.

Resentment momentarily flowed through me as I recalled giving her too many coins to begin with, half-expecting her to not spend them all. It seemed that she had spent quite a lot on these daggers. The tip of the handle was shaped like a small clamshell, and the handle itself twisted in a corkscrew pattern of silver.

Aqeara eyed the black glittering metal at her hip in distaste. But I would be damned not to admit those were gorgeous blades.

She had discarded her ripped and bloody dress for tight black pants that hugged her curves and a dark blue shirt with billowy sleeves. The neckline was too low for respectable women's fashion, and several passersby gawked at her. A black corset with blue patterns threaded onto it was tied tightly around her torso. A brown belt sat atop her pants and pinched her waist even further.

I breathed in sharply while Dalton gave her an impressed look. Her red hair was still down, contrasting beautifully against her dark outfit. I shook my head at my line of thoughts.

She was a siren sympathizer. A complete lunatic. It didn't matter how attractive she looked. Or how... ugh.

"Now, *this* is an outfit! I wish I could pull that off... actually, I probably could." Dalton made a face like he was considering it, and Aqeara giggled.

My jaw clenched, and I turned to leave, motioning for the two of them to follow me.

She had *giggled*. This woman wouldn't last a day at sea, especially in that ridiculous outfit. I didn't trust her, and I was not at all appreciating how quickly Dalton let his guard down. Physically, she looked dainty and frail. But mentally? Who knew how cunning she could be?

Aqeara slung a large satchel over her shoulder that was stuffed to the brim with more clothes. I had also purchased better-fitted clothing back in Avalon before we left. Dalton had mentioned how men's fashion was beginning to dominate the markets for women, and I was curious to see how they held up. The new clothing was still loose and comfortable, but unlike the men's clothing I spent the last year adorning, these pieces of clothing did more to accentuate my body's best features. I wondered if the two of us were similar sizes.

"Let's head back to the ship. These sirens aren't about to off themselves, you know," I ordered.

Aqeara grumbled something incoherent as she eyed the *zephlum* pearls at my neck and moved further away from me.

I rolled my eyes.

Our unlikely trio walked toward the harbor, mostly in silence. Aqeara occasionally asked a question about a building or something else I felt she should have already known. I remained silent, but Dalton entertained her questions.

As we reached the docks, I noticed Ruff standing to the side. His facial hair was covered in a white powder. In his hand, a Zephlus delicacy: fried dough completely powdered in sugar.

"And where did you get that?" Dalton called out in his own form of greeting as he skipped over.

Ruff looked up with guilt written on his face and eyed Dalton as he made his way to him. He shifted his gaze over to me and then to Aqeara. Ruff then quickly shoved the remaining piece of dessert into his mouth before Dalton could snatch it out of his hand.

Dalton crossed his arms over his chest and feigned annoyance.

"Idiots," I muttered.

Aqeara scrunched her nose, but said nothing in response.

"Find everything okay, Ruff?" I asked as I made my way over to him.

Ruff fiddled with his burlap sack filled with *zephlum* arrows. Aqeara eyed them nervously, like she feared them. Or she was thinking of a way to stab us all with them, perhaps.

"Yeah, the lass even threw in a couple extra bolt arrows when I bought the more expensive crossbow. Says it'll be easier to shoot with this one. She better be right." Ruff wiped his hands and face free of sugar, using his shirt to clean up.

"You certainly have a way with the ladies." Dalton said.

Ruff huffed in return, as if Dalton had insulted him. He picked up his burlap sack and heaved it over his shoulder. We all followed him up the boarding dock and onto my ship. Atty was already sharpening knives on board.

"Captain. Boys. M'lady," Atty greeted us. Dalton and Ruff made a face at the denunciation but walked over to show off their new weapons.

Aqeara stood motionless, unsure of what to do with herself.

"How long have you been sailing?" Aqeara asked right as I was about to walk into my room.

"I've been captain for over a year now," I answered, not bothering to elaborate.

Aqeara only nodded. She looked like she had just swallowed a lemon. She also looked like she wanted to ask more questions. Before she could get the chance, I disappeared into my room and closed the door behind me.

Safe in my quarters, I plopped down on my bed. My heart was racing, which was odd because there was no present danger.

It was Aqeara. I couldn't wrap my head around how someone could love the creatures I hated and hunted for so long. She was intolerable.

My blood started to boil.

If I mentioned how they killed Edmonde, would she still worship the demons? I shook my head and swung my feet over the side of the bed. Crouching down, I crawled onto the floor and lifted the loose floorboard. My extra unspent coins settled with the other jewels.

I leaned against the wall next to my bed and tilted my head back. I needed to compose myself. To gain control. I was her captain now. I was the one in charge of situations. Emotions gave away information, and Aqeara was not to be trusted with them. The crew had to be protected at all costs and despite our deal; she was not yet part of the crew.

I would keep a silent, watchful eye over Aqeara and learn as much about her, as she was no doubt learning about me.

Chapter Eleven
Kae

Shouts and chatter filled the air outside my quarters. Everyone was trickling back onto the ship. It was about time; we were nearly due for departure. Hours had passed since I boarded my ship.

I grabbed my hat off my desk and placed it on my head. I eyed the mirror that hung on the wall as I fixed the triangular headpiece, not caring if any of my curls poked out. There was no need to hide who I was anymore.

Then I stepped back outside to greet my crew.

Aqeara was making conversation with Dyer as he hoisted the sails. She watched him pull the levees with an intensity that matched a curious child. I walked up the stairs toward Barnes at the helm. He was already giving out orders. Barnes smiled sheepishly at my having caught him.

"We'll be sailing south toward Naivia." I said in a stentorian manner, addressing everyone as they stared up at me. "I heard at a pub last night there have been several siren sightings along the route. We'll reach the southern kingdom in just over two weeks' time if things run smoothly."

As the ship was prepared for departure, I held a hand out against the beating sun. Not a cloud in sight.

Aqeara looked shy as the rest of the crew came to terms with her joining us on our journey. She clasped and unclasped her hand in front of her multiple times before letting them hang at her sides. Her eyes darted away from all the staring, and they met my own.

I beckoned her to come up and join me.

"This is Aqeara of Soledel." I exclaimed. "I know, I know she's from the siren asylum, but be nice. She's going to train as a fighter and give us insight on the sirens. We've seen her fight. She'll be useful with a bit of training." I looked at Atty and Birch as I spoke.

Aqeara's would-be trainers nodded. All our fighters trained under the duo as they were the best we had. The rest of the crew stared at Aqeara in a way that made her squirm.

"And I'm sure if any of you try anything on her, she'll enjoy breaking off your fingers as well," I added.

The men went wide-eyed and nodded fervidly. Aqeara's lips twitched upward. My crew was comprised of only the most respectable men. While I knew Aqeara had nothing to fear from them, I wanted her to know it as well.

"Aqeara, allow my crew to introduce themselves." I motioned out.

Aqeara composed herself like she was bracing for battle.

"Well, I obviously am the captain of the ship," I said sort of feebly.

Aqeara blinked at me like I had said something foolish. Dalton cleared his throat.

"If we're stating the obvious, the name's Dalton." Dalton said with ease as he winked at Aqeara. "Again. I'm the Captain's secondary and navigator."

"I'm Ruff. Captain's first mate and right-hand man," Ruff stated in a gruff voice.

He crossed his arms in front of his chest, displaying his muscular, tattooed arms fully.

"Don't be too intimidated by Ruff. Deep down he's a big softie," Dalton interjected, and Aqeara let a smile slip through.

Ruff only rolled his eyes in response.

"I'm Barnes. I'm a navigator-in-training of sorts. Dalton's teaching me while he learns cartography." Barnes waved beside Aqeara, still behind the wheel.

His cheery, boyish demeanor earned a small smile from Aqeara.

"That over there is our doctor, hence the nickname Doc. He's stitched up all of our wounds from battle," I said in a proud voice.

Doc gave a sly smile. His cheeks were rosy red and there were already some gray streaks in his hair, despite only being in his twenties. He was one to be in a constant state of stress, and having to take care of us didn't help.

"I must admit, Captain, that most of the wounds seen on this ship are more from drunken accidents," Doc said.

I smiled and nodded in agreement.

"Hello, I'm Rigby. I'm the chef, and I know about twenty different ways to serve fish," Rigby, one of the scrawnier members on board, spoke up.

Doc punched him in the shoulder. The two had grown close since they both tended to stay away from any violence.

"Thank the heavens for that. I'm Atty and this here is Birch. We'll be your trainers." Atty gave a big smile, flashing his teeth, and Aqeara shivered.

Birch was silent as usual.

"There's no proper way to describe their talents. It's like they're two halves of a whole." I said just to Aqeara in a low voice. "The way they both move while fighting, completely in sync. The best tutors you'll ever have."

She nodded. I could tell she was trying hard to commit all names to memory.

"Oi! I'm Arden, one of the gunners on board. I do explosives." Arden's grin was too enthusiastic for comfort.

He was on the taller side amongst the crew, with lean muscles and thick, curly hair. His foot tapped anxiously on the deck. Kenley slapped a hand to his face, clearly not enjoying the restless energy coming from Arden.

"And I'm Kenley, the other gunner. I man the cannons. And keep an eye on Arden." Kenley spoke in a deep voice that made him seem twice his age, despite him only being twenty.

He was two years older than Arden, but three inches shorter. Kenley's wavy hair was tied back and away from his sweaty face.

"There's a rumor a certain explosion that destroyed an old, abandoned building back home in Avalon was done by a young man. They never caught the culprit." I tried speaking in a low voice to Aqeara, but Arden heard me, anyway.

He grinned even wider.

"We all sleep better knowing Kenley keeps the boy in check," Ruff stated.

Arden walked over and punched Ruff in the shoulder as hard as he could. Ruff didn't budge. I pinched the bridge of my nose and let out a huff. The last thing we needed was a fight.

"Lastly, we have Marsden and Dyer. They're in charge of…" I paused, eyeing Aqeara as I considered my words carefully pointed to the last two unintroduced men. "They make the ship go."

Marsden and Dyer both waved at Aqeara from their posts and continued to tie down or loosen up ropes. It was like the two were polar opposites. Dyer, who was thin with long limbs. Marsden, with a stocky build and a round face.

"It seems like everyone is paired up with their roles," Aqeara noted.

I nodded.

"Working together helps keep us from going at each other's throats. It creates a sense of unity. We are all one with the ship," I said and waved a hand at my crew.

They saw the signal and got back to work. Several headed below deck. Aqeara's face was still scrunched up like she was deep in thought.

"I can give you a tour of the ship, too, if you'd like," I offered, motioning my hand out toward the main deck.

"That sounds lovely." Aqeara's voice was soft.

She seemed far away despite standing right next to me. Her gaze was captivated by something on the main deck I couldn't see.

"Well, up here obviously is where Barnes and Dalton spend most of their day. And down on the main deck," I led Aqeara down the small staircase, "is where most of the crew spends their day. We have fishing rods and nets to catch our meals. Marsden and Dyer are constantly up here monitoring the wind and listening to Dalton or Barnes on where to shift the sails. It allows us to keep our course," I explained.

Aqeara still had that look of marvel that made me want to trust her. Almost.

"Do you not get bored? The ship is large, yes, but what is there to do for fun?" Aqeara's eyes flickered to the men that went about their business.

I wasn't sure if that was a euphemism.

"We eat, drink, train, dance, and sleep. Sometimes they like to place bets on the most obscure events, like how many days Birch goes without bathing or the sort. We also try to make plenty of pit stops to nearby kingdoms along the route. We'll dock on land for a few days and relax while trying to get more info on siren sightings. It never really gets boring out here at sea. I mean, not for me at least." I was rambling and stopped myself from going on.

Aqeara looked at me wistfully. It probably sounded silly to her, but what did I care?

I remained quiet as I led her down the steps to below deck. Aqeara blinked several times as her eyes adjusted to the dim lighting.

"Over here are the rum barrels. See how they're painted red on top? That differentiates them from the ones that have freshwater inside. Those are painted blue." I pointed toward one corner of the ship, where multiple barrels were lined up.

Aqeara looked taken aback.

"You are surrounded by water. You mean to tell me you do not drink ocean water?" she asked, looking at me with that scrutinizing gaze.

Now it was my turn to be taken aback.

"You drink ocean water in Soledel?" I asked.

Aqeara grimaced at my reaction, like she said something wrong. I mean, she did. Gross.

"Well... we clean it?" She struggled for the right words as a pink tint rose on her cheeks.

I wasn't certain if Soledelians spoke the same common tongue as the rest of us. I could tell from her thick accent and the way she paused between phrases she struggled with her words at times. Given that Soledel closed itself off from the rest of the world, it made sense that they developed their own dialect. The official language of Avalon was the same spoken in all the other kingdoms, though it was only named our official one just a generation ago.

"Oh, so you boil the water to drink it. I mean, yeah, you can do that. Our water is fresh from the rivers that flow from waterfalls just outside Avalon. The snow-capped mountains are their source, but we usually never feel the cold because we're right by the ocean. It's just humid all the time. The waterfalls are only a short hike away, so we get our fresh water from there and just bring it back to the kingdom." I was rambling on again.

So much for the lack of trust. Here I was, spilling my guts. I couldn't possibly imagine what this woman would get out of waterfalls to betray me with, so I relented.

Aqeara was intently listening as she looked around at the rest of the ship.

"That seems beautiful, the waterfalls. I have swum under several that pour over cliffs into the ocean. They are fun." She smiled in a daydreamy sort of way.

I coughed and made my way to the crew's quarters. "These two rooms are where the crew sleeps."

The two large rooms in question looked as if one of Arden's explosions had gone off. There were heaps of clothes everywhere. Each cot and hammock were a tangled mess of sheets. Several were occupied. Aqeara peeked in and made a face of disgust, whether at the visual display or the smell, I wasn't sure.

"I am most grateful for my own room," Aqeara observed, and I held back a laugh.

We then walked to her room, passing storage crates and cannons that leaned against closed windows.

"This is where I slept last night." Aqeara pointed to her room.

I nodded, mostly to myself, while she walked in. It was a small space, but it was all we had. I wasn't sure we could squeeze her with the men even if we wanted to, and she certainly wasn't sleeping with me.

Aqeara sat down on the bed, and I was suddenly aware of how hot and stuffy it was down here—how tight and cramped the space felt. I left her without a word, ending the grand tour at that.

She didn't follow me back up the stairs.

I didn't see Aqeara until the next day around midafternoon. She had spent the night and most of this morning in her room. It wasn't until Atty and Birch went over to accost her into beginning her training that she emerged. When she did, I chose to go below deck, dragging a protesting Dalton with me to do some practice of our own.

We worked on some stances for all of fifteen minutes before winding up slightly tipsy behind the rum barrels. Barnes had taken over his shift at the helm, needing more practice behind the wheel. I despised change. Routine kept me sane at sea, and having a damsel board my ship threw me off.

When I voiced my thoughts to Dalton, he stared off into the distance.

"It's just that you pride yourself in being so detached and breaking hearts before yours could get broken. Do y'know it took us forever to become close friends? You like to be on the defensive side with your guard up. So, in comes this lass with ideas completely contrasting your own, and everyone else's, quite frankly. Of course, you won't trust her immediately!" Dalton moved his arms while he spoke. As if they helped emphasize his words.

I used to tease him about it until he turned on me and said I did the same thing when I got lost in thought.

"I suppose when you put it that way…" I took a swig of my drink.

"Just give her a chance. Like you said, she could be useful. Besides, she seems spoiled. I heard bets going on that she wouldn't last with the smell and squalor," Dalton said and cleared his full glass in a matter of seconds.

I laughed at that. My movements were a tad delayed while I set my glass down.

"You're right. I'll try to be more open. She's a member of this crew now. Trust is essential for function," I said, repeating the simplified version of my mantra for the hundredth time to Dalton.

It was more for my own sake than for his. I would show my trust to Aqeara's face, but be watchful of her at all times.

Dalton smiled approvingly at my response and swung an arm around my shoulder, pulling me in close for a one-armed hug.

"I am proud of you, young one, for your maturity." Dalton tried to age his voice.

I laughed and pushed him away. For someone only eleven months older than I was, he liked to gloat about being the elder, more mature one in our duo. As if. It got to his head far too much. It also got to mine, in a worse way. It reminded me of Edmonde.

Dalton sensed my drifting thoughts and leaned back against the wall, closing his eyes. The movement distracted me, and I stared at him, perplexed.

"Remember when we got arrested in Eayucia for stealing bread?" he reminisced, with his eyes still shut.

I shot him another nonplussed look—which did nothing since he wasn't looking at me—and leaned back against the wall with him. I placed my hands behind my head for comfort.

"How could I possibly forget when Ruff reminds us every other day about how heroic he was for breaking us out?" I asked and Dalton smiled fondly.

"Smug bastard," Dalton said.

His mouth remained curved upward as he insulted Ruff.

"He earned the right to hold it over our head," I ignored the way Dalton's eyes shot open with an accusatory look, "but only for that first week. After that, it became excessive. It's not like we were being selfish. We stole that bread for a starving kid."

The image of the little blonde girl with dirty hair came to mind. Her stomach had rumbled right when I caught her trying to pickpocket me. Dalton and I didn't hesitate trying to get some food for her.

Dalton lifted a shoulder. "He thinks it reckless that we were so irresponsible. S'not our fault that he's done nothing rash in his life."

I grinned at the way Dalton pouted. It was true. Out of the three of us, Ruff was the cautious one. He kept Dalton and me in check whenever we were on the verge of doing the rashest things.

"You nearly skinned me alive for getting frustrated that we were in that awful, hot cell for hours on end," I accused.

The memories came rushing in vivid colors—the bright sunlight streaming through the cell window, the raw scent of dead rats and sweaty bodies in the building, the sounds of drunk men trying to woo the guard dog that held the jail keys.

"I would have if Ruff hadn't blown up the damn wall of our cell," Dalton said.

I could still hear the explosion and the ringing it caused in my ears. How we all ran as fast as we could back to the ship. We hadn't been to Eayucia since then. Odds are, we were banned from the kingdom. Though we hadn't stayed long enough to find out.

Dalton and I both broke off into laughter, sharing more memories and smiles. Until I forgot about Aqeara and sirens and lost ones, even for just a short while.

Chapter Twelve
Aqeara

The first ten days at sea flew by in a blur. I spent most of my afternoons under the brutal sun, learning new fighting stances and training with the professionals, Atty and Birch. Though I had no intention of harming any sirens, I was all for acting my part while on board the *Mar Daemon*.

What a ridiculous name. Sea demon. A name that described sirens in the ancient tongue. It took all of my strength to not make a face when I was told the name.

The second day at sea was one of the most wretched. They forced me to run laps all around the main deck, up and down the stairs at the helm, up and down the stairs to below deck, and back around again. It made my legs feel like jellyfish. I wished to saw them off and be rid of the searing pain they made me push through.

Though, it was strangely exhilarating, the moments just after I was done with my exercises. My body never felt more alive. When they gave me large sacks of dry food to carry while I ran, however, my exhilaration depleted.

Playing my part in this was also not the only reason I grew eager to learn the ways of the dagger. I also wanted to learn to defend myself. As a human, I was constantly reminded I could not heal as quickly, nor sing for my protection. I did not wish to feel vulnerable, especially being on a vessel surrounded by mostly men. If they found out what I really was, I would be dead in a heartbeat.

My two trainers had learned about the incident back in Zephlus. They used my own fears against me, smiling those mischievous smiles to make me uneasy as they approached. It made me freeze in place instead of raising my weapons to defend their onslaught. It took several days before I overcame my initial fear of men. I grew to know better than to believe their false, dangerous flirtation.

After another few sessions, I even met their smiles with a dark one of my own. The clash of *zephlum* on *zephlum* no longer frightened me. The blade felt surer in my hand. My skills were developing faster than the two men had expected. It coaxed my ego, being able to adapt to new moves so easily.

Any sense of self-worth would disappear at night.

I avoided interactions with the other men and spent most of my days in my room where I rested my tired, sore muscles. Having my own space to collect my thoughts at the end of each day kept me from going insane.

Being surrounded by my enemies at every hour of the day had proven to be exhausting. Though, having them train me helped ease a bit of the nerves. At least in close proximity, I knew how they fought. They unknowingly gave me tips to use against them should I ever need to defend myself.

Though I enjoyed nights to myself, I was alone in an entirely different way. My much-needed sleep was riddled with nightmares. Hyrissa's dying face was always present the moment my eyes were closed. Noerina, yelling at me as I trained in the ways of the warriors would transform into Kae's dagger, ending her life. My insomnia served as motivation to be twice as alert the next day to not raise any suspicion to myself.

"Hey! Wherever your mind's going, pull back. Focus." Atty snapped me to attention.

He was right. I was thinking of Hyrissa again. I ducked from his oncoming swing and thrust my hand forward, clashing my daggers against his. Fighting required less concentration and more muscle memory now. I was improving.

Atty's long sword had a greater range of motion and allowed him to stay back while still on the offense. My daggers required me to get close enough to wound him. I jumped as he attempted to slice at my knees and took a few steps forward.

"Have you slept well last night? You seem slow today," I countered.

Atty's face stretched into a wolfish grin as he swung, causing me to bend back in a way that surprised me. I did not know humans could be this flexible.

I flipped over and lunged, only to be met with his sword again. That was the thing with Atty and Birch—they were impossibly good. The two moved together like liquid, always in sync, always sure of themselves.

"Don't mess up, princess. We seem to have an audience," Atty sneered and sliced at my sleeve, tearing the cloth in a shallow rip.

I huffed in annoyance and retreated two steps. How was *princess* an insult? Clagoria was the fiercest and deadliest siren I had ever known.

I stole a glance to see that several of the crew had stopped their duties to watch us. It was common for the men to watch how I fought. Some found it interesting, others did not seem to care much. Kae was always the latter. I never caught her watching as I trained, not once. The captain always had something more important to do while I trained with Atty or Birch.

"I would not dream of it," I replied to Atty's non-existent insult and lunged at him with my daggers.

As I noticed before, Atty darted to the right when he attacked. I faked another lunge and swept my leg out, knocking him over. Atty let out a surprised noise while I held my daggers just over his heart. Birch clapped from the sideline. His eyebrows were raised, but he looked impressed.

I grinned and extended a hand out to Atty to help him up.

"Unbelievable." Atty said as he clapped me on the back. "You've improved so much! I like the little false move at the end."

Though I tried my hardest in the days that I spent with my trainers to remain impassive, Atty grew on me. He was friendly and patient while I struggled to learn how to defend myself. Birch still intimidated me with his wordless prowling and blank stares, but I knew he was like Atty—patient and cautious—around me. He just had his own way of showing it.

That sort of thinking led me to scowl at myself for letting my guard down. These two were the most lethal hunters on board. They were not my friends.

Another round of clapping in the distance reached my ears, pulling me away from my thoughts. Dalton was applauding from behind the wheel. He saluted at me and I laughed. Out of all the men on board, I trusted him the most. He seemed the most at ease, the most laid back. I fed off that energy to drive away the monsters in my head.

"Nice job, Aq—" Kae had emerged from below deck without my notice.

She had cut herself off from an unfinished compliment as her eyes went wide. Dalton, who was still looking down at us, followed Kae's gaze out into the sea. They were both looking at something in the water. Something that was floating just above the surface.

No, *someone.*

Kae whipped out her telescope and began shouting orders. There was a siren in the water. *A siren.*

This was too soon. It was all too soon. I did not even have time to discuss sirens with them. Primarily my fault, but they also made no effort to interact with me.

I was so obtuse. This was my *job.* It was the reason I boarded this ship instead of killing Kae immediately. To convince them that sirens were good. And now look at them. They were so eager to catch and kill this innocent being.

Repulsion, fear, and stress engulfed me.

My pulse quickened and my heart plummeted deep into the pit of my stomach. The next few minutes whirled by without sparing a second for me to process. Though my thoughts were racing a thousand miles a minute, everyone moved in a hazy blur. Men were running around the ship, stuffing something in their ears. Their weapons were drawn and all my sessions getting over my fear of *zephlum* vanished in an instant. A cold feeling crawled down my spine. I was frozen in place. Sweat dripped down my temple.

I began to process the words being shouted.

"Make sure your ears are covered!"

"Ruff, read my lips! Fire your crossbow at it!"

"What?"

"Arden is about to fire the cannon. Brace yourselves!"

"Shit!"

"The ship just lurched. Are we dying?"

"Read. My. Lips."

"Dalton's in the water!"

"Captain, don't you dare jump in after him. *Dammit!*"

"Earbuds out! Okay Barnes, bring her steady."

"Someone, lower a lifeboat!"

The voices echoed distantly in my ears, like I was not there at all. Yet, I could feel myself shaking.

I regained my composure, snapping out of whatever spell I'd been under. I rushed to the railing and looked down to see a gagged siren bleeding out on a smaller boat. Sitting across from her, soaking wet but unharmed, were Dalton and Kae.

The two had really jumped overboard to retrieve her. Marsden and Dyer hoisted the ropes to bring the boat back up toward the ship's level.

They had not killed her. Hope sparked in me. Perhaps they did not want her dead after all. A small voice in my head hoped that they would listen to me first. I began internally rehearsing a speech that would sway them to my side.

They hoisted the siren's body onto the main deck, right by my feet. I stared at the weakened siren. Her arms were bound behind her back. Strands of seaweed-green hair were sprawled across her face. Her tail thrashed pathetically against the deck.

Even in her vulnerable state, she was beautiful. The siren possessed a beauty that made you want to stare at her forever. A powerful urge to protect her rose in me, and I wondered if it was from being human prey or former kin.

I was not prepared for the feeling that washed over me when she looked up at me. Our eyes locked, and it felt like a swift kick to the stomach. A glimmer of recognition passed through her eyes. We'd met before. Her name slipped my mind, but I knew her. I had studied with her many years ago.

She was a fish trader, harmless to humans. She was more innocent and far less volatile than all the men on this ship.

The siren struggled against her gag, wanting to speak. There was a mortified expression on her face that I was certain mirrored my own. I shook my head in the slightest of movements. My cover could not be blown this early.

The siren stopped her resistance.

How had she recognized me in this new form, when none of the other humans could?

"Move out of the way." Kae barreled past me to get to the siren.

She harshly grabbed the siren by the throat and yanked the cloth gag out of her mouth.

"Where are the others? The ones that attacked us. The ones that killed Kipp. *Tell me where your home is!*" Kae growled at the siren, who was turning a shade of purple as Kae continued to squeeze her neck.

I lunged forward and tried to pull Kae off of her.

"Stop!" I yelled. "Stop! Leave her alone, she was not even hunting!"

My grip was futile as Kae shoved me back with little effort. I landed on my bottom and stared at the trembling lips of the siren. She glanced at me again briefly before turning to Kae. Her eyes hardened.

"You and your men are doomed." The siren smiled as she spoke in an accent that I hoped did not sound too similar to mine.

Her eyes turned black as her pupils were immersed in the inky color of our hunting state. Green scales appeared on her cheekbones, and I knew she was about to strike.

I crawled forward just as the siren clamped her mouth down on Kae's arm. Before she could sink her teeth too far into Kae's bicep, Kae ran her sword through the siren's seaweed covered chest with her free hand.

"NO!" I shouted in protest as the siren's eyes went wide.

Her body dissolved rapidly until nothing but a small pile of sand remained on the damp ship deck.

Birch rushed forward and poured alcohol on Kae's shallow wound. She shoved him back and then turned to me.

I was filled with rage.

That could have been me, I thought to myself.

If I were in my true form, my cheeks would have been covered in red scales, but I wasn't. I was human, and I had human defenses.

I did not think twice before I lunged at Kae, dagger in my hand. I tilted the blade under her chin, forcing the captain to meet my eyes. Several men stepped forward to intervene, but Kae held a hand up to halt them. Her eyes held an equal amount of rage when they met mine.

"You said you would let me speak—teach you about the sirens." I shouted, aware of the crew slowly and silently inching forward. "You have avoided me this entire time and killed one before I even had the chance to say a word to you!"

They had all taken their ear coverings out; the threat of the siren was no longer present. I dug my blade deeper until a singular drop of blood welled over the thin slice I made. A flicker of anguish crossed Kae's eyes, but her expression did not betray her. Her face remained stoic.

"And you said you would do nothing to interfere, yet here we are. Get your fucking blade off my neck before I throw you overboard!" Kae shouted, the tone so cruel that the small hairs on the back of my neck rose.

I lowered the dagger, knowing I was outnumbered. I kicked the pile of sand into the ocean, returning the siren's body to the seas. Her soul would be at peace.

My feet carried me down the stairs that led below deck before my brain could give in to my temptations of gutting Kae right then and there.

Pure hatred radiated off of me like steam. Everything in my vision was red. I was so close to ending all of this. All I had to do was lower the blade several inches and plunge it into Kae's heart. Her crew would have murdered me before I could escape. There would probably not be enough time to carve her heart out and throw it into the ocean. I shuddered.

Calm down.

I witnessed a siren being gutted right before my very eyes.

Be sensible.

Nothing made sense anymore. I threw my daggers into the wall with such force that the blades embedded themselves halfway into the wood. I walked over and retrieved them, pulling them out in a way that did the most damage.

As I got my daggers, I noticed a small bedding in the corner below the holes I made. I plopped down and tried to steady my breathing, resting my head against the wall behind me.

"*You have to stop overthinking and let the song come to you naturally. Like I said before, the melody is easy. The words are harder,*" I said in the most mature voice I could muster.

Hyrissa had grown frustrated with my teachings. I could not blame her. The entire day had been spent helping the young princess discover her luring voice, and she was failing miserably.

"*Maybe I should get a professional mentor. Learning at home is so awful. I want to go outside the castle,*" Hyrissa muttered, and I tried not to let her comment hurt my feelings.

I sighed.

Princesses were always taught at home, especially when they were not yet of age. The less they left the castle, the better. At least, that was what the Queen had decreed.

I knew better than to go against her orders. For the most part.

It was also decreed that I stay here and teach Hyrissa during my time off duty. When the Queen was not overlooking our sessions, I had a little fun expanding Hyrissa's curriculum to cover hunting and human behavior.

"*Will you stop being dramatic for five seconds? Do not actually count out loud. That was an expression. I am going to harmonize your melody with you. Try to think of the words I taught you, and let them flow through you. Imagine a human man right in front of you. How will you lure him into the water?*" I motioned for Hyrissa to close her eyes as I spoke.

My own eyelids snapped shut. Hyrissa hummed. Her voice emitted an electrifying power. I joined her and hummed at a higher octave.

My brave and cunning sailor
Who has crossed the many seas?
Will you be a maiden's savior?
And join the water with me?

I opened my eyes at the same time that Hyrissa did. I stopped humming and grinned. Hyrissa exclaimed with glee at her first verse and clapped with as much enthusiasm as a youthling.

"That was great! It might be just enough to lure a man in with you. Remember, eye contact and intention are important. Perhaps tomorrow we can work on the second verse. You are off the hook for today." Hyrissa beamed at my compliment and swam in circles, creating a ring of bubbles in her excitement.

"Wait until I sing for Clagoria! Oh, and Mother! They shall be thrilled!" Hyrissa spoke in a shrill voice and kissed me on the cheek.

She swam out of the cave and left me alone to my thoughts.

In my alone time, I worked on a new song and hummed a lulling melody. I laid down on the ocean floor as I created lyrics to match. My hair flowed in front of my face. I daintily swept it back with my hand and closed my eyes. It had been a successful day.

Today had been a horrible day. I snapped out of my wandering thoughts when the cook, Rigby, if I remembered correctly, came into view. My chest still ached.

"Do ya mind if I sit here?" Rigby motioned toward the space next to me.

I stared ahead, not saying a word or looking at him. He did not seem to get the hint and plopped down next to me. I stared at him incredulously. He had soft brown eyes with equally brown skin. I noted that his hair was red, similar to mine, but a lot darker. I sighed and looked away again, hoping this would spell it out for him.

"Look, I heard about what happened earlier, and I'm sorry on behalf of the crew. I think, knowing where yer from, they should've handled it better. Ya shouldn't have seen that. I know yer people look at sirens like deities." Rigby was looking at a fraying piece of his shirt as he spoke. He fiddled the strand of cloth with his fingers.

These words coming from a pirate, even if he was only a cook, were shocking to hear. My silence stretched on.

"I'm not entirely a huge fan of killing sirens meself. All living things are valuable and placed on this earth for a reason. We shouldn't be harming creatures unless in self-defense or for survival," Rigby rambled on, and I wondered if I was hallucinating.

"Then why join the ship? Or eat fish as often as you do?" I could not help but voice my thoughts, despite my attempt at remaining silent and aloof.

"I eat fish because that's the only way I'll survive on this ship. It's necessary protein." Rigby did not answer my first question, not right away.

"I grew up as a dirt-poor kid in Avalon. When I heard about this crew being put together on the down low, I knew I had to join. It was the adventurous life I had always dreamed of, ya see. The escape plan from living a dull and drab life in poverty. Aye, me morals aren't completely aligned with everyone else's, but I wouldn't trade this for the world. These men, and Kae, are family." Rigby said with such a fierceness, I could not help but trust him.

I sighed, understanding his perspective.

Initially, I had not wanted to join the warriors when the Queen sent me off. Being treated like one of the princesses was more appealing than going off to hunt and track. It had taken me several decades before I was a confident warrior. My natural talent was enough of a motivation to stay. I had enjoyed my warrior status a lot more after that.

"I brought one o' these in case ya wanted something to eat. It's a delicious Zephlus fried dough pastry. I snuck some onboard before we departed, so don't tell anyone else or they'll kill ya in yer sleep for this." Rigby smiled as he reached into a satchel slung against him.

He produced the food that Ruff had been eating before by Zephlus' harbor. I stared at the delicacy, my mouth watering. My stomach rumbled at the heavenly scent.

I was about to accept when I made eye contact with Rigby. His kindness reminded me too much of Hyrissa. Of why she died. I had to think twice about why I was here and what I was ultimately going to do. My anger rose again as the faces of fallen sirens flooded my vision.

My hand dropped. Rigby noticed my sour mood and stood. He placed the pastry beside me, despite my obvious rejection. I stared bitterly and waited for him to disappear from my peripheral vision. After a few moments, when I was certain that no one else was going to invade my space, I quickly strode toward my room and shut the door behind me. I plopped the pastry down on top of my things and slumped into bed.

Chapter Thirteen
Aqeara

If I was avoiding Aqeara before, it was nothing compared to the effort I was making now. Aqeara had spent most of her time the past few days wallowing in her room. She didn't even emerge when Atty and Birch tried to fetch her for training. None of the crew had seen her leave her quarters.

I honestly wondered if she was even in there or if she somehow jumped ship without our notice.

Though I was right in my initial assumption not to trust her, I was still surprised the girl had it in her to nearly cut my throat open over a *siren*. It shouldn't have been as surprising. She was doing fairly well in her sessions with the two hunters.

Still, I'd marked her as a pretty smile and nothing more. How wrong I was. I should have known someone from Soledel would kill their own kind over a murderous sea creature.

Aqeara was not dainty or frail, and I was a fool to think otherwise. She was cunning, like a warrior. When she trained, it was like she had years of experience shimmering beneath her, waiting to be used. Not that I watched her train with Atty and Birch. At least, not where she caught me.

I was assessing.

What threw me off the most, despite everything else, was how distracted I had gotten. I was paying far too much attention to Aqeara's reaction to notice the siren's intent to strike.

After killing it, I was too caught up in my wound and anger that I hadn't expected her to react with such malicious intent. There was little doubt that Aqeara would have sliced my throat open, yet all I did was stare into her amber eyes that so reminded me of whiskey. Useless. She was devastatingly tempting, and I had let her get past my guard.

I'd stalked back and forth across the floor of my quarters after the attack, debating on what to do with Aqeara's treacherous act. The temptation to simply throw her overboard rose, regardless of any little morals I had left in me.

But then days passed and my anger faded ever so slightly. Aqeara remained out of sight, locked away in her room. It helped keep my temper in check. Not looking at her, even with the wound on my neck healing, made it easier to let it go.

Once we reached Naivia, I could be rid of her and hopefully discover where the lost siren city was located. Though it would be a shame to lose such a skilled fighter, Aqeara could not be trusted. I was grateful she'd taken her rage out on me. She could have easily turned her blade on any of my crew. I would never let anything happen to them.

I grew quite lonely. In my rage post-incident, I rarely left my quarters. With Aqeara keeping to her room, my crew was on the blunt end of my wrath, and I wanted to avoid taking it out on them. The only times I left were to eat or check in with either Dalton or Barnes—whichever of them was at the helm.

The ceiling above me provided no distraction as I laid on my bed. My heart was racing. In my whirlwind of thoughts, Rigby's knocks had gone unheard. My attention was slipping when it came to the insensible Soledelian.

"Captain?" Rigby's voice floated through my room.

I tried to compose myself.

"What is it, Rig?" I asked as the cook entered my quarters.

I appreciated a distraction from my destructive thoughts.

His shoulders tensed, and I mentally prepared for any bad news regarding supplies.

"It's Aqeara. I'm worried about her. Lass hasn't eaten in days. Not since the... incident." Rigby was right to be tense.

My anger welled again. The almost-healed bite mark pulsed on my arm. I would forever have a scar in the shape of that siren's teeth.

"If she starves herself, I fail to see how that's my issue." I snapped. "I'm not her mother. She's perfectly capable of making her own decisions. Once we're in Naivia, she's off this ship."

I didn't realize how cold my voice became until Rigby flinched at my tone. I fought hard to keep any guilt from showing on my face.

"Maybe just talk to her. She won't open her door for anyone, but she might listen to her captain." Rigby was oblivious to my rising rage.

Leave it to the soft-hearted kid to make friends with everyone. Even a siren sympathizer.

"She deliberately disobeyed my orders of not interfering. She tried to *kill* me, Rigby. I don't think I'll be too inclined to give her another opportunity," I deadpanned.

He stared at me with large pleading eyes that watered.

Damn him.

"Fine! I'll talk to her. You better cook up something spectacular for us tonight." I sighed as Rigby nodded eagerly and left.

My feet started walking out of the room before my brain could think how terrible of an idea this was. Closing the door shut behind me, I stalked over to the middle of the main deck, ignoring whoever was swabbing the deck and went downstairs. There were several men at the dining table, yet none greeted me. One look at my face sent them to busy themselves and remain unnoticed.

I was a lit stick of dynamite waiting to explode.

I didn't even know what I would say to Aqeara when she opened her door. If she even opened her door. I doubted I could remain neutral instead of releasing all my repressed anger at once.

When in front of Aqeara's door, I hesitated. The reluctance startled me. I was the captain of a ship of ruthless pirates that hunted creatures far scarier and more dangerous than a redhead who drank ocean water.

My anger was rising again. Would she have defended her sirens if she knew Kipp? Blood boiled within my veins as I pounded on her door and shouted her name.

"What do you want?" Aqeara called as she ripped her door open like she'd been standing on the other side and expected this.

There was a hint of annoyance to her tone, like I had interrupted something important. As if *she* had the audacity to be cross with *me*. The thought of throwing her overboard crossed my mind again.

"What I want is for you off my ship at our next docking," I spat.

"Anything else?"

"Rigby seems concerned with your overdramatic antics of starving yourself. He told me to talk some sense into you. Personally, I don't care."

"Duly noted. I am so thankful for your concern." Sarcasm dripped from Aqeara's voice as she spoke.

Her red hair was down and her amber eyes bore into mine. There was a fire behind them as she stared at me. I slammed the door behind me and walked toward her. Aqeara tried not to seem phased, but she was breathing heavier.

"Learn to talk to your captain with more respect. It takes zero effort for me to just toss you in a lifeboat and leave you behind," I said in a voice as stiff and cold as I could muster.

I took another step forward and Aqeara took one back. She had nowhere to go. Her back was pressed against the wall—the rise and fall of her chest gave away her rapid breathing. Amusement coursed through me when fury lit up in her eyes. I had made her feel vulnerable, like she had done to me with that dagger at my throat.

When Aqeara didn't answer, I turned around and headed back to the door, satisfied with myself. Electricity bubbled within me at the proximity.

My hand barely touched the door handle when a whirring sound shot past my left ear. The same dagger that was at my throat several days ago was now stuck in the wood panel of Aqeara's door. The blade was lodged a considerable amount deep in the paneling. It had gotten eerily close to hitting the side of my head. She was either aiming for me and was a terrible shot, or she was aiming for the door and had better aim than I thought. The handle of the dagger still vibrated from impact.

My eyes widened when I turned to face her again. She smirked, and I knew she meant to scare me. Her body tensed, ready for attack. Aqeara ran forward, arm raised with her second dagger in hand. My hand shot up and grabbed her wrist before she could bring the blade down on me.

Aqeara let out a frustrated noise and twisted her wrist free. I kicked at her legs and she brought me down with her, both of us tumbling to the ground.

I gasped when I hit the floor. She rolled out from underneath me and came back to pin me to the ground before I could get up. Aqeara straddled me with her dagger still in hand. Her eyes glinted with murderous intent, and my heart raced.

I tried not to think of how she felt on top of me. I'd been in this exact position before for far different reasons. My thoughts betrayed me, as if they'd somehow been displayed on my face. She leaned forward, smirking at my reaction.

"Am I treating you with respect now, my *captain?*" Aqeara spoke with feigned concern and spat out the last word.

The tip of her blade was once again on my neck. I ignored the way her words rolled off her tongue, how it sounded when she called me her captain. Anger and shame overcame me.

I grabbed Aqeara's thighs and rolled us over so that I was now straddling her. I twisted her hand that held onto the dagger until it fell out of her grip. She yelped in pain.

"I have the authority here," I said in a low voice.

My fingers reached out for the fallen dagger, barely grasping its hilt.

"Yes, well, I am taller," Aqeara said with a coy smile.

I let out a frustrated noise as she shoved me right as my hand clasped around the hilt.

The dagger skidded across the floor, and I hit the wall behind me. I gasped in pain. Aqeara quickly pinned my hands at my sides. She was a lot stronger than I'd assumed. And much more skilled than I had originally given her credit for.

I tried wiggling myself free, but it only made Aqeara tighten her grip on my wrists. Her chest rose and fell with each breath she took. Her tongue swiped across her lips. Realizing the dangerous line of thought that would lead, I looked up at her eyes. They twinkled with some familiarity that I could not quite place.

Aqeara stared back at me. There was no longer rage behind those amber eyes, but instead... shock? As if neither of us expected to wind up in this position. We both just stared at each other, neither of us speaking nor moving. I wondered if she noticed the quick, shallow breaths I was taking.

I almost could have sworn Aqeara leaned in toward me, her lips slightly parted, before I heard several shouts coming from outside her door. I pulled away, successfully this time, and ran out of Aqeara's room without a second glance back.

Once I was out, the door slammed shut behind me.

Chapter Fourteen
Kae

Ruff's normally calm voice rose above the other shouts, far more tension to it than I was accustomed. Most of my crew were on the main deck. The men pointed at something not too far off into the distance as they shouted.

A ship much larger than the *Mar Daemon* was approaching us at full speed. It was close enough I could see the dark blue sails, clearly pointed toward our ship.

Dalton was barking commands at Barnes, who looked as if he was seconds from wetting himself. I ran over to the helm and grabbed the small telescope that was attached to Dalton's belt. A symbol of a fish and a siren swam to form a circle on their flag. That was Soledel's crest.

Why were Aqeara's people approaching us?

"They haven't changed their course since we spotted them," Barnes said and allowed Dalton to take over the steering.

At the rate of the ship's speed, there was no possible way of fleeing. They were going to hit my ship if they didn't slow down.

"They could be targeting us for hunting sirens," Dalton called out.

"Whatever it is, they're going to hit us before we can turn away. Dalton, I want you downstairs to flank me while I greet the captain. Barnes, whatever happens, keep at the wheel and be ready to get us out of here at my signal," I ordered in an exasperated tone that had Dalton down the stairs in a flash.

Barnes saluted me and kept both hands wrapped tightly around the wheel.

I set aside all emotion. I was the captain. I had to act like it.

I ran about the ship, helping others out where they needed a hand. We had to be ready to flee or fight should the opportunity arise. My heart was pounding, but my hands were steady.

"They're slowing down!" Ruff called from below.

I looked back to see that they had noticeably slowed, proving my assumption correct: they were here to talk first and maybe fight later. We rarely encountered ships. The ones that we ran into never seemed inclined toward a friendly conversation.

A sinking feeling in my stomach grew at the thought, persisting in a way that made me want to hunch over. I choked it down, hoping it did not show on my face.

"Men, be ready for a fight! To your stations and look alive!" I shouted loud enough to ensure everyone could hear me.

The other ship approached, turning slightly as it did. We were now parallel to one another, with their helm facing the opposite direction of ours. This positioning was common in ship battles. I knew that, thought we'd yet to be a part of one. I knew battling ships would align parallel and unload their cannons until one—or both—sank.

I tried to calm my racing thoughts, but I was nearly knocked over by a jolt that rocked the entire. The Soledelians shot anchors directly into the windows that were used to fire cannons, and three thick chains disappeared into the side of my ship. We were secured and trapped.

"Arden, Kenley! Get those anchors out of my ship and prepare the cannons!" My voice bellowed over the shouts of my crew.

I walked down the stairs and over to Ruff, who was ready to jump into battle. His long sword was unsheathed. The fierce look in his eyes made me realize I had to assume the worst and be ready to fight. There was a chance this wouldn't be a civil conversation.

A large plank stood upright at the edge of the other ship, looming several feet in the air. Three men flanked it. The ship was so close to us that even the details of their waistcoats were within my view. The men were trying to knock down a plank to provide easy access across ships. Ruff and I backed away just enough before the slab of wood crashed down between us.

All my men halted their scurrying at the noise. Everyone stood in silence as their footsteps echoed across the plank. Eerily quiet given the number of men around me. All I could hear was the sound of boots on wood.

"They're boarding us, Captain!" Barnes yelled from behind the steering wheel.

Dalton was back up at the helm beside him. He held up a large telescope to survey the other crew. Dalton whispered something to Barnes and then descended back down the steps with his swords drawn. Barnes turned the wheel in the opposite direction of the Soledelian ship.

My sword remained sheathed as I approached the man assumed to be the captain. He hopped over the railing of my ship as several of his pirate crew swung over using ropes. Men who did the utmost over-the-top entrances were the ones who compensated for something they severely lacked. This was nothing more than a show of power they did not have, I was sure.

The captain and I stood face-to-face, waiting for the other to speak up.

"Pardon the intrusion and allow me to introduce myself. I am Captain Xander of Soledel." Xander spoke with an unmatched sense of authority. "My crew and I are bounty hunters. It is our duty to track down any civilians that have tried to abandon our kingdom. It is forbidden to leave our city's walls, as you may have heard. We were informed by a seamstress in Zephlus that a Soledelian has sought refuge on your ship. Give us the girl, and we will gladly leave you to your course."

There was a pause where I considered Xander's request. I could give Aqeara up and be done with her. After her second attempt on my life, I very well might. I had planned on dumping her at the next port, regardless. What did it matter to me if we got rid of her now or later?

As I regarded Xander, I noted he was a lot taller than me and twice my size. He was burly and dirty and covered in bloodstains. Several of his teeth were missing and replaced with silver ones. His smile was false and threatening. A glance at his flank showed me that his four men were equally menacing.

I tried to picture Aqeara on a ship with these men and shuddered. I would let her make her own path once we made our next docking, but as captain of the ship, I couldn't let these men forcefully take her away. The thought went against so much I stood for, but I knew refusing would not end well.

I did not have to turn around to know Ruff and Dalton were flanked on each side of me. Were the Soledelians analyzing us as I was them?

If they underestimated us, we might have a chance in a fight. It took me less than a few seconds to come to my conclusion. Aqeara would stay with us, damned if we had to fight our way out of this. To Xander, it would appear that I took this time to process his words, but I was doing so much more. His shoulders were lax, his demeanor easygoing. As if he expected submission immediately in his presence.

"I am Captain Kae of Avalon. The Soledelian in question is on my ship and therefore under my protection." My voice did not falter as I crossed my arms in front of me while I spoke, though I was shaking internally. "I am not so willing to hand her over to complete strangers, no matter how intimidating they try to be. I don't appreciate the show you've made in damaging my ship, and I certainly don't appreciate the unwanted boarding. Please make your way off my ship at once."

If he had an issue with it, he would be the one inciting a battle.

I locked my gaze on Xander. His own hardened while I spoke, and his smile dropped into a scowl. Xander took a step toward me, stopping when Ruff and Dalton took one step forward as well.

"Don't talk down to me, *girl.* Who let a *woman* take charge of such a... respectable vessel?" Xander held his arms out wide as he turned to address everyone. "Do you *men* not feel ashamed listening to this girl? She is not a lady nor a figure of authority. Have you no pride in yourselves that you would take orders from the likes of her?"

"Don't you dare speak of our captain like that," Atty said in a low growl.

Each of my men wore a similar expression. They snarled with furrowed brows and hands firmly grasping their weapons. They would stand by me. A rush of pride swept over me.

Xander's thundering voice kept the rest of my crew still and silent while he spoke. "Listen to me, brothers. Bring me the red-headed traitor, and a fight need not occur today. Fail to do so, and you will be sweeping the floorboards clean of your own blood for days."

"Like I said before, you're not touching a hair on her head, you mangy lowlife," I said.

The anger in my voice surpassed any formal neutrality. Pride may have sparked this fury, or perhaps it was protecting a passenger on my ship. Or stupidly enough, maybe it was just Aqeara's pretty face I wanted to stare at a little while longer. Even if she kept trying to kill me, even that was somehow growing on me.

Stop that.

My tone snapped Xander's attention back to me.

"So much for formality. Expected, coming from a woman. This is why none of you lasses should be in positions of power," Xander spat.

"Call off your men and *get the fuck off my ship!*"

"Men…attack!" Xander roared as he brought his sword up and swung at my head.

Instinct kicked in and I ducked out of the way, avoiding his strike by a hair's length. I unsheathed my sword with an effortless flourish and lunged forward as the rest of Xander's men rushed onto the *Mar Daemon*.

Chaos ensued.

I was instantly overwhelmed at the sounds of weapons clashing and shouts of pain and anger mixed through the air as the two crews fought against one another.

Xander brought down his sword with strike after relentless strike. My heart raced, blocking out the sounds around me. A punch to the jaw left a metal taste in my mouth I had to ignore as I blocked his never-ending attacks.

With a fleeting glance, I saw Ruff and Dalton fight off three men while they pressed their backs against one another. I glanced back at Xander, feeling the wind of his sword against my cheek before I dodged his swing and blocked him.

"I expected you to be a better swordsman," I said breathlessly as I kicked Xander in the back of his knees.

He stumbled forward before regaining his balance. He spat a wad of blood in my direction.

"I'll carve my name into that pretty face of yours," he said with a grin.

Xander brought his sword down on me, missing me by centimeters before I dove into a roll to avoid his blade.

Strike. Duck. Strike. Block.

I dove forward into a roll and looked up at the helm. Barnes was still at the wheel with Atty guarding him by the stairs. I only had seconds to check on how my crew was faring before Xander was on me again.

Duck. Roll. Strike. Grunt. *Shit.*

Xander knocked my sword out of my hand and it slid across the floor, far from my reach.

As I ran toward my blade, I made eye contact with Birch. He was surrounded but still holding his own. Arden's approaching shout caused a smirk to crawl on Birch's face as he welcomed the backup.

With most of the men occupied up here, I hoped that Aqeara remained hidden below deck. Though I knew she was capable of holding her own. She'd shown me first hand just how well she could—*strike.*

Xander sliced at my side, taking full advantage of my concern for my crew. I gasped in pain at the blade digging into my flesh. Sweat beaded my forehead, the scent filling my nostrils. The world quieted to background noise while I stared at his blade.

In a quick maneuver, I swiped my sword off the floor and raised it to meet Xander's blade. Xander held himself like he'd fought with his weapon for many years, more so than I. Perhaps he'd had better trainers than I'd had, as well. His burly muscles allowed him to fight with brute force while I relied on agility and strategy.

I leaned back as a blade swiped above me. My muscles were beginning to ache, while Xander had not wavered once. No amount of sparring with Dalton had ever quite prepared me for an all-out battle such as this.

Swipe. Miss. Strike. *Ouch.*

A shallow stream of blood spread from my right thigh, leaving a burning sensation in its wake. I grimaced and nicked Xander in the chest. He smiled with wild eyes, ignoring his bloodshed at the sight of my own. I backed up as he pounded on my blade with fury.

A scream caught my attention from the fight. My foot collided with Xander's groin, and I turned around while he was momentarily distracted.

"Get off of me! Let me go, you foul monster!" Aqeara was shouting as two men carried her across the deck.

Aqeara thrashed wildly against their grip—one man hooked his arms under her armpits while the other grabbed onto her legs. Aqeara tried dropping her weight to no avail. She was shouting insults like no one's business. Some seemed to be in her Soledelian dialect since I had no idea what the words meant.

Movement in the corner of my eye snapped my attention back to Xander as he ran toward me and knocked me sideways. I groaned and punched the weak spot above his shoulder multiple times while we rolled on the ground. Xander kicked me and got up on his feet. I scrambled away as his sword plummeted into the floorboard just inches from my head.

Back on my two feet, I blocked another offensive strike and got a good jab into Xander's side.

"Bitch!" he roared and kept at it.

I dodged and ducked while swinging with more vigor. Aqeara's cries for help rang loudly in my ears. Xander turned his attention from me for a quick second, and I followed his gaze as Aqeara and the two men stood halfway on the plank.

Wait.

There was only one man now clutching tightly onto Aqeara. He looked over the plank into the water below. She had knocked one of the men overboard.

A small smile formed as I brought my sword up with a flick of my wrist. Xander expected the movement and blocked it with ease, his focus back on me. A frustrated noise escaped my lips as I continued the back-and-forth rally of our swords.

"Captain, they've got Aqeara! They're retreating!" Barnes cried out from above me.

The other pirates backed away toward their ship. Xander flashed his teeth in victory. I drove my sword forward, and he flicked it out of the way with his own.

Strike. Duck. Block. Strike.

There was a pattern to Xander's movements.

Strike. Duck. Swerve. Duck. *Strike.*

My sword drove into Xander's stomach. He let out a yelp, but did not seem to falter for long. He removed the blade and tossed it to the ground. To my dismay, Xander charged forward and butted my head with the heavy handle of his sword. I fell backward and hit the ground hard, the air fleeing my lungs.

My vision blurred and black spots appeared.

"Hey! Get up! He's getting away!" Dalton rushed over to me, no longer occupied with fighting.

I reached for his outstretched hand as he helped me to my feet.

I grabbed my sword and ran toward the plank without a word or plan. Jumping over the railing, I sprinted across the plank. On Xander's ship, I was outnumbered. It was a death wish.

"Release the anchors!" Xander shouted as he strolled over to Aqeara who was tied to their mast with rope.

She spat in his face, and he slapped her.

"Don't touch her!" I yelled and brought my sword down on him.

He was losing blood, but the hit to my head had blurred my vision. My sword missed him by a long shot. Xander swiveled and punched me square in the temple. My head hit the floor.

"Kae!" Aqeara shouted, her voice distant, like it came from a long tunnel despite her being a mere feet away.

I crawled back blindly as the black spots grew bigger and bigger. Everything was blurry. The sun reflected off of Xander's sword as he swung for my head. I lifted my hand to block him, averting my gaze.

When no blade came in contact, I looked and saw Aqeara had somehow managed to break out from her bonds. She ran into Xander and knocked him over with surprise on her side.

"You're done for, traitor!" Xander shouted, but Aqeara had grabbed my sword from the ground where I fell.

She blocked Xander's blade with mine. I was shocked and impressed as she kept up with the bleeding Xander. Dalton's shouts were coming from behind me, growing closer.

Consciousness slipped away from me. The last thing I saw through sluggish blinks was Aqeara's face, mere inches from mine. Her amber eyes, full of concern. Why would she be concerned for me?

Chapter Fifteen
Aqeara

Xander's head was resting somewhere at the bottom of the ocean now. Dead by my hands, but I felt no regret. I hadn't thought twice before beheading Xander. And once their captain was dead, Xander's crew had retreated, heading back the way they came, like further bloodshed wasn't worth the fight.

My body continued on the next few days while my mind remained frozen in time, unable to fully comprehend what had happened.

I couldn't remember if I slept in the days that followed. The blur of events catching up to me made everything fuzzy. Flashes came to me—Kae's unresponsive body on the ground. Helping Dalton carry Kae to her quarters while the Doc treated her. Walking down to eat while the rest of the crew cast me looks of concern. Ruff quietly handing me a towel to wipe the blood from my face.

Xander's blood.

I was unsure what to feel just yet. I had nearly died, and it gradually settled in like frostbite in the northern waters.

Kae had remained unconscious for nearly five days. I came with the Doc every day when he checked on her and dressed her wounds. I learned in our chats that his real name was Crowell, though we hadn't talked about much else.

It shocked me that the ruthless siren killer would risk her life to save mine. Without hesitating, she had run after me onto a ship where she had been outnumbered... to save *me*. Despite my trying to kill her only moments before the attack.

Perhaps in her eyes, I was a traitor to my kingdom. I had run away for a reason I had not yet come up with. More lies.

I had hoped that saving Kae's life would make us even. It was the only logical reasoning I had for striking Xander instead of allowing him to kill her.

But I owed her one. Didn't I?

Sirens disapproved of the concept of debt. I could have easily let her die. Thrown her body overboard and carved out her heart to be done with it all. It would have been so easy. It would have been over. But I was in her debt. I could bide my time for a little while longer.

"Will she wake soon?" I asked as the Doc placed a wet towel on her forehead.

He felt her jugular with two fingers, trying to locate a heartbeat, and I wondered what would happen to me if he didn't find one.

"It is hard to say. The mind is a complex thing," the Doc replied, his voice sounding so mature, it made him seem ageless.

Every day I asked when she would wake and each time the Doc would respond with wisdom instead of a solid answer.

The rest of the crew had fared fine from the fight—most of them had made it out of the battle with minor injuries that were healing well, but I felt indebted to them as well. They stood by Kae's side to fight off the threat on my life. They'd tried to protect me.

In the time since the fight, I spoke with them more. They seemed to enjoy prattling about their lives, and I listened. The conversations were what humans called "small talk", but I enjoyed them nonetheless. They were kind enough not to ask me too many questions about my life. Which meant less lies I had to tell.

"She looks a lot less angry when she is sleeping," I noted while I observed Kae in her most vulnerable state.

The Doc laughed at my comment.

She was peaceful, the hard lines on her face smoothed out to leave her expressionless. It was hard to connect the ruthless siren killer to the slumbering woman in front of me, though I knew they were one and the same.

I could kill her once the Doc left—leave her body with a cavity in her chest where her heart should be. But something pulled within my own chest. It had to be my gut telling me to wait just a little longer. For what, I was not sure yet.

"The captain seems hard-headed at times," the Doc said. "But she's kind-hearted when she wants to be. She just needs to warm up to you before she lets you in. Once she does, she will fight tooth and nail for you,"

My shoulders shrugged at his comment, but something moved within me. There were less than two weeks until I had to carve Kae's heart out before it was too late to complete the spell. For once, I repressed the thought. There was plenty of time to worry about that later.

"Yeah," was all I said in response.

Kae stirred in the slightest of movements, a flutter of her eyes and a shudder in her breath, and something within me stirred.

"Let the others know she will wake today." The Doc smiled and fussed about.

He fluffed Kae's pillow and adjusted her shoulders on top of it. Not wanting to be there when she woke, I quietly left Kae's quarters and shut the door behind me.

"How's she doing?" Ruff approached me as I was halfway down the stairs, hoping to head back to my room.

I paused. He asked me every day when I reemerged from her bedroom. He did not once question what I was doing in there. I would always have my excuse of being the Doc's assistant ready on my tongue if he ever asked, but Ruff was not one to ask questions. He just simply knew the answers to everything.

"She is just waking up." I softened as Ruff—the man who was all muscle and hardness—let out a large sigh of relief.

He truly cared about his friend. It was sweet.

I thought of the other crew members I'd gotten to know. They all cared about her. Guilt struck sharply in my stomach like a pang of acid from poisonous fish. These men had feelings. They were not the near-constant violent storms I had once thought them to be. At least, the ones on this ship.

I shook my head to clear of that line of thinking. They were hunters, the lot of them. They were only at sea to hunt me and my people.

Ruff went into Kae's quarters. A glance upward, and I made eye contact with Dalton, who was behind the steering wheel. He quickly looked away.

It was very odd. Out of everyone on board, we had originally got along the best. Dalton was a kind, extroverted man that always offered company and friendship. He had been acting strangely since the fight, but I could not blame him. Near-death experiences make us all strangers to ourselves. His gesture felt cold, but I ignored it and continued on the way to my bed.

The rest of the crew were enjoying lunch down below. Blast whoever decided to place the eating table right next to the staircase. I was spotted before I even made it halfway down. There was no making a quiet getaway.

"Hey Aqeara!" Rigby waved at me and motioned toward a full plate of grilled fish.

My stomach grumbled at the smell of spices and the familiar scents of the ocean.

"Thanks, Rig." I said, the nickname feeling odd on my tongue. "I should change first." I swept a hand up and down my body at the grime that I felt covered me head to human toe.

"You broke into a sweat because you haven't been keeping up with your exercises," Atty chided from his seat.

My eyes threatened to roll out of my head. Atty had swept me off my feet this morning during training, quite literally. My back was beginning to bruise.

My mind had been a bit occupied the past few days. Nearly dying and all that follows afterward does that to you.

I strode over to my bedroom and clicked the door shut behind me. The smell of sweat mixed with saltwater was becoming a permanent scent on me. I barely noticed now. The ocean smelled differently to humans than it did to sirens. To us, the smell was like breathing in fresh air. To them, it reeked of fish and other things I could not quite place.

My dirty and tattered clothes hit the floor—I had not changed since before the fight, and that was days ago. I pulled on a white top with long and billowy sleeves as my mind drifted to Kae. She was awake and that very fact lit my nerves on fire.

How would things be between us now that we had saved each other's lives? Would things be different? Could I allow myself to care? I absentmindedly threw on the rest of my clothes, not paying close attention to what I shrugged into.

I looked at myself in the small, dusty mirror that never seemed clean no matter how many times I scrubbed at its surface. Dressing in human clothes had not ceased to create joy for me. I was absolutely stunning. If only bright colors were acceptable in fashion.

I was still missing something. I grabbed the purple cloth from my bag of purchased goodies from Zephlus and tied the cloth around my head. It kept my hair back and out of my face.

Most of the men wore cloths on their heads as well. Dalton and Ruff were the only ones to wear hats, indicating their rank as first and secondary. Though, their hats were not nearly as large and ugly as Kae's.

Dalton had told me the day before that having our heads covered would shield us from the unyielding heat that came from the sun. It protected our skin. I had never known that human skin could get burnt just from the sun's rays. Humans were so strange.

I may have stared at myself in the mirror for a longer time than deemed normal. It was odd looking at my face, knowing it was my face, while also noticing the subtle differences made by Salophine. Small splotches of dirt mixed with my freckles. I watched my reflection frown at the observation. The thin cut below my jawline had scabbed over, but was healing. The bruises that I also obtained from the fight were yellowing and fading away.

A sharp knock on the door startled me, and I looked away from my reflection. I fixed my hair and went to open the door.

"Hey, uh Aqeara. Were you planning on eating the fish that Rigby put aside for you?" The man named Marsden, who worked with the sails, leaned against my door frame.

He was bigger and stockier than Ruff, but a lot less threatening. I'd had little interaction with Marsden, but I assessed him as docile for the most part.

"For heaven's sake, Mars, let the girl eat! Don't try and take her food." Rigby threw his hands up in the air from where he stood.

A few other men were still seated. Marsden grew still at the scolding, his cheeks turning red. I gave him a soft smile before disappearing into my room.

The pastry that Rigby had given me a few days ago sat on the small stool near my bed. Handing the food to Marsden, I held up a finger to my lips and winked. He smiled brightly and split the delicacy in two. He handed me one piece while he munched on the other. We ate our shares and returned to the table.

It was strange how quickly I had fallen in step with the crew. How I barely noticed that shift from the men that stared at me like I was a stranger to the ones that welcomed me to their gatherings. To them, I had protected Kae from Xander's death blow. I had earned their respect by saving their captain. The thought should not have made me as content as it did.

Rigby set a full plate in front of me as I sat down. The food was cold, but still edible. I guess I took a little too long changing.

"This is delicious!" I exclaimed after taking the first bite.

I'd grown accustomed to hunger after several days of not eating. Hiding and sulking and starving. Clagoria had often said that I would take my spite with me to the grave.

I devoured the rest of the fish while Rigby nodded approvingly at me. He had always been so kind. I should not have been cold to him when all he did was care about my well-being. After all, he wasn't one of the hunters, not really.

"So, since you're from Soledel, have you ever seen a siren?" Kenley asked.

This was the first time the gunner had spoken to me.

Arden and Marsden—their names were difficult to distinguish at times—were the only others at the table. They both shot their heads up at the mention of sirens. I hesitated, unsure of how to answer in a way that did not seem suspicious. After all, I had no idea about Soledelian culture. I was banking on the fact that they did not either.

"No, but I have heard many stories of others who have encountered sirens. It is how we know so much about their kind." I took a sip of water from the cup in front of me after I spoke.

Rigby sat down across from me, enjoying his own plate of fish. He did not eat until he made sure everyone else was served first. A wave of guilt washed over me at so long to change and making him wait.

"There're people that have been close enough to sirens without falling prey? Seems impossible to me," Marsden commented and raised his eyebrows at me.

"Well, yes. Especially with women. The songs of sirens do not affect women since they are not attracted to other women… for the most part. Or at least, that was what I always thought until recently," I added at the end, thinking of Kae and the way she was pressed against the wall of my bedroom, how her eyes had lingered on my lips. How her expression had changed when she looked into my eyes again.

It seemed that previous siren knowledge had been faulty.

"We didn't know sirens could hunt women. It makes sense. We always thought sirens only hunted men. But as long as you're attracted to women, fair game as prey," Arden said, and I knew he was talking about Kae.

It was the confirmation I needed that she liked women. Though I was unsure why it comforted me. What did it matter? My treacherous thoughts of the way she'd looked at me during our…scuffle came up with a reason why it could. A hopeful reason. I internally rolled my eyes.

Judging by the way he alluded to Kae, liking the same sex was not the norm in human cultures. Peculiar, but I had never given it much of a thought becoming human. Other sea creatures mated with the same sex. It was quite common.

"There is much that you lot do not know," I said. "Like how most sirens tend to avoid humans as much as they can out of fear. It is why not even most Soledelians have seen them."

The three men nodded, and I held back a sigh.

These were the wrong men to talk to about sirens. I had to convince the actual hunters, not the crew. I was sure none of these men had killed a siren. Though, the preaching had to start somewhere.

"Captain's up. She's starving." Dalton poked his head in from the top of the staircase.

Rigby rose to his feet and began heating a fish at the little match-lit contraption in the far corner. Dalton sauntered down the steps and sat in Rigby's seat. He smiled at me in greeting. His entire demeanor had changed from just half an hour ago. It seemed the old Dalton was finally coming back to us.

"How's Barnes holding up?" Marsden asked of Dalton's mentee.

Dalton poured himself a glass of water and chugged it.

"Better. He's a lot more confident in himself after steering clear of the Soledelian bounty hunters," an indecipherable glance at me, "Also, Dyer's been asking for you. He said the wind's picked up, and he needs help with the pulleys." Dalton hadn't even finished speaking before Marsden was already scurrying up the stairs.

Kenley and Arden were arguing about whether an unnamed object was flammable. Dalton did not avert his gaze, even when I made unwavering eye contact. He narrowed his eyes, studying me. I scrunched my nose in discomfort.

"Did you want seconds, Dalt?" Rigby asked as he flipped the flounder over in a pan.

Dalton looked away from me.

"I'm alright, thanks, Rig." Dalton flashed his dazzling smile.

Rigby would not let Marsden have seconds, but did not hesitate in asking Dalton for more. Dalton had that certain aura of charm to him that could enamor anyone. He combed his fingers through his hair lazily as he leaned back in his chair.

Footsteps creaked, and I did not have to look up to know who it was.

"Well, if it isn't the woman of the hour," Dalton announced toward Kae, who had appeared at the bottom of the steps.

The Doc was by her side, making sure she made it to the table alright. She thanked him and plopped down in the empty seat next to me. I straightened in my seat.

The Doc disappeared into one of the men's bedrooms. Kenley and Arden stood up, saluting Kae when they saw her.

She chuckled and motioned for them to sit back down. The dismissive way she went about it made me think she did not care for her authority too much, especially in more familiar settings. I tucked away that information, not sure what to make of it.

"I keep telling you guys you don't have to stand up every time," Kae said. Arden shrugged.

"Arden and I were just about to test out a theory. We'll be above deck," Kenley said, still standing.

"Just don't blow anything up," Kae said.

The two nodded and left us. From the way Kae spoke, this was a reasonable thing to be worried about. It only sparked curiosity in me. I wanted to see just how such a theory could lead to something explosive.

"How are you feeling?" I asked in a small voice.

Every time I spoke, I was reminded of how much of an outsider I was. It was why I much preferred listening to the men talk and gathering whatever information from them I could, instead of voicing my own stories and giving them parts of myself. The feeling of being on the outside looking in grew tenfold, with Kae sitting mere inches from me. I was not sure if my presence was wanted. And her authoritative energy made things seem more formal.

"Better. My stomach's sore from the stab wound, but I'll live." Kae began eating as soon as Rigby set her plate in front of her.

"I want to express my gratitude to you for protecting me, despite the times we have fought before. You all did not have to, and I appreciate it," I said, twirling a strand of hair in between my shaky fingers.

Kae looked over at the sudden movement suspiciously, as if expecting a dagger to be dangling between us.

"I could say the same." Kae said what I was hoping to hear. "You fought off and killed Xander just as he was about to do me in. We're even."

We were not indebted to one another. I was hopefully gaining her trust. With trust, I could learn all that she and the hunters knew about sirens. How they tracked us down, if it was calculative or just by pure luck. Perhaps I could sway her mind away from hunting, but that would be like asking the moon not to go through her routine phases. Still, with gathering intel about humans and the hunters, every delayed second would count.

I nodded, and the room grew quiet.

Dalton's gaze shifted between Kae and I. He remained silent, but his eyes appeared warmer when he drank from his glass again.

"Everyone's served, the kitchen is closed, and I'm taking a nap. If anyone wakes me up, I'll be pissed," Rigby grumbled.

"What if the ship's sinking?" Dalton asked with feigned sincerity.

"Well then obviously wake me up." Rigby crossed his arms in front of his chest.

"If we're being boarded by pirates?" Kae quipped.

"The ship catches fire!" I added.

Kae gave me a look of approval, and I cursed myself for the way my cheeks burned.

"I hate the lot of you," Rigby said and retreated to his bedroom.

He left the three of us laughing to ourselves. For the first time since aboard the *Mar Daemon*, or maybe for the first time *ever*, I felt at ease.

"That's the first time I heard you laugh, I think," Dalton observed as he looked at me.

I was the sole focus of their attention now. My cheeks flushed a deeper red.

"It is because you two are not funny. I am warming up to the idea of a nap." I got up and bowed ridiculously at Kae.

Dalton chuckled, and Kae rolled her eyes at me.

"Sweet dreams," Kae said as she took a swig from her glass.

I walked over to my room and shut the door behind me. I pressed an ear against the door in case I could catch a conversation between Dalton and Kae about me without my presence. The loud waves crashing against the ship drowned out any other sound.

With a defeated sigh, I crawled into bed and stared at the ceiling. The sun was just setting, so it was still too early to call it a night. In my short time as a human, I learned that they required far more rest than sirens did. While we could last with two or three hours of sleep, humans needed at least six for maximum energy. It was wasteful to spend a third or fourth of your day asleep. There was training, exploring, hunting, and the like to spend my time doing. Even the boring political conversations the Queen and princesses allowed me to sit in were more productive.

Still, the calming sounds of the ocean drifted my thoughts to nothing as my eyes fluttered shut.

Chapter Sixteen
Aqeara

I was barely dozing off, my dreams unable to form, when a steep rock of the ship threw me out of bed. I sat up and tried to steady myself.

My stomach turned with the slightest movement. I ran to the wooden bucket near my bed and emptied my stomach of the only food I had eaten all day. The wretched sounds coming from my throat were foreign. My thoughts raced. Was I dying? The ship rolled again, and I grabbed onto the bucket to steady myself.

"Hey, are you alright? You sounded hurt." Dalton's voice called out from behind my door.

The noise I made in response resembled that of a wounded animal. I was too dizzy to form a coherent sentence.

The door swung open, and Dalton walked in on me heaving again. With the odd way he had been acting lately, his presence frightened me. Had I been poisoned?

"It's okay. You're okay. There's a nasty storm rolling in." Dalton rubbed my back soothingly.

I tried not to think too much of the current situation—it was exceptionally embarrassing. Being comforted like this while I was weak and vulnerable, heaving up a disgusting mess.

"Look, I need to get back up to Barnes and help out. I'll send someone else down. Deep breaths," Dalton said in a calm voice.

I tried to relax and wiped my mouth with the back of my hand.

Dalton made no noise when he left. A glance up, and he was gone. My door was wide open. I started coughing when I tried to take a deep breath. My stomach flopped like a fish out of water. The ship went over another large wave. I held on to the bucket filled with my sick, desperately trying not to let it tip over.

Footsteps approached and from the corner of my eye, I saw a familiar pair of navy-blue boots.

"Oh dear, it looks like you have not gotten your sea legs yet. Not to worry! I have this for you." I turned my head to look at the Doc approaching me.

The Doc sat down beside me and handed me two small objects. I stared at him in confusion. I had already rid myself of my sea legs and replaced them with human ones; that was the whole point of Salophine's spell.

"Put these in your ears if you can manage. They can help with the imbalance of the ship. If you can stand, I recommend going up and looking out into the ocean. It may help with the nausea." The Doc stood up and nearly toppled over with another harsh jerk of the ship.

My stomach rolled, but I did not get sick again. There was nothing left in my stomach to heave.

"I am feeling this way because of the ocean's movements?" I asked as I looked down at the wax objects in my hand. This was what the men wore when they encountered sirens.

"Yes, it's common to get sick when the ship rocks this drastically, especially during severe thunderstorms. You can probably stay up on the main deck for a little while before any lightning strikes." The Doc smiled at me as he looked expectantly at the wax coverings.

I placed them into my ears and noticed the dampening of that ringing in my ears.

The Doc offered his arm for balance, and I looped mine with his. Together, we exited my room and headed up the stairs slowly, much to my relief. As someone who spent their entire life underwater, it was difficult to wrap my head around a couple of rough waves being my undoing. It was humiliating. If anyone in Meyrial heard about this, I would never live it down.

The staircase railing was my vital crutch as I climbed each step with care. The Doc was patient, allowing me to lean on him when needed. He was kind, seeming unconcerned that I might get sick on him.

The Doc led me to the edge of the ship where I threw myself onto the railing. I leaned over and stared into the horizon. The skyline was barely visible from the opaque clouds and sky as dark as the sea. Still, the familiar smell of the ocean breeze and the raindrops on my face calmed my nerves. I breathed deeply, feeling ridiculous but glad that the wave of nausea rolled away.

A siren getting seasick. How laughable.

I removed the wax from my ears when I felt slightly better and put the two objects in my pocket.

"Doc! Dyer got hit in the face with the lower mast yard. Can you check if his nose is broken?" Marsden shouted over the growing winds.

He pulled down a rope and tied it to the railing. I looked past him where I located a bloody-faced Dyer, who was clutching his nose, wincing slightly. Flashes of lightning and the small flickering flames encased in glass lanterns were the only light source. The Doc turned to me with uncertainty.

"I am fine. Go help him," I spoke through gritted teeth as the ship rolled over yet another enormous wave.

The Doc left me on the railing. My knuckles were bone white where I held on. It was pouring now—the storm was picking up. The rain drenched my hair in an instant. A clap of thunder rumbled in the skies above.

"This is going to get ugly fast." Kae shouted from the helm next to Dalton. "Everyone below deck besides Dalton and Marsden! Make sure everything loose is tied down. Now!"

A bolt of lightning struck somewhere on the horizon. It lit up Kae's features in a flash of light. Despite the sun having just set, it was already pitch-black out. Another boom of thunder sent everyone scurrying down the stairs below deck.

I still held onto the railing, afraid I was going to fall over or get sick and make a fool of myself. The rain came down even heavier. I could barely see my own hands out in front of me. It was rare for storms to pick up as quickly as this one had. Someone had put out the fires in the lanterns. With such winds, the flames could easily escape.

Kae descended the steps from the helm and briskly made her way over to me.

"You need to get below deck. It's not safe up here!" Kae yelled over the storm.

She did not seem angry, maybe concerned, as a look of alarm took over her face. I nodded meekly and let go of the railing with one hand. I was too frightened to come up with a retort. My whole body would not stop shaking.

Humans were so weak. Suddenly, the thought crossed my mind, and I feared falling overboard and drowning. What a fitting and ironic death that would be for me.

As I let go of the one thing that steadied me, another bolt of lightning lit up the sky and the ship rolled to one side. We were climbing up a tall wave. Dalton was shouting something from behind the wheel, but I could not hear what he was saying, nor to whom his shouts were directed.

Kae shot a hand out to steady me, gripping my forearm tightly. She gasped as her eyes went wide at something behind me. I turned around to see that the wave Dalton was trying to steer us over had grown in height.

The ship tilted even further back.

I stumbled onto the ground and brought Kae down with me. We slid across the wet deck and hit the railing on the other side of the ship. The force knocked Kae over the side, and I had no time to think before I grabbed her hand.

The ship was almost at a ninety-degree angle now. I was laying nearly flat on the railing as I held Kae's weight in my hands. If I let go now, she would drown. I could jump in after her and bring her body to Salophine. It would be easy.

Yet again, something stopped me.

I still had time. I did not have to rush, and if her crew sought revenge, my siren sisters would be in danger. I pretended that was the sole reason I still held on to her. The way she stared at me holding her life in my hands had nothing to do with it. I was lost in the intense contact of her steel gaze. Silver eyes glistening with worry, as if she expected me to drop her.

"Marsden, help them!" Dalton shouted.

His voice cracked, nearly an octave over his usual tone. He could not leave his post until we were over the wave. The wheel would not listen to his movements as he struggled to gain control of the ship.

"Hang on!" I called to Kae, who was trying to swing her body to reach the railing.

There was a flicker of fear in her eyes, but it could have just been the lightning playing tricks. It was gone in a flash, replaced by sheer determination.

With a grunt, I got up and pushed my feet against the railing as I pulled on Kae's arm. She swung her body again and with the momentum of the swing, I grabbed her as she clung to the railing. She rolled onto the ship and landed beside me, and the ship evened out as it got over the wave.

"Shit!" Marsden called from the middle of the ship. He was still trying to tie down ropes. I did not think he even saw what happened nor heard Dalton's call. This storm was too intense to see or hear much.

"Are you okay?" I asked breathlessly.

My heart thumped violently in my chest for more reasons than one. Kae caught her breath and nodded.

"Thank you," she said.

"Well, I was not about to let you drown. Who else would I torment?" I asked, and Kae let out a dry laugh.

Without another word, she got up and rushed over to Dalton. His face was paler than usual, his eyes wide. He turned his head down to speak with Kae when she got to him.

I ran toward the stairs, stumbling on the slippery wood and the thrashing of the ship, and descended below deck. That was a little too much for one day. Kenley and Birch were gathered around the dinner table. It was bolted to the floor, and they held the edges of the table to steady themselves. The rest must have retreated to their beds.

"Are the storms usually this bad out at sea?" I asked, addressing the gunner and my trainer. I sat down and grabbed the edge of the table to steady myself while the ship continued to rock.

"Not really. It usually gets this bad near Naivia. Last time we traveled here, a huge storm cycle raged a few days away from the kingdom," Kenley answered.

He took a deep gulp of what I thought was water out of a mug. The trickle of brown liquid on his stubble proved to be rum. Half of it soaked his shirt, probably spilled from the harsh wave.

"We should be through the whole thing come morrow," Birch said as he twirled one of his sheathed throwing daggers in his hand.

His voice was rough and gritty, probably from neglect—he rarely spoke.

My stomach churned at the thought of feeling like this all night.

"I have never experienced this sickness before," I admitted, feeling vulnerable but also not caring as much as I had before.

If I were to gain everyone's trust, I might as well be more open. Though I doubted I could change everyone's minds about hunting, perhaps just one would be enough.

"It's normal for newbies. Heck, I even get nauseous sometimes still. It's why I drink. The rum soothes the nerves," Kenley explained, and lightly shoved his mug over the table to me.

The waves had settled, at least for now. I gladly accepted a remedy and took a sip. The liquid burned my stomach, making me feel warm inside. I handed the mug back to him. Kenley smiled, finishing the remains and then got up. He stumbled right as the ship lurched over a wave.

"Ya shouldn't have more than four pints. Ya always get horribly sick on yer fifth," Birch said and eyed Kenley as he went to refill his glass.

I laughed as Kenley tried sputtering a response.

"You're too observant, old man," Kenley said.

"I'm only five years older than ya," Birch deadpanned.

His face never showed an ounce of emotion. I grinned as Kenley sighed. He retrieved his sliding chair and sat down with an empty mug, earning a satisfied hint of a smile from Birch that Kenley did not notice. But I did.

"You all seem so close in age," and younger than most sailors I had encountered at sea. "How did you meet?" I asked, curiosity getting the best of me.

How did the great Kae of Avalon round up this motley crew?

"It happened a little over a year ago. Word got out this guy was trying to throw together a crew to sail the seas. The captain was seeking to hunt sirens. Truthfully, I didn't even believe in the sea creatures. But the money he was offering was to die for. I went to the meeting place where all potential crew members gathered at a tavern. That's when we all met Captain Kae." Kenley looked at a blank spot on the wall as he spoke, lost in memory.

"That is right! You all thought she was a man at first," I said, remembering when I also thought the same.

"We thought so until two weeks ago." Birch said matter-of-factly, not an ounce of bitterness to his voice. "She's aloof, that one,"

"I also thought she was a man at first," I said.

"She enjoys dressing masculine. Can't blame her. Women's clothes are so heavy and time-consuming," Birch said, as though he spoke from personal experience.

I disagreed with him. I'd had fun fighting at the bar in my emerald dress. I missed it.

"It doesn't matter what Kae's in, she'll cut your throat whether she's wearing trousers or a dress. Ruthless thing," Kenley said with fondness and respect in his voice.

As I listened to the way they all spoke highly of Kae—how she had earned their loyalty—another thought came to mind, taking me away from the trailing thoughts of Kae.

"If you are all from the same kingdom, why do you speak so differently?" I asked, noting that Birch and Rigby were the outliers compared to the others.

"It's because Rig and I are originally from Evrelon. Their accent differs from Avalon. I moved to Avalon when I was eleven," Birch said.

I nodded.

"So, whoever showed up at the tavern is on the ship now?" I questioned.

They seemed patient as I jumped from one topic to the next.

"Well, no. See, the pay was *really* good. A lot more men showed up than there were spots to fill. Nearly thirty men. We each had to prove our skills to Captain Kae. Marsden and Dyer went through knot tying, Atty and Birch showed off their fighting skills. Myself and Arden shared our knowledge of explosives—though we were asked not to do an actual demonstration. Rigby prepared a meal of trout—" Kenley was cut off as the Doc sat down beside him.

"And I stitched up Atty, who had been cut by Birch in their fighting demonstration," the Doc said.

Birch smirked at the memory, and I raised a brow.

"We were close friends long before meeting the rest of the crew. There were no hard feelings from Atty. He's gotten me back plenty of times since then," Birch explained.

This was the most I had heard him speak since meeting him. He appeared more relaxed when he was not my trainer.

"The rest of us had not met each other beforehand. Captain Kae didn't even know Ruff or Dalton before that night," Kenley said, excited to be the one telling the story again.

"Really? The three seem inseparable," I wondered aloud.

"They had to grow close. Ruff is the captain's first mate, and Dalton's the navigator and secondary. I don't know why Captain Kae and Dalton are so close, but they're attached at the hip," Kenley answered with a shrug.

"Dalton and Ruff don't seem to get along much. Well, they always bicker over pointless things," the Doc chimed in with a whisper.

"Those two are always at each other's throats," Birch said, followed by awkward glances that fell on me, "But who wouldn't when yer in such close quarters with someone else all the time," Birch added.

"Not everyone can always get along," I muttered, thinking of when I almost slit Kae's throat open.

The three men's thoughts seemed to align with my own. The room grew quiet.

"Ugh, this storm is still making me woozy," I said in a lighter tone to avoid ruining the mood.

The Doc got up and disappeared into a corner of the room where he kept his healing supplies.

"If you aren't feeling better, you can chew on this plant leaf. It'll knock you right out and hopefully you can sleep through the rest of the storm." The Doc returned with a bright orange leaf that had many red spots on it.

Surely the healer would not poison me. I trusted him. That thought startled me to my core. I trusted a man. Perhaps I hit my head during the storm and did not remember.

"Uh… sure. Why not?" I shrugged.

The Doc nodded at my response and dropped the leaf into my outstretched hand. The bright color and patterns reminded me of poisonous fish. I tried not to think of it as I laid the leaf on my tongue and chewed.

"Got any extras lying around, Doc? This storm's doing a number on me," Kenley said as he eyed his empty mug and then glanced over at Birch.

"Yes, give me a moment. Aqeara, let me lead you to your room. We wouldn't want you passing out on the chair." The Doc extended his arm out again for support, and I followed him toward my bedroom. He walked me inside and helped lower me into bed.

"Thank you for all your help today." My words slurred as my head hit the pillow.

My eyelids grew heavy. I was struggling to keep them open. This leaf worked fast.

The Doc smiled and nodded. He made his way toward the doorway. As he was about to close it shut, his eyes roamed to the dent in the door where I had thrown my dagger at Kae's head. The Doc ran a finger over the damage and then shrugged, like he had no explanation for it.

My eyes shut just as the door clicked.

Chapter Seventeen
Kae

I slept the entire morning and part of the afternoon. I had been up all night captaining the *Mar Daemon* through the brutal storm, helping Dyer tie down ropes and adjust the sails once the crazy winds died down, and exchanged shifts with Dalton at the wheel. My ship had suffered only minor damage, much to our surprise. We would be in Naivia by the next afternoon.

Things could have gone much worse.

I held up a hand to my face as I exited my quarters. It was just past high noon, and the sun shone brightly against the damp wood. There was no sign of the raging storm that had passed hours ago. The faintest of breezes caressed my cheek. A few white clouds littered the sky. Even the seagulls had returned, cawing at one another.

"Afternoon, Captain!" Dyer called out from his post.

He adjusted sails for the slight wind.

There were deep bruises on either side of his nose, just underneath his eyes. His nose wasn't broken, but definitely looked like it was.

"How's the nose feeling, Dyer?" I walked over and inspected the masts for any signs of damage.

Not that I was a professional in any way when it came to the specifics of sails. It put me at ease whenever Dyer or Marsden would explain things to me in a way that did not make me feel unintelligent. None of the books in the royal library had prepared me for this.

"Doc put a nice balm on it and numbed the pain. Should heal up in a couple of days. I can smell Rigby's raw fish scent sleeping in the cot above me, so it still works," Dyer said cheerily.

I smiled and shook my head at his jest.

"I heard that, asshole!" Rigby called out from an unseen location.

Dyer and I chuckled.

Marsden walked over, tilting his head down at me in greeting. He and Dyer broke into conversation about knots and wind speeds. I took that as my cue to move on and left them to their work.

I glanced up at the helm, looking for Dalton, but found Barnes behind the wheel. He noticed my gaze and waved enthusiastically. I waved back, thinking Dalton must have been sleeping off the day. He deserved it. He had also been up most of the night.

I headed down below, where more men were lounging about. At the dining table sat Dalton, Ruff, Atty, Birch, and Aqeara. They were all heads bent down and discussing something serious. The only open seat was next to Aqeara. A fact that left my hands slick with sweat.

I could still feel her firm grip on my arm from last night. For the smallest of seconds, I thought she would drop me to my death.

A look had passed over her face, like she'd considered it at the very least.

"Captain!" Dalton spoke up as soon as he saw me lingering by the stairs. "We were just talking about training today. Atty and Birch were working with Aqeara all morning, so I decided it's my turn to show her some moves. Care to join?"

Atty and Birch stopped their own separate conversation to wave me over toward the empty seat. Ruff leaned back in his chair, tilting it in a way that made me concerned it was going to fall over. I sat down beside Aqeara, who said nothing at my arrival. She hadn't even looked up at me. It shouldn't have bothered me, but the avoidance stung.

Rigby walked over and placed a plate of toast smothered in jam on the table. I beamed at him and dug right in.

"I think I'll just watch for today." I said, my mouth mostly full. "I'd love to see how far our novice hunter has come in her combat skills."

Aqeara flinched beside me, and I regretted the word "hunter," as soon as I said it. Great. Right when it seemed we could be amicable toward each other, I had to remind us of our stark differences.

"Are you sure you would not want to duel me? I recall we had an *incredible* fight last time." Aqeara leaned close as she spoke in a low voice meant for me.

I froze and unfroze, desperately trying to hide the hitch in my breath, not wanting to give her any satisfaction in my response. I hated how my breathing quickened. Surely, she must have known what her words would do to me.

Back to square one, I thought bitterly. I didn't even know why I wanted her to like me now when I'd loathed her before.

I recalled when Dalton had said it was because I had a thing for redheads. That was during the first day at sea after departing Zephlus. I wondered if his arm was still bruised from when I had *accidentally* punched him.

I chugged Dalton's glass of rum and burped in Aqeara's direction. She scrunched her nose in disgust.

"Oh, I'm positive, dulzura." I winked at Aqeara and got up.

She rolled her eyes. She seemed to hate the nickname I had given her, and I reveled in it. As if *sweetheart* was an insult. Dalton had a goofy grin on his face as he watched our spat.

"Let's get to it!" Dalton called and led the way back upstairs.

Ruff and Aqeara were right behind him. She glanced back at me just once, and I swallowed hard at the feeling that rose in the pit of my stomach.

"Thanks for the breakfast, Rig," I said to Rigby, who nodded and sat down to join Atty and Birch with their second plate of food.

I allowed my two hunters to be given second portions, with all the exercising and training they did on the daily.

I left them, slipping back up the stairs without another word. Back on the main deck, Dalton and Aqeara were a few feet apart, facing each other. Ruff stood further back, observing. I walked over and stood next to him, crossing my arms over my chest as I tried to mimic his stoic expression.

"Alright, Aqeara. I've been watching you during your training sessions. Now, I'm no better than the two *professionals*, but I figure it'd be good for you to learn various moves. Especially after you were nearly kidnapped." Dalton unsheathed his twin swords as Aqeara put a hand on her hip.

Aqeara scoffed at the insult, but I knew Dalton's play.

He wanted to see how she'd react when she fights based on emotions rather than instincts. He'd tried this move on me plenty of times.

"I mean, you tried slitting the throat of our captain, which proved you got guts. But getting dragged all the way onto the Soledelian ship? Seems like you're slacking in certain areas." Dalton flashed his teeth in a predatory grin.

Aqeara bared her teeth back at him and lunged forward, daggers already in hand.

I watched as the two engaged in combat. Dalton had struck first with the smile still etched on his face. Aqeara had learned how to get close enough to use her short blades against longer ones. She was ducking and swiping against Dalton's strikes with apparent ease. But her anger meant her head was clouded. She was not thinking as clearly as she could have.

The two knew when to pull their strikes to avoid actual damage, but my heart still raced watching them. Ruff sucked in a breath as Aqeara went for Dalton's neck. He swerved out of the way at the last second.

"C'mon, I'm not even breaking a sweat! Is that the best you can do, siren lover?" Dalton barely ducked in time when Aqeara struck again.

Her face was red and scrunched in anger, but Dalton was faster on his feet. He jabbed at her and she backed away. When she was out of range, Aqeara paused and had a calculating look in her eyes. She was learning, sizing him up, picking up on his habits.

"I'm not sure, pretty boy. Are you even trying to hit me?" Aqeara hissed out her comment as she ran and slid across the deck, bending back to avoid Dalton's swing.

She used the flat side of her blade to tap against Dalton's calf, indicating that he would have been stabbed had this been an actual fight.

Aqeara was using Dalton's own tactic against him. She had figured him out. Dalton grumbled at being the first one to get struck and brought his blade down to hit Aqeara's side before she could spring back up onto her feet. Aqeara let out a frustrated noise and tumbled forward, using the momentum to hoist herself back up.

I had to admit; I was impressed. She had greatly improved in her short time aboard. Then I thought of what that might mean if Aqeara decided to get stabby with me again. Chills ran down my spine as I thought of our fight in her cabin, yet I wasn't sure if it was entirely from fear.

"I could never bring myself to hit a little girl!" Dalton spat as he swept his long leg across Aqeara's feet.

She fell over and got the wind knocked out of her.

Dalton took the opportunity to basically straddle her. Ruff made a choking noise beside me. Aqeara flashed a dazzling smile up at Dalton. She leaned forward and kissed him, taking him completely by surprise. Dalton broke away from the kiss and blinked several times. It gave Aqeara enough time to knock him over and gain the vantage point.

Aqeara tapped the dagger right over Dalton's heart. It was silent for a moment before Aqeara stood up, beaming at her victory. Dalton's eyes were still wide in shock.

"Nice going, Aqeara," I said, trying not to seem too impressed even though I thoroughly was.

Aqeara smiled and held out a hand to help Dalton up. He took it and shook hands with her, slowly, like there was a numbness that hadn't subsided.

"Thank you, Captain," Aqeara said slowly as she smoothed out her shirt and made her way over to Ruff and I.

Aqeara's blazing red hair had freed itself from her bandana during the fight. Several strands were falling wildly across her face. She tied her hair back again and ran fingers through the ends, and I couldn't take my eyes off her while she did.

She noticed.

"That was a cheap shot, but I like it." Ruff clapped a hand gently on Aqeara's back. "Way to go, Soledel."

She smiled at him and nodded her thanks.

"Cheap shot indeed. Though how could I blame you? I'm irresistible." Dalton sauntered his way over to us, and Aqeara rolled her eyes.

She extended her foot and caused Dalton to nearly trip over. He shoved into her and the two giggled like children.

"If you are up for it, Ruff, I would love to go against you," Aqeara said.

Dalton had only just recovered from his wide-eyed, shocked face, only to regress back to it. Even I was taken aback. Ruff had a certain aura about him that screamed dangerous. It surprised me Aqeara felt cocky enough to challenge him.

"Why the heck not?" Ruff grinned and took a step toward Aqeara.

He had no weapon on his person.

"Are you not going to draw a sword?" Aqeara raised an eyebrow as she brought her daggers up in defense.

Ruff's grin grew ominous. He was always the most skilled in a fistfight. Aqeara tilted her head at him and shrugged, letting out a breath. She flipped the daggers over in her hands as she rolled her wrists.

"Your move," Aqeara called out and bent her knees into a fighting stance.

She had the perfect form. It was… my heart hammered in my chest just looking at her. I forced my attention to Ruff as he mimicked her moves and advanced.

Even with Aqeara's daggers, Ruff would be a hard opponent to beat. Ruff launched at Aqeara with a right hook. She barely ducked in time before she swiped her blade and missed Ruff by mere inches. The two twirled and struck around each other, close to dancing.

"Why is this literally the hottest thing I've ever seen?" Dalton said, mostly to himself, it seemed, as he stared at the two of them fighting.

I tried not to join him in staring at Aqeara. But the girl knew how to move.

I flinched when Ruff hit Aqeara's striking arm hard. She winced and backed away. For someone staring at Aqeara, Dalton didn't seem to notice her injury. His eyes were focused on Ruff.

"Watch out!" I shouted as Ruff reached out for Aqeara's neck while she had her back to him.

She was anticipating this move and bent back almost in half—wow, she was flexible—and tapped her dagger against Ruff's stomach.

Ruff grabbed Aqeara's waist, spinning her around to face him. She maneuvered out of his grip in a fluid motion, but he expected it. He side-stepped to where she went and then grabbed her neck.

"Snap," Ruff called out.

Aqeara stopped moving. Had this been an actual fight, she'd be dead.

Realizing her loss, Aqeara straightened and smiled wickedly at him. She held her hand out, and the two shook hands before making their way back to us.

"I cannot believe you bested me with just your fists. I expected you to win, but to win weaponless was a bold move. I like it," Aqeara praised Ruff, and he laughed.

Dalton raised a brow, and I found myself smiling.

The sun beat down on us, but the weather was beautiful. Though summer was my least favorite season, I enjoyed the heat. A salty breeze arrived at just the right time when the heat became a bit too much.

"All this fighting has made me thirsty. Anyone down to kill an entire barrel of rum? We're going to be refilling them with fresh ones in Naivia anyway," Dalton voiced his idea, already backing toward the lower deck.

He made an excellent point. Ruff and I followed him, and Aqeara muttered to herself something I didn't hear.

"I am covered in dirt and sweat all the time! How do you people just go on about your day like this?" Aqeara lifted her arms to sniff at herself and grimaced.

I gave her an annoyed look. Dirt and grime helped me cover my smooth features and appeared like a man for over a year. We had all grown used to our filthy state.

"Well, we rarely have access to clean water to rinse ourselves until our next destination. You'll just have to wait another day." Dalton, ever the man to care about appearances, looked at Aqeara, perplexed.

Aqeara pointedly ignored his comment and removed her vest. Ruff and I paused in our tracks to stare at her. What on earth was she doing? The Soledelian removed her boots, oblivious or uncaring, as we watched her. She then removed her dagger belt. Then her corset.

I inhaled sharply as she plopped it on the growing pile of her garments. We stood silent. I was frozen in place. She was underdressed. In front of men. And she didn't care.

Aqeara winked at me before running toward the side of the ship. She gracefully leaped over the railing, stood at the ledge for a few seconds, and then jumped into the water.

Ruff, Dalton, and I shouted in surprise and ran over.

This woman was going to be the death of me.

Chapter Eighteen
Aqeara

It was the first time since becoming human that I returned to my home—that large, never-ending body of water. I did not even consider what that would feel like. The grime that covered my body was begging to be disposed of.

When I hit the water and sunk several feet, blood surrounded me like a dark cloud. To a human, such a sight would scare them. But I knew better, and despite being momentarily startled, I realized what it really was: magic.

I swam into the cloud of blood—which was a thin layer of red liquid—and found myself peering into Salophine's cave. Only, I was not actually there. It was an illusion; I was sure, a way of communicating. I had seen this sort of portal communication done twice by the Queen. It was no surprise that a powerful sea witch possessed this power as well.

"Salophine?" I called out and was shocked to find that I sounded normal.

My voice was crisp rather than muffled, like I expected it to be. Humans couldn't speak the same underwater.

I knew I had a limited time down here. My body was human, after all. I would need to resurface to catch my breath.

"What is taking so long? Are you aware of the fact that it is day nineteen?" Salophine sneered as she came into view. Her crimson eyes never failed to startle me. "You have less than ten days before the spell cannot be performed. I would have contacted you sooner, but you seem to be content surrounded by *humans*."

"I am spending time with these hunters to teach them the gentle ways of the sirens. I hope to change their minds about my kin. Gaining Kae's trust has been difficult," I said in a shaky voice.

Could she see past my hesitation? Look deep within me to see reasoning that *I* did not even know?

My fear ebbed as Salophine mused. Though speaking should have taken more air out of my lungs, whatever magic Salophine was using helped me neither gain nor lose oxygen while I spoke. I was only running on time.

"You want to learn the ways of the humans. You seem to be enjoying your new body," Salophine guessed, and I could tell she was growing angry at my shortcomings.

Her demeanor had shifted, turning colder with each exchange.

"Well, yes. But that is only because the more time I spend as a human, the more I learn about their species. The Queen would want to know every detail about my experience." I was halfway through speaking when Salophine's eyes narrowed.

Her fury exploded out of nowhere.

"Yes, the *Queen* would want to be updated, would she not?" Salophine's voice raised higher as she scolded me. "While you worry about her majesty, why not worry about the fact that you will never see Hyrissa again should you fail to bring me the heart of that captain by the full moon's rise?"

I cowered and swam back from her wrath.

"I will not fail. I promise you that. I will not let Hyrissa down," I said, and knew my time was up.

My lungs were bursting for air. I kicked my legs up and away from the red billowy cloud, away from the ominous eyes of the sea witch. Just before breaking the surface, I looked down one last time. There was no sign of blood nor magic. It was as if I had merely conjured up the conversation. But I knew better.

"Win the trust of the captain. Take her heart for the spell."

The voice of Salophine's illusive anglera hissed in my ears, but they were nowhere in sight. I tried shaking my genuine terror and relaxed my tense muscles. No one could know of the conversation I just had.

I kicked my legs rapidly and gasped as I broke the surface, taking a deep breath of fresh air.

Chapter Nineteen
Kae

"Woman overboard!" Barnes shouted from behind the wheel.

I ran over to the railing from where Aqeara had disappeared, my heart thundering against my eardrums. Though the water was clear, I couldn't find any sign of her, as if the ocean had simply swallowed her.

"What in damnation!" Ruff exclaimed from behind me.

Dalton was speechless, peering over the side of the ship next to me with a worried expression. Several other crew members looked at us to see what all the commotion was about.

Moments passed—too many, and a hush fell over the ship as if we were all holding our breath. I considered jumping in after her. I was growing worried with every passing second that Aqeara had hurt herself in the fall. She was drowning. A shark got to her. She had been dragged under the ship by an undercurrent.

After what felt like eons, Aqeara's head bobbed above the surface. Though I could have sworn I saw a fearful look on her face, it was gone as quickly as it had appeared. Aqeara broke out into laughter when she spotted us peering down at her, the maniac.

"Come on in, the water is great!" Aqeara called from down below, waving her hand at me.

She struggled a bit to keep herself afloat. Her face twisted with concentration.

Relief flooded through me, relaxing my shoulders and easing my stomach pain. I didn't dwell too much on what my worry meant, but I was also justified for being afraid that Aqeara might have died from a simple accident. Trust her or not, I didn't want her to die.

Dalton and Ruff flanked my sides as they leaned over the railing to see the Soledelian still alive, and shook their heads. I could not believe my own eyes. The fall alone could have killed her.

"Lower a lifeboat immediately," I ordered Ruff.

"After all that, and we still have to rescue her," he grumbled, but his voice shook.

He couldn't deny that he also feared for Aqeara's life.

The small vessel made its way toward sea level, floating just a few feet away from Aqeara. I couldn't help but be amused at her spontaneity and recklessness. A smile tugged at my lips, and I let it form. Despite myself, this woman was growing on me.

"What a woman," Dalton stated in a way that questioned her sanity more than anything else.

He shook his head and chuckled as he went over to aid Ruff in lifting the boat back up. Aqeara swam over and hoisted herself on board with ease. I walked over as the two men pulled on the ropes to bring her back up.

"Is she mad?" Dyer called from his post across the ship.

I shrugged with genuine bafflement and turned back to Aqeara, who was now taking Ruff's outstretched hand and jumping back on board.

"Well, that was refreshing!" Aqeara wrung water out of her hair and wiped her eyes clean.

A puddle pooled around her. She was dripping wet as she walked over to her discarded clothing. I shifted my gaze anywhere else but on her. The way her wet shirt was clinging to her body was definitely an invasion of privacy, despite her nonchalant attitude about it. The fact that it was white did not help the matter.

"Go get changed. You can meet us by the rum barrels," I stated, trying not to act flustered, but even I knew my cheeks were burning.

Dalton whistled low to himself, and Ruff smacked him on the arm.

"Hey!" Dalton rubbed his arm, pretending to be hurt.

Ruff rolled his eyes at Dalton's kicked-puppy expression.

Aqeara laughed at the interaction as she made her way to the stairs, leaving a trail of salty water in her wake.

"Dyer, mop this up," I called out, pointing to the puddle of seawater on the deck.

Dyer looked at it and then raised his eyes to the sky before nodding and making his way to the small closet where we stored supplies.

We followed Aqeara downstairs and stopped by the rum storage corner. Aqeara kept walking until she entered her bedroom and closed the door behind her. My cheeks flushed at the thought of her changing. I walked up to Atty and Birch, in hopes of distracting myself from that line of thinking.

"We're done training for the day if you want to use the main deck for fighting." I addressed the two hunters. "But watch out for puddles. Or join us for some drinks."

"Excellent. I may take you up on that offer later. C'mon, Birch." Atty signaled to Birch, who sat beside him.

The men saluted me and then ascended the stairs, weapons already drawn for hunting practice. I shook my head at their retreating figures before I turned back to Dalton and Ruff.

I made my way over and sat down on my cushion. Ruff and Dalton were bickering about where the best rum was imported, with differing opinions. I smiled up at Dalton from my seat, batting my eyelashes at him to get glasses and pour drinks. Ruff sat down beside me and mimicked my expression.

Dalton rolled his eyes at us, but we both knew he would give in. Our pleadings were answered as he left and soon returned with four empty glasses. Ruff and I watched as Dalton filled the glasses to the brim with the delicious brown drink.

"If you get as drunk as you did the night before we reached Avalon, I'll kill you," Dalton warned as he handed me a glass.

I beamed up at him, remembering that he'd been sick just from the sight of me getting sick from over-drinking. Dalton despised vomiting. When he found Aqeara sick in her room the day before, he had left her and sprinted up the stairs to hurl over the railing.

"We'll be in Naivia tomorrow. I'm not getting drunk on the *Mar Daemon* when I can get alcohol poisoning in the most beautiful city in the world," I deadpanned.

The three of us cheered to that and drank deeply.

I sighed in content. Nothing could beat the taste of rum save for ice-cold rum. I couldn't wait to get my hands on a refreshing cup once we got to Naivia.

Dalton sat on the other side of me, despite there being plenty of room next to Ruff. I had hoped, after a year on board a ship together, these two would stop acting weird around each other. Ruff got up a bit abruptly and refilled his glass. I wasn't the least bit shocked he had finished his drink already.

We were on our third glass—Ruff, his fourth or fifth—when Aqeara moseyed over. The way her new black corset was tied around her waist could tempt the gods themselves.

Pathetic, I scolded myself.

Aqeara sat down next to Ruff, who handed her a drink wordlessly. He got up for a refill. Aqeara smiled and sipped slowly. Her face did not falter against the rum's smooth taste.

"Do they have alcohol in Soledel?" Dalton asked, leaning over me to look at Aqeara as he spoke.

Ruff sat down and blocked Dalton's view of her. Dalton didn't seem to mind in the slightest. He even smirked at the gesture.

"No. We have, uh… these plants that cause hallucinations when ingested. They sort of feel like what this drink is doing, only a lot more intense." Aqeara took another long sip.

I narrowed my eyes at her. It sounded a lot like the stuff in Avalon that some got addicted to. I hoped that was not the case. Though, Aqeara did not have the demeanor of an addict reliant on anything.

"How strange," was all Dalton said as he finished his drink.

He stood up for a refill and Aqeara held out her own glass in her hand, empty, with a look of innocence plastered on her dangerously not innocent face.

I was surprised at her ability to down the rum so fast. Ruff seemed pleased as he gave her a warm smile and an encouraging clap on her shoulder.

Dalton shrugged and took the glass. He filled the two cups, handing Aqeara's back to her. He then shoved the rum barrel closer to us, turning it so that the nozzle was right in front of our feet.

"You are nothing if not innovative," Ruff said and barely stretched to fill his glass again.

I couldn't tell if there was sarcasm laced in his tone, but when it came to those two squabbling idiots, it was almost always venomous.

"Thanks," Dalton replied as he sat back down again.

His cheeks were tinted pink.

I ignored what that might mean as I finished my drink and refilled it with ease.

Dalton stretched his long legs out in front of him. Wanting to also be comfortable, I took off my tricorn hat and placed it on my lap. I ran fingers through my freed curls.

Aqeara scrunched her face at the hat like she had some unspoken vendetta against the headpiece. I ignored her expression. It was silent for several moments while we all drank. While I could hold my own with rum, its effects still clouded my mind.

"You all constantly ask about me and my kingdom, yet I know nothing of yours. Tell me something about yourselves," Aqeara said.

I turned in my seat to fully stare at her. I wanted to know who has been asking her questions because it certainly wasn't me. I knew next to nothing about her. I'd only just begun to tolerate her.

"I'm an orphan," Dalton offered, breaking my train of thought.

There was neither merriment nor resentment in his voice. Ruff looked over at him with sadness in his eyes. I awkwardly traced the rim of my hat with my fingers. Dalton never enjoyed talking about his life before we met him.

"I am not sure I am aware of the word," Aqeara admitted after a lapse of silence.

I raised my eyebrows. Soledelian dialect was something I had to get used to.

"It means I have no mother or father. They gave me up when I was a baby. I was born in Avalon, but my parents definitely were from another kingdom. It's why I have paler skin than the rest of the crew. I don't know where my parents were from," Dalton explained in a toneless voice.

I finished my drink over a lump that had risen in my throat.

When I first grew close to Dalton, I knew from the start he had no family to leave behind. He didn't seem to mind it—he considered the crew his new family.

What bothered Dalton the most was he did not know where his family was from. All he knew was that he was dropped off at an Avalonian orphanage before he could walk. Avalonians had darker, more tanned-brown skin. Dalton's skin tone was light, his dirty blonde hair a clear giveaway that he was from another kingdom.

Ruff cleared his throat, breaking the awkward silence.

"I emigrated from Eayucia to Avalon. Figured I could make more money and have a better life in a kingdom nicknamed the Golden City," Ruff said.

Aqeara looked equally intrigued.

"And you all met at that tavern the night Captain Kae called to form a crew," Aqeara said.

In the time we spent avoiding each other, it seemed Aqeara spent it with the rest of the crew. I wondered how much they told her—if they talked about me. I would be lying if I did not admit I was a bit jealous. They seemed to be able to talk to the Soledelian with ease.

"Yes. And we've been jolly friends ever since." Dalton said with a huge grin.

Ruff coughed at the statement.

"What about you? You left your family behind in Soledel, I assume." Ruff shot an empathetic look over to Aqeara.

He knew the feeling.

"I am like Dalton. An orphan." Aqeara spoke in a smaller voice than usual. "My mother died giving birth to me. My other mother, I am not entirely sure what happened to her. I know she committed high treason and was killed for it. My aunt raised me, along with my seven cousins. They are not of my blood, but I still consider them my family. I am so grateful for her kindness. Honestly, I do not even remember the faces of my mothers."

There was a heavy silence, and my heart ached for her. But wait—

"You have *two* mothers?" I questioned.

"Had," Aqeara corrected.

"What about your father?"

"I had no father."

"Surely you must have—it doesn't matter. Is Soledel really okay with women loving each other openly? Raising children together?" I was completely caught off-guard by the implication.

In every kingdom I had been to, same-sex couples were frowned upon. It was punishable in certain regions. Everything was done in secret, behind closed doors. It was a laughable irony that the one kingdom that worshiped the very creatures I hated with every ounce of my being would accept me for who I was.

"They do not seem to mind. Besides, my mothers did not raise me together. One died before I took my first breath. The other was taken from me before I could remember her face." Aqeara's mood shifted while she spoke.

She was upset in a way that wasn't the type of grief that developed over the years. No, whatever that was upsetting her had happened recently. The raw expression of loss on her face was fresh.

"I am sorry for your loss," Ruff said and patted Aqeara's shoulder.

It was one of his scarcely few ways of showing affection. Aqeara smiled softly.

"It is no matter. The past is the past. We must only look forward."

There she goes again with her wisdom. No wonder she got along with Doc.

Dalton was hanging on to every word. I tried not to show my disagreement on my face. I very much enjoyed thinking of my past. It was how I kept Edmonde with me.

"Oi! Are you lot seriously going at it without me? Bunch of sardines, you are!" Arden called out as he appeared from nowhere.

Aqeara frowned and cast me a puzzled look.

Sardines? she mouthed at me.

"Arden loathes sardines. Whenever he finds something we do offensive, he feels compelled to throw the *insult* at us. Kenley's usually at the receiving end since I put him in charge to make sure Arden doesn't blow us all up," I explained.

Aqeara snorted.

"You'll do better than to address your captain like that, Arden," I called out after him.

Arden grew red in the face. He had not noticed me among the others without my hat on. He stammered, and I smiled at his flustered state.

"Apologies, Captain. I was merely suggesting perhaps we take the drinking upstairs? I'm sure the others will join. We've just swabbed the entire deck." Arden stood up straight and held his arms behind his back.

I got up and walked over to the gunner. We were barely a foot apart. Arden shrunk back, intimidated even though he had a couple inches on me in height.

"Excellent idea!" I shouted, startling him. I grinned. "Prepare the barrels. Everyone! We shall celebrate our last night before reaching Naivia. We killed a siren on our quick journey so far. We won our fight against those dreadful bounty hunters. This calls for a drink!" My voice boomed throughout the ship.

My men scrambled from wherever they were to get up to the main deck. Several grabbed the few full barrels we had left in stock. Aqeara glided past me and up the stairs as she clutched her glass close to her. I had not realized until then what my words of the siren's death would mean to her. What memories it would spark.

I kept my vision focused on the railing of the staircase as I followed behind her. I tried my best to ignore the way her pants hugged her legs.

Pathetic. Snap out of it. You're already drunk.

I hadn't kept track of how many drinks I'd had. I should have.

When I emerged on the deck, the men were all set up, drinking heavily from their mugs already. The songs of different sea tunes filled the air.

Aqeara seemed enchanted by the songs. There was no other way to describe it. A dreamy smile crossed her face and her eyes closed as she swayed to the music.

Doc and Rigby were playing the accordion and violin, respectively. Though they weren't much in a fight, the two were the most entertaining when it came to music.

Atty lent his voice to sing a popular song about love and war. His voice carried strong over their melodies. It was quite a show.

Marsden and Arden were dancing along with exaggerated moves that made the rest of us laugh. There were smiles all around. My crew was always prepared for a party, no matter the circumstance.

I sat atop an empty barrel and crossed my legs in front of me.
I watched the small celebration in silence, drinking in the group's
energy.

Long after the sun had set, my vision swayed back and forth. I
feared if I left my perch, I would lose my footing. As captain, I
never much liked showing weakness or vulnerability in front of my
crew. Only Ruff and Dalton had seen a glimpse into that side of
me.

A captain was supposed to be respected and even feared. Or
so I thought. So, I had not joined in the singing or dancing tonight.
I stayed back and watched, soaking my organs with more glasses of
rum than I could count.

Aqeara made her way over to me, stumbling slightly. She had
been seated next to the musicians the whole night, nodding her
head to the beat of each song. I'd been kicking myself for thinking
how beautiful she looked in the lamplight.

"Why do you not join your men in their revelry?" Aqeara
asked, leaning against the barrel I was on.

She was awfully close, and I was awfully drunk. I scanned the
crowd of pirates to see if anyone was looking at us. They were all
too invested in their dancing and drinking to notice anything. Not
that anything was happening. Or would.

"I don't sing," I answered and internally flinched at the poor
excuse.

My words were slurring. Dammit.

"No offense to Atty or the others, but I do not think any of them are that good either. Except maybe Dalton." Aqeara said.

I knew she tried to be reassuring, but it made me feel something else entirely. The two always seemed to be flirting. And I wasn't jealous. There was nothing to be jealous of. I shouldn't care if they flirted. I didn't care.

"I enjoy sitting here and watching my crew have fun," I said.

Aqeara sighed at my response and leaned closer to me. She still faced the dancing men. Her gaze was on the crew. But it didn't feel like her attention was on them at all. Mine certainly wasn't.

With Aqeara this close to me, I could smell hints of sea salt and, oddly enough, coconuts. I inhaled deeply and tried to mask it with a sigh. Aqeara did not seem to notice. I'd never felt such a stronger desire to just grab this woman and kiss her.

What was wrong with me?

No. This was the alcohol, muddling my thoughts.

It didn't matter how attractive I found Aqeara. She was a siren sympathizer. And I was a siren hunter. She'd even tried killing me on more than one occasion. Even if she'd saved me twice since then.

Aqeara was still potentially dangerous and not worth tangling the sheets with. My mind trailed off at the last thought while my heart rate picked up. Aqeara's hand casually rested atop my thigh. My breath hitched.

"So why don't you sing?" I asked an octave above normal, barely giving space between words while I tried to steer the mood away from whatever she was thinking.

Sadness flashed over Aqeara's face at my question. She removed her hand and fiddled with a loose strand of hair instead. My thigh felt cold where her warm touch once was.

"I cannot. I lost my ability to sing."

"How is that even possible?"

"It happened in Soledel. A man tried fighting me while he was drunk. He slashed my throat. Only the vocal cords responsible for singing were damaged." Aqeara spoke in a well-rehearsed manner, like she had been practicing this explanation for a while.

I ignored the robotic tone in her voice. There was no visible scar on her throat. I wasn't the most educated on anatomy, so I couldn't really dispute the logistics of her story.

I didn't bother to comment, and at this point, I was not even sure I could. My head still spun with an equal mix of intoxication from both alcohol and Aqeara. I squeezed my eyes shut, hoping the spinning would cease. I opened them again, not wanting Aqeara to be aware of just how drunk I was.

"Are you alright? You look like you have seen a corpse," she said it like she was concerned—like she cared.

She looked me in the eyes, giving me her full attention.

My gaze fell to her lips, red and full. Her cheeks were flushed. I met her eyes and wished I hadn't. Her pupils were fully blown as her amber irises stared into mine, a hint of the lamplight catching them with a captivating glimmer.

"I'm retiring for the night. Please continue your fun without me," I spoke in a louder voice, tearing my gaze away from Aqeara's parted lips.

My statement was directed toward the crew. A synchrony of well wishes and bids of goodnights met me in return. The men returned to their night, switching up songs and celebrating as they were before my brief interruption.

I hopped down from the barrel. Before I could make my way across the ship, Aqeara grabbed my arm and spun me toward her. She was only a few inches taller than me. My heart stopped as she ran her fingers up and down my arm, leaving a trail of goosebumps behind. I swallowed hard.

Aqeara locked her gaze on my lips. I was either about to pass out or do something I knew I would regret.

Instead, I twisted free from her grip and hurried across the deck toward my quarters. I shut the door behind me and sunk to the ground.

I slapped my hand across my face if only to pull me back to my senses. It worked. Slightly.

I was foolish. Running away like I wasn't in control of myself. An absolute idiot.

Once in Naivia, I could avoid Aqeara and enjoy myself. I could go off and find dozens of women to fill my bed space. And make sure none of them were from Soledel.

I crashed on my bed and slept alone, not a single dream filling my head.

Chapter Twenty
Aqeara

I had no headache the morning after drinking, despite Dalton's warnings that I would. In truth, I felt perfectly normal, if it were not for the fact that I encountered an all-powerful sea witch yesterday. My nightmares had been riddled with her crimson eyes and Kae's beating heart in my grip.

I was the first one on deck in the morning. Waving a hand to Barnes behind the helm, I walked over to the railing and leaned over. We were just two hours away from Naivia.

Somehow, the arrival at this destination solidified Salophine's warning—I only had a little over a week to steal Kae's heart.

Though I went about the rest of the day like nothing had happened, *something* had happened. And so, I spent my time after our conversation trying to grow closer to the captain. I knew Dalton trusted me, and Ruff was warming up to me. The rest of the crew tolerated me, at the very least.

Kae was the only one left.

Time passed while I was lost in my thoughts. The morning men awoke and began their duties before we docked, allowing the night shift to catch some rest.

Kae emerged shortly after Kenley and Arden finished swabbing the deck free of spilled alcohol from the night before. She grumbled about a headache to Ruff, and the two disappeared from sight. I knew she noticed me standing at the edge of the ship, but Kae did not acknowledge me.

Back to avoiding me, I supposed. But this was different. Kae was more awkward, like she was suddenly unsure of herself. She tripped over a bundle of ropes and apologized to it, before glancing up at me and down casting her eyes again.

She was not at all angry like before. No, the captain was avoiding me because I had gotten so close to seducing her last night.

I was getting under her skin. The back-and-forth flirting with Dalton was hopefully working. I knew it annoyed her at the very least and made her jealous at the most.

It meant nothing to me, though he was very handsome. I knew the false flirtations meant nothing to Dalton either. Being alive for so long gave me wisdom in knowing what the look of being in love was. And that man was certainly enamored by someone. Someone who was not me.

"How'd you sleep?" Dalton asked me as he jogged over to my thinking spot.

I looked at Dalton and the bags under his eyes.

"Like a youthling," I said without a second thought.

Dalton laughed at my choice of words, and I realized my siren lingo probably came off like Soledelian expressions.

Eight days, I thought to myself. I would be a siren again in eight days. I would have Kae's heart in eight days. My stomach flipped, but I couldn't quite tell why.

"There she is! Naivia. We're here!" Barnes called out and Dalton rushed up the stairs to his mentee's side.

The two navigated the *Mar Daemon* into the port of Naivia.

The kingdom was made of colorful buildings from where I could see. Someone let off fireworks as if they celebrated our arrival. The loud, colorful *pops* dazzled me. Sometimes sailors would let those off at sea, their celebrations heard even from below the water's surface. The tiny variegated explosions were always so fun to watch.

The crew rushed about to prepare for our docking. The anchor splashed into the ocean, as the sails were tied into place. I tried not to think of the fleeting time I was running on. Instead, I thought of what this new kingdom would look like. What new things I would see and learn? What potential stories I could witness and tell my little cousin when we soon reunited?

Kae was milling about, barking orders and making sure the ship was angled right for docking. Most of it went over my head, like why there were stars on board or how the placement of the sails affected the ship.

"Ship's docked!" Marsden called out.

Kae reemerged on the main deck, followed by Ruff and Atty. The three lowered the plank, and Kae got off.

The harbor of Naivia was structured similarly to both Zephlus and Avalon. Many boats of differing sizes floated along the jutted ports, anchored and temporarily abandoned. People everywhere went about their day. I marveled at the sight.

"What is she doing?" I asked Dyer as he tied up the final loose ropes.

"Paying the toll for the ship. We have to pay to keep the *Mar Daemon* docked in this spot," Dyer explained.

I frowned.

What silly little customs humans had. As if they could own— temporarily or permanently—part of the sea. The ocean belonged to all that lived in it. Such a concept was foreign to humans.

"Has anyone seen my will to live? I seemed to have misplaced it this morning," Arden muttered as he walked across the deck while rubbing his temples.

I let out a giggle at the gunner's dramatics. Really, I was not sure if I just did not consume as much alcohol as the rest of them or if my human body could just handle it better. I could easily get through three training sessions.

I noticed then that all the men had their things on them. I raced back down to my room to grab my satchel full of clothes, securing it over my right shoulder before I climbed the steps two at a time to the main deck.

Kae appeared at the top of the landing plank. She was in a better mood than earlier this morning. Her face was lit with anticipation, hands eagerly fumbling at her sides as if she could not contain her excitement.

"Ship's secured! The lot of you, follow me. We'll be heading to the inn first. Then you're free to do whatever your heart pleases." Kae's voice boomed across the deck.

The men hurrahed and joined her in exiting the ship. I almost let out a squeal at the feeling of my feet on solid ground again. No more rocking on waves or nearly plummeting to my death in rainstorms.

"How long are we staying here, Captain?" Rigby called out as Kae led the way deep into the heart of Naivia.

"Ideally, a week. The supplies must all be restocked and there's some information I need before we leave. Don't worry, you'll have plenty of time to drink merrily here," Kae answered.

I tuned out the rest of the chatter as I drank in the city before me. Buildings, made of stone, were painted the most vibrant colors. I had never seen such a variegated kingdom. Not even Meyrial had this many colors.

Hyrissa would love it here. Shops that sold jewels and cloth and other small trinkets lined one side of the main street while food and drink were sold in the bars on the other. I hoped Kae would supply me with coins again. There was so much I wanted to buy, and I regretted spending them all in Zephlus.

I should have kept one or two, just in case.

Everyone moved in almost perfect synchrony. The people flowed from place to place in rhythm, like a song. They dressed in the most colorful frocks. I saw smiles on almost every face. Music flowed out from the open windows of several buildings and from musicians that fiddled with instruments in the streets. It was all so joyous. And almost overwhelming.

"Hey! Watch where you're going, lass!" a man's loud voice boomed above me.

In my astonishment of looking around, I had bumped into a man twice my size. His hand was on the handle of the sword that rested against his hip. I seized up and froze in place.

"Sorry! My sister's partially blind." Marsden appeared and grabbed my arm.

We both ran from the man as he led me back toward the group. Relief flooded through me. Though I would not hesitate to fight the giant, I was glad Marsden came to my rescue.

"Thank you. I seemed to have been distracted by the beauty of this place." I smiled at him.

He offered a grin in return. We flanked the back of the pack, trying not to cause any more trouble.

"It can get a bit risky here. You always have to be on guard. It's the most beautiful city in the world, but also the most dangerous. Naivia is basically lawless," Marsden explained.

I nodded and decided to make sure I paid more attention to my surroundings. Dyer was just ahead of me, and I knew he would not mind getting bumped into, should I lose myself to distractions again.

Kae was out of sight in the front of our group—she was shorter than the taller crewmates that separated us. If she wanted to play hard to get, I would not be opposed. This was a challenge that I was sure to win. I wanted to have some fun in my last days as a human. Besides, it was clear with her stammering and flustered state the night before that she was not invincible to this attraction either.

I smiled at the thought.

After an indefinite amount of walking, we finally stopped in front of the first ugly building I had seen since arriving. The walls on the outside were once painted a light green, though time and weather had chipped the color away, leaving a drab gray behind. Several chips of the lime-colored paint littered the ground beneath the walls. A few had fallen out, replaced by growing weeds.

"This is the inn where we'll be staying." Kae shouted to us. "I know, I know, it's not the same one as last time. The man at the harbor said this was the only one with rooms available. Apparently, we've arrived during the Festival of Music and everywhere else is all booked."

The exterior displeased me, and I could not even imagine the disarray that the inside held. Marsden did not hide his discontent by our choice of lodging and pointed out its many flaws.

"Last time we stayed at the Whaler's Inn. It was so much better and *clean*," Marsden grumbled as he kicked a loose stone out of his path.

Kae opened the front doors wide. We all filled in after her as she headed to the front desk. After a brief exchange of words and coins, the woman in charge led the way to a staircase at the far end of the room. She waved us to follow.

Several men carried satchels filled with their personal belongings. I envied the way their bags were filled to the brim. I'd brought only three outfits. The want for more coins from Kae crossed my mind again.

"This hallway should have enough rooms to occupy the lot of you. Two to a room. There you go now." The woman directed the crew to break off into pairs.

Kae tried to walk into the room with Dalton but was stopped.

"I don't see a ring on your finger, miss. Unmarried men and women cannot share a room. It is simply forbidden," the woman said with judgment in her tone.

I almost let out a laugh.

Dalton gave Kae a meager shrug before continuing into the room. The rest of the crew paid no mind as they paired off much as they did aboard the ship. The group dwindled down until only women were left—myself, Kae, and the owner.

"You two will stay in this last room. It may be the furthest from the stairs and exit, but look at that view! Enjoy your stay." The woman beamed at the two shocked faces that Kae and I wore.

She disappeared down the hallway, leaving us in silence.

"Are we to share a room?" I asked with a flicker of hesitation, trying my best to hide my triumph.

Kae's frustration was evident, letting air *whoosh* out from her nostrils as she huffed. She nodded, swung her old bag over her shoulder, and entered the room. I walked in after her and surveyed the place.

Kae threw her bag onto her bed—well, our bed—and looked out the window. There was only one large bed in the center of the room. It was twice as big as what I slept in back on the *Mar Daemon*, looking like it would be a lot more comfortable than my cot. It could easily fit two people with some space in between.

"Perfect. This is just perfect," Kae muttered and threw herself on the bed with a creak.

I stood awkwardly by the small dresser, uncertain of where to go or what to do. Kae ignored me and stared up at the ceiling.

Unsure if I should opt for some light flirting or silence, I dropped my bag on the side of the bed that was opposite where Kae was laying. If I made a move now when she was in this state, it would only drive a wedge between us.

A new idea lit up in my head.

"How about instead of moping about our sleeping situation, you give me a tour of the kingdom?" I suggested. "Everybody has been raving about Naivia for days. I would like to see it for myself."

I was not sure if Kae would take the bait. Spending time and getting close to her during our week here was the top priority on my agenda. Second on the list was indulging in anything and everything human. This would solve both on my list. Two fish, one spear.

There was a moment's hesitation before Kae answered. "Sure. I'll get Ruff and Dalton to join us. I can never leave those two alone without them quarreling," she mumbled and sat up on the bed.

Disappointment coursed through me. I would not be getting alone time with Kae, but the presence of her two loud friends always made things more entertaining. After all, she did agree to this little excursion. That was a step in the right direction.

Kae sat up and turned to me.

"Before we head out, I should warn you. This place, while breathtaking, is lawless and can get dangerous, especially at night. It's swarming with pirates and gamblers and everyone in between.

Be on guard at all times," Kae warned me in a similar way that Marsden did before.

Though I did not sense danger while in Naivia, I nodded anyway.

"I know," I said as I got up from the bed. "Marsden told me already."

Kae straightened up at that. "Since when do you talk to Marsden?"

"Should I not? Is something wrong with him?"

"No, it's not that. It's just..."

"What is it?"

"Nothing. Forget it."

I rolled my eyes at Kae's curtness. Despite my display of annoyance, I was secretly pleased with whatever this was. Jealousy? Protectiveness?

I walked to the doorway of our room and ran fingers through my hair. I would never grow completely used to how it felt dry, not flowing around me, suspended in the water. Kae stared at me, her face blank. I wished to read her thoughts, to know exactly what she was thinking.

"Well, are you just going to stare at me all day, or are you coming?" I asked with a slight uplift of a smile.

Kae grumbled and grabbed a few things before joining me out in the hallway.

I realized I had not been paying attention to where each person picked out a room as I contemplated where the two were staying, and I paused. Kae strode past me to the room that was next to ours. The door was wide open.

Dalton and Kenley occupied this room. Kenley was passed out cold on the bed, recovering from the night before most likely. Dalton tucked folded shirts into drawers. He handled his garments with precise care.

"Aqeara and I are heading out to tour the town. Care to join us?" Kae asked in a quiet voice as to not wake up Kenley.

Dalton shot his head up at us, startled, as though he had not noticed us standing in the doorway. The proper way of folding dress shirts was far more intriguing.

"I do expect food and debauchery will be involved. Of course, I'm coming." Dalton stripped as he talked, removing the shirt he was wearing and quickly replacing it with a billowy black linen one.

It was slightly open in the front, revealing a well-toned chest.

Kae scoffed and left the room to find Ruff.

"Too much skin?" Dalton questioned with a faint hint of insecurity as a few chest hairs poked out.

He looked at his reflection in the mirror.

I shrugged.

"If seduction is on your agenda, then I think you will fare well," I said, and Dalton laughed.

"Excellent," he replied, and left to follow after Kae.

I was right at his heel.

Several doors down and across the hall, Kae was leaning on the doorframe and talking about something I could not hear. Dalton peered in and made a sound of shock.

"Hey, no fair, you get your own room!" Dalton cried out.

Ruff laid in bed, tossing a large silver coin up in the air and catching it. He rolled over so that he could properly see us.

"Heard you lot were going on a little adventure. Will drinks be involved?" he asked.

"Yes, now get off your ass and let's go." Kae rolled her eyes and walked back into the hallway.

Ruff rolled out of bed and followed her out. His eyes widened at the state of Dalton's attire. Blood flushed Ruff's cheeks and neck as he gave Dalton a once-over.

"Nice outfit," Ruff said neutrally.

Dalton raised an eyebrow but smiled, anyway. He fumbled with the buttons of his shirt.

I led the way back downstairs to the main lobby of the inn while the three pirates followed suit. Dalton brushed past me and led the way, his shirt catching the air as he brusquely pushed open the double doors and walked out into the bright sun.

The busy streets were teemed with people carrying about their lives. Naivia was filled with echoes of musicians celebrating the Festival of Music. Sweet scents floated out of a shop that had pastries lining the windows. They looked similar to the one Rigby gave me from Zephlus, covered in the white powdered sugar. My stomach grumbled at the sight.

People chattered, catching up with those they have not seen in a while or bartering with owners of various stalls. Beaded necklaces hung from one stall, clinking against each other in a way that sounded as though they called my name.

Walking amongst the crowd as I trailed behind my new acquaintances, I felt completely and utterly human. Everyone appeared to be from all walks of life. From the way they looked to the way they dressed, there were no two people that were the same. It was wonderful. I fit right in.

For the first time in twenty days, I think I enjoyed being human. Perhaps... even loved it.

Chapter Twenty-One
Aqeara

The tour of the kingdom was more silent than I had expected. It took me a while to notice the lack of commentary. I was so engrossed in all the unfamiliar sights, sounds, smells, I constantly had to catch up with the others, nearly getting lost in the crowd more than once. As we headed toward the heart of Naivia, the density of the crowds increased. We had come during the most popular time of the year to visit the City of Song, as a passerby nicknamed it.

"Usually on tours, you are supposed to name and point things out as we pass by," I shouted above the noise of the crowd.

A woman wearing a green coat lined with pearls caught my attention. I almost drifted away and followed her.

"This area is all temporary housing and inns. Nothing is interesting here. Once we get to the Square, it'll be a lot better," Kae replied and pressed on.

"It all seems very interesting to me," I said, mostly to myself, but followed, anyway.

Dalton and Ruff paced back and forth to several stands, buying food and trinkets and other things I had no name for. The two offered Kae and I bites from their food each time. I tried something that tasted like an overcooked plant and declined all offers afterward. It was disgusting.

Ruff bought small silver hoops for his pierced ear and placed them in one on top of the other. I envied them and their coins but had enough pride to not ask Kae for spares.

Kae saw me watching the two men buying things, anyway. She caught my eye and wordlessly handed me two gold coins before she stuffed her hands back into her pockets and carried on as if nothing had happened. I smiled and pocketed the coins, knowing I should be wise and save them for later.

My attention wandered back to the enchantment that Naivia radiated. Ropes were strung up, distanced by every few buildings. They crossed over the streets, and on them hung unlit lanterns that were covered in colorful insignias that represented the flag of Naivia – a violin with a flute for a bow. I just knew that once the sun set, and the lanterns were lit, this city would glow.

The sun had passed its peak three hours ago. Sunset would reach us within another four.

And then it would leave me with just a week left.

The bitterness in my thoughts left me in a sour mood. I was enjoying my time here and did not want to think about murder. I tried my best to ignore the growing guilt at the thought of my mission and remained silent as we continued on.

The narrow street eventually opened up to a large town square. Shop stands and little tables were scattered around a large structure made of stone. I gasped at the contraption. Small streams of water shot up into the sky and back down into beautiful arches. I sniffed the air and smelled the ocean, despite being so far inland.

In the center of this oddity was a marble man half-submerged in the water. He held a large spear with three prongs attached, not too far from that of a fork. Something about it recalled a memory, though I could not quite place it.

"They built this fountain to honor Idros, the sea god." Dalton's voice crept up behind me. "The people of Naivia don't have an established religion, but they are superstitious. Their legends say that the sea god will protect them while they cross the ocean."

I turned to him, painfully aware of the frown on my face.

Idros was worshiped by the sirens, but it had never occurred to me he was a god to the humans as well.

"Like you said, superstitious," Kae said dryly to the fountain at my other side.

"You do not believe in any higher beings?" I questioned.

It was to our knowledge that humans had gods for nearly everything—that some groups of humans worshiped certain gods while others had their own higher beings to look up to.

"No. Avalon worships their own beliefs with the sun god, Atdia, but I have serious doubts that there's something up there watching over us." Kae spoke with indifference as she pointed up at the sky.

I looked at Dalton and Ruff expectantly.

"No one on the crew is all that religious save for Doc. He prays every night. The rest of us, well with the lives we lived, it's hard to believe there's a higher-up controlling everything," Ruff said.

I pursed my lips, considering his words.

It was a novel experience, encountering faithless beings. Though, it was intriguing to learn about people's diverse viewpoints.

"What do you believe in?" Kae asked, with a hint of judgment in her tone.

"Idros. He created sirens, so we worship the sea god," I said defiantly until I realized I was speaking from the standpoint of a siren.

I fought to maintain composure, hoping that my slip-up had gone unnoticed.

"Is everything in that rotten kingdom about bloody sirens? Have you brainwashed people no thoughts of your own?" Kae questioned, and her eyes widened in surprise when she finished speaking.

A sense of rage welled up inside me. I was through with her judgmental superiority complex. I turned and stalked away from her. Kae did not get to act like this. Not when I was contemplating on whether I would clench her heart in my fist in a matter of days.

You will kill her. There is no doubt.

But what if…

Stop. Think of Hyrissa.

I let my internal thoughts battle out and grew frustrated that I was even considering anything other than the only choice that I had. I weaved through the sizable crowd, trying my best to ignore Kae calling out my name. Shoulders bumped into my own and apologies were lost on me. My anger was simmering.

Take deep breaths. Calm down. How will you earn her trust by shoving her out?

I ignored the voice in my head and ducked down to squeeze past two pairs of legs. I was glad to not see a familiar face in sight. I longed to be back home, but losing myself in an unknown land with unknown beings brought a thrilling joy to me. I recognized no one or even where I was going.

A firm grip held on to my arm, and I did not turn around to face her. She had no right to seek me out. No matter how hard I tried to shrug the hand off, it did not budge. I spun around, ready to slap Kae in the face. I was so caught up in my swirling thoughts I had not realized how heavy and large the hand felt on my arm.

The face did not belong to Kae. An astonished breath escaped me as I craned my head up to see who the face belonged to. A giant man, nearly double the size of me, stared down at me. A large, red scar ran down one side of his face, leaving his iris white and cloudy. The other eye was black, void of any color. It narrowed at my cowering form. A cold smile stretched across the man's face, and I shuddered.

My daggers were in my bag back at the inn. Foolishness made me think I would be fine without them. I helplessly tried to yank my arm free again, to no avail. The man tugged me after him as he began walking away. His tall stature cast a shadow over me.

"My darling wife! I'm so glad to have found you. Thank you, kind sir. She tends to wander off on her own, the little deviant! How about some gold for your trouble?" Dalton's voice sent a wave of relief so strong it made me weak in the knees.

The man sneered as Dalton looped his arm around me. He pulled me closer to him and craned his neck upwards, something I was certain he had not done much before with his height.

The man glared at the two of us, but reluctantly let me go. He accepted the small bag of coins Dalton handed to him and disappeared back into the crowd of people.

I wilted against Dalton as my tense muscles relaxed, though my heart still raced.

He still held me close to him, his grip firm like the man might try to steal me away regardless of the money.

"I am sorry I lost you your coins," I said as we walked in the direction opposite the giant man.

Dalton brushed it off, but his shoulders sagged in relief. He was equally terrified of the situation I had landed myself in. I shuddered at the thought of him not finding me in time.

"It's nothing, just do me a favor, will you?"

"Anything. What?"

"Don't run off at the first sign of bickering with Kae." Dalton looked at me while he spoke. "She's stubborn and can be a handful at times. I get it. But it takes a while for her to fully trust someone."

The irritation must have shown on my face.

"And if you need space, at least make sure Ruff or myself are with you. I don't like admitting it, but this wonderful place can be very dangerous for a pretty face," Dalton said as he gestured to himself and smirked.

I laughed at his attempt to lighten the mood.

"Alright," I agreed.

"And don't go anywhere without your daggers!" Dalton groaned when he saw my lack of a sword belt.

I smiled sheepishly as we kept walking until we returned to the clearing by the fountain. Kae and Ruff lit up when they saw us, but both of their faces fell at Dalton's arm looped around me.

I broke away from Dalton and strode over to Kae. Time to be the bigger person.

I'd rather choke on rotten seaweed.

"Apologies for my outburst. It was unwarranted and rude," Kae said as soon as I was within earshot.

I was taken aback by the intensity in her manner. She had been worried about me; I could tell just by the look on her face.

"All is forgiven," I replied.

Compared to nearly being abducted by a seven-foot-tall man, a small spat with her was nothing.

Kae only nodded in return. A small smile that was meant to be reassuring broke out on my face. Kae returned it.

"Okay, now that we're all together again, we have to head to the western side of Naivia next. That's where all the good eateries are!" Ruff exclaimed and Dalton's features warmed up, probably at the thought of eating and drinking.

We continued onward, resuming our tour as though nothing had interrupted it. I was grateful, ready to put the giant man behind me, even as I eyed the crowds for him once again.

Time was lost to the four of us as we huddled over a table. This eatery was by far the one with the best food. Certainly, better than the last, though the third one was a close second. Our bellies were full of rich foods beyond what I could ever have imagined eating. I had never known human food could taste like this.

A man played an accordion in the corner of this quaint little place. It was a lovely background noise that drowned out the rest of people's chatter. The turn of the night elicited a delight in me that seemed long gone. Though I always tried to find the little pleasures in life, I had never felt like this since before Hyrissa—

"And the berries! It's a gift from above to be this talented at baking." Ruff interrupted my thoughts as he continued his praises for the dessert he had demolished.

He licked his plate free of crumbs. Dalton opened his mouth but shut it without saying a word. He looked away from Ruff as a faint blush spread across his face. Kae shook her head in silent laughter. Everything was so much funnier when there was wine sloshing in you. We had consumed two bottles' worth of the dark red liquid since we'd sat down.

I timed when Kae's attention was on me to lick my spoon clean of the fruity syrup. She looked away too quickly and stammered something unintelligible.

I smirked. Wine brought out all secrets.

"Oi! We're closing for the night," the man that brought our food earlier shouted at us from across the room.

His shouts brought out a round of laughter, but all of us stood up from the table regardless, myself a bit too hastily. I laughed again as I tried to regain my balance.

"We should probably head back to the inn. It's well past midnight." Kae tried her best to enunciate each word.

I giggled even harder. She shot me a look, but then burst into laughter so hard she snorted. I never heard her laugh like this before. It was genuine.

"I think we've been had," Ruff said as we all snickered our way out of the building.

My drunk brain had trouble translating the meaning of his phrase.

"What? Pfft, no," Dalton said, trying to compose himself.

It was a futile attempt, his words slurred dramatically. Kae cursed under her breath.

"Did that guy slip something into our drinks? Dammit. Naivians and their *good times* motto." Kae reached out and yanked a wandering Ruff closer to us.

The wine did not help with my state of confusion.

"What... are... you... saying?" I spoke slowly, as if that would stop my vision from spinning.

"Our server slipped elixirs in our wine goblets so we would feel the effects tenfold. They do that sometimes to get people to party more," Kae explained.

"He probably saw your serious face and thought to lighten us up," I mused and laughed.

"I think we all just drank too much," Dalton added.

Kae rolled her eyes and looped her arm around my waist. I gasped, and all my thoughts were muddled beyond reason. Perhaps it was to keep me from wandering or finding danger. Or perhaps it was something more.

I pulled free from Kae's grip, causing her to frown. The lanterns twinkled like stars against the night sky, and I wanted a closer look. I twirled beneath the bright lights, feeling like a youthling again.

The walk back to the inn faded from memory as we stumbled on our own feet. I kept close to Kae, even considered letting her wrap her arm around me again, as I worried that I might drift off or pass out on the cobblestone street.

Dalton began singing wildly off-key, and he swung Ruff's hand back and forth. Ruff looked down to where their hands were entwined and let out a huff of air before he laughed at Dalton's cheery mood.

"If we make it back in one piece, I will be surprised," Kae said, her eyes trained on the lanterns.

I giggled as I saw the inn appear within view, just a few buildings away. My head spun and my feet felt like they floated along.

We returned to the inn, barely conscious. I was exhausted and drunk. Anything else my senses picked up faded in the background like white noise. I bid Ruff and Dalton goodnight as they left into their respective rooms.

I was as light as a feather.

"I can sleep on the floor. I don't mind at all," Kae said after I plopped down on my claimed side of the bed.

I laughed and brought the covers up to my neck.

"Just get in the bed, Kae." I muttered through a yawn. "Stop being so dramatic."

The bed swayed like a ship out at sea, and Kae murmured something too low to distinguish. But the dip in the bed told me I had won this argument. I smiled and wrapped myself tightly in the thin blanket.

My dreams were filled with music—a blend of Naivian tunes mixed with siren lullabies.

I awoke to sunlight pouring onto my face. My eyelids fluttered open, and I basked in the warmth the morning brought me. It had been freezing when I had gone to bed, I could remember that.

Something on my stomach twitched. I looked down at an arm wrapped around my waist. My breath stopped mid-exhale. I was no longer on my side of the bed, but in the middle. And Kae was wrapped around me, our legs tangled.

How much wine did I have?

I coughed, and Kae jolted awake. A dagger was drawn and pointed at my neck before I could take another breath. We'd been in that position before.

I rolled my eyes and pushed it to the side with a single finger.

"You keep a weapon on you when you sleep?" I asked, irritation laced in my voice.

It was too early for this. I blinked away the grogginess and eyed the death threat still hovering near my face.

"Of course, I do." Kae said as she eyed our entwined bodies. "Did you move in your sleep?"

She retracted the dagger and placed it back under her pillow. With a shuddery sigh, she untangled herself from me before sitting up on her side of the bed. Kae's curls were all over the place, creating a halo around her head.

Feeling cold in her absence beside me, I rubbed my eyes and sat up.

"No. We must have been cold." I reasoned, and swung my legs over the side of the bed. "It was freezing last night."

Kae faced away from me, her head tilted toward the window. I quickly undressed out of my nightgown and threw on a shirt with a vest over it. I slid on the first pair of pants I could find and my dagger belt before I hurriedly strapped on my boots.

I did not like the feeling that welled in me at waking in Kae's arms. After all, I was planning on seducing Kae and winning her trust, anyway.

Why did it feel like she was seducing me?

"I'm going to get something to eat," I called over my shoulder as I practically ran out of the room.

Kae had no time to respond.

The two gold coins felt warm in my pocket, though I did not want to spend them just yet, especially on just food. I walked down the hall, seeing if anyone else was awake and wanted to venture out with me.

"Aqeara! Wanna grab food with us?" Atty's voice rang out from down the hall.

I smiled and nodded, making my way over to where a small group of the crew had formed. Perfect timing.

I needed time away from Kae to get my priorities straightened out, to plan my next move. A move that *I* would be in control of. It would be impossible to think straight with those cunning silver eyes staring at me.

And that very thought gave me doubt I could not afford.

The rest of the day I found myself in the company of the hunter and gunner boys. Atty, Birch, Kenley, and Arden proved to me that they were the most dangerous when put together. I had never met a more chaotic group of individuals. The life-threatening things done in the name of adventure led me to believe I would meet my maker by nightfall.

I peered down three stories to the street below and shuddered. Standing on the ledge of a rooftop made me feel like I was simultaneously on top of the world and one step from my grave.

"Come on, Aqeara! It's not that far of a jump," Arden called from the roof across from the one I was on. Atty and Birch stood beside him, egging me on. It was just Kenley and I left on this rooftop. He wanted to make sure I jumped before crossing himself. I thought it a kind gesture.

"If it's too much, I can lead you back down. But trust me, it's not that long a distance. You can do this," Kenley murmured in my ear.

I nodded. So, this was how I died. Not fighting off hunters or drunk men, but dropping to my demise. I hesitated.

Inhale. Exhale.

Who would have thought a siren to be fearful of heights?

"You got this, Soledel!" Arden exclaimed.

I could do this. I had to prove myself to these men. In a matter of hours, I had already become a part of their little group.

The things I do for you, cousin, I thought to myself as I took several steps back.

My feet carried me as I ran toward the ledge and leapt. My arms flung helplessly, grasping at nothing but air. The warnings Birch had taught me came to mind. I did what he told me to do and tucked my body into a ball, bracing for impact as I rolled onto the other roof. Birch whooped at my survival, the sound of it surprising me.

I stood up and dusted off my clothes. Kenley tumbled more graciously beside me.

"Heck, yeah!" Atty said, and clapped me on the back.

We walked to the opposite ledge and jumped in unison. There was no hesitation the second time. Nor the third or fourth time, either. By the fifth, I did not even think about what I was doing. My veins were pumping with adrenaline.

Having legs was proving to be one heck of a gift.

That evening was not as blood-pumping as rooftop jumping, but fun nonetheless. We stole several things from larger stands. I almost protested against it, but even Birch, the most mature out of the bunch, reassured me it was okay. Or rather, as okay as theft ever gets.

Pirates stole from the rich. And who was I to go against that? I wanted to be on their side, after all.

I was now in possession of gold hoops for my ears and a thin black bracelet that had a pearl in the middle of it. I held out my wrist and admired my new accessory.

With their deepened trust of me, I weaved talk of sirens in a way that would not appear too excessive. Atty and Birch were reluctant to keep the conversation going, probably out of discomfort from being the ones that did most of the killing.

Arden and Kenley, however, were thrilled to discuss them.

I had half a mind to believe that most of the crew did not really care much for siren hunting. They all had less-than-ideal lives back in Avalon and jumped at the first chance to explore the world.

Even with Atty and Birch, the pair enjoyed fighting in general, and had no personal vendettas against my kin. Perhaps I could convince them to hunt sharks instead. Idros knew I could do with less of those foul beasts roaming the waters.

"Today was fun. Thank you for letting me tag along," I said as we all headed back to the inn.

The sun had set hours ago. My feet drug on my way up the stairs as if the soles would split open if I took a single step further.

"Thanks for joining us. It's nice getting to know you more," Kenley said, and Arden nodded in agreement.

"One more reckless addition to our group," Atty cheered, and we all smiled.

I had steered clear of Kae for the entire day. Though I strangely missed our bickering, I knew it was for the best. Testing the waters to allow her to miss me was essential to my plan. Sleeping with her was the only way to solidify her trust in me.

Or you're just attracted to the captain.

I groaned and ignored my thoughts. They were probably right, but it did not mean I had to face the truth just yet. It was my desire to be with Kae, and yet I needed to justify why I kept prolonging the inevitable.

I shook my head and walked down the dimly lit hallway.

Bidding the boys goodnight, I made my way over to my shared bedroom. The entire walk back, I mentally prepared myself for what I would say when I returned.

It was wasted.

Kae was out cold, her hand dangling over the side of the bed. The faint snore of a deep slumber emitted from her peaceful state. This was a delightful turn of events. I was too exhausted for conversation.

I threw my stolen goods down on top of my bag and laid on my far side of the bed. My body would regret all the excursions tomorrow, but for now I could revel in the excitement of the day.

I stared again at Kae's slumbering state. She was vulnerable here. Yet, beautiful. None of my goddesses would compare to this one sleeping human. I turned my head, glancing at my daggers that rested near my bag. One swift plunge and this could all be over.

Why did I keep hesitating?

Tomorrow. I shall deal with this tomorrow.

As I closed my eyes, the song of my people filled my ears once again. It called to me.

Come home, Aqeara.

Soon.

Chapter Twenty-Two
Kae

"So, you're telling me that you've never seen the siren city?" I didn't hide my annoyance.

It had been twenty minutes since I walked through this fisherman's door. Twenty minutes of hearing his prolonged anecdote about how he claimed to have the location of the hidden siren city.

I had gotten word in Zephlus that this fisherman was the one to talk to about sirens. And yet, when I entered the small home on the other side of Naivia, I knew this conversation would not pan out well.

Garbage littered the floor. Random trinkets that appeared to have been fished out of the sea adorned the walls. Nonsensical scribbles filled the pages of open journals. I had refused the coffee he offered for my own safety.

"Well, no. But that would be rather impossible for a singular sailor like meself to see the city and make it out alive, wouldn't ya think?" he said.

"If you hadn't made it out, my day wouldn't be wasted here," I mumbled out of earshot. I had been polite to hide my frustration at the lack of solid intel at first, but my patience was dwindling.

"Listen, seeing a pod of sirens has got to mean something. That many at once? I'm telling you; southeast is where you wanna head. You'll find their home. Promise on me mama's grave." The fisherman crossed his heart before pressing his lips to his hand.

I rolled my eyes.

"Well, if that's all you have." I got up from the dining table in the tiny kitchen. The whittled wooden table looked as if it had weathered one too many storms.

"I hope this was useful, Captain Kae."

"Two hundred gold coins for such valuable information? I couldn't think of a better way to spend my day." Sarcasm oozed from my voice as I painfully slid the pouch of gold coins across the table.

"Pleasure doing business with you, lad," the fisherman said.

I pulled my tricorn hat lower on my head and tipped it down in farewell. The man did not get up from his table to see me out. I strolled out of his front door into the nearly empty street of northern Naivia.

Most of the revelry and businesses were further south, where we were staying. I was *not* looking forward to the hour-long walk back. Part of me wanted to turn around and slit the fisherman's throat to keep my coin, but I forced my feet to keep walking.

He wasn't the kind we stole from, and a deal is a deal, no matter how awful the terms.

On the walk back, I let myself get lost in the bustling life of the kingdom. The day was not faring to be the best, but in my solitude, I could truly think about the next move. I would keep the news to myself and let my crew enjoy a few days here. They deserved as much.

As for Aqeara, I wouldn't dare tell her I had potential news about where her pious sea demons are located. She could find out at the very last second before we dropped *zephlum* bombs on the city. It was a cowardly move, but I felt as though we were finally on good terms. I didn't want to ruin that just yet.

On the way back to the inn, I walked into the nearest bar and sat at the high stools. Before I knew it, hours had passed into the night. I had been lost in my angry thoughts, fueled by revenge to eradicate sirens, but hesitant to do just that.

I had spent so many long months searching for this siren city to wipe out the creatures once and for all. Why now, did I feel so hesitant?

It was getting late. I threw some silver down on the table and headed back out. My hand rested on my sword's handle the entire walk back, daring any passersby to try something. None did. When I returned to the inn, I had enough spirits in me to ease any feelings of awkwardness in confronting Aqeara. But she was not there, despite it being so late.

Part of me grew worried, hoping she was with some of the crew and not dead somewhere in the back of an alley. The other part of me was puzzled. When had I begun to care so deeply about the Soledelian's whereabouts?

I laid down, intending to wait up on Aqeara to see if she would get back alright. My thoughts drifted to flashes of bright orange and a lullaby.

I woke up once in my slumber to Aqeara dipping the bed ever so slightly as she laid down. When I closed my eyes, it was her face filled with pure joy, laughing at the dazzling lanterns that greeted me in my dreams.

The next morning, I woke up on my side of the bed and not curled up with Aqeara. A small wave of disappointment annoyingly washed over me. She was fast asleep on her side of the bed, wild hair covering her face like flickering flames. I could have nudged her awake, asked if she wanted to spend the day with me.

Nope. Don't go there, Kae.

I shook my head and tiptoed out of our room. I strode down the hall and grabbed Dalton and Ruff for some adventure. As we walked down the streets of Naivia, I internally kicked myself when my heart fluttered upon seeing any woman with red hair.

I needed serious help.

"You alright, Kae?" Dalton inquired when he noticed me staring at a woman with wavy red hair for a second too long.

My cheeks reddened. "Yes. F–Fine."

Dalton and Ruff provided the perfect distraction to get my mind off things. We ate, drank, shopped, and talked about pointless things. I always wondered if we would be friends if I hadn't put together my crew. Would we have even crossed paths? I couldn't imagine a life without either of them. It would be a boring life indeed.

And yet, I knew there would come a day when the three of us would separate. Live our own lives. Or at least, I would be separate. Taking over for my parents, a lonely life in the castle.

I shivered at the thought. Today was a day of merriment, not thoughts of the future.

This kingdom was the perfect place to lose yourself... but also to find yourself. The colors were excessive and even a bit distasteful, but it made Naivia seem even more surreal. Several hours of wastefully spending money found our trio in a bookshop. I perused the aisles, hoping to find something on sirens or Soledel.

There were about six bookshelves in total in the shop, all filled with books of various lengths. The warm tones of the place reminded me of when my mother would sit me and Edmonde by the fireplace and read bedtime stories to us—mostly hoping that our energy would dwindle and we would go to sleep at a reasonable hour.

My heart lurched at the memory.

"Excuse me, miss? Can you grab that book off the top shelf for me?" A young boy tugged on my shirt and looked up at me with expectant eyes.

He was skinny, with clothes that looked much too big on him. There was no sign of the boy's parents in the shop. My eyebrows furrowed.

"Sure. Which one?" I asked.

The boy smiled and pointed to the large brown book with a thick spine. The title read, *Fairytales of the Lost Kingdom*. Now that was something I didn't believe in. Fairytales.

Still, I stretched up and grabbed the book off the shelf and handed it to the kid. He smiled widely and gaped at the cover. It was filled with mythical creatures. One of them was a siren.

I frowned.

But sirens are real.

"Is that the Naivian flag on your shirt?" I asked and immediately questioned why I bothered.

I normally wanted nothing to do with children.

"Yes! I wear the flag wherever I go. This pin was my mother's, and she loved this kingdom, so now I love this kingdom as well," the boy said, sounding well beyond his youth.

"It is a very lovely pin," I noted.

"Thank you. I know that this place will always be my home. My uncle says we are to leave soon for another kingdom, but I don't want to leave. I want to stay here." There was a hint of sadness in his eyes as the boy spoke. "No matter where I am, I will keep this pin on me and be reminded of home."

I found myself relating to the kid. While I loved the sea, I knew deep down that Avalon was my home. I was proud to be from there. I missed it. The thought of my place in line to the throne crossed my mind, and I shook it away.

"Hey, here's a couple of bronze coins. You can pay for the book with them," I said in a knowing voice.

The boy's eyes widened. "I wasn't going to steal it!" he said in a defensive tone.

I winked and continued my search.

"Thanks, miss!" the boy said and before I knew it, he was gone.

"Hey! You have to pay for that!" the clerk shouted from behind his desk, though he made no move to chase after the young thief.

I smiled to myself and glanced up at the shelf to see if there was another copy of the book. So far, it was the only one that I could find that mentioned sirens. No sign of a duplicate.

I sighed and walked over to the next stack of books. Ruff thoroughly examined each book on the middle shelf. I scanned the titles and concluded that this was the fictional literature section. Most of the men on my ship could read, whether they learned at the academy in their youth or by others on the ship during our first year out at sea. I considered literacy to be essential, so as not to be conned by more knowledgeable thieves.

Ruff paused to admire a famous romance novel, seemingly avoiding my gaze. I made no comment. Dalton walked over from the opposite end of the aisle. He peered at the book Ruff was looking at and made a face.

"Wait, you can read?" Dalton asked.

"I hate you," Ruff answered with a blush creeping up on his neck, still holding tightly to the book.

I laughed and slung my arms around the two, hugging them both.

Day turned to night. We would soon have to leave for the siren city. Or where some messy old man thought it might be. I hated how fleeting time was, slipping away from me before I could gather my bearings. Time passed differently while in Naivia. It rushed by like a sharp gust of wind, leaving me disheveled and disoriented.

The entire crew was enjoying dinner at a tavern a few blocks from the Square. Discussions of exhilarating days and sinister nights were all anyone talked about.

I had no updates to give, and it was already our third night in Naivia.

The tavern was filled with patrons, all buzzing over their days like we were, stuffing themselves with greasy delicacies and spirits. It made for a pleasant background noise.

Atty and Birch sat closest to me, lost in their own conversation about something unheard. Marsden was across from me, telling a story to anyone that would listen of how he sampled enough free sweets at the local vendors today to count as a meal.

I nodded along, my eyes drifting every so often to Aqeara down the table, who seemed to be listening to each conversation in bits and pieces.

"Any word on siren sightings, Captain?" Barnes asked from across the table.

I froze but shook my head, trying my best to look solemn.

"No one's heard anything yet. As soon as we get even the slightest rumor, we can head out," I replied in an even tone.

Several of the crew grumbled, solidifying my intention of waiting a few days before breaking the news. It was the Festival of Music. Everyone was having a glorious time. They didn't need me and my drive for vengeance to rain on their parade.

Aqeara seemed oblivious to our conversation. She leaned over in her chair to speak with Arden and Kenley, laughing at a joke that I did not hear. I sighed and downed my rum as I attempted to look at anything else.

"Well, no offense, but I hope these rumors hold off on another day or two. I want to hit the tables," Ruff said, and a few men cheered.

I rolled my eyes at the statement—I loathed gambling.

"Here, here!" Birch said and clinked his glass with Ruff's.

The rest of the meal was filled with animated chatter about the night's plans. Several wanted to visit brothels, others were to head to the gambling tables. Dalton, though not keen on gambling as I was, took a sudden interest in it.

After our meal, we all split up, heading in entirely different directions.

"Please, just make it back in one piece," I said with a grin on my face.

They laughed and departed into the night. None asked if I was going to join them. They knew my answer and how I felt about gambling

"Will you accompany me on a walk?" Aqeara asked.

We were the only two standing outside the restaurant.

"Sure," I replied.

She smiled and led the way, though I doubted she had a destination in mind.

We continued in silence for two blocks, admiring the lanterns and the nightlife. The way the colorful lights bounced off Aqeara's admiring face had me considering that maybe colorful things weren't so bad after all.

The silence grew the longer we walked. I decided to be the first one to break it.

"Did you know Naivia is my favorite kingdom? Besides Avalon, of course. It has its flaws, but it is my home kingdom, after all. Anyway, even when there aren't any festivals, this city is always filled with music. There are constant parties and light shows and fireworks. Everyone does their own thing. And sure, it can get dangerous, but also no one cares about what you look like or how you dress or who you sleep with—I'm rambling."

I hated how I couldn't stop talking whenever I got excited. And how awkward I felt with Aqeara looking at me while I spoke. But she made no face of disinterest. She nodded her head and gave me a look of understanding, maintaining eye contact.

"It sure is beautiful. I love the music here. Back home, we would always make up our own songs. It was something I loved doing," Aqeara said in a somber voice.

She kept looking up at the lanterns, lost in thought. I remembered our earlier conversation when she told me she could no longer sing. She wore the same look of longing and sadness on her face. It pained me.

"I used to sneak out of the castle at night to hear the local bands play," I said, trying to steer the conversation away from singing.

Aqeara snapped her attention to me.

"You lived in a castle?" she asked with raised eyebrows.

"Yes... wait, you didn't know I was the princess?"

"The what—of course not! You never mentioned that before!"

"I assumed someone told you. Probably Dalton, at least."

"Well, no one did. And why Dalton, of all people?"

"Nothing. Never mind." I sighed. "Allow me to formally introduce myself. I'm Princess Kaelyn Amarant of Avalon," I bitterly said my full name.

Aqeara stared at me like I was a ghost.

"I like Kae better," Aqeara replied after some consideration.

I laughed and agreed with her. The way she brushed over my status like it was nothing was refreshing. No bows or second thoughts.

We found ourselves at the mouth of the Square. A band played in front of the fountain. People danced in a tight-knit crowd, clapping to the beat.

"Kae felt more like me, in a way. It helped me conceal my identity whenever I snuck out. Edmonde was the one to come up with it." I smiled at the forgotten memory.

Aqeara shot me a curious look as we went to sit at the small tables that bordered the Square.

"You're betrothed?" Aqeara asked in a voice that almost seemed to quiver.

I scoffed at the idea, momentarily pulling me out of my grief.

"No, he was my brother." The past tense with Edmonde always stung.

Aqeara tilted her head. "Was," she repeated. "What happened to him?"

It hurt, talking about Edmonde. It had taken me a while to tell the crew that the reason behind my vengeance against sirens—the "someone close to me" that I had lost to the sea demons was in fact my brother. Talking about his death aloud made it all the more real. It didn't matter that a year had passed. Whenever I thought about the fact that Edmonde was gone, it felt like that awful day when I received the news all over again.

"He died in a siren attack." I paused long enough to see Aqeara's face fall and then quickly compose again.

"I avenged his death." I murmured. "I killed the siren who murdered him. The day before we sailed off to Zephlus, actually. It killed another friend of mine, Kipp. I think you would have liked him. He loved Naivia's colorful lanterns."

Trying to stop the tears from forming in my eyes, I looked over at the dancing couples, and I could feel her eyes on me.

Aqeara stared at me with an oddly familiar intensity. I couldn't quite place it. She opened her mouth as if to say something, but closed it again.

After a beat, she spoke.

"I lost my little cousin before I left Soledel," Aqeara started and then trailed off when tears welled. She swallowed harshly before continuing. "Her death was the reason I left. She was killed, and I could not save her. The one responsible was killed by another... person. I thought with the murderer's death, I would feel at peace. But her avenger died as well. It's a vicious cycle, revenge. It eats away at you until there is nothing left." Aqeara's eyes glazed over as she stared off into the distance, where the people danced with glee.

"You always seem a lot wiser for an eighteen-year-old," I said, and Aqeara smiled like I had told a joke, "But I am truly sorry for your loss."

I offered a comforting hand on her arm. She looked down at it but said nothing. This was the first time Aqeara had opened up to me. I didn't know what it meant, but I was glad for it. It meant there was some sort of trust between us. That she didn't quite hate me as much as she once had.

"When I miss her, I try to think of the good times I had with Hyrissa. Like this one time..."

We recounted childhood memories with our lost ones and some just on our own. Though we both had different upbringings, we shared a love for music and the sea. I felt surprisingly giddy as we talked about our lives. With each story, I was able to piece together the puzzle that was Aqeara.

As I spoke of Edmonde and a fencing exercise gone wrong, I waved my hands to exaggerate my words. Aqeara laughed and though she could no longer sing, it sounded like a melody. She challenged which of us had a more reckless life and told me stories I would never have associated with her.

"You two nearly got killed by a shark? More than once?" I blinked several times, like I might have heard her wrong.

She must have been an exceptional swimmer. Aqeara laughed and nodded. Suddenly, I wanted to tell endless jokes just to hear her laugh a bit more.

"Hey, you nearly got your hand chopped off for stealing an apple for an old man. That seems more reckless to me," she countered.

"In what world is that more reckless? I was giving back to the poor," I defended myself.

"You actually got caught," Aqeara responded with a devilish smile that raised goosebumps on my arms.

I grinned back.

"Tell me one thing. Your people are obsessed with sirens, right? Hold on, don't make that face. I'm not trying to be mean here. If you worship the sea creatures so much, have you ever seen one personally before boarding my ship?" I questioned before Aqeara could protest my line of talk.

"Well, no. But many people in my kingdom have had peaceful encounters with them. Even conversations," Aqeara answered defensively.

"So, you believe sirens to be inherently good despite your only encounter with one being when that siren bit my arm?" I was dubious about Aqeara's priorities.

"Kae. You love the sea, correct?"

"Of course, I do."

"And the sea has given you terrible storms that threaten to capsize your ship." She stared at me, her amber eyes glowing in the lamplight.

I could see where she was going with this.

"Well—"

"It can also drown you. Should you stick your head underwater long enough? Yet despite its dangers, you appreciate the beauty of it. You only see the good of the ocean." Aqeara leaned back in her chair, satisfied at the way my brows furrowed.

She had a good point.

"The ocean isn't constantly trying to kill me," I replied.

"Sirens are not always out to get humans. Most are peaceful and merely hunt, when necessary," Aqeara said.

"How would you know?"

"Soledelian culture worships sirens. Surely you must not think that we would see them as deities if they were mindless killers?"

"They *kill* humans. Tear their flesh off and end their lives. Innocent people, dead."

Aqeara nodded in understanding when my voice caught.

"I wonder, who struck first? The sirens killing the humans that hunt them down? Or the humans killing the sirens for trying to survive?" Aqeara raised an eyebrow while she spoke, as if she herself didn't have an answer.

I said nothing and let her have this one. The conversation wasn't going anywhere. We both felt too strongly about our side. Though I did wonder, who struck first.

It had to have been sirens. We were their prey, their next meal. Humans only killed them in self-defense. I wished I could better understand Aqeara's viewpoint on the matter. I wished I wasn't so personally affected by the sea demons. I wished things were different.

The music surrounding us lightened my mood. I found I had grown tired of the spats I had with Aqeara. This right here, the discussions and the laughter, was something that felt comforting and safe. Feelings that I only felt when surrounded by my crew. Sure, there had been other women in my life, but none of those hidden nights lasted long. Whispering names like secrets and oaths. None felt like how I felt now.

Aqeara's eyes wandered back to the band and the dancing couples. She became so captivated by the songs, her lips curving upward when the lyrics to one talked about a forbidden lover. Her fiery hair framed her face like a halo. Amber eyes glazed over as she nodded along to the music. She was absolutely radiant.

"Dance with me," I said.

Aqeara gazed back at me with a raised eyebrow. I extended my hand and her confusion was superseded by fear.

"I do not know how to dance." Aqeara twirled a strand of hair between her fingers. Her red hair looked nice down without a bandana tying it away from her face.

"You can't be serious. Soledel worships sirens. They're all about music. And you can't dance?"

Aqeara crossed her arms in front of her chest. "I never tried. I am quite clumsy on my feet," Aqeara said in such a serious tone.

I almost laughed. I'd seen her fight with Ruff. That was practically a dance in and of itself.

"Let me guide you. C'mon." I walked over and dragged her out of her seat.

Aqeara squealed, but followed me toward the makeshift dance floor. She entwined her hand with mine as I led her to the middle of the crowd. Aqeara's breath hitched when I pulled her closer to me and rested my hand gently on her hip.

Who's the one making moves now, I thought smugly.

"What now?" she whispered in my ear.

I shivered and started moving my feet, absentmindedly falling into a waltz. The song was slow and reminded me of ballroom music that I had spent years learning to dance to.

Aqeara's look of pure concentration was adorable as she followed my footsteps. I had half a mind to bring up how she went from throwing daggers at me to this, but refrained from the comment.

"Ouch," I said when Aqeara stepped on my foot.

She smiled apologetically, but said nothing as she continued twirling the floor with me.

Our bodies were basically touching, pressed against one another. I tried to focus on my breathing, but whenever our eyes locked, it was as if all the air had been suctioned into a vacuum. With our faces this close, I couldn't help but picture how Aqeara looked, pinning me against the wall in her room. Her eyes darted to my lips, and I knew she was thinking the same.

The waltzing continued for a few minutes, and then the song ended much too soon. Aqeara didn't pull away. She stood there and waited to see what came next.

"Thank you for being an amazing crowd tonight! Now on to a more upbeat tune we came up with just yesterday. Drallon, hit it!" the singer shouted to us.

He motioned to the one playing the brass instrument, and the band picked up in tempo.

People started swinging with their dance, moving at a faster pace. This type of music always played at the local taverns back home. A memory of a blonde woman teaching me how to dance with her came to mind.

I smiled and pulled Aqeara toward me. I dipped her low and brought her back up. Aqeara gasped, and her eyes were full of mischief. She pushed away and spun me around, mimicking the other couples' moves. She was a quick learner.

We spun and twirled and stomped our feet to the rhythm. I laughed, twirling Aqeara despite her being a few inches taller than me. She giggled and allowed me to lead again.

The song ended faster than I would have liked. We were both panting, trying to catch a breath as the opening notes of the next song filled the air. Aqeara's smile was dazzling as she flashed her pearly white teeth at me.

"What now?" Aqeara asked in between shallow breaths.

She swept stray hairs back behind her ears. I looked up at the dark sky and then around at the dwindling couples. It was late in the night.

"We should probably head back to the inn," I suggested.

Aqeara frowned but followed me as we left the Square.

"Naivia is more dangerous, the later it gets," I explained, only half-lying.

Truthfully, I was dizzy from the buzzing onset of emotions. Desire. Confusion. Hesitation. I was also exhausted.

Aqeara nodded, and we walked the whole way back without a word.

As we went down the hallway of our inn, I stopped in front of Dalton's room. Aqeara kept walking. His room was still empty. Not even Kenley was there, and I knew he was an early sleeper. I walked to Ruff's and found it empty as well.

It was well into the middle of the night, but I needed someone to consult my feelings with. I would have woken them up if they had been in their rooms. Perhaps I would have spilled my guts about how tonight made me feel.

This is a sign to just keep everything in and deal with it later, I reasoned.

With that, I let out a sigh and walked back to my room.

I paused in the doorway. Aqeara was fast asleep on her side of the bed, her clothes discarded in a neat pile on the floor. She had time to change into a nightgown.

I frowned, disbelieving that someone could fall asleep so quickly. Her shallow breaths and parted mouth indicated otherwise. She was even snoring ever so slightly.

I quickly changed and stretched my joints, feeling satisfied when I heard the pops and cracks. I smiled to myself and climbed in on my side, not caring if I wasn't all the way on the edge. I fell asleep instantly and dreamt of rainbows.

Chapter Twenty-Three
Kae

"Will you wake up already?" Aqeara's singsong voice interrupted my dream. By the time I opened my eyes, I had forgotten what it was about.

Aqeara crouched next to me, so close that her liquid amber eyes filled my vision. I was startled and moved back. I didn't realize how close to the edge of the bed I was because the next thing I knew, I was tumbling onto the floor.

Aqeara giggled and peered over the bed.

"Good morning!" She smirked at my rude awakening.

I sighed and stood. A groan escaped my lips when I saw that the sun was well-risen. It was high noon.

"Was I out for that long?" I questioned.

"You were tossing and turning in your sleep. At one point in the night, you slapped me," Aqeara grumbled and got out of bed.

I smiled at that. I tried to conjure up memories from my dream, but all that came to mind were lightning bolts and stormy weather.

"Hello, darlings. That's one way to waste a day away. Had a bit of fun last night, did you?" Dalton materialized in our doorway and waggled his eyebrows seductively.

Aqeara tilted her head as if puzzled. My cheeks heated for absolutely no reason, and I threw my pillow at him.

"Hey!" he cried out when it hit him square in the face.

I grinned.

"We danced a bit in the square. My legs are exhausted," Aqeara muttered and massaged her thighs.

Now it was Dalton's turn to be confused. He shot me a look as I grabbed my things and headed for the door. I wasn't in the mood for him questioning why I decided to dance now when I never had before.

"What's on the agenda for today?" I asked.

It did not slip my mind that half my crew had been out far later than I had. And I'd been out late enough.

"Back to the card tables! You should've seen Ruff last night. He was on a roll. He won double his betting in gold. Even Birch didn't win nearly as much." Dalton beamed.

I was impressed. Birch was by far the best out of all of us in cards. His constant state of silence meant he had an excellent poker face. Ruff was a close second. Though I hated playing cards, I knew I was the third best out of the crew.

The two of us walked out of the inn. I tried to keep up with Dalton and his fast pace. He never had enough consideration for those with shorter legs.

"The rest are already at the tables. I had to come back to fetch more silver. Have you ever played before, Aqeara?" Dalton turned his attention on the sneaky redhead who had been silently following us this entire time.

I whipped my head around to see hers shake in decline.

"Is it a form of betting?" she asked as we continued to walk down the street.

"Yup. It's actually how Kae won the *Mar Daemon*," Dalton answered.

I rolled my eyes. As big of a win as that had been, that game was the last time I had played cards. I'd lost so many jewels that day in my desperation to win the ship. I vowed to never feel that weak or out-of-control again.

But in my paranoia about how easily it can be to fall into a gambling void, I figured I would pay my crew a visit at the tables to make sure all was well.

"Wow." Aqeara said lowly, but she didn't press on the subject. I was grateful for it.

We continued to walk toward the gambling halls located just before the Square. The owners were smart in having their businesses so close to the inns. It meant less travel time and more frequency for customers. It was also close to restaurants and shops. Most visitors never left the area during their stay.

I made us stop along the way to buy some spiced tuna and ale for our lunch. My stomach grumbled as I devoured the entire meal in minutes. Aqeara even made me buy seconds. The sweet spices were a Naivian specialty.

As we headed west, Dalton pointed out things that we hadn't seen on our tour when we first arrived in the kingdom. Aqeara's eyes remained wide the entire way.

We stopped right outside the major hub. Ruff was eager when he spotted us approaching. He bounced back and forth on his feet, like a ship over rocky waves.

"Hey! Did you get the extra silver?" Ruff asked, his eyes immediately going to the pouch that Dalton pulled out of a hidden jacket pocket.

"Yes, and I'm charging interest, so you better win," Dalton replied and tossed the coin pouch over to Ruff's expectant hand. Ruff grinned and scurried back inside. The rest of us followed suit.

Loud shouts of victory and defeat filled our ears as we entered the building. It was dark and dingy with the smell of booze and sweat and misery. I grimaced.

"You don't like to gamble," Aqeara guessed when she saw my face.

She stood behind me while Dalton joined Ruff, Birch, and Atty at a table. Other men surrounded it as well, trying to win their share in gold.

"No. I don't really like leaving things to chance," I replied.

"That makes sense. We sometimes make bets through games where I am from, though it differs greatly from here. I never liked it," Aqeara said with a scowl on her face.

"Because you would lose?"

"That, yes, and because my cousins always cheated." Aqeara's bitterness made me laugh.

She rolled her eyes at me, but even in the dim lighting, I could tell that her mouth quirked up ever so slightly.

We walked over to the tables, watching as the men carelessly threw down their earnings that were either won, stolen, or bartered. Birch was winning this round. A deep bruise that covered his right eye nearly closed it shut.

"What happened?" Aqeara asked her trainer at the sight of the black eye. Atty frowned.

"Got myself into a wee fight at the bar. S'nothing," Birch said before placing his cards down in another win.

He whooped and collected the earnings.

"Some people can be real judgmental jerks," Atty muttered.

Birch sighed. I drew my eyebrows together. I was about to ask for details, but was interrupted by a tap on the shoulder.

"Can I get you ladies anything while you watch your boyfriends?" a servant asked from behind Aqeara and I.

Aqeara turned to the man and then back at me, unsure of how to respond.

"Is there a bar? We'd love to sit there instead of watching our *boyfriends* waste our dowries." I flashed my teeth after I spoke.

The man frowned and pointed toward the back of the place, mostly out of sight from the tables. I tilted my head in thanks and led Aqeara away from my crew. We sat on the small, rickety stools that threatened to tip over if I shifted too much weight onto one side, and I waved the bartender down to order us drinks.

"I do not particularly like these bar tables. It reminds me of…" Aqeara drifted off, frowning as she eyed the other men sitting further down.

It reminds me of that night in Zephlus, I finished her sentence in my head.

"We can leave if you want. We don't have to stay," I said.

Despite hating the place, I would not leave Aqeara alone here.

I studied her face, trying to read her emotions as the bartender brought over two cups filled with fruit-infused rum. I took a sip, relishing the ice-cold taste of the local Naivian spirit.

"It is fine. I just wish they had some music," Aqeara said.

She was right. The only song here was the chorus of shouts at the end of each game. I downed my drink and ordered more.

Aqeara and I laughed together as I recalled my jailbreak story to her. I tried not to make it noticeable when I clutched onto the bar counter for balance. Naivian rum can seep into your bones if you're not paying attention.

"You always get in trouble for helping others. The apple for the elderly, the bread for the little girl. You are selfless, like a princess from tales," Aqeara said between sips of her drink.

I scrunched my nose. I was a fearless pirate captain and siren hunter, not some sweet fairytale princess.

"I've severely hurt people before." I pouted comically.

My head spun at Aqeara's proximity.

"So have I," Aqeara said with a straight face.

I raised my eyebrow at her, not sure if she was joking or not. I certainly wasn't, but I wondered what sort of violence she had encountered. I didn't bother trying to pry. We continued back and forth some more, sharing stories and tales of our lives. Aqeara seemed to have endless memories.

Aqeara was in the middle of telling me a story of how she discovered jewels in a shipwreck not too far from Soledel when we were interrupted by Dalton. He ran up to us, white in the face— well, paler than usual.

I immediately tensed at his forlorn expression.

"Hey, uh, don't get mad, Captain," Dalton said, and his formal greeting toward me was sobering.

This was not good.

"What did you do?" I asked with an immediate suspicion that Dalton got into some sort of trouble.

"Ruff got hauled away! I couldn't stop them, there were so many. They claimed he was cheating, but I was watching him play the entire time. I think he's been set up. There was a guy with a nose ring that was moving his hands too fast the entire time! He said he'd free Ruff for five hundred gold coins." Dalton was exasperated as he spoke.

He tugged at the bottom of his shirt. Despite his tall stature, Dalton seemed small. This was unsettling for him.

Dalton's face fell as I felt mine turning red.

"Are you *insane*? I don't have that kind of money on me! What did you guys get into? Where are the others?" I demanded.

I was seething, rising out of my stool so fast that the metal scraped against the floor with an unpleasant groan, which might have made me wince had it not been for the steady ringing in my ear. Dalton flinched back. He knew this was precisely why I hated gambling.

"He was feeling confident and wanted to play at the higher tables! I advised against it, but you know how damn stubborn he is. The others left a while ago. They have no idea any of this happened." Dalton avoided eye contact.

I could not even form the proper words to express myself.

"Nose Ring Guy told me where to meet up with the money by midnight. I know where he is. Maybe if we snuck by earlier...?" Dalton trailed on, either not sure of a plan or too afraid to make one.

He let out a quiet "please" and I could tell how frightened he was, not of me, but *for* Ruff.

Aqeara shifted in her seat beside me. I had forgotten she was there, listening to all of this.

"What if we broke him out? Like how Ruff broke the two of you out of jail in Eayucia. I can distract whoever while you free him," Aqeara suggested in a quiet voice.

I regretted telling her that story if a dangerous jailbreak was all she got from it.

"No, the last thing we want is to be on a hit list if this *Nose Ring Guy* turns out to be one of Naivia's aristocrats. We have to play it safe. If we show up, we might be able to work something out," I said, though doubt had already planted its seed in my mind.

I thought of the strange nickname Dalton had used for the man that kidnapped my friend. It made him seem less of a threat, to be distinguished by only a piercing.

Dalton frowned at my statement. He already knew what I was thinking. We had to act soon, and we had to act fast.

"I'll lead the way," Dalton said, and he led us out of the bar.

Dalton's twin swords were strapped to him. My cutlass sword was on me. Aqeara's daggers were either hidden or forgotten as her belt was not tied to her waist like it usually was. This slimmed our odds if only two of us were armed.

No plan, money, or numbers. My blood chilled.

We hurried as we cut through the Square. It was less crowded than usual, but we still had to push through several people before we made it to the other side.

My worry for Ruff's safety grew as we continued to dash block after block after block. I once again thought of the nickname. Surely a man whose only distinguishable feature was a nose ring rather than a scar or something sinister meant he wasn't as intimidating as Dalton was making him out to be. I ran through several scenarios in my head, mentally preparing how the three of us could get out on the other side of this with Ruff unscathed.

While we ventured onward, the buildings gave way to large warehouses. The crowds thinned until only a handful of people remained on the streets. I had a sinking feeling about this part of Naivia. I had never been there before.

"This one. The one with the red X on the side." Dalton said. He pointed to what looked like an ordinary abandoned warehouse.

The painted X was not what I'd initially thought it to be. As we drew closer, it was obvious that it was drawn with fresh blood. The symbol reflected the more dangerous groups that prowled Naivia. The ones that tourists and natives alike avoided at all costs.

I groaned at the sight. Few rules were imperative to learn upon arrival in such a lawless kingdom. One of them was staying away from these types of symbols.

"Oh no," Aqeara gasped.

She frowned at the building.

Dalton's face turned a pale shade of green. I pulled him away before he could make guesses on whose blood it belonged to. We walked through the open entrance into dim lighting. There were staircases, multiple hallways, and presumably many doors. I hadn't the faintest idea on where to start. The place looked like a labyrinth. The eerie silence only added to the swell of worry resting in the pit of my stomach. My heart was racing, and it felt as if the blood drained from my head. I kept fumbling my grip on my sword handle, standing near Aqeara in case she wandered off.

Dalton led the way as we tiptoed deeper into the place, turning right down a large corridor. Our backs were braced against the wall to remain unseen, blending in with the shadows. As we marched on, muffled screams sporadically broke the silence. Every muscle in my body tensed. The sounds didn't seem to belong to Ruff, but the fact did not ease the rapid beating of my heart.

"I don't think I can charm my way out of this one. We need to break him out and get far away from this place," Dalton whispered as he stopped in his tracks.

Aqeara breathed quietly behind me.

"Go around the corner down there. I will go to the screams and seduce someone into letting Ruff go, or at least distract Nose

Ring Guy long enough for you two to set him free." Aqeara's voice was eerily resolute.

I questioned her sanity.

"You can't be serious. Do you know how *dangerous* that is? You'd be outnumbered," I said in disbelief.

A flicker of anger washed over me when Dalton did not join in my objection.

"Dalton is a man, and you look way too intimidating. Now I do not know what these men prefer, but I am guessing someone who looks dainty, delicate, and vulnerable like myself can get close enough without suspicion." Aqeara's voice grew steadier as she spoke. "I can take them."

"You don't even know how many men are down there! And where are your daggers?" I hissed at her.

I could tell from her huff that she was growing annoyed with me. I didn't care. This was out of the question. I wanted to reach out ahead of me and smack Dalton for remaining silent. I couldn't see a damn thing in here.

"On me. I can take care of myself. Besides, I will not *need* them. I told you, I know how to seduce a man," Aqeara whispered.

I sighed, knowing I'd lost this argument. I should be the one coming up with a plan as captain that didn't involve putting anyone else in danger. But this was our only plan, and I knew it.

Using her as bait could work.

By the state of this warehouse, no aristocrat would be caught dead owning a place like this. It had to belong to someone with a terrible status—otherwise, why risk ransom for five hundred gold coins? It would mean that if we broke Ruff out, no law or those in power would come after us. Just a cowardly band of thieves.

Dalton's voice interrupted us before I could answer.

"Okay, so there's about twelve men in the room down the hall to the left. It connects to another room adjacent to that one, which is where I think they're holding Ruff. We would have to get through all those men to get to him. The screams came from that room, but stopped before I could get a good look. I think that person is dead and Ruff might be too if we don't hurry." Dalton breathed his words out so fast, I hardly understood him.

He had scouted ahead, and I hadn't even noticed from arguing with Aqeara. I cursed under my breath.

"Let's do a roundabout, so we come from the side. There might be another door leading to Ruff's cell. Aqeara, you're our bait. Distract them while we try to get to Ruff. Yell 'coconuts' if anything goes south and you need immediate help. Understand?" I ordered.

Aqeara might have nodded, but I couldn't see a thing.

"Yes," Aqeara said.

"Good," I replied.

Despite being blind in the dark, I felt the moment she left, like she sucked all the warmth out from the dingy hall. I held tight on to Dalton's sleeve as he led the way down the hall and around a bend. We kept veering left until we were certain we were parallel and on the opposite side of the room Dalton had discovered.

"If anything happens to her…" I trailed off, not wanting to finish the sentence.

How would I react? Things had changed so much between us since arriving in Naivia.

"I've fought against her. She kicked my ass, remember? She can handle herself. You just have to trust her," Dalton whispered as we trudged on.

That was the thing, though.

Did I trust her?

Did I even have a choice? Ruff's life was on the line.

We kept walking down the hall that hopefully had another door to Ruff. This building was intentionally designed to confuse unwanted visitors. I took in several deep breaths, trying to not let my nerves get the best of me. Surely Dalton could hear my heartbeat thundering in the damp silence. My rapid breathing left me dizzy.

I refused to lose another friend. We would be okay. Soon we would drink ourselves sick, laughing over this whole affair.

A few torches hung from the walls, flickering every few feet. I squinted and walked over to the first door we encountered. I pressed my ear against the wooden door, straining to hear any familiar voice. Dalton did the same at the next door down.

"Anything?"

"No."

"I think their room was further down, come on," Dalton said and crept slowly.

I trailed right behind him.

He halted and quickly pressed his back against the wall. Not knowing the reasoning behind his sudden movement, I flattened myself beside him, anyway. Our shoulders were touching, and I could feel Dalton breathing rapidly. I peered into the darkness where we were hidden, out of reach of the light from two adjacent torches.

A man walked down the hall, not noticing us as he passed. He had a round belly and no hair. I squinted to see if I could locate a nose ring. I held my breath.

"Not him," Dalton whispered once the man rounded a corner. It wasn't *him*.

We pressed on, shaken up by the close encounter. I kept my hand firmly on my sword's handle in case we were surprised again. A shrill voice spilled down the hall. It was familiar.

I paused.

"How about we go somewhere a little more private? I am sure you do not wish to share me with your other men." Aqeara's voice carried through an open door ahead of us.

It was a higher pitch than usual—almost childlike.

Dalton and I were just underneath the light of a candle when someone walked out of the room. I pulled Dalton back into the safety of the shadows right when Aqeara exited with a man. The man had a golden nose ring and Dalton sucked at descriptions. This man was *enormous*. He was as tall as Dalton, but far more broad. He wore a tricorn hat with a feather attached.

Pirate captain.

A shudder ran down my spine when he wrapped his arm around Aqeara's waist and pulled her against him.

"This way to my bed chambers," he said in a deep voice as Aqeara allowed herself to be led further down the hall. I stared in shock.

"She'll be fine. We have to get Ruff out," Dalton said through gritted teeth.

I could tell just from his tone he was equally disturbed by the thought of Aqeara fighting a man twice her size. He seized up, breaths coming out in pants. If I were a betting woman, I'd wager my coin on Dalton wanting to strangle the man responsible for kidnapping Ruff and towing Aqeara away.

We entered the room they'd just exited. Lanterns lit up the place, allowing little shadows to blend in. The walls were made of damp concrete, as if the many bodies inside captivated all the heat and moistened the air.

A sleeping man slumped in a wooden chair in front of a jail cell, doing an awful job of guarding it. Past iron bars, another room was connected by the small cell. A dozen men sat in the far room, seated at a table with liquor sloshing in their cups and scantily clad women dancing around them. The hoots and hollers left a chill in my bones.

On one side of the cell, a dead man lay in the corner. His eyes were glassy as he stared up at nothing. Blood pooled from the back of his head. On the other side sat Ruff.

His arms were tied behind his back. A cut ran down his cheek. His shirt was also covered in blood splatters, and his arms were bruising. His head hung so that blood dripped off his lips straight into his lap.

I sucked in a breath.

"I'll kill every single one of them," Dalton said in a murderous tone.

I was already planning on it, but his sentiment softened me a bit. I'd always assumed Dalton genuinely disliked Ruff with the way they bickered. It was nice to know crew loyalty rose above all else.

"Who the fuck are you?" a man's voice called out.

Dalton and I froze in place. The shouting from the other room had woken the slumbering guard. He stared at us, his face turning down into a scowl. The other men all looked up at us.

Ruff lifted his head and grinned when his eyes landed on us.

"Here we go," I muttered as Dalton, and I unsheathed our swords in synchrony.

Chapter Twenty-Four
Aqeara

I was going to enjoy killing this man. Despite no longer being in my siren form, I still knew what men desired. It had been way too easy to waltz in and blend among the women they paid to be there. I was only in a corset now—my long-sleeve shirt had been discarded in the shadows of the halls.

The nose-ringed man named Garroway was a brutal maniac. He kidnapped, tortured, and killed for fun. His crew of miscreants were just as guilty. I heard them saying as much as I hid in the shadows on my way to the room, passing a pair of them discussing their *activities* from the past week. I had a feeling I knew that despite whatever sum of money the men paid those dancing ladies; they did not know was to become of them.

I shuddered at the thought as Garroway led us out and away from the others. As we walked down the hallway, I could not shake the feeling that we were being watched. I could only hope that Kae and Dalton were somewhere close by, lingering in the shadows.

"Here we are, my sweet." Garroway's breath was hot against my skin.

I had no time to react as he threw me onto his bed.

The force knocked the breath out of me; the quickness taking me by surprise as my head hit the soft mattress. Before I could get up, the pirate captain was on me like a shark on a seal pup. I squirmed beneath him, no longer bothering to keep up any pretenses. Garroway kept me pinned down with ease—he was double, if not triple, my size. I could not breathe.

"You're so gorgeous." His mouth was at my ear, and I shivered in disgust.

He mistook it for pleasure, placing rough kisses at my neck, making his way to my mouth. I turned my head to the side before he could crash his lips against my own.

"Allow me to undress you." My voice was hard to steady in my stress, but it worked.

Garroway broke away and sat up.

I got up and unbuttoned his shirt slowly, feeling his ravenous eyes on me. I tried to think of ways to get out of this, if I had taken enough time for Kae and Dalton to break Ruff out. Garroway was breathing rapidly, distracted by my half-exposed breasts that spilled at the top of my corset.

The monster shrugged out of his unbuttoned shirt. I reached behind me as if to pull on the strings of my top. Instead, I grabbed the dagger handle that was locked between my corset and its lacing. It had remained hidden beneath my hair.

I pulled the weapon free with ease and slid the blade across Garroway's throat in one swift motion. He jumped back in shock and fell off the bed. I rushed over to see if I had cut deep enough. I had not.

"You little bitch!" He gargled on his blood. Garroway got up from the floor with little difficulty and swung a fist at me.

I ducked out of the way and swiped at his kneecaps. He screamed more in anger than in pain as he toppled over.

I lunged at him, driving my dagger into his heart, hearing the crack of his ribcage. I stabbed him five more times for fear I had not killed him. I felt no remorse. Never for men like him.

I ran out of his bedroom and did not stop running until I made it back to Ruff's prison cell. The shouts of fighting led my way in the dark, though I was cautious of each step. One wrong turn, and I would be lost in this puzzle of a building.

I knew I had finally found the room when a man was thrown out of the open doorway. His unconscious body skidded inches in front of my feet. I stumbled over him and regained my balance. Candlelight reflected off the hilt of Kae's dagger, buried right above his heart. I wiggled the weapon free and peered inside.

Dalton was fighting off two men at the same time. He was bleeding profusely through his shirt, but it did not appear to affect him. Ruff, now free, had his sword in a man's back. He wrenched it free and continued his onslaught. Kae stumbled backward after bashing her head into that of another man.

Her head tilted toward me. Her lips moved soundlessly, and her eyes were wide. I noticed a beat too late. A man appeared from behind and hurled himself at me. I yelped as we both went down. A sharp sensation filled my side, like I had been punched. He had stabbed me in our fall.

"Ugh!" I shouted at the sight of my torn corset.

I was dangerously close to being topless.

I slipped the dagger out and winced as a sharp pain kicked in. I slid my blade across his throat and shoved his body off me. My left side was throbbing. I put a hand to it and came back with blood dripping down my palm.

It was only a scratch.

"Dalton!" Ruff called out.

I turned and saw Dalton outnumbered four to one.

As Ruff tried to reach him, he was knocked over by another man. He winced in pain as his arm was twisted back. Kae's head shot up and looked for her friend mid-fight. It had cost her a cut on her arm. She was too busy to break free and help.

I rushed over and brought my dagger down on the back of one of Dalton's assailers. It was too late. Dalton dropped to his knees after a sword ran through his stomach. I screamed and blocked a punch before plunging my two blades into the man's eyeballs.

Dalton fell over while I fought the remaining two men. Ruff and Kae were still preoccupied.

"You fight a useless battle. Garroway is dead!" I exclaimed to the minions.

They hesitated before bringing their swords down against my daggers.

"You and the other bitch are ours." A blonde man whose hair was matted with blood spat at me.

Dalton, though gripping his stomach on the floor in a puddle of his own blood, tripped the blonde. I threw a dagger at his friend, aiming right for the heart. I then doubled back and stabbed the fallen blonde man.

A hand on my shoulder made me whirl around, dagger raised for attack, but it was only Kae. She grabbed her dagger from my hand and wiped it clean of blood. I ran back and freed my thrown dagger.

"Dalton!" Ruff cried as he knelt in front of the injured man.

I looked between Ruff's agonized face and the way Dalton stared at him as if he were the sun. Something clicked from watching the two of them, but I had no time to process it.

Bodies surrounded us. Blood mixed and pooled together, creating a thin layer of red liquid across the entire floor of the room.

"I'm fine. Get off me," Dalton grumbled and swatted Ruff's hovering hands away.

Kae and I exchanged a look. He was not fine.

"They nearly killed you!" Ruff cried. "You shouldn't have come here. I'm grateful that you all did, but this was my mistake to deal with."

"Sometimes you can be so dumb-witted!" Dalton exclaimed and winced at the effort.

"It's dim-witted, genius," Kae interjected, with worry lines creased in her face.

"What does light brilliance have to do with intelligence?" Dalton questioned before passing out.

"Shit!" Kae said and knelt down.

Dalton was losing a lot of blood.

"We have to get out of here. Now," Ruff said, on the verge of tears.

Kae went to work, ripping the bottom half of one of the unconscious men's shirts off. She used the cloth to bind Dalton's wound.

"Help me carry him," Kae said in a detached, monotone voice. Her eyes darted around, giving away her rising panic.

Ruff picked up Dalton and hoisted him over his shoulder. His strength should have been deterred by his injuries, but he was determined to walk out of the place.

"Lead the way," Ruff grumbled through strained breaths.

He must have been blindfolded on the way here. He seemed to have no knowledge of where the exit was.

Kae had a look on her face like she wanted to chew Ruff's head off, but remained silent as she surveyed the bodies on the ground. She shifted a few with her foot and let out an exclamation when she found a familiar-looking cloth pouch. It was the one Dalton had given to Ruff filled with silver. Kae held it out to Ruff before realizing his hands were full, trying to keep Dalton from falling off his shoulder. She pocketed it and looked down the hallway for more of the crew, but we ran into no one on our way out.

"Where do we go?" I asked once we were out of that madhouse.

"Back to the inn and hope that Doc is there," Kae said, a frantic tone in her voice.

We remained silent the rest of the way back. At one point, we stopped to check Dalton's pulse. His bleeding had slowed, but so had his breathing. I was worried sick with each passing minute.

Our pace hastened, driven by the fear of losing Dalton. He remained unconscious the entire way.

Kae and I ran ahead into the inn to scout for the Doc. Relief flooded through me when I found him applying ointment on Dyer's healing nose.

"Help us! Dalton was stabbed," I said, with tears already flowing down my face.

The Doc and Dyer ran past me and down the hall where Ruff had just reached the top of the stairs. Kae explained to Dyer what had happened, tumbling over her words like they could not leave her mouth fast enough.

"Bring him to the nearest bedroom and place him on the bed. Let me get my supplies," the Doc said in a solemn voice, and he ran to his room.

Dalton groaned as they placed him on the bed. Ruff's forehead creased with worry, but he didn't look away. Kae seemed dazed, but I was still riding my adrenaline high.

"Leave us. I need to assess the damage." The Doc instructed and kicked the three of us out. "Dyer, help me stitch him up,"

Dyer closed the door behind them, with an apologetic shrug.

"This is all my fault," Ruff said and slid down the wall.

He pulled his knees to his face. I was about to go comfort him when a sob broke out of him, pulling Kae out of her trance.

"You're damn right it is! I can't believe you selfishly went to those higher-up tables. You know they're always cheating, so why gamble with your own fate? Aqeara nearly had to sacrifice herself as bait. You could have been beaten to death. If Dalton dies, it's on you." Kae spat out venom.

Ruff and I flinched. Her face was red. Ruff said nothing in response, but kept his eyes on Kae. Her face was plastered with worry, and I knew she was more terrified than angry.

He stared at a spot in front of him. A tear streamed down his face. I looked back at Kae with reluctance, scared she would yell at me, too.

Kae was crying. She slid down the wall like standing was taking too much out of her, and sat beside Ruff, who embraced her while she sobbed.

"I'm sorry. You know I am. This was all a huge mistake. If it weren't for you three, I would be dead. Dalton will make it. He has to," Ruff murmured, repeating that last sentence over and over to himself.

I wanted the ability to teleport as I stood there feeling like I was interrupting something. The raw emotion between the two was overwhelming. Suddenly, my own face was wet with tears.

Here I was, crying over a human. Not just any human—a man. I wiped the ocean-like water from my cheeks and stared. These were ordinary tears, but the mere existence of them proved extraordinary. I cared for these humans, whether I wanted to admit it or not.

The bleeding had stopped in my side but the pain lingered. Kae had a cut on her cheek. Ruff was bruised everywhere. The three of us sat against the wall, too scared to utter a word. Time passed by slowly, as if it were trying to catch up with us from the way that warehouse fight had blurred.

After what felt like an eternity, Dyer opened the door and walked out to us. His hands were covered in Dalton's blood, but his face showed no sign of worry. There might have been a hint of a smile on his face.

"He's going to be okay." Dyer said with a sigh. "Doc gave him a strong numbing salve and stitched him up. He's resting."

The three of us shot to our feet. We went inside while the Doc left to get more supplies.

"Dalton!" Kae exclaimed, and carefully gave him a one-armed hug.

Ruff and I stood in the doorway.

"Ouch, Kae. I'm fine, really. Stop fussing." Dalton said in a raspy voice.

"Dalton, I feel—" Ruff's apology was cut off.

"It's over. Put it behind us. Though you do owe me for nearly dying. How about you fetch a round of rum on you?" Dalton said with a hopeful smile.

"Dyer, would you mind going with him?" Kae asked, casting a sideways glance at Ruff.

He seemed bent out of shape, frazzled and pale.

"Sure, I—" Dyer said but was cut off.

"I'll be fine. Promise," Ruff said and strode out of the room.

"I'm assuming you yelled at him while I was knocked out," Dalton said to Kae.

She looked offended, but she nodded, anyway.

Dalton frowned.

"It was *his* fault." Kae said. "But he is forgiven."

She turned her attention to me.

"I am glad you are okay," I said.

Dalton made a face when he looked at me, his eyes focused on my aching side like he could somehow sense our nearly matching wounds.

"You're bleeding," Dalton noted, pointing to my cut.

I was still covered in blood, though most of it was not my own.

"It is shallow. I will live," I said just as the Doc returned.

Kae took in my torn corset and walked over. She pressed a hand to my side and frowned at the fresh blood on her palm. The cut must have reopened when I hastily stood from the hallway floor.

"Let me sew her up," the Doc said and sat me down on the edge of the other bed.

I winced as the needle threaded through my skin. A small yelp escaped my lips, despite wanting to appear strong when before these pirates I had only just stopped loathing.

"Hey," Kae said softly, bringing my attention away from the blood and to her face, "it will only hurt for a little bit longer."

She did not once look away as we held eye contact. I bit my lip as the needle went back into my skin.

"Are you hurt?" I asked Kae.

She assessed her injuries and shook her head. "Nothing a little time can't fix," Kae answered with a grim smile.

The Doc snipped the extra thread and gave me an encouraging smile. I looked down at the thin black stitching on my bloody side.

It was not too bad. Definitely not as pleasant as healing in my siren state.

"I do hope Ruff went to that shitty bar down the street. I don't care if it looks run-down. I don't want to wait an hour for some alcohol," Dalton complained, and I laughed at his pout.

"If any of you need me, grab me from down the hall. I'll come back in a few hours to change your bandages," the Doc said and left the room.

"Thanks, Doc!" Dalton called out.

It was then that I relaxed. Dalton was okay. We were all okay. It was over.

I let out a big exhale, and Kae's face softened. I was aware of how rumpled and unbecoming we were, but neither of us left Dalton to change. Dalton dozed off for a bit while we waited for Ruff. Kae and I remained silent, not wanting to wake him. We kept roving our eyes over the other, making sure no other injuries were in sight.

Fifteen minutes passed before Ruff entered with four mini barrels. They were each twice the size of a regular glass.

"That crappy bar is actually not that bad. I got these fruit-infused rum drinks for cheap. Look, they even came in these little barrels to travel with!" Ruff exclaimed. Dalton jolted awake and blinked several times.

"Oh, sorry mate," Ruff said.

Dalton waved him off and made a grabbing motion with his hands for the drinks.

Ruff passed around the drinks, and we all stared at our mini barrels before opening the lid and taking our first sips.

"This is super strong." Kae coughed.

"It is delicious," I said.

"I like it," Ruff noted.

"I guess this makes us even for Eayucia," Dalton said between sips.

He looked at Kae, calculating whether she would explode at the mention of the fight. Kae took a large swig in response.

"Yes, yes, of course we're even," Ruff said in a serious tone. Dalton smiled and continued drinking.

"Why?" I asked.

"It's a long story involving a loaf of bread and a prison break," Dalton said in a casual voice, as if he were discussing the weather.

A faint memory came to mind. Kae had mentioned that Ruff used to hold his prison break over Kae and Dalton's head for the longest time. Now he could no longer do it.

Ruff was red in the face from the alcohol. From his queasy look, I was certain he would be spew out the rum any minute. Dalton had passed out after twenty minutes, not even finishing his.

Kae's words slurred, though she tried so hard to keep herself steady. I was seated next to Dalton's resting body. I pushed his matted hair away from his face. He looked so peaceful sleeping.

"I'm going to bed before I vomit," Ruff said and stumbled out.

He gave one last soft look at Dalton before leaving.

"Goodnight!" I called out.

Kae stared at me with a frown on her face. I did not tear my gaze away until she broke first. She got up and left the room with a soft huff that left me intrigued.

I followed her.

Kenley passed by us as we headed to our room.

"He doing okay?" Kenley asked.

"Yes, he's sleeping. Wake Doc if you need anything," Kae instructed.

Kenley nodded and disappeared into the room.

Kae kept walking, not offering so much as a glance behind her. I peered into where Kenley and Dalton's former room was, expecting to find an open door with Atty and Birch inside—they were the ones to swap rooms with Dalton and Kenley—but only found a closed door and silence on the other side.

In fact, the whole floor felt quiet. A pin drop would sound like an explosion there. I wondered if they were all sleeping, or if they remained inside in fear of stepping out of line.

Kae was tense as I shut the door behind us in our bedroom. I hoped we could talk or something. Anything. I was wide awake and filled with rum. The nightmares from today would haunt my sleep, and so I did not wish to embrace them.

"You are angry," I concluded when Kae forcefully let her cutlass clatter to the ground.

She sat down on her side of the bed, legs touching the floor with her back to me.

Kae said nothing.

"Back to the silent treatment again? I thought all the dancing and laughter we shared meant something," I grumbled and placed my dagger on the floor next to the one I had left behind.

Kae huffed a sigh and laid down on her side of the bed without a word.

"Fine. I am going out. Maybe I will check on Dalton," I said as I discarded my torn corset and slipped on a dark blue shirt.

Kae's back was still to me. I had no intention of going back down the hall. I just had a sneaking suspicion that he was the reason Kae was cross with me. I was too tired and too sore and too drunk to deal with childish antics.

"Great! Why don't you go sleep with him while you're at it?" Kae muttered. I almost did not catch it.

"What?" Shock tinted my voice at her forwardness.

The moonlight shining through the window was the only thing that allowed me to properly see Kae as she sat up and faced me. Her eyes challenged my own, and I did not look away.

"Do you seriously think my being nice to Dalton and caring for him means I want to sleep with him?" I asked when Kae said nothing in response.

"Yes?" Kae responded meekly.

Her gaze sharpened on me.

"Kae, he is not the crew member I am attracted to," I said.

Even in the dim moonlight, she was radiant. Like a promised death if I kept staring at such beauty. I could not look away, could not deter my wandering thoughts as I continued to gaze at her. My nerves frayed at the thought of finally admitting how attractive I found Kae, even to myself. How much I wanted her; spell be damned.

"Oh. *Oh.*" Kae's voice was shrill. She ran a hand through her curls and sighed. "I'm sorry for being cross with you. It was immature. You can sleep with whoever you want."

Kae said, as if she still did not understand. My frustration grew at her obliviousness.

"For Idros' sake, it is *you!*" I exclaimed and leaned onto the bed.

My lips crashed against hers.

Kae made a noise that I would cherish forever as she pulled me onto our bed. Her lips were everything I imagined and more. She tasted of fruit, leftover from the drink. I swiped my tongue against her lower lip and broke the kiss. Kae shivered as I placed gentle kisses down her throat. I kept trailing my lips down her skin until I reached her collarbone. With a flip that was too fast to register, Kae was on top of me. My back was against the soft mattress. She kissed me, and this one was deeper and electrifying.

"Are you alright?" Kae breathed against my throat.

I'd forgotten how to speak. I barely managed a nod of my head when Kae flashed me a dazzling smile. It turned sinister, and my heart raced.

Kae tugged at the bottom of my shirt and lifted it over my head. I did not feel vulnerable, but I did feel conscious of being laid bare to this woman. My worries dissipated when Kae's lips reached my throat.

I gasped and felt her smile against my skin. She kept up with her trail of kisses as she made her way down to the hem of my pants.

"Kae," I breathed.

She shuddered at her name escaping my lips. I was enjoying the way she reacted to me. I wanted this to last forever. To think we could have been doing this so much sooner.

There's not enough time.

"Aqeara," Kae murmured against my thigh, breaking me out of my meddling thoughts.

My head tilted back into the pillow. I was afraid I would pass out. Kae undressed herself with swift ease. She was experienced in this. I stared at her bare chest and pushed her back onto the bed, keeping the wound at my side in mind as I carefully hovered over her. Our lips met again. And again.

Chapter Twenty-Five
Aqeara

We had stayed up until the sun rose before passing out in each other's arms, doing our best to remain as quiet as we could so as not to give the crew something to talk about later.

I felt relaxed and at peace, something I had not felt in weeks—if ever. I wanted this feeling, this moment, to last forever. The tendrils of sunlight were the last thing I saw before drifting off to sleep.

A knock at the door interrupted my dreams. I was continuing the night with Kae while I slept and was annoyed that I had been awoken. I grumbled and stretched my arms out in front of me. It was still morning.

Kae had been unfazed by the knocking. She snored carelessly beside me. I smiled at the sight.

Another knock rapped against the door, this one more impatient than the first. I got up and quickly slipped into my discarded clothes. I lifted the sheets to cover Kae's body before opening the door.

"Hi, Aqeara!" Atty greeted me cheerily.

I smiled and tried not to look too suspicious as I closed the door behind me.

"Good morning, Atty," I greeted in return.

"I was actually hoping to speak to the captain."

"She is still asleep. Should I wake her?"

"Oh no, it's fine. We can wait. It's just, we're all so excited. Dalton was telling us about the big fight and filled us in on all the details. He mentioned that Kae told him about meeting with a guy who knew where the siren city was. We figured we'd be leaving as soon as possible to the southeast heading, but wanted her approval first before packing up." Atty saluted me and walked off.

My ears rang with an imaginary shrill noise. I reopened the bedroom and disappeared inside, barely hearing the *click* of the shut door.

I sat down on the bed, ignoring the creak under my weight, and tried to collect my bearings. My head spun; my thoughts ran rampant. I knew that several hundred miles in that direction was where Meyrial was.

The siren city. My home.

How had they figured it out?

Kae knew. She knew their location. She was *looking* for the city. This entire time.

Someone must have miscalculated. We have rules in place that sirens could not breach surface unless after a certain distance from the kingdoms. It was to protect us and Meyrial's location. But even if Kae sailed directly above the city, Meyrial was deep below the waters. It would be impossible for a human to dive that far down without oxygen.

"Up so soon?" Kae called to me in a way that made my skin tingle.

At the moment, I could not distinguish whether it was excitement or fear. It did not calm me in the slightest. Acute awareness that I had slept with the captain of the siren hunters dawned on me. And yet, my heart tugged at imaginary strings. The lines representing everything I knew and stood for were blurred.

She killed Noerina.

She was avenging her brother and friend.

I sighed at the small voice in my conscience. It did not change the fact that she killed multiple of my kind. Planned on killing more. In three days' time, this would all be over with. It had to be.

At that, my stomach dropped. It was too soon. I had to make a decision that either resulted in the death of Kae or the permanent death of Hyrissa. A numbness settled over me.

"Is something wrong?" Kae asked as she dressed herself.

I knew she would find out the cause of my mood shift soon.

"Atty came by and said the crew wants to know if we are leaving today." I spoke in a robotic tone, trying desperately not to show any emotion. "They know you received word of a possible location for the siren city."

Kae stiffened at my words and stared at me. I knew she was trying to search for any sign of disapproval, but I refused to give it to her.

"Right. I suppose it's time to depart Naivia," Kae said flatly and grabbed her things before walking out of the room.

I remained sitting at the edge of the bed, staring at the blank wall ahead. Whatever euphoria I felt the night before was a distant memory. I had gotten what I wanted. I seduced the pirate captain. I gained her trust.

Why did I feel so empty inside instead of triumphant?

Hyrissa's face bubbled to the surface of my thoughts and remained there.

I would do anything for my cousin. For my kin. I looped my dagger belt onto my pants as my fate became more concrete. I tied a black corset onto my body and put on the jewelry I had stolen a few days ago.

It felt like another lifetime.

I tied back my hair mechanically and tucked away any loose strands. With another sigh, I grabbed my extra clothes and stuffed them into my bag.

I exited the bedroom, closing the door and any joyful memories behind me. It felt like being sent to a watery grave.

"The rest are waiting downstairs," Ruff said when I passed his room.

He shut his door and slung a satchel around his shoulder.

I nodded.

"Listen, just because we're heading toward sirens doesn't necessarily mean we'll find any." Ruff tried to comfort me.

The kind gesture threw me off guard. I glanced at him and could tell his intentions were sincere, but it made him uncomfortable. To him—to all of them—I was just a passionate siren lover. To them, this would only sadden me, perhaps even anger me deeply. But I would get over it. Because I was a human. If only they knew their new friend was one of the very things they aimed to wipe out.

I followed Ruff down the staircase that led to the lobby. There, the rest of the crew had gathered. Kae stood by the front doors. She looked up at Ruff and me as we made our way over to the crew.

"Okay, everyone's here! Let's move out. I know, I know our trip was seemingly cut short, but it's time we get back out on the sea," Kae addressed us.

A few grumbled, but all raised their fists in the air.

My arms remained down, holding on to my belongings.

We all marched out of the inn and toward the harbor. I studied each man carefully and thought back to the many interactions and conversations I had with them.

To them, this voyage meant freedom and a better, more adventurous life. A life away from poverty. It was only Kae who really harbored an everlasting grudge against sirens. The thought did not make me feel any better. They would all still follow her every command, even if they trusted me and my judgment.

If I were to appear before this crew in my true form, would any of them hesitate to kill me?

Would Kae?

I did not like the answer that filled my thoughts. Hypocrisy crossed my mind as I mentally filtered through different plans to take her heart.

Being back on the *Mar Daemon* made everything feel real. They were going to sail toward Meyrial and unknowingly float right above my home. I knew they would never find it and probably turn around to visit another kingdom in a circle of hopelessly following leads that may or may not put them on the path of a siren. Perhaps after some extended amount of time, Kae's crew would grow tired of her antics and suggest a new motivator for their journey. One could only hope.

But they would never get the chance. Their captain would be dead soon.

"Hoist the sails and bring the supplies below deck." Kae hollered her orders. "Arden, raise the anchor. I want people swabbing the decks immediately. It's filthy and reeks of raw fish. Barnes, plot our course due southeast. We're ready for departure!"

Everyone scurried to their respective positions.

I grabbed a crate of food and brought it below deck. I did not want my resolve to waver by looking at Kae's infuriating, symmetrical face or risk thinking of the way it felt to have her steel gaze on me.

"Put that over here, Aqeara. Thanks." Rigby led the way to a corner where I piled my crate on top of his.

I walked over to my room to drop my things off, unsure of what to do next. How was I to act normal with these men when I would take their captain—their friend—from them?

I needed more time.

There was a bucket half-filled with water next to my bed. I thought it strange. I remembered cleaning my sick from the bucket and emptying any remaining contents. I peered down at the water and gasped when it turned a bloody red.

Salophine, I thought with a strike of fear. She was trying to contact me again, probably to rush me in finishing the job.

No. There was still more time.

The sea witch would just have to wait until the last possible second. Grabbing the bucket, I left my room and climbed up the steps to the ship's railing. I dumped the bloody water over the side of the railing into the ocean, hoping no one noticed the contents.

"Hey, Aqeara! Grab a mop and bring the bucket over." Atty grinned and waved a hand toward me.

I smiled and walked over, wanting something to do that would take my mind off things.

Sweat trickled down my temple as I swept my mop back and forth. I occasionally glanced toward the horizon behind us as Naivia shrunk in the distance. Soon, it was out of sight, taking all the fun and joy with it.

As day turned to night, I found myself amongst friends as I sat at the dinner table with Atty, Birch, Arden, and Kenley. The dangerous bunch were talking—arguing—about explosives, debating whether grease from cooked fish could catch fire and be wielded as a weapon. At some point, Rigby had joined and offered us his two coins.

I sat back, for the most part, delighting myself in the simple pleasures of being human. This was what I would miss the most. The banter, the drinking, the laughs.

Sure, sirens had fun, but when warriors were on duty, laughter meant relaxation, which meant we were off our guard. Even a chortle would cause a verbal lashing.

Dalton had stopped by for a bit as he left his hammock for the first time since we departed. The Doc had ordered him to rest, with Kae agreeing. Though he winced every so often when his movements were too swift, Dalton was tough.

Ruff constantly trailed behind him, fretting over him and making sure he was okay. I smiled at the pair and wondered just how deeply their feelings ran. It seemed that they had not yet confessed them to one another.

I would miss them. Even the exhilarating fear of not knowing whether I would make it out of that warehouse alive was something I would miss. The dangers of Naivia made me feel as though I had not lived for a century and a quarter, but merely for the four weeks I was given a pair of legs.

Though I avoided Kae, all thoughts that led back to her and the sacrifice I would make. It did not stop me from entering her quarters late that night after everyone had gone off to bed.

Chapter Twenty-Six
Kae

Damn me to the depths of the sea. If my mind wasn't already made up about Aqeara, it sure was now. The first morning at sea after leaving Naivia left me feeling groggy.

I woke up before Aqeara did. She slept peacefully on her side of the bed, tangled in bedsheets. Her chest rose and fell with each deep breath. Her red hair was splayed wildly across her face. She was beautiful, captivatingly so.

Not wanting to wake her from her peaceful slumber, I crept from the bed and quietly dressed myself before padding out of my room. The door shut with a soft *click* behind me.

Ruff, Arden, and Kenley were on the main deck, peering over the railing. They greeted me before returning their attention to whatever was in the ocean. Each of them held a fishing rod in hand.

"Morning," I said and walked over to them. My steps paused mid-track when Arden dropped a *zephlum* bomb into the water. I frowned.

"What are you doing?" I questioned and walked over to look over the side of the *Mar Daemon*. I was hoping they were fishing, not experimenting with explosives.

Several dead fish floated to the surface near where Arden dropped his bomb. A net lifted them up, pulled by a bitter Kenley.

"You know how he is with his ideas, Captain," Kenley muttered as he brought the net onto the ship.

They collected the fish into a small bucket with a mischievous set of snickers.

Ruff ignored the two gunners as he reeled in his own catch, a respectable flair about his stance.

"Just be sure we don't find any *zephlum* pieces in our meals," I said.

The two nodded at me.

I left them to their fishing and checked in at the helm. Dalton sat cross-legged on the floor, studying a map. I knew that he had fresh bandages beneath his loose shirt. His bleeding had stopped and Doc had said that Dalton would be all healed up within the next few weeks. It still upset me to see my friend flinch whenever his pain flared up.

Barnes steered with swift a confidence that lightened my mood. He had come a long way from the nervous, jittery boy he was when we first started out.

"All good, boys?" I asked.

Barnes gave me a smile and Dalton, a thumbs up.

"Aye. Heading southeast as ordered, Captain. Weather is ideal," Barnes reported.

I peeked at the map Dalton was studying. It was of the southern kingdoms. The direction we were heading didn't have any markings of discovered land. We would be on our own without proper navigation.

Staring up at the cloudless blue sky, I thought of what we might discover. The weather was more than ideal—it was perfect.

I descended the steps and tried to take my mind off things as I made my way down below. My stomach growled at the scent of food, and I remembered I had not eaten the night before.

"Morning, Captain!" Rigby was oddly cheery today.

I smiled and sat down at the dining table.

Dyer, seated across from me, looked up from the book he was reading. He nodded his head at me while he chewed on his breakfast. I glanced down at the book, noticing sketches of different knot-tying techniques with small captions beside them.

"Fresh tropical fish should be ready in an hour if you want to wait. Otherwise, there are eggs for now." Rigby placed a plate filled with two hard-boiled eggs and a slice of bread in front of me.

"This is fine. Thanks, Rig," I said and immediately dug in.

Salt and pepper were the only seasonings we could restock in Naivia, but I was grateful we found any at all. There had been a scarcity of spices in Zephlus.

As I gulped down the fresh water in front of me, Aqeara descended the steps. She was quiet with her head down, not wanting to draw attention. Her red hair cascaded over her face, shrouding her in fire. Her shirt was rumpled, as if she had hastily thrown it on mere seconds after waking up.

I watched from the corner of my eye as she swiftly walked to her room, unnoticed by anyone but me.

Rigby moved food crates while Dyer concentrated on his book. I smirked under my cup as Aqeara emerged a few minutes later. Her hair was combed, and she wore a new outfit. She shot me a dirty look at my amusement but sat down beside me.

"Morning, Aqeara! We have eggs and toast for breakfast today." Rigby said as he placed a plate down in front of her.

"This looks delicious, thank you," Aqeara said.

She daintily ate her meal in a way that would have raised suspicion to anyone if they were paying attention, exaggerating every move. She lifted her fork with the precision of a royal, going about the motions as if a teacher were watching her every move—a memory I wasn't too fond of.

Aqeara pointedly ignored me. I smirked and gave her a sideways glance. She sighed into her drink, trying to hold back a smile. I got up and looked at Aqeara and her half-eaten plate. She was focusing way too hard on it.

As I gave Rigby my plate and headed upstairs, I wiggled my fingers in a certain way that had Aqeara blushing furiously before I left for the main deck.

"Captain! We've caught all kinds of colorful fish, come see! The waters here are incredible." Arden shoved his bucket in my face before I could adjust my eyes to the sunlight.

I frowned at the putrid smell of raw fish. The carcasses of blue, red, and yellow striped fish filled Arden's wooden bucket. I walke over to investigate the other buckets to find their contents equally colorful. Some of them were only half of bodies.

"How many of these fish did you blow up?" I asked skeptically. Arden's mouth twisted into a wicked grin as he hauled the buckets downstairs for Rigby.

"Too many," Kenley muttered.

He grabbed two buckets, one in each hand, and brought them down.

Ruff leaned over the railing, lost in thought as he stared out into the sea. I stood next to him and followed his gaze. Dolphins jumped alongside the ship. Their blueish-grey skin shimmered against the bright sun.

"How have you been?" I asked.

"I'm fine. Tired, I suppose." Ruff sighed, and I sensed something was bothering him.

I knew better than to pry; if Ruff wanted to voice his thoughts, he would.

"One can never be sad in the face of dolphins," I noted, staring at my favorite sea creatures.

They zoomed underwater and roamed wherever they pleased. I envied them.

Ruff chuckled and placed a warm hand on my shoulder. He left to retrieve the last of the fish buckets and vanished below deck. The sounds of the dolphins calling to one another masked Dalton's approaching steps.

"I couldn't help but notice Aqeara running out of your quarters 's morning. Did you request an early meeting with her?" Dalton's voice appeared over my shoulder.

I shuddered at his implication and turned to him. He had a shit-eating grin on his face.

I rolled my eyes.

"Yes, we discussed what actions to put in place should we spot a siren. It seems we thoroughly disagree, as per usual. I assume she stalked off long after I left," I lied through my teeth, knowing damn well that it was no use when it came to Dalton—he knew me too well.

"Hmm, indeed. She had a guilty look on her face when we made eye contact, so I'm sure that was why." Dalton ran a hand through his hair.

His grin hadn't faltered.

Disinclined to talk about it, I shoved against his shoulder and stalked off. I climbed up to the crow's nest to get some peace and quiet away from Dalton's maniacal laughter. Few had been up in the crow's nest. Occasionally, Marsden or Dyer was stationed as lookout, but it was rarely used.

Whenever I craved solitude away from everyone, including Dalton, the crow's nest was my oasis. Dalton was terrified of heights, only following after me if I was behind the rum barrels.

The never-ending horizon stretched out before me. Miles and miles of deep blue sea surrounded the *Mar Daemon*. Nothing else was in view. Not even the dolphins swam alongside my ship. Only a fine line where the sky met the sea was visible. A slight breeze pressed coolly against my skin.

Time slipped away from me up here. There were no distracting faces or existential thoughts, only the breeze that left me at peace in my solitude. The sun had reached its peak and started to descend back toward the horizon.

An equal beauty that rivaled the sun stood directly below me. Her fiery red hair was pulled back, and I couldn't quite read her face from this high up, but I knew Aqeara was staring at me. When she didn't avert her gaze, I climbed back down with caution to avoid slipping in front of her.

"Find anything interesting up there?" Aqeara asked, her tone split between curiosity and worry.

"Nope. Nothing but clear skies," I replied and jumped the last few feet onto the ground.

Aqeara leaned against the mast and frowned.

"You left me in your bedroom this morning," she said flatly.

I couldn't decipher the meaning behind it.

"I didn't want to wake you," I replied.

"I am pretty sure Dalton knows."

"I know. I'll talk to him later."

"Do you regret it?"

"The sex? Of course not," I answered.

Aqeara gave me a brief smile, letting it fade as she eyed the horizon again. The worry was still behind those amber eyes. I desperately wished to read her mind.

"Good," was all she said before returning below deck.

The pull to follow her was strong, but I knew something was troubling her, and I didn't feel it my place to press. Instead, I walked back up to the helm. I checked in on Barnes, feeling the gust of wind breeze through us.

"Wind is picking up a bit," Barnes said while looking up at the sky.

"Have Marsden keep an eye on it," I said, and Barnes saluted the command.

I crouched down to where Dalton poured himself over parchments. Dalton had stayed up here for most of the day. He sketched our heading, making note of the vast expanse of sea we were crossing. This was unknown territory for most, and he took it upon himself to create a new map.

Once Barnes' shift was over, I would take the wheel while Dalton continued to rest, an order he'd protested increasingly.

"If you want to take a break, would you consider having a chat with me in my quarters?" I asked sweetly.

I may have laid it on a bit thick. I was nervous. Dalton raised a brow but shrugged. He rolled up his parchments and tied them with a thin piece of leather.

"Lead the way." He motioned to the stairs.

I led him to my room and closed the door behind us. The last thing I needed was someone eavesdropping. I lowered myself onto the edge of my bed, suddenly full of nerves. Dalton sat down in my desk chair and tilted it back.

"Is this about you and Aqeara? You know I can keep secrets," Dalton reassured me.

His face was creased with worry.

"I know you can. I just... I don't know." I huffed a sigh of frustration.

Talking about my inner thoughts and feelings was proving to be a lot harder than I'd expected. It wasn't something I did often. How were people so vocal all the time? This was exhausting.

"When I'm with her, I feel different. Not in a bad way, I don't think. Just different. And it was in a bad way before, but now so many things have changed. Am I making any sense?" I threw my hands up in the air, wishing what I wanted to say could be transferred easily into spoken word.

Dalton stood up and sat on the bed beside me.

"You care for her, though you hate to admit it, because the two of you are just so different when, in reality, you're more similar than you think. You act rudely to her in hopes she'll hate you, but deep down, you desperately want her to like you. You seek her approval and when she shows you any contempt, you avoid her in hopes of never seeing the hateful look in her eyes again." Dalton did not look at me while he spoke. His eyes were glossed over as he stared at a random spot on the wall across from us.

"But you can't keep away for too long. It drives you mad. Not even in your own thoughts will you admit to yourself the way being with her makes you feel. She makes you feel alive. And, when you start to realize you truly care for her—beyond words—you isolate yourself in the crow's nest all day. Because deep down, you're terrified if she cares for you as much as you care for him... her." Dalton slumped back and cursed under his breath.

I whistled as the silence got heavy. His words rang true, way too true. It was scary how well he articulated my feelings. Though I wondered how much of that was meant for himself than me, I could feel his words turning in my head.

"Wow," I said, incapable of any other words.

My thoughts fluttered about.

Dalton placed a comforting hand on my knee. It was an anchor to steady my down-spiral. I leaned against him and took a deep breath.

"Be brave and tell her how you feel. Don't keep quiet and regret every passing moment," Dalton said with what sounded like regret.

I couldn't help but wonder if he was talking about Prince Zecheriah of Zephlus or someone entirely different. I hadn't let the little gender slip of "him" go past my notice. There was double meaning woven in his speech.

"That's the thing, though. I don't think I just care for her. I think—" I cut myself off from saying the final three words when I heard Aqeara's peals of laughter just outside my door.

Her words and Barnes' response were muffled. Dalton gave me a little shove toward the door. His smile was sad, but encouraging. My muscles tensed. I would have to inquire later about who this mystery man was that held Dalton's affection.

"Oh, for my own sake, get out there and tell her before I tell her for you," Dalton said.

He opened the door and pushed me out.

Aqeara was leaned over the railing, admiring the sunset. I walked over to her and stopped. She looked ethereal. Her lips were parted as she marveled at the colors of the sky, and I felt my breath hitch. It was seeing her like this that made me realize.

I loved her.

Chapter Twenty-Seven
Aqeara

The warm colors of the sunset flooded my vision when the familiar sound of Kae's boots slapping the deck echoed in my ears. She stopped abruptly beside me as I turned to look at her, but could barely register that soft look on her face before a strong wind gusted through the ship.

It blew the sails inside out, steering us completely off course, and I heard shouts from whoever was at the helm. Kae shouted at Barnes. Marsden and Dyer came running from below deck. Everyone seemed equally confused. The weather had been perfect—too perfect, even.

Dark clouds swallowed the sky and its enticing colors whole, as if one blink had turned the vibrant sky a dismal grey.

This was not natural.

Another gust of wind, stronger than the previous one, blew directly at me. I slammed into the railing and then plummeted over the side of the ship into the churning waters below.

"Aqeara? *Aqeara!*" Kae's frantic voice carried over the screaming winds.

I spit out the ocean water and tried to stay afloat. A crash of thunder boomed in the sky above. Something wrapped around my legs, pulling me underwater. In a moment of panic, I choked on a gasp of salty water.

The water was dark and opaque—I could not even see my own legs. My nails dug at the restraints, and I nearly gagged when my fingers brushed against a slimy substance. I kicked my legs back and forth with as much strength as I could muster. Nothing was working, and I was running out of air.

Pressure began to build in my head as I was pulled further into the depths of the ocean. I desperately tried to push my arms toward the ever-fading surface. There were only seconds left before I passed out.

To my horror, a portal appeared below me. Bioluminescent light flooded out of it and suddenly everything was bright and clear. Salophine's chimera was wrapped around me. I froze as the demonic anglera dragged me through the portal and out the other side.

Pain shot up my spine. Bones cracked. I gurgled a scream as I felt torn open and put back together. My scream became more vocalized, and I reached down my side to feel the gills. I took a deep breath and cried out when my legs went numb and morphed together. A tail took their place—*my* tail. Little needles prickled at my face, and I reached up to touch the scales.

What was happening?

"My sweet, Aqeara, you have done it!" Salophine clapped her hands in glee. "I knew I could rely on you. You have stolen the heart of the one who hated you the most."

Her words were not registering in my head. I could not tear my gaze off my tail. None of this made sense.

"But I do not have her heart! I could not kill her," I said with hopeless confusion clouding my thoughts.

Was Kae hurt? Did she fall overboard too?

"Your little hunter fell for you, and thus her heart is yours. Such a strange loophole, I must say, but I shall take it. Now that the heart has been stolen, figuratively at least, I am free to tell you the truth, *my daughter.*" Salophine stared at me with her crimson eyes.

I shuddered and swam back several feet from her, trying to process what was happening. Surely, she meant daughter as in kin and not offspring.

"What are you saying?" I said slowly as I stared at my siren state.

"Long ago, I fell in love with a siren named Nemeria. She was the most beautiful being to ever exist. Her hair was close to your red, and she was just as fierce as you. We soon married, and then she fell pregnant."

"Halfway through her pregnancy, she grew ill. It was not uncommon for pregnant sirens to fall sick, but we both knew something serious was wrong with her. She died giving birth, but the youthling, our daughter, survived. I had grown inconsolable with grief, unable to rule my kingdom. Unable to look after our youthling."

"That was when I met *her*. Salophine, the ancient sea witch. She whispered lies into my ears that she knew how to bring Nemeria back. All I had to do was seduce a king into the waters and cut out his heart. It proved to be rather easy. The whole affair was over in minutes. I was so excited to bring Salophine his heart that I failed to notice the signs." She picked at something under her nail as she told her story. I had never listened more intently to something in my entire life."

"Once I arrived in her cave, in *here*, I realized she had tricked me. A flash of green light erupted between us, and I awoke in this body. *Her* body. She awoke in mine and fled back to Meyrial as queen. There, she conceived seven daughters, all younger than you." She had a sad expression while she spoke.

I stared numbly back at her. Her red eyes were less threatening than I once thought them to be. If this was not Salophine, then that meant…

"I can tell by the look on your face that you understand my tale." She said with a sigh. "I am Amalis, Queen of Meyrial and ruler of all sirens. I am also your mother. I am so sorry, Aqeara. I never meant to abandon or lie to you."

I swam back in shock.

"When Salophine tricked me, she placed a curse that forbade me to leave this cave or tell another soul about my predicament. My only chance was to recreate the spell through you. I only figured out how to use those portals because your soul called out to me on that day Hyrissa died. It was my one chance to return home."

Salophine, or well, Amalis… my mother, placed a tender hand against my cheek.

I tried not to lean into it.

"You tricked me." I said as the thought dawned on me. "Hyrissa cannot come back,"

Amalis looked at me with those same sad eyes. My little cousin—*sister*—would never return. I wanted to break down and cry, but a part of me deep, deep down had known she was gone. I'd accepted her fate when I realized I could not kill Kae.

"No. She cannot. The only reason I can tell you all of this is because you tricked that hunter into falling in love with you, thus gathering all the ingredients I need for this spell. Salophine's curse is nearly broken," Amalis said with newfound excitement.

Her eyes lit up as she brought forth the pearl that gave her vision.

I ignored her as Hyrissa's smiling face lit up in my mind. Raising the dead was too dark of magic to work without severe consequences. I knew that—I should have known that. In my grief, I did not consider any other option.

Amalis' words about Kae came back to me. She was in love with me. That was the only way the spell worked. This insignificant loophole meant the entire world to me. But I had not tricked Kae. I fell in love with her just the same.

I blinked back tears.

"Now, with the hate-filled heart won by my daughter's hand, I summon my return from a queen's command!" Amalis shouted, and a bright flash of green erupted in front of us.

I yelped and scrambled back, not wanting to be struck by whatever that light was capable of.

Amalis cried out in pain. Her eyes squeezed shut. I watched as she sank to the sandy floor. I rushed over to aid her, but I could only watch helplessly as her body convulsed.

She snapped her eyes open, and I swam back when Amalis sat up. The red eyes that met my own held a fire I had not seen before. Sadness, excitement, and fear were replaced with anger, fury, and rage. The spell incantation had worked. Amalis successfully switched back to her own body, meaning that she was far away in Meyrial.

Which also meant a very pissed-off Salophine had returned to her own. After a hundred and twenty years, she no longer had to pretend to be queen. She was fully back in her sea witch form.

The real Salophine reached out and grabbed my throat in an iron, choking grip. I struggled against her as she brought my face mere inches from her own.

"You *ruined* me!" Salophine hissed at me. "I cared for you, I raised you! And how do you repay me? Conspiring with your wretch of a gullible mother to end me. Well, if you want to take my power over the sirens, perhaps I can show you something worth losing."

I thrashed my tail wildly at her. My sharp nails sunk deep into her arms at the comments about my mother, but her grip did not falter. She smiled wickedly and opened a portal, using her own power for the first time in decades. We both traveled through the other side before I could blink.

Though I was out of Salophine's grip, the pain of it lingering on my throat. The sea witch was nowhere in sight, but her disappearance left a sinking feeling in my stomach.

I breached the surface and took a deep breath. The *Mar Daemon* loomed overhead. Rain poured in buckets down on the ship. I tried to find a way to climb up, only to realize I was still a siren. I no longer had legs. This was a ship full of siren hunters. Fear sparked inside me.

"Human hunters, you need not be alarmed." Salophine's voice boomed against the thunderstorms clapping above. "I am Salophine, sorceress of the sea. I come bearing the swift gift of your deaths, all thanks to a treacherous friend."

I swam back and looked up at a sight blocked by the *Mar Daemon*. To my horror, Salophine had grown to about sixty feet in size—larger than the mast of the ship. The crew shouted as several arrows struck the belly of the sea witch.

She screamed, and an enormous wave washed over the main deck. I swam toward the hull, desperate to find anything to climb on to. Several anglera dragged me backward. They were all tripled in size. There had to be hundreds of them—an entire army. Lightning struck the ship's mast, lighting it aflame.

Kae.

A twister of water swept me up and out of the ocean. It lifted me to the height of the deck. Atty and Birch ran toward Salophine, clutching small explosives in their fists. Ruff had been the one to shoot the arrows but was knocked off his feet from the wave. He crawled toward his dropped crossbow. Kae and Dalton bellowed at each other, probably arguing over strategic moves. I only hoped that Arden and Kenley were below deck, readying the cannons.

"This traitor is the very thing you hate the most. The creature you have sworn to hunt and kill. The one who haunts your nightmares. Behold your precious Aqeara!" Salophine flicked her hand to bring me forward.

Lightning acted like a spotlight, cracking as she spoke, bringing all attention to me. Everyone on board saw me struggling against the swirling waters. Kae nearly dropped her sword. Recognition flickered across her face, followed by disgust. My true form was on display, and she rejected me, an outcome I'd already fearfully predicted.

My heart shattered into a million jagged pieces, nonetheless.

"Please," was all I said.

A whisper, a prayer.

The loving look I'd seen briefly on Kae's face had been wiped clean. What a sick twist of fate this was. For the first time in my century and a quarter of being alive, I was in love. Only for that love to be spit back in my face.

The other faces of the crew were mixed with shock and hurt. A wave of guilt at my mere existence overwhelmed me when I met the eyes of Dalton. The first person on the *Mar Daemon* to trust me and come to my rescue back in that bar all those weeks ago. He wavered from looking at Kae to me and back to Kae.

Salophine's sinister laugh filled the air like she was thoroughly enjoying herself. I wanted nothing more than to just disappear forever under the weight of the stares of my friends.

Then she did something unexpected. Something that horrified me beyond words. Salophine opened her mouth and sang.

O sailor in the lonely night
Whose ship has crossed the ocean
Fierce as you are with all your might
May join me with your devotion
Come one, come all
Don't worry, don't be afraid
Come, let the water stand tall
And join a pretty young maid
Let go of your worries
Let go of your fears
Join hastily with hurry
Let me wipe away your tears

That was *my* voice! My singing voice, the one I gave up as payment for the spell, came out of her mouth. Salophine was singing my song, my words, in a voice so smooth and soft, it could put an insomniac to sleep. I had never wondered what my song would sound like to my own ears like this.

Salophine was mocking me. She was a sea witch, not a siren, and had no such power to lure humans into the sea, even with my singing voice in her possession. I was powerless.

Kae's eyes had gone wide, and she stared at the sea witch in terror. Then, as if a flicker of recognition crossed her mind, she shot me an angry look. I grimaced under the weight of it.

I stopped resisting the water, and it dropped me back to sea level.

I looked up to find the *Mar Daemon* was completely engulfed in flames. Salophine brought down her tail and cleaved the ship in two. It was worse than most shipwrecks I had discovered. Several men, too distant to make out their identities, dove headfirst into the water near to where I floated, watching helplessly.

Others had tied barrels together as a makeshift lifeboat and pushed it overboard. The anglera saw a chance for potential prey and stalked toward the men. I snapped out of my grief and swam forward, grabbing several by the tails and yanking them toward me. They hissed and tried to attack, but I bit down hard. The anglera evaporated into nothing once my teeth touched their flesh.

Barnes reached out into the water to help the Doc and Rigby board the lifeboat. They looked at me floating there in the water, but didn't reach for their weapons. A tiny flicker of hope filled me. I still had a chance to prove what I'd been trying to convince them all along; sirens could be good.

"Look out!" Rigby shouted and pointed at something behind me.

I turned as an anglera shot into me, shoving me against the barrels before dragging me down into the waters. I struggled and chomped on slippery skin. The anglera disappeared.

Screams pierced through the water. I broke the surface and saw blood pooling over the barrels. An anglera had leaped out and struck. Before they could attack again, I grabbed their tail and dug my fingers into their eyeballs. My teeth sank into scaly flesh.

Looking back up, Rigby stared back at me, frozen in shock. The Doc had stripped off his shirt and tied it around the stump where Barnes' forearm had been. It had been chewed off by the anglera. Barnes was deadly pale and unconscious. I wanted to do something, but no amount of healing could bring back an entire limb.

"Go!" Rigby shouted at me.

There was no malice in his voice as he pointed toward the others. It was pleading almost. He wanted me to help them.

I swam back to the sinking ship, desperate to find Kae. Even if she hated me with every fiber of her being, I refused to let her die, not when there was a chance I could save her.

Another makeshift barrel boat landed beside me. Two actual lifeboats were cut from their ropes and fell, crashing into the ocean, nearly crashing into me. The anglera immediately sprang on the rest of the crew, and I heard the familiar sounds of metal as the men whipped out their *zephlum* weapons in defense.

I spotted Ruff, Dalton, and Kae in one of the lifeboats as it tossed and turned against the stormy waves. A flash of lightning illuminated their determined faces. I swam forward, looking for any way of helping them, a way to get them out of here, out of this mess I had created.

I reached the side of the boat, unnoticed by any of them when Salophine spoke again.

"These humans will die tonight, Aqeara, all because of you. I will regain my full power in their bloodshed. And you, too, shall join them on the other side." Salophine's voice echoed, seeming to come from all directions at once.

Another flash of lightning allowed me to meet Kae's eyes. They were wide with trepidation at my siren form, but I did not have the chance to process the hurt look in them before I was jerked back by one of Salophine's anglera, a single yelp slipping out of my throat.

They had wrapped their tail painfully tight around my waist. I dug my nails into the flesh, but it was no use. I couldn't bite down.

My eyes wandered for Kae again in desperation to see her one last time. I caught sight of her as she jumped from the lifeboat, her sword raised and a steel look in her eyes. I closed my eyes when she swung down, but could not feel the blade pierce my heart. The grip on my waist slackened, and I peeked out to see that Kae had cleaved the anglera in two.

I met Kae's eyes for a brief second in the dark water before Salophine cried out in anger at the failed attempt to bring me to her. She whipped her long tail toward us and struck Kae.

The force sent Kae flying into the hull of the overturned ship. She hit the side hard and my stomach lurched at the bone-crackling noise that was made at contact. Kae slipped into the ocean and did not resurface.

I dodged the tail that came after me and swam below water. When I resurfaced on the other side of the lifeboat, I turned my attention to Ruff and Dalton. The two had just killed an anglera.

"Give me your daggers. *Now.*" I barked orders like I had any ranking over either man. "And get Kae!"

Ruff dove into the ocean the moment the words were out of my mouth and swam to where Kae had fallen. Dalton scrambled to the side and hesitated. We stared each other down for several seconds before Dalton reached into his belt and procured a set of daggers. Not just any set. My daggers. He slowly placed them into my hands.

"Save us." Dalton whispered. "Please."

I nodded and swam to where Kae had dropped her sword when she was thrown.

The sword reflected underwater from the light of fire and lightning. It had not sunk too deep yet. I placed the blade between my teeth and bit down, trying hard to avoid the burn of the metal on my skin.

Salophine was nearby, wreaking havoc. With a dagger in each hand, I swam up her long tail until I was fully breached above the water. I dug a dagger into Salophine's flesh and used the other to cut into a higher spot. I alternated using the daggers to climb up to where her tail reached her torso.

Had it not been for Arden and Kenley firing cannons off the other lifeboat, Salophine might have noticed the annoying stings at her side. I nearly lost balance a few times as the slick handle slipped from beneath my wet fingers. I held strong, knowing that everyone's lives depended on me. It was not until I reached the top of her stomach that she noticed what I was doing.

"Get off me! Get off of me, you wretched, wretched girl!" Salophine screamed.

She tried batting me away with her arm, and I slipped. My grip on one of the daggers faltered. I hung by one hand and my weight cut a larger wound into the sea witch. Salophine reached for me again but missed when I swung out of the way. I used my momentum to hoist myself back up onto the other dagger still lodged in her chest. I kept swinging with one arm and used the other to dig a new hole, higher until I was right above her heart, the now increasingly more rapid fire of the canons preventing her from knocking me back into the ocean.

With one hand wrapped tightly around a lodged dagger, I grabbed Kae's sword out of my mouth and drove it as far into Salophine's chest as I could.

From the sound of her agonizing screams, I had successfully pierced her heart. Salophine slowly shrunk back down to her normal size, letting out a frustrated shout as she did. She grabbed me and threw me hard into the water, the force of which left an ache from my neck to the tip of my tail.

Salophine continued to shrink when I breached the surface again. She was much smaller than I was and kept getting smaller.

The sea witch wailed and tried to swim over to me. I flapped my tail backward, unsure what contact with her would do to me. I stared in shock as Salophine was no bigger than a guppy. She eventually popped into a cloud of sand, disappearing from this life forever.

Chapter Twenty-Eight
Kae

It had been nearly twenty minutes since Aqeara fell into the churning waters below when a nightmare spawn appeared from the depths of the sea. A giant sea monster was threatening to destroy my ship and kill my crew. As if I was living inside one of my worst nightmares, the girl I had grown to love was my worst enemy: a siren.

At first, I thought the siren presented before us was the one who had killed Edmonde and Kipp. The heart I drove a dagger through. It had bright orange hair that almost appeared to glow. But this siren was different. Fiery red hair and a face that I could recognize in a crowd of thousands.

Hurt. Betrayal. Anger. A flash of disgust. She had lied to me. She had tricked me into loving her. And she had brought this demon with her to eradicate us. My heart was daggers, piercing its way through my chest.

"Oh shit," Dalton said when he saw Aqeara in… whatever that twister was.

He looked back at me, as if trying to gauge my response. After all, I had confided my feelings to him mere moments before Aqeara fell into the ocean.

My heart lurched at Aqeara's broken face as she mirrored how I internally felt. For just a moment, she looked heartbroken, too, the soft plea barely reaching my ears. I was torn away from her tear-streaked face when that demon sang. It sounded an awful lot like Aqeara. The recognition in her eyes confirmed my growing suspicion. I did not look at her again. I couldn't. It was all too much.

There was no time to process any feelings. The *Mar Daemon* was on fire and cleaved in two. Both sides of my ship were burning and sinking. I stood frozen in place for a bit too long before the reality of it all dawned on me. I had to protect them.

"Get on the lifeboats!" I ordered as Rigby had fashioned a lifeboat out of barrels.

Several jumped overboard.

"Kae!" Ruff called and motioned for me to join in the lifeboat with him and Dalton.

I ran down the stairs and did a quick sweep to make sure none of my men were still on board. Half of the staircase was destroyed. My knees buckled as I tried to maintain balance, nearly slipping into the tumultuous waters below. The floor was collapsing as the ship sank and I could only hope that there was no one left down there.

Rain soaked through my clothes, making it harder to move as they clung to my skin. Thunder cracked ahead like the gods themselves were yelling at us.

"Hurry!" Dalton shouted when I ran to them. I swung my sword and cut the ropes as soon as I stepped onto the boat, plummeting us down into the black waters below. My stomach dropped during the fall and it took me several seconds to make sure I wouldn't retch.

I couldn't see anything in this infernal storm. I only hoped my crew was still alive and safe, and not knowing was consuming. Fear seized me as my blood turned to ice, my heart pounding in time with the strikes of thunder.

As if a gigantic sea monster wasn't enough, giant murderous sea demons flooded the waters. My sword became covered in black goo from cutting their bodies in half. The only saving grace was how quickly they disappeared under the metal of our blades.

As I searched for any sign of my men other than their distant screams, I realized I was searching for Aqeara despite everything. She floated just above the surface, several feet away. Her eyes were filled with tears as she stared at me, though I don't believe she noticed—the tears or me.

A large demon zoomed toward her. Before I could shout a warning, she was hauled away from me, out of my reach once again.

I didn't hesitate before I leaped after the thing and cut Aqeara free. For a brief moment, it was just me and Aqeara in those dark waters, the flames from the ship reflecting perfectly in her eyes that still reminded me so much of whiskey.

It was only a moment, a brief moment in which I knew she was still… her. Then there was only adrenaline and fear and a loud crack when my head hit the hull of the *Mar Daemon*.

I woke with a start and coughed up more seawater than I thought humanly possible to store. I was on the lifeboat without a clue how I'd gotten there.

Aqeara.

My eyes scanned the waters for any sign of her. She had tried to save us. At that point, I didn't care if she betrayed us or wanted to hurt me. She could carve my heart out, and I'd let her.

I sat up too fast and nearly tumbled backward. My leg was broken. A shallow pool of blood covered the bottom of the lifeboat. A quick assessment of my injuries told me it wasn't mine.

Dalton sat on the bench opposite me. His gangly legs were just below my own bench. He was sobbing uncontrollably, ugly sounds heaving from his chest like I hadn't heard since losing Edmonde. He was cradling Ruff's head in his lap as Ruff faced the sky.

I let out a sharp cry when I saw the large gash in Ruff's neck, splattering blood at an alarming rate. His skin had turned ashen, like a corpse. Ruff was still shallowly breathing, but his eyes were glassy.

"You idiot, you absolute idiot!" Dalton sobbed between words. "Why? You should have just let it kill me."

He pressed his hand against Ruff's throat to slow the blood flow, though it continued to seep through his fingers.

"Who else would annoy me to death if you died?" Ruff's eyes were rolling in the back of his head.

Dalton inhaled sharply. This strange exchange between the two seemed out of place. They were always bickering like an old married couple... oh. *Oh!*

"You keep fighting this, Ruff. Do *not* leave me! Stay alive, for me." Dalton shook from the sobs heaving through his body.

Ruff's eyes desperately tried to focus on Dalton.

"My heart is yours. It always will be. Even if you don't love me back," Dalton murmured as he stroked Ruff's hair.

"I have always loved you, dimwit," Ruff said with almost a smile on his face.

His eyes fluttered shut and his head lolled back.

For the first time in my life, I prayed to whatever gods who listened. I prayed I would never hear the guttural scream of agony that came from Dalton again. My own eyes filled to the brim and spilled tears.

I cried and stared at the limp body of my friend—my first mate. Dalton's sobs broke my already torn heart. Dalton seemed oblivious to his surroundings. I doubted he noticed I had witnessed this interaction at all.

Our sorrow was interrupted by the booming voice of the monster echoing across the sea.

"Get off me! Get off of me, you wretched, wretched girl!" The sea demon swatted at something on her chest that was too far to see.

I squinted at the small figure that clung on, and horror overtook me when I saw a flash of red hair. Of course, she was trying to take down a sixty-foot monster by herself. I don't know why I expected anything but recklessness from her.

The scream shook through my bones as the monster began to shrink.

If I had not witnessed it with my own two eyes, I would not have believed in such magic. As the sea demon sunk into the ocean's depths, she dragged Aqeara down with her. I almost jumped in after them, but my leg would have only hindered me.

So, I waited. I waited as Dalton sobbed. I waited as the voices of my crew began to carry over the ocean's angry crashing. I waited until the waves grew calm. Time wore on. The clouds parted and moonlight shone through.

Still, Aqeara did not emerge.

Don't make me lose her, too. Please. Bring her back to me.

I was doing an awful lot of praying tonight for someone who did not believe in the gods. My gaze did not waver from where Aqeara had disappeared. I couldn't bear to turn around and watch Dalton cradling Ruff's lifeless body. It was too much.

Just as I started to lose hope, Aqeara's head popped out of the water beside me. I jumped back, and she smiled tiredly at my surprise. She looked over to Dalton and Ruff and the smile vanished.

"Hoist me onto the boat." Aqeara's voice trembled in fear.

I hesitated, but determination set in Aqeara's expression. She would climb on board if she had to, maybe knock the lot of us into the sea by trying, and then we'd all be in worse off.

I reached down and grabbed her by the waist, lifting her up and onto the lifeboat. I took in her soaked red hair, her green shells and green tail, her striking yet determined face as she propped herself up in front of Dalton.

She was beautiful, even in this form, and I knew I'd never tire of thinking so, even if I wasn't ready yet to consider what that meant.

Dalton parted his gaze away from Ruff to see what caused the lifeboat to rock. He did not move as Aqeara placed a tender hand against Ruff's face. It was like Dalton wasn't registering what was happening before him. He was hallowed and numb.

Aqeara turned Ruff's head so that the open wound faced her. I couldn't tear my eyes away, despite the pain it caused me to look at Ruff's body. Dalton stared with empty but curious eyes as Aqeara shed tears. My heart ached at how easily the tears flowed from her face. She truly cared about us.

A small glow appeared at the cut on Ruff's neck where Aqeara's tears had landed. Dalton and I stared at the shrinking cut. Blood stopped flowing and new skin formed. The gaping hole healed until there was no sign of an injury. Dried blood over smooth skin was the only indication that Ruff had even been hurt.

The three of us stared at our fallen friend until his eyes shot open and he gasped for air.

"What in the blazes are you lot looking at? Oh, hi Aqeara," Ruff greeted Aqeara.

She beamed and threw her arms around him. Ruff was taken aback but returned her hug in a tight embrace.

Aqeara then broke away and turned to me. She shifted her weight so that she loomed over my leg. Her tears cascaded on my broken bone, and I flinched when it snapped back into place.

Dalton sobbed and gripped Ruff in a tight embrace. Ruff had a smug grin as he allowed himself to be smothered in kisses. Aqeara slipped off the boat just as Dalton yanked me by the sleeve to pull me in for a group hug.

"No hard feelings on the whole siren thing, Aqeara." Dalton said as he faced the ocean. "You saved us."

The color slowly crept back onto his face, though that haunted look behind his eyes did not fade. He regarded Ruff like he might not be real—this might be an illusion.

Ruff sat up beside Dalton, still several inches shorter than him, even sitting down. He didn't seem fully aware he had died, or had been nearly on the brink of death.

Aqeara nodded and turned to swim away.

"Wait! Where are you going?" I called out after her.

She stared at me without blinking. I couldn't decipher the look in her eye.

"Salophine and my mother were tied together for many decades." Aqeara said. "I need to make sure she is alive back in Meyrial. Besides...you're all safe. My work here is done."

"You'll come back though, right?" I asked.

I didn't mention that Aqeara had previously told me her parents were dead. It was probably all part of her cover story. The whole thing had been a lie, from her stories of Soledel to her entire past.

"What do you care?" she shouted at me with a trembling voice.

A lump formed in my throat, making it impossible to swallow down the building emotion. Tears welled. Dalton and Ruff turned into awkward statues. At the weighted silence that ensued, Dalton kicked my bench and shot me a look.

"Because I love you." I said, painfully aware of how soft and small my voice sounded. "And I want to learn everything about you, the *real* you. I want to make sure you're safe. I want to spend every waking moment of my life with you." I spilled my heart out and ignored the way Ruff was looking between me and Dalton.

Dalton who was smiling for the first time since the monster had appeared.

The tears flowed freely down my face, blending with the last drops of rainfall.

Aqeara's gaze softened.

"Even if I'm a siren?" she asked in a small voice.

I hesitated.

"I don't care," I said, and it was the truth, somehow.

Aqeara swam forward and pulled me overboard. I crashed into the water beside her, letting the warmth of her body wash over me.

She kissed me deeply underwater. I almost choked when I breathed in, but sighed into the kiss. We floated in the ocean, together as one, with our tight embrace. My worst nightmare had turned into my heart's wildest dream.

Aqeara pulled me up for air before I remembered I needed to breathe.

"I love you, Kae. Even when we die, and our souls cross over, I will love you then. I shall return as soon as I can," Aqeara whispered, and kissed me again.

I shuddered at her soft, silky voice.

Aqeara broke away and helped me climb back onto the boat with ease. She was even stronger in her true form.

Ruff and Dalton murmured to each other behind me.

"Meet me at the port of Avalon. I'll wait for you," I said.

Aqeara raised a brow, and I wondered if she remembered that was where we'd first met. It seemed like a lifetime ago to me. Aqeara nodded before she dove into the depths of the ocean. I stared after her, longing to join her.

The sound of kissing brought my attention to Ruff and Dalton, who were heatedly going at it. Splashes of water surrounded us as the rest of my men rowed themselves into view.

Atty wolf-whistled at the kissing pair. They broke apart, looking sheepish and embarrassed under the gaze of the rest of the crew. The hard look in Birch's eye as he sat beside Atty made me fear he would say something negative toward two men kissing. I nearly fainted when Birch whipped Atty around and kissed him deeply. Atty grinned into the kiss.

"Are you *kidding* me?" Dalton exclaimed to the hunters. "I hid my preferences for a year, and you two have been together this whole time!"

Ruff shook the entire boat with silent but hearty laughter.

"S'not our fault ya aren't observant," Birch said with an elated voice.

I laughed and joined the whoops and shouts of victory from the other men.

They were all injured and bloody, but would be okay. As my eyes went over each of them, I was grateful we all made it out alive.

I faltered at the sight of Barnes waving with one arm, a stump where his other should have been cradled against his chest. It didn't wipe the smile from his face as he joined the hollering.

Seagulls circled overhead. We were near land. We would be alright.

"Aqeara! Aqeara! Aqeara!" my crew shouted in unison. They praised the siren who had saved us all. My Aqeara.

I smiled proudly and joined in, hoping even with how far she'd likely already swum below the water's surface she could still hear us.

.

Chapter Twenty-Nine
Aqeara

The intel on Meyrial's whereabouts had proven to be close to the truth—I knew these waters where Salophine sunk the *Mar Daemon*. It was only a short swim away. The swift currents did most of the work while I drifted along, lost in my thoughts. Fatigue weighed me down like a tangible pressure on my sore body, but I pressed on.

I worried that I would not make it in time, that Amalis—my mother—would be gone. Her life energy had been connected with Salophine's for over a century. Their souls were more interwoven with one another than two strands of a single seaweed plant. I only hoped I had not lost my mother before even seeing her one last time. Such a strange feeling to discover you have an entire family when you were thought to be an orphan your entire life.

Death loomed where hope once flourished. I could feel the coldness it brought with the increasing intensity as I got closer to home.

Hyrissa calmed my thoughts of despair. Her laughter rang in my ears and my heart ached once more. My half-sister was gone too soon. The grief that coursed through me was not as forceful as it had been before. I had found happiness in my time as a human. I knew Hyrissa was on the other side watching over me, happy that I was happy.

Then there was Kae. Her furrowed brows and sharp wit. I missed her and her kisses already. She did not care that I was a siren. She loved me.

I arrived at the border of the siren city and stopped. Clagoria's banishment rang in the back of my mind. As I slowly swam forward, I did not feel the tug of her command pulling me in place. The truth had made me immune to her compulsion—I was actually her older sister; I ranked above her.

With a kick of my tail, I bolted forward into the heart of Meyrial. Sirens waved and greeted me as I swam past them in a blur. I had no time for greetings. I kept swimming until I finally reached the castle. I swam into the large opening of the cave and kept treading until I reached the Queen's chambers.

"Aqeara!" Clagoria wrapped me in a tight hug.

It caught me off guard. She grabbed my hand and led me to the back of the Queen's cave. There was no anger in the way she greeted me, like I was a long-lost friend rather than a formally banished siren. I didn't have time to decide how I felt about her change of heart.

Amalis lay on her seaweed-covered slab of rock. Her eyes unfocused past me, her breathing shallow. If life was a fire, there were few embers left smoldering in Amalis' wake. She was leaving this world, soon to cross over to the next.

It was strange to see her with the same face as the siren who had raised me and my sisters all this time. There was kindness in her eyes that Salophine never had when she was in my mother's body. I knew that if Amalis had raised us, our lives would have never known sorrow or misery.

The other five princesses surrounded their biological mother. I wondered how much they knew, how much my mother had told them before I could reach Meyrial.

"My daughter," Amalis breathed out.

I swam over to her side and allowed her to hold my hand. The knot in my stomach dissipated beneath her touch. All the angry words I wanted to spew out at her vanished into thin ocean. The life draining from her eyes transformed my anger into loss.

"I am here. Salophine is dead," I reassured her.

She smiled weakly and nodded.

My sisters remained silent as they floated in the corner of the room. Amalis reached a hand out and placed it on my cheek. Her fingers were cold as ice when they touched my skin—practically lifeless.

"I am sorry, Aqeara. I know that is not nearly enough to make up for everything." Amalis spoke in a rough, quiet voice. "You will make an excellent queen."

I stared in shock at her words. I turned to Clagoria, the supposed heir to the throne. Clagoria only nodded.

"But I—"

"My trident. It will give you great power as queen, something that spent decades hidden from Salophine." Amalis coughed harshly and I squeezed her hand with my own. "Clagoria fetched it for me."

Clagoria swam to the corner of the room and picked up the so-called trident. Though I had never known what it was before, I always felt a pull that the trident radiated, like I'd known it was meant for me. The object in Clagoria's hand was familiar.

I remembered Hyrissa picking up the trident in a discovered shipwreck. She had tried to use it to comb her hair long ago, when she was still alive. I shed a tear as I remembered my sister's incessant need to make me laugh.

Clagoria placed the trident in my hands. She smiled and swam back to allow me a chance to admire it. My tears stopped when I clasped the handle. Blue light glowed around the trident in my grip, and I marveled at it.

When I looked back at my mother, she was gone. Her eyes glossed over and stared at nothing. I sobbed alongside my sisters as we watched our mother's body turn to a colorful cloud of sand.

"We must announce the queen's passing. Your coronation will commence soon afterward, Queen Aqeara." Clagoria squeezed my shoulders as she spoke.

I threw my arms around her and she returned my hug.

The other sisters joined in until we were nothing but one big blob of tangled tails and scales. We would come out of this stronger than ever. I had a blood family to call my own. The thought made me cry even more.

"Clagoria," I said, and cleared my throat.

Everyone broke apart and turned to me.

Their Queen.

"I want to make you the new head of all the warrior troops. There shall be no more killing of humans. The war between our kind is over. Too many of us have died seeking revenge. I will no longer allow it." I kept an unwavering gaze on Clagoria as she blinked back shock at my words.

She regained composure. The warriors would dislike giving up human flesh and that indescribable burst of energy it gave us, but we had survived off fish for hundreds of years. We could do it again. If the other sirens in our kingdom lived that way without complaint, the resilient warriors could, too.

"Although, the men that crave violence and inflict pain on others… those are fair game," I added, thinking of men like the one at the Zephlus bar.

Clagoria snarled in agreement.

"Our new troops will protect the city and sirenkind. No longer will we live in fear of traveling beyond Meyrial's borders." I spoke with conviction. "The warrior troops will aid in travel and explore the seas. We must be open-minded. It will make us stronger than ever."

Clagoria's eyes went wide, but she bowed her head at me.

I was not entirely sure if I was ready to be Queen, but I knew I had the support of my family on my side. Salophine lied about my age and my rightful place as heir to the throne to lessen my power should I seek the truth. The more I thought about the throne, the more I knew it was the right place to be. It was my duty to serve my kingdom.

"One with Meyrial. One with the Queen," my sisters chanted.

They left me to get ready for my coronation. Clagoria was last at the entrance of my new cave. She glanced at me over her shoulder.

"Words cannot describe how proud I am of you. Hyrissa is smiling down on us," Clagoria said in a warm voice.

I smiled and bowed my head in thanks, and she quickly swam away.

Clagoria was never one to outright apologize, and I knew this was as close as she would get. Grabbing the trident, I swam out to the top of the castle of caves. I floated right outside the large entrance and took in the view of Meyrial. Sirens traded gems and other found goods in our market. There was a hoop show tonight where several swam in and out of carved rings made of rock. Others enjoyed fresh tropical fish. The city was full of life, full of my kin, vibrant as I had remembered it.

My gaze fell to the trident in my hands. I laughed to myself, noting how it resembled a human fork. I tightened my grip and focused on the trident until it glowed blue again. Its power radiated in small waves. I wished that the one person I wanted beside me was here right now, seeing all of this. Hyrissa would have been ecstatic.

I looked back out at Meyrial, glimmering with life. My city. My home.

Chapter Thirty
Kae

"Are you out of your damn mind?" My father's voice rose as he stared at me, red in the face from his bubbling anger.

I flinched from where I sat at the small tea table. My mother sat beside me, head in her hand. A deep sigh escaped her, the only sign of any sort of emotion coming from her since the beginning of this conversation.

A nearby fisherman had given us refuge on his boat and sailed us to Avalon. The trip had cost me the last of my gold coins and stash of jewels, which I'd nearly lost my life retrieving from the sinking ship.

We had no other choice. The *Mar Daemon* was gone.

My royal "welcome" home had been received by the entire fleet greeting me at the harbor. My parents were nothing if not excessive. It was when I'd arrived at the castle just over an hour ago and was brought to this small, cozy room I was completely forthcoming about my whereabouts—both in the past month and the past year.

I was a pirate captain, seeking revenge for Edmonde. I had led a crew, and we'd spent the last year hunting sirens. I left out the last battle against a sea witch in fear my parents would think I'd gone mad and have me locked up. Sirens were believable, giant sea creatures were not.

"Possibly, but that's beside the point," I joked with a humorless laugh.

My father shattered the glass cup in his grasp, and I winced at the bleeding slice in his hand.

"Honestly, dear," my mother murmured as she handed him a linen napkin.

My father wrapped his hand with it but did not once take his eyes off of me.

"Is there anything else you would like to confess on top of lying, stealing, and countless other crimes?" He asked.

"I hardly think piracy should be a crime if I'm stealing from the wealth—" I cut myself off from the murderous look my father gave me. We were the wealthy.

My mother looked as if she would rather be anywhere else but here. That made two of us.

"There is also this woman… who means a lot to me… she—I…" I trailed off as my father knocked over all the plates on the table, sending them flying across the room.

He had never been violent, and this display sent chills down my spine.

"That is enough!" my mother said and rose to her feet.

At first, I thought it was in response to my coming out and saying I was in love with a woman, but she strode over to her husband. My father opened his mouth and was greeted with a slap on the cheek by his wife. I stared in shock at the outburst of emotion, frozen in my chair.

My father was equally taken aback as he brought a hand up to the stinging skin. My mother rushed over to me and embraced me in a tight hug.

"I am so proud of the confident woman you have become," she said into my hair.

My throat tightened, and my father stared at us like we were ghosts.

"I don't care who you love so long as they cherish your heart as if it were their own. You are my daughter, brave and ruthless. You bow to no one." My mother lifted my chin with a finger. "And though it saddens me, you hid so much from us, I understand."

My father's mouth gaped open. My mother shot him a stern look, and he closed it. For the first time in his life, the King of Avalon was at a loss for words.

"This doesn't mean you are without punishment." My mother walked to my father's side and took his hand in hers.

He saw a silent question in her eyes. They whispered to one another, completely out of earshot. I tried to decipher what they were saying from their facial expressions. My father's gaze softened. He nodded once and then turned back to me.

"Your mother and I have talked about this for quite some time now. It seems with your reckless abandon that this would serve as a proper way of reprimanding you for your behavior," my father started.

I straightened in my chair, waiting for them to give the order to have me locked away or something dreadful.

"We are retiring."

"*What?*"

"Kaelyn, as heir to the throne, you are to be crowned in three days' time. You will be the new Queen of Avalon, free to marry whoever you desire so long as you one day have a proper heir to replace you." There was a twinkle in my mother's eyes as she spoke.

Now it was my turn to gape like an idiot.

"It is time your mother and I step down and go on our own adventure. We can't let you have all the fun," my father joked.

He actually *joked* with a smile on his face. I must have been hallucinating. Perhaps I died back on the *Mar Daemon* and this was some strange limbo.

"You're both serious," I said.

They nodded and looked at me for my answer.

Once, a long time ago, I would have shied away from such responsibility. And yet, I smiled, much to my surprise.

I thought back to the boy in the Naivian bookstore, who had worn his kingdom's pin with pride. I could be the change for Avalon's children to feel the same, that they could be their true selves without being reprimanded. I would have power with this position and spread positive tales of sirens so that no human dared to hunt them ever again. So, Aqeara could be safe.

I stood up and looked into my parents' eyes before taking their hands in my own.

"I accept."

The sun began its descent, marking a week since I returned to Avalon. It looked different somehow, despite being the same sun I watched rise and fall my entire life. Avalon seemed different, in a good way. It was my home and I would defend it and its people. Time away from it had kindled my love for the kingdom.

I sat beside Ruff as we both stared out at the horizon ahead. There had been no word on the red-headed siren in the days I spent as the new Queen of my kingdom. I had stood by the docks every morning in hopes she would return. She crept into my dreams and took over my thoughts.

I missed her terribly and hoped she would come back to me soon. Having her far away after all the time we spent together in close quarters was hard. I had taken our time together for granted.

"Still no sign of Dalton?" I asked.

"Nope." Ruff sighed.

I frowned. Our friend, well now Ruff's boyfriend, had disappeared as soon as we anchored in Avalon. He left without a trace and none of us had heard from him since.

"I'm sure he's just drinking to cope with the traumatic events of nearly getting killed by a giant sea monster," I said, hoping to get Ruff's aching heart off of Dalton.

He shrugged, but his brows furrowed, and a flicker of tension moved across his jaw.

I opened my mouth to offer relationship advice when a glimmer in the water caught my eyes. My feet carried me before I even knew where I was going. The red hair floating like a crown around Aqeara's head was the only thing I focused on.

She gave me a dazzling smile that left me breathless.

Aqeara beckoned me to lean over the edge of the dock, and I was happy to oblige. Our lips crashed in a deep kiss. Her laugh sounded like hundreds of small bells ringing. It made me feel warm inside. If I could only hear one song for the rest of my life, it would be her laughter.

I laid on the dock, not caring if the damp wood soaked through my suit, while Aqeara floated in front of me. She hummed the tune of her song that once haunted my nightmares. I gasped at the memory.

"Your singing voice, it's back!" I exclaimed.

Aqeara simply nodded and brought forth a trident. It looked exactly like the one from the fairytale books my mother read to me when I was younger. She held the golden trident tight in her hand, and I scrambled up when it glowed a blue hue. The light enclosed her in a bubble that slowly lifted out of the ocean.

I crawled up to my feet and took several steps back while the strange bubble landed in front of me. The light was so bright, I could not see Aqeara at all.

Ruff cried out as he approached, eyes wide and mouth hung open in a perfect circle.

When the light faded back into the trident, Aqeara stood in front of me in a sparkling pale green dress, the same color as her shells. A crown of colorful jewels rested atop her head. Pale pink coral was carved around sapphires and rubies and emeralds.

Her hair was dry and cascaded down her back in loose waves. She was a goddess, leaving me entranced by her beauty, momentarily stunned. She had human legs and smirked at my reaction.

"Your crown is much better than that ugly hat," Aqeara noted, not an ounce of humor in her tone.

I laughed at her seriousness and pulled her close to me. She threw her arms around my neck and kissed me.

Ruff made an awkward noise and walked back to the tavern while we stayed in our embrace.

"Sorry!" I shouted to him, breaking away from the kiss.

He waved me off, shooting us a smile over his shoulder.

I turned my attention back to Aqeara, soaking in the feel of her arms around me again. I smiled as she kissed me, feeling the happiest I had felt in ages.

The Queen of sirens and the Queen of Avalon. Finally, together.

Everything was absolutely perfect, and together, we'd make sure it stayed that way.

After

A woman walked on the sandy beach of northern Zephlus. She strode from the depths of the ocean, shoulders squared back, and feet trudging with relentless certainty. She wore a long, black sheer dress that was bone dry, despite having just been submerged in the water. Her face was etched in a twisted expression of fury.

Black hair rested on the small of her back. Her crimson eyes glowed as she took in the island, her pale skin nearly translucent. Perhaps she was a ghost, especially with how swiftly she moved.

She did not need to accustom herself to legs, but she did hyperfocus on the way the grains of sand felt beneath her bare feet. She wondered if *Aqeara* felt this way when she washed up on this very shore weeks ago. The name flitted through her thoughts like a curse.

The woman walked up to the mouth of a cave and was delighted to find the man already waiting for her. She had not been sure she still had enough power left to control him, but was pleased to find that he stood here, having traveled all the way from Avalon.

His clothes were askew and missing buttons in his shirt that allowed her to see his torso was tightly wrapped in bandages—the cloth stained with dry blood. His irises were void of any color and his mind was blank, waiting for her to place her own thoughts inside.

He had been a pirate, part of the crew that had killed her. Until now.

The man looped his arm with hers and led her deep into the cave. The woman dug her nails across the stone and let the horrifying screech fill the void. The man said nothing. He was tall and handsome with dirty blonde hair that made the woman envious of such good looks and youth. She appeared just as young, though magicked appearances held nothing against the eternity of life.

"And what's your name, my new apprentice?" the woman asked the dazed man.

He turned to her with his blank stare.

"Dalton," he replied without emotion.

The two stopped short when the walls of the cave gave way to glittering black metal that begged to be harvested. A wicked smile crossed the woman's face.

The sea witch cackled as her plan formed in front of her very eyes.

Acknowledgements

It not only takes a village, but an entire kingdom, to bring life to a book and I couldn't be more blessed with having my support system throughout this entire process.

First and foremost, I would like to thank my parents and brother for allowing the obsession of Pirates of the Caribbean to fester throughout my childhood and for constantly introducing me to new stories. This book wouldn't exist without our countless rewatches. I love you all to the moon and back.

To my friends and family, thank you for listening to me shyly rave about this book and continue to support me throughout it all. Without each and every one of you, I would feel lost at sea.

Sara, you were the very first person to read this book in its entirety and it means endless amounts to me.

Michaela, you gave feedback on the earliest–and roughest–draft and for that I'm grateful.

Alex, thank you for listening to me talk nonsense about this book.

Ally, thank you so much for your support of listening to me talk endlessly about my book and for all the TikTok love.

Thank you to my incredibly talented writing group, The Spaghetti Throwers. I would not have gotten this far without each and every one of your encouraging words. The support you've given me and each other has helped me get through the hardest challenges. May the spaghetti forever stick!

To my lovely beta readers, whether you read one chapter or the entire manuscript: your feedback got me through those rough middle drafts where all hope seemed lost. To Danai and Melissa, you have helped shape this book for the better.

he lovely Hansen House family that made this queer book (and myself) feel right at home from the start.

Elizabeth, the number of thankful words I want to say could probably outlast this book. You have challenged me in the best way and I am so, so grateful that you took a chance on this sapphic story. Your patience and kindness are beyond appreciated, thank you.

To my editor Kaitlin, I can't thank you enough for making A Song of Silver and Gold shine.

Finally, words can't describe how grateful I am for you, treasured reader, in joining Kae and Aqeara on their journey at sea. May your compass always point to where the adventure is.

About the Author

Melissa Karibian grew up obsessed with reading.

What she wished more than anything was to be able to see herself in the worlds she immersed herself in. Now, she aims to add to the growing collection of sapphic stories out there so that hopefully others can see themselves in her characters.

Melissa was born and raised in New York, where she grew up with both Hispanic and Armenian culture. She studied at Stony Brook University where she got her degree in Psychology. Now, she studies Behavioral Neuroscience at the graduate level. Her writing tends to contrast her studies, filled with fantastical worlds and of course, women with swords.

When she's not writing, Melissa loves to read young adult fantasy and any genre with queer characters. She also enjoys watching all kinds of movies, ranging from rom coms to Disney movies to action and horror (somehow, her top three comfort films are "Coraline", "Captain America: the Winter Soldier", and "17 Dresses).

Melissa continues to live in New York with a threatening, growing tower of to-be-read books.